A SONG IN THE MORNING

'A marvellous thriller. There is not a slack moment in the action. With consummate skill, [Seymour] keeps the reader on his toes right to the last breathless page' – *Sunday Telegraph*

'Pitches headlong into the turmoil of modern South Africa. Exciting and entertaining' – *Sunday Express*

'Seymour keeps all in doubt up to the last gasp . . . streetwise with a difference' – *The Sunday Times*

'Achieves a resonance beyond the headlines' –*Guardian*

'Enthralling . . . Very exciting' – *Daily Mail*

'Keeps the suspense going right to the very end' – *The Times*

HAVE YOU READ . . . ?

HOLDING THE ZERO

Saddam Hussein wages a savage war against Kurdish guerrillas. English marksman Gus Peake is drawn into the deadly conflict by an old debt of friendship. Against him is pitted Major Karim Aziz, the deadliest sniper in Saddam's army. The duel between these two killers soon becomes an obsession, and only one man will walk away alive . . .

KILLING GROUND

The US Drug Enforcement Agency is desperate to capture Mario Ruggerio, and the mastermind behind a multi-billion dollar international Sicilian drugs trade.

When Charlotte Parsons, a young English schoolteacher and the Ruggerio's former nanny, is asked to resume her old job she is excited to return to Sicily. But Charlie doesn't realize that she is the live bait in an American trap, and that she has just entered the *killing ground*.

KINGFISHER

Four Ukrainian Jews are fighting for recognition within the Soviet Union. When one is captured, they know time is running out. Their only hope is to hijack a plane, fly to the West and then on to Israel.

Britain is the only country that allows the hijacked aircraft to land. Intelligence Officer Charlie Webster is brought in to negotiate with the hijackers. But, as the British government prevaricates, the hijackers become increasingly desperate, losing patience – and control.

THE JOURNEYMAN TAILOR

There is a rumour of an informer within the Provisional IRA's most active Brigade. But to collaborate with British Intelligence means certain death. If identified, he will be ruthlessly inter-rogated, tortured and executed. The MI5 agents running the informer must protect their man at all costs, even if that means innocent people will die.

ABOUT THE AUTHOR

Gerald Seymour spent fifteen years as an international televi-sion news reporter with ITN, covering Vietnam and the Middle East, and specialising in the subject of terrorism across the world. Seymour was on the streets of Londonderry on the afternoon of Bloody Sunday, and was a witness to the massa-cre of Israeli athletes at the Munich Olympics.

Gerald Seymour is now a full-time writer, and six of his novels have been filmed for television in the UK and US. A SONG IN THE MORNING is his ninth novel.

For more information about Gerald Seymour and his books, visit his Facebook page at
www.facebook.com/GeraldSeymourAuthor

GERALD SEYMOUR

A SONG IN THE MORNING

HODDER

First published in Great Britain in 1986 by Collins Harvill

This paperback edition first published in 2013

1

A CIP catalogue record for this title is available from the British Library.

Book ISBN 978 1 444 76017 0
eBook ISBN 978 1 444 76018 7

Printed and bound by Clays Ltd, St Ives plc

Hodder & Stoughton policy is to use papers that are natural, renewable
and recyclable products and made from wood grown in sustainable
forests. The logging and manufacturing processes are expected to
conform to the environmental regulations of the country of origin.

Hodder & Stoughton Ltd
338 Euston Road
London NW1 3BH

www.hodder.co.uk

To Gillian, Nicholas and James

For all that this novel seeks accurately to portray the events described in it in present day South Africa, all the characters in the book are fictitious. The author acknowledges with gratitude the help that many people have given him, not a few at risk to themselves, in the writing of this book.

(From the 1986 edition.)

A SONG IN THE MORNING

Foreword by Peter Hain

Nelson Mandela still had four years to serve of his long prison sentence when *A Song in the Morning* was first published.

Apartheid – the worst racial tyranny the world had ever witnessed – was still supreme and, as a fan of all Gerald Seymour's thrillers, I read this one at the time with a special, personal interest.

It gripped me even more than his page-turning writing normally does. Because Seymour's hero awaits his fate in the same macabre, grisly Pretoria gallows where a family friend, John Harris, had been hung in 1965 – the only white amongst 134 political prisoners executed there in the struggle against apartheid.

Frustrated that all peaceful protest seemed futile in the face of an omnipotent police state, Harris had planted a bomb on Johannesburg railway station. He intended it as a spectacular protest and telephoned a fifteen minute warning to the police urging the concourse to be cleared.

His message went straight to the Police Minister John Vorster who, with his Security Chief General H.J. van den Bergh, decided deliberately to ignore it, anticipating that the resulting horror amongst the white community would provide an excuse for even further repression.

It did, forcing my anti-apartheid parents to leave their beloved country, taking me and my younger brother and sisters with them. They vehemently disagreed with Harris's act. But they refused to desert a friend and took in his wife Ann and baby son David, bringing the wrath of the state upon us, and leading to exile in Britain.

A few years later I found myself, aged just nineteen, leading a British campaign of militant protests to disrupt whites-only South African rugby and cricket tours. Gerald Seymour interviewed me often for ITN. We got on well, but then lost touch – except of course indirectly through his thrillers.

This one is right up there, with an uncanny yet professionally objective feel for those fraught apartheid times and also for Pretoria Central Prison where the infamous gallows were housed. There, during the hundred years before the death penalty was finally abolished, over 3,500 condemned inmates had ascended the fifty-two concrete steps to the pre-execution room, ready to be lined up, often seven at a time.

The hangman then turned down the flaps on their freshly laundered white hoods, checked all was ready, and pulled the lever, plummeting them through huge trapdoors. In a gruesome medieval ritual the rope jerked with such force that it not only broke their necks but left severe rope burns. John Harris's hangman, Chris Barnard, had a personal tally of 1,500 executions by the time he retired.

We now take it for granted that apartheid is history, after Nelson Mandela famously walked from prison to freedom in 1990, and four years later was elected President of his country.

A Song in the Morning is not only a brilliant read like all Gerald Seymour's thrillers. It is also testimony to the bad, dark times of apartheid and the bravery of those who fought against it. Forgive, said Mandela, but never forget.

Peter Hain, Neath, June 2013

Peter Hain MP is a former British Cabinet Minister and anti-apartheid leader. His memoirs *Outside In* were published by Biteback in 2012, and his short, popular biography, *Mandela*, by Spruce in 2010.

I

They were four.

They walked abreast, dodging the lunchtime crowd. They were unremarkable to the point of anonymity. When their line broke it was to let a White through because even for these four that was ingrained instinct. They all wore jogging shoes and loose shapeless trousers and long overcoats and their woollen caps were tight down on their skulls. The Whites passing between them, ignoring them, were still clothed for the remnants of the drought summer, girls in light frocks and cotton skirts and blouses and the men in shirtsleeves. But these four had started out on their journey to the city long before the Whites had stirred in their suburban beds. They had moved out of the township before the sun had glimmered onto the electricity pylons and over the horizon of galvanized tin roofs. When they had caught their first bus the frost was still on the ground, crystal lights on the dry dun veld.

They didn't speak.

A security policeman or an interrogator might have noticed the tightness at their mouths, or the brightness in their eyes, or a certain stiffness in their walk, but the secretaries and the salesmen and the shop girls and the clerks saw nothing. For each of them it was the first time that they had been given a mission into the very centre of the city.

A security policeman or an interrogator, any man who was accustomed to the scent of fear, might have noticed the way that one of the four held in two hands the strings of a duffel bag that was heavy and bulky. He might have seen that two others each had a hand thrust deep into the side pocket of their overcoats as if to guard or hide something of importance.

But the city was at peace and at its lunch hour, and the four young men aroused no attention as they made their way along Pritchard, going west.

For the Whites who shared the pavement with these four young Blacks the sun was high, and the violence of the townships was beyond sight, out of mind. A relaxed and safe and comfortable warmth shimmered on the fast traffic flow and the rough pavement on Pritchard. There were queues at the sandwich bars. There were men with their heads in the afternoon newspapers, not searching for the statistics of the previous night's unrest but for the selections of the local rugby teams. There were women eyeing the big plate glass windows of the department stores and the clothes that came by sea from London and Paris and Rome.

Together, at the same moment, the young Blacks saw the cream and grey Combi van that was parked against the kerb on the junction of Pritchard and Delvers. And they looked at each other and saw that they had all found the van.

A White man lounged behind the Combi's wheel.

The White couldn't have missed the four Blacks as they hesitated on the pavement, their faces split with nervous smiles, and stared at him. He couldn't have missed them but he gave no sign of having noticed them. He looked ahead and sucked the wet filter of a cigarette. The engine of the van was idling. The four Blacks went on, and one turned and saw that the rear doors were marginally open. It was all as they had been told it would be.

They waited for the green pedestrian light and crossed Van Wielligh.

Each of the four would have wanted to run now, to charge on the target, but the discipline held and so they waited for the light and then walked across the wide street and past four rows of cars. Past the Methodist Church offices and the bookshop. The one with the duffel bag stole a glance at the books in the window because he had been educated to Grade 3 at a church school, and the books in the window were something familiar to him where nothing else was familiar. The ones with their hands in their pockets and the one with nothing to carry in his tight, clenched fists were of the townships round the city. The one with the duffel bag was a country boy and a member of this cadre only because of his especial training.

The pavement narrowed, its width cut by high wooden boards, filled with advertising, that marked a building site. They were jostled by Whites and Blacks alike hurrying against their flow.

The one with his hands clenched went first, a ram against the tide. He was followed by the one who held in his overcoat pocket a Makarov automatic pistol. Next was the one whose fingers were coiled round the smooth metal of an RG-42 fragmentation grenade. Last was the one with the duffel bag. They were past the building site, and the pavement opened out and in front of them were the tended lawns and the mock Gothic mass of the Rand Supreme Court.

They had all stopped. One thing to walk past the court when they were clean, carried nothing. Different now because three of them were the escort and the fourth carried a duffel bag that held a 5-litre can of petrol that was strapped with adhesive tape to nine sticks of explosive each weighing 250 grams, and taped to the can and wired to the explosive was a battery for the electrical timing device manufactured to provide a 30 second fuse. They all waited on one of the others to take a step forward.

The courthouse was an attractive building, wide steps and a dominating portico, entered through double doors. The front part of the building housed the courtrooms. Behind and towering was the eight storey administration block, the work place for the clerks and their records. Two years earlier comrades of these four young Blacks had smuggled a limpet mine into the administration. It had been defused before it exploded, but it remained something of a symbol. Not enough of a symbol for the men who had sent this cadre back for a second attack. Inside the courthouse the sentences were handed down on the comrades, on the captured cadres, on the broken cells. One year's imprisonment for playing an audio tape distributed by the African

3

National Congress. One year and six months for engraving a tea break mug with the words MANDELA – THE PEOPLE'S LEADER. Six years for singing at the university a song in praise of Mandela who was in gaol and Aggett and Biko who had died in police custody. Eight years for membership of the banned underground African National Congress and being found in possession of T-shirts with the logo VIVA MANDELA. Ten years for collecting political information for the African National Congress. Fifteen years for possession of firearms and explosives. Twenty years for sabotage. The sentence of death for the man who in the name of the African National Congress executed a policeman. On their way to the gaols the comrades had come in their tens and in their hundreds to the Rand Supreme Court on Pritchard Street.

It was a good target.

They were beside the sweeping entrance road that went down the side of the court building and then turned sharply into the tunnel that burrowed under the tower. It was the way the prisoners went, and the informers who gave evidence against them, the most secret of the state's witnesses. A White stood at the mouth of the entrance road, blocking it, short cut hair, pressed slacks, a club tie neatly knotted, and his arms crossed and cradling a personal radio. They had seen this policeman each time that they had come to look at the court, they would have to run back past him after the bomb. They had been told that everyone would be dazed after the bomb, that the Boer too would be confused, and they had the Makarov and the RG-42 fragmentation grenade.

The bustle and swim of the city eddied around them. The sun shone down on them. The noises of the city drifted between them. The one who carried the duffel bag closed his eyes, seemed to look upwards and his lips moved in silence as if he repeated a single word again and again. He was the country boy who was fearful of everything that was beyond the farm where he had been raised. He was the country boy who had stifled that fear and travelled by aircraft two years before from Tanzania to

4

the great city of Moscow, who had gone to the camp outside Kiev and who had flown back with his knowledge of explosives and his expertise in detonators and fuses. The others huddled close to the country boy and they heard the whispered hiss on his lips, the one word.

The word was *Amandla*, meaning Freedom.

Muscles strained under the overcoats, veins swelling from under the woollen caps. They were together, they were as one.

The country boy took a great gulp of air into his lungs and his hand loosened the mouth of the duffel bag and slid down inside it.

They walked along the pavement, beside the low wall that bordered the court's lawns. They saw the Blacks who lay on the grass on their backs, servants of the court and outside because it was the lunchtime recess. They saw a barrister trotting towards the doorway with his gown folded like a raincoat over his arm. They saw the Japanese cars parked at the kerb immediately in front of the doors and their high radio aerials which showed they were driven by the security police and the crime squad detectives. They saw a White youngster kiss his White girl. They saw a Black man wobble and swerve on his bicycle when he was cut up by a shining Mercedes. They saw the dark open doorway of the court.

The country boy wondered if the White in the Combi would really wait for them after the blast and the fire . . .

The country boy led.

On the skin strip between the collar of his overcoat and the wool of his cap he could feel the separate breath of the one with the Makarov and the one with the RG-42. He knew what the bomb would do. At the training camp he had seen the scattering flame of the bomb. He liked what he had seen. What he did not like was the order that the timing of the attack should be for the lunch hour. There had been a fierce argument between those who would carry the bomb and those who gave the order for its use. Those who gave the order had said they wanted only damage to the buildings, not casualties. Those who carried the

5

bomb had insisted on damage to the buildings and also to the Whites who were the apparatus of the state and the Blacks who were the accomplices of the state. The compromise had been the lunch hour . . . He led up the path between the lawns. His right forefinger rested on the switch inside the duffel bag, when he pressed the switch they had half a minute. The two doors were open. The lunch hour, so they said, was the likeliest chance that the lobby of the court would be empty. The country boy thought it was a wrong decision. A heavy wooden bench was placed across the doorway leaving only a small entrance through which the court's visitors could be filtered by the police when the adjournment was over, when the friends and relations of the accused would be admitted.

On the first floor judges were clustered round the table in the chamber of the most senior of them, talking not of law but of bloodstock form. In the Whites' canteen, waitress service, barristers briefed by the state sat with their poorer *Pro Deo* colleagues who would make the defence case, seldom successfully, for their Black clients, and chewed over disinvestment and the slide of the rand and the collapse of residential property prices. In the basement cells a White businessman charged with fraudulent conversion ate the fried chicken sent in by his mistress, and in their separate cells there were Blacks who squatted against the cold concrete walls and bowed their heads over bowls of porridge.

The country boy was on the bottom step. The doorway yawned in front of him. His finger was rigid on the switch. They were panting behind him. He pressed the switch. Again the draught of air sank in his throat.

'It's closed.'

The Boer's voice. The enemy's voice. His hand snaked back out of the bag. The arm that was to hurl the bag into the lobby of the court was frozen useless.

'You can't go in there for another eighteen minutes.'

He spun his head. He saw the one with the Makarov and the one with the RG-42 and the one who had nothing at all gawping

6

back down on to the path. The uniformed warrant officer stood in the centre of the pathway, his arms were clasped behind his back on a short leather-coated swagger stick. An immaculate police tunic, knife-edge trousers, shoes that a servant had polished.

'Seventeen minutes actually.' The warrant officer grinned cheerfully. 'For now, get yourselves away.'

The country boy flexed his arm, turned and threw the bag into and inside the doorway.

He ran.

He cannoned into the one with the Makarov, felt the bite of the barrel into his thigh, and he ran. Across the grass. Jumping the wall. All of them charging together. None of them hearing the shout of the warrant officer. None of them seeing him stagger from the shoulder charge of the one who had nothing, and then go as if from instinctive duty through the doorway, none of them seeing him grope for the duffel bag under a table deep in the lobby and take it in his arms and twist again for the bright sunlight of the doorway. All of them sprinting. None of them seeing the fast sweep of understanding chisel the face of the plain clothes policeman with the personal radio.

They were past the building site. They were running, swerving, sidestepping, jumping into the traffic on Van Wielligh, going chicken with a bus driver and having him brake when the bomb exploded.

A bomb detonated in the centre of a safe city, in the middle of a safe lunch hour.

A bomb that spewed fire, showered glass, ripped at plaster and concrete and brickwork.

All four would dearly have loved to have seen the explosion. Only the country boy had an exact idea of the scale of the flame blown outwards in a blazing spray. They would dearly have loved to have seen the warrant officer disintegrate when he was a yard from the door, when he was at the moment of throwing the bomb away from him and onto the grass. In the few seconds that the warrant officer had screamed of the danger of the bomb

7

he had attracted enough attention for there to be seven civilians and two policemen in the court lobby. They would dearly have loved to see those nine persons bowled over by the blast and the smoke cloud and the fire draught. They saw nothing of the devastation, and nothing of the policeman chasing after them, the radio in one hand and a revolver in the other.

They reached the Combi van.

They flung open the door and scrambled inside in a confusion of knees and elbows and shouts, and the van was accelerating into the wide spaces of Pritchard before they'd managed to close the doors. The last thing the country boy saw before the doors were shut was the policeman on the pavement, panting, heaving, yelling into his radio.

Jeez drove like he hadn't a tomorrow.

And he didn't reckon he had, a tomorrow.

Shit, and he'd heard the explosion. Couldn't have missed it. Half choked on his cigarette, and the windows around him had rattled fit to break and he'd seen the heads on the pavement spinning to stare up the street. He'd been facing away from the explosion, he'd had only the shock wave, none of the sights . . . left into End, up past the Kerk junction, left onto Jeppe . . . Jeez going hard, and with the frown slashed on the old weather-stained skin of his forehead. He was going hard because he'd heard the bang and a bang like that at midday in central Jo'burg meant a bloody big show.

Nobody had said anything other than that he was to be parked in a Combi van on the corner of Pritchard and Delvers, north side, looking east, back doors unfastened. Done as he was told, because that's what they all did in the Movement, Blacks and Whites. Shit, nobody had said it was a bloody headline grabber they'd be running from . . . Right off Jeppe and into Rissik. He was burning the tyres, hitting the turns. Way ahead, up Rissik, was the railway station, that's where he'd been told he had to get. Four kids to catch a train, that's all. He had been told that if there was a police block then a White in a commercial van would sail through.

But this was an arsehole.

Because of his initials James Carew had always been Jeez. He rather fancied it. He used that name on the telephone, used it to anyone who knew him marginally. He'd had the name since the time he left school, since he was in the army. The name was his possession, his style, like kids who had a ring in their ear, or a tattoo. He was Jeez, had been for more than thirty-five years.

He heard the siren.

Shit . . . Jeez saw the traffic in front of him swerving for the slow lane, and that told him that the bells and the whining were behind, and his ears told him the bastards were closing.

Nobody had told him who he would be driving. Hadn't said it was a getaway. Just that four kids who were a bit hot needed picking up on the corner of Pritchard and Delvers and needed dropping off at the station. When he'd seen them earlier, he'd thought: bright lads, these, not piling into the van straight off. They'd have been checking for a tail. Well, now they had a tail all right.

He'd been on the road of bells and sirens before, more than twenty years before, but the memory was still sharp, not the sort of sound that any bugger ever forgets. What was sharpest was the same dingy old thought, that when he heard the sirens and saw the uniforms then there wasn't a hell of a lot of point in beating your guts out and running faster.

A bloody shambles the clowns had dropped him in. Shit up to his nose.

In the back was a babble of screaming for more speed. He looked into the side mirror. The unmarked car had the bell going, and the yellow police wagon had the blue light going and the siren . . . right up to his bloody nose and down his bloody nostrils. When he looked again through his front windscreen he saw the police jeep that was slewed across the road a bit over a hundred yards ahead. There were no side turnings between him and the police jeep. Back to the mirror. The car and the wagon weren't trying to get past him, didn't have to, were sitting on his arse, shepherding him.

The poor bastards were frantic in the back, spittle on his neck the way they were shouting through the close mesh grille.

You win some and most often you lose, that's what Jeez reckoned.

He eased his foot onto the brake pedal. He changed down. He could see that there were pistols aimed at him from behind the cover of the police jeep. Down again to second, and his foot harder onto the brake and stamping.

'Sorry, boys,' Jeez said softly.

If they hadn't been making such a hell of a rumpus they might have heard the genuine sadness in his voice. He brought the Combi to a halt. He took the keys out of the ignition and tossed them out of the window, onto the roadway. He looked into the side mirror. The policemen were spilling out of the unmarked car and out of the wagon, crouching and kneeling and all aiming their hand guns at the Combi. Nobody had told Jeez what the hell he was into.

Silence in the van.

'Let's have a bit of dignity, boys.' An English accent. 'Let's not give the bastards the pleasure of our fear.'

Jeez opened his door. He stepped down onto the street. He clasped his hands over the top of his head.

In front of him and behind him the policemen began to run warily forward.

Johannesburg is a hard city. It is a city where the Whites carry guns and the Blacks carry knives. Not a city where the pedestrians and shoppers cower on their faces because the police have drawn revolvers and have blocked off a Combi and are handcuffing four kaffirs and a kaffir lover. A crowd had gathered inside the minute that it took the police to hustle their five prisoners towards the wagon and to kick them up and slam the doors on them. There was something to see. The White guy was the something to see. Must have been more than forty, could have been more than fifty, and wearing decent slacks and a decent shirt. The crowd wondered what the White guy was doing with those Black bastards, what the hell he was at.

Four long blocks away a cloud of slow-moving smoke was settling above Pritchard Street.

Mr Justice Andries van Zyl had passed the sentence of the supreme penalty on 186 men, of whom his clerk had told him recently 142 had been executed. It would have been beyond him to believe that an innocent man had ever been convicted in a court over which he had presided. He attended church every Sunday morning and sometimes went back in the evening. When he retired in two years' time he would devote his energies to a charitable society supporting children afflicted by the spina bifida disease. Privately, in his room, after passing the death sentence, he would say a prayer for the condemned man; not a prayer that the man should be reprieved, but that he might go to his Maker with true repentance in his heart.

On that late afternoon in the Palace of Justice on the north side of Pretoria's Church Square he dealt first with the four Blacks deemed guilty by himself and his two lay assessors of murder. There was no theatricality. The black cap had long before been dispensed with in the Republic's courts, and his sentencing voice was a racing monotone, that of a bowls club secretary getting through the minutes of a previous meeting.

As Happy and Charlie and Percy and Tom stared back at him from the dock, expressionless, exhausted of hope, he shuffled his papers, then pressed his metal-rimmed half moon spectacles tight onto the bridge of his nose. He allowed the murmurs to subside in the public gallery.

He looked up at Jeez Carew.

Mr Justice van Zyl saw a man only a few years younger than himself, and well dressed in a dark grey suit and a white shirt and a silk tie. He saw a face which seemed to say that there was nothing new to be learned. He saw the way that the shoulders were pulled back, and the way that the man's arms were held straight down to his sides. He saw that the prisoner's bearing was more militarily correct than that of the prison service guards at attention behind him. Mr Justice van Zyl had watched this

White accused through seventeen days of courtroom business. He thought he had detected an arrogance. He disliked arrogance. The previous day he had decided that when he passed sentence on the White he would make a fuller statement than was usual for him. He would break that arrogance.

'James Carew, you have been found guilty of murder without extenuating circumstances. There is only one sentence that I may pass upon you. It was your own decision that during your time in custody you refused to co-operate with the officers who have diligently investigated a quite appalling criminal act. You chose to remain silent. You have also rebuffed the efforts of a very able and conscientious counsel to present a defence on your behalf. I understand that you chose not to brief him, and also that you refused the opportunity offered you of going into the witness stand to give the court your own version of events on that horrific day in Johannesburg. By these actions I am forced to the conclusion that in your case extenuating circumstances do not exist which would mitigate your guilt.

'I have heard in police evidence that you came from the United Kingdom to the Republic of South Africa twelve years ago. In the time you have resided here perhaps you have acquired the belief that different standards of justice obtain for our varied ethnic groups. You may have believed that the colour of your skin offers you some protection from the consequences of your actions. You would have deluded yourself, Mr Carew, if you believed that.

'The crime of which you have been found guilty involved a quite dastardly act. You acted together with terrorists of the outlawed African National Congress, one of whom had been trained in sabotage and murder in a communist state, to set off a bomb inside the Rand Supreme Court in Johannesburg. The bomb consisted of explosives and petrol to which had been added a quantity of household liquid detergent, the effect of the latter being that the flaming petrol would fasten itself to any clothes or flesh it came into contact with. The casualties would have been even more severe but for the devotion to duty and the personal sacrifice of warrant officer Prinsloo. In taking much of the blast of the bomb the warrant officer without doubt saved many others from the savagery that you intended. As the driver of the getaway vehicle your guilt is equal to that of the man who made the bomb and the men who delivered it. You were an essential member of a murderous conspiracy.

'We live in a time when it is more than ever important that in our beloved country God-fearing men and women should support the legitimate forces of law and of order. No benefit to any person in the Republic, whatever his colour, can come from an outrage such as you helped to perpetrate. I truly hope that the sentence that I am about to pass on you will deter other foreigners from coming to our country, taking our hospitality, and repaying us with murder.

'I believe, Mr Carew, in the efficacy of the deterrent. A few years ago a distinguished colleague of mine said, "The death penalty is like a warning, just like a lighthouse throwing its beams out to sea. We hear about shipwrecks, but we do not hear about the ships the lighthouse guides safely on its way. We do not have proof of the number of ships it saves, but we do not tear the lighthouse down." Mr Carew, we will not permit our country to be used as a playground of mayhem by foreigners who conspire with such hate-consumed organizations as the African National Congress.

'James Carew, the sentence of the court is that you be taken from here to a lawful place of execution and that you there be hanged by the neck until you are dead.'

There was no entreaty for the Lord to have mercy on James Carew's soul.

Had Jeez slumped or even dropped his eyes from the Judge's face, then there would have been. Mr Justice van Zyl was vexed by the prisoner's composure. He thrust his papers together, propelled himself from his chair.

'All rise,' the clerk intoned.

Mr Justice van Zyl stamped out of his courtroom, his assessors after him.

13

A guard tapped Jeez on the shoulder. Jeez turned smartly and down the steps from the dock to the courtroom cells, followed by Happy and Charlie and Percy and Tom.

In prison lore they were the 'condemns'. While they were driven under heavy escort to that part of Pretoria Central prison a mile and a half away that was reserved for these men who were condemned, a police major sat in the emptied courtroom filling in with a ballpoint pen the specific details of the printed form that was the death warrant. The form would go later to the sheriff of the capital city for his signature and in due course to the hangman as authority for his work.

An age later Jeez sat on the end of his bed and stared down at the sheet of writing paper, blank as yet, that lay on the table that was fastened into the cell wall.

An endless time later. Countless days, more than a year. Long enough for the Rand Supreme Court and the ride up Rissik Street to be just a hated memory, a smell that was everywhere in the mind but couldn't be located.

It was the first time that he had asked for writing paper and a pen.

What to write? What to say? . . . He could hear the singing. Many, many voices in a slow dirge. Couldn't escape from the bastard singing. Shit, when it was his turn, who'd be singing for bloody Jeez?

On the top right hand corner of the sheet of paper he wrote the date.

2

He let himself in through the front door and the atmosphere hit him.

Before Jack had his key out of the lock and the door closed behind him, he could sense catastrophe.

The vacuum cleaner was in the middle of the hall rug. His mother always did the carpets straight after Sam and Jack had gone to work and little Will to school. There were dirty clothes at the foot of the stairs. She would have put the yesterday shirts and socks and pants into the machine straight after she'd done the carpets. Down the hall the door into the kitchen was open. The saucepans and the frying pan from last night's dinner and the morning's breakfast were in the sink.

Had to be a catastrophe.

Sam gone bankrupt? Will hurt? . . . But Will was sitting glumly at the top of the stairs, still in his school blazer, and he too had his routine and always changed out of his blazer, chucked it on the bedroom floor, as soon as he came in, and that would have been two hours back . . . Sam couldn't have gone bankrupt. What recession? Business never brighter, Sam was forever saying.

The boy on the stairs shrugged dramatically, like no-one had bothered to tell him what was biting his Mum and his Dad.

Jack heard Sam's voice through the closed living room door.

'Get it into your head, it's nothing to do with you.'

He heard his mother crying. Not loud weeping, not crying for sympathy. Real crying, real misery.

'Whatever the bastard's done, Hilda, whatever he's going to get, that's not your concern.'

He turned to close the front door. Behind him was wretched, normal Churchill Close. Nothing ever happened in the dead end road where the cherry trees were in blossom and the pavements were swept and the mowers had been out once or twice already on the front lawns and the rose beds were weeded. Tudor homes set back from the road, where nothing ever went bad and sour. You could get a funeral moving out of neo-Elizabethan Churchill Close with half the residents not knowing there'd been a death. Jack closed the door behind him.

'He's gone out of your life.' He heard the anger in Sam's voice.

Jack knocked and went into the living room.

His mother sat on the sofa beside the fireplace. Yesterday's ashes. She had a crumpled handkerchief tight in her fist and her eyes were red and swollen. She still wore the housecoat that was her early morning gear. Sam Perry was at the window. Jack didn't think that they could have been rowing between themselves, they hardly ever did, and never when Will could hear them.

Jack was 26 years old. His quiet love for his mother was the same as it had been from the time he could first remember, when there had only been the two of them.

'What's happened, Mum?'

Sam replied for her. 'There's been a letter.'

'Who from?'

'There's been a letter come from a gaol in South Africa.'

'Will you, please, tell me who has written us a letter from South Africa.'

'A letter to your mother from a condemned cell in Pretoria Central prison.'

'Damn it, Sam, who wrote it?'

'Your father.'

Sam turned to stare out of the window. His wife, Jack's mother, pointed wordlessly up to the mantelpiece, fresh tears on her cheeks. Amongst the delicate china pieces, next to the flower vase, was a small brown paper envelope.

16

His mother's voice was muffled through the squeezed handkerchief.

'You should read it, Jack. They're going to hang your father.'

He went slowly across the room. He stepped over the brimming ashtray in the middle of the carpet. She had been there all day with her cigarettes and her letter. It was an envelope of flimsy paper with a blue airmail sticker and a 25 cent stamp which showed the bulged bloom of a protea plant. Tight, joined handwriting had addressed the letter to Mrs Hilda Perry, 45 Green Walk, Coulsdon, Surrey, Great Britain. A different hand had crossed out that address and replaced it with Foxhaven, Churchill Close, Leatherhead, Surrey. No-one had seen a fox in Churchill Close for six years. On the reverse side of the envelope was overstamped 'If Undelivered Return to Commissioner of Prisons, Pretoria', and there was a post box number. The envelope was featherlight, for a moment he looked again at the mantelpiece.

'It's inside, Jack,' his mother said. 'They don't seem to give them much in the way of paper.'

Sam said tersely, 'You don't have to read it. Not after what he did to your mother and you.'

'If it's my father I'll read it,' Jack said quietly. It wasn't a put down. Jack knew that Sam Perry had done his damndest to be a good proxy father to his wife's son.

He drew the single sheet out of the envelope. Across the top of the sheet was written in capital letters JAMES CAREW – C2 3/86.

'My father's James Curwen.'

'It's the name he's using there,' his mother said.

Jack turned the sheet over. The letter was signed 'Jeez'.

His mother anticipated him. 'It's what he always called himself. He was always Jeez to me and to everyone.'

To himself almost, but aloud, he read: 'Dear Hilda, This comes a bit out of the blue I'm afraid, and I have to hope that it doesn't upset you. God knows that once I did enough to upset you and I've no right to repeat the dose. I suppose that it's because of my present situation, because I am sentenced to hang, that I thought it would be good to tie down some of the loose strings of my life, that's why I'm writing. About going out of your life, well, I'm not saying anything about that. What happened is gone. No excuses, no whining, it just happened . . .'

'And, Christ, did it happen,' Sam snapped. 'Walked out on a fine lady and a two-year-old child.'

Jack ignored him.

'. . . A lot of years later I came back to the UK and I found out that you were well and married, that Jack was well, that you had a new baby. I didn't see the need to drag up the past. You were in good shape. I was OK. I reckoned you were best left alone . . .'

'And why couldn't he leave her alone now?' Sam couldn't let go of it. 'Suddenly, twenty-four years after he's dumped your mother, it's a sob story.'

'. . . So, I'm in a bit of a mess now, things aren't looking too good. As I used to say, you win some but most you lose. If you read in the papers that I'm going for the early walk then please just think of me that morning, and remember the better times. As I will. If nothing comes up at the last minute, this has to be goodbye to you and the lad. I watched him at sports once over the fence. I thought he was OK. Things aren't always what they seem. When I'm gone, ask the old man. He'll tell you. Yours affectionately, Jeez . . .'

'Got all that's bloody coming to him.'

Jack put the letter back into the envelope. He was very pale. His hand trembled as he gave it to his mother.

'Why should he have written to you, Mum?'

'Perhaps there's no-one else he could have written to.' She stood up. Jack knew she wanted to be out of the room. She didn't want her husband and her son to see any more of her tears. She laughed in a silly, brittle way. 'There's jobs. Will's tea. Our dinner. Have to be getting on.'

She was going to the door.

'Do you want a hand, Mum?'

'You talk with your father – with Sam.'

She went out. She couldn't help herself, she was sobbing before she'd closed the door.

'Sponged for sympathy, that's what the bastard's done. Old man, indeed. I'd give him bloody old man.'

'Steady, Sam. He's my father.'

'I've put it together, what he did, what it said in the papers. He was involved with communist terrorists and murder.'

'You're talking about my father.'

'He treated your mother like dirt.'

'He's still my father.'

'He's not worth a single one of your mother's tears.'

'Do you bloody well want to hang him yourself?'

'Don't swear at me, son, not when you're under my bloody roof.'

'Isn't it enough for you that they're going to throw him in a pit with a rope round his neck?'

'He made his bed. He'd no call to bring his problems into my house, into your mother's life.'

'He's still my father,' Jack said.

Sam dropped his head. The hardness was gone from him.

'I'm sorry, Jack, truly sorry that you ever had to read the letter.'

They had a drink together, large Scotch and small soda, and another, and there was time for one more before Hilda Perry called them to dinner. They talked loudly of business, Sam's garage and showroom and Jack's work. They sat at the dining room's mahogany table with candles lit. The man who was in a cell fifty-five hundred miles away was thought of but not spoken about. When they were having their coffee Will came in and sat on Hilda's knee and talked about the school soccer team and there were bellows of laughter.

Jack pushed his chair back and stood up. His father was going to hang. He thanked his mother for dinner. He said he had some work that had to be sorted by the morning. In a gaol on the other side of the world, dear God. He said he'd go to his room and put his head into his papers. Was so alone that the one he wrote to was the one he had most hurt. He told Will that he should learn to kick with his left foot if he ever wanted to be any good. He had no sense of his father's face. He rested his hand on Sam's shoulder, and Sam patted it. The man he didn't know was his father, and his father was going to hang.

He went up the flower-carpeted staircase to his room.

It was a little under four miles to work, across on the London side of the town. Jack Curwen was employed by Richard Villiers and his son, Nicholas. The office was an unlikely place for D & C Ltd (Demolition and Clearance). There was no yard for JCB diggers and bulldozers and heavy earth-transporting lorries; there weren't any cranes; there weren't any workmen. Villiers was a shrewd man, which made him a good employer, and he'd long before decided that the way to the maximum profit and minimum outlay was to be in the art game of sub-contracting out. He hunted out the business and then pulled in the freelance operators that he needed. A few local calls could bring in a million pounds' worth of plant and transport whose maintenance and upkeep was some other bugger's headache. D & C Ltd liked to boast that nothing was too small, nothing too large. They could clear the foundations of a 5,000 square yard warehouse in dockland. They could take out the stump of an oak tree. Villiers came into the office in the morning to ferret into the balance sheets and retired with a huge handicap to the golf course for the afternoon. Nicholas Villiers looked after the sub-contracting side of the business, and Jack was there to sniff out new contracts. There was a business manager who kept the books, two secretaries and a receptionist. Nice and lean, was how Richard Villiers described D & C Ltd, no waste, no fat. He liked young Jack because he didn't have to pay the lad that much, and because the lad kept the cheques rolling. When he retired there might be a directorship for the lad.

D & C Ltd were housed in the ground floor of a Victorian

building. They shared with a solicitor, an accountancy practice, a chiropodist and two architects.

Jack would have preferred to have just slipped in that morning, shut himself away. No chance. Villiers had an office where he could keep his clubs and his wet weather anoraks and leggings. The business manager had his own territory. Nicholas Villiers and Jack and the two secretaries shared what had once been the ground floor drawing room.

The girls and Nicholas Villiers stared at him, like he looked awful.

'Been on the piss, have we?' Villiers asked loudly. Janice giggled, Lucille dropped her head.

'Didn't have a very good night,' Jack muttered.

He'd had a tossing, nightmarish, sweating night.

He'd nicked his right side nostril with his razor.

He'd missed breakfast.

'You look pretty rough.'

'Didn't sleep much.'

'Not got the 'flu?'

Hadn't been on the piss, hadn't got the 'flu, only problem was that his father was going to hang. Nothing else was wrong.

'I'm fine, thanks, just didn't sleep much last night.'

Only problem was that his father was going to kick it on the end of a rope with a load of crap-arse foreigners around him, with no-one of his own around him.

The girls were all eyes on him. He was a good dresser, took care of himself. Wasn't every day that Jack Curwen looked as though he'd slept in a hedge. He thought they both fancied him, but they were too close to base. No future in a typists' pool relationship. Best keeping the ladies separate from work. And he was on the rebound anyway. Last girl had been with him for four months, good kid and good looker and occasionally good in the back seat of his motor, till she'd upped and offed with a doctor to Canada. She had looked him hard in the eye and said he was sweet and said her new fellow had more of a future with a medical degree than he had working at a nothing place like

D & C Ltd. It was a comfort to think that Janice and Lucille fancied him, but he wasn't doing anything about it.

'Please yourself . . . The pillbox on the Downs, they can't do that today. The blaster isn't free before tomorrow. Too expensive keeping the plant hanging about. Going to go tomorrow afternoon. Does that mess you?'

'Not particularly. I've other places I can be.' It wasn't a lie. 'There's a line of elm stumps I'm chasing near Dorking. A bit of chasing'll fix it.'

'And afterwards try sleeping it off, eh?'

Jack smiled weakly. He was on his way back to the door.

Nicholas Villiers said, 'Anything I can do to help, Jack?'

'No.'

Janice watched through the window as Jack walked to his car. She typed two lines and looked up again. She saw the car turn in the road and drive away.

'He's not gone to Dorking,' she announced, proud of her keen observation. 'He's taken the London road.'

He had the wipers on, shovelling the rain off the windscreen, for the drive into the city.

By luck he found a parking space near the street market behind Waterloo station.

He walked over the bridge with the rain lashing his face, soaking his trousers and his shoes, and he hadn't cared.

His father had never been mentioned since his mother's second marriage. What he knew of his father was what he had been told when he was a child. A bastard of a man had walked out of his mother's life, told her that he would be away for a few days and had never come back. Jack had been two years old. He had had it drilled into him that his father was a callous man who had opted out and left a young mother with a child that was little more than a baby. There was nothing accidental about it because money had come to his mother all the time that she had been bringing up the child, and had kept on coming right up to the week of her registry office marriage to Sam Perry.

Jack knew that. Never a word from his father, only the cruel mockery of a monthly stipend. He had never asked about how the money was paid or where it had come from. But it had arrived, sufficient for the household bills, food and electricity and heating oil and a caravan holiday each August, right up to the time of the wedding. It was as if his father had watched their lives from a safe distance, and stopped the money when he'd known it was no longer needed. Jack had kept his father's name and it would have been hell's complicated to change it to Jack Perry. He had been Jack Curwen at grammar school, and Jack Curwen at college. But of Jeez Curwen there was never a word in Sam Perry's household.

He turned left onto the Strand. He knew where he was going. He knew that he had first to go to Trafalgar Square.

He knew nothing of this man who was condemned to die in South Africa but his name and his age, and that he was his father. He didn't know his face, nor his habits. He didn't know whether he drank, or swore or whored. He didn't know whether he laughed, whether he cried, whether he prayed. He hadn't the least idea what he did for a living.

He had to fend off the spike of an umbrella tent, and the woman who was powering out of Simpson's didn't notice him, so didn't apologize. He came into the square. Weather too awful and season too early for the tourists. The column and the lions and the statues were granite grey in the rain.

Sam Perry had been good to them. Good to his mother by marrying her, kind to her son who had no blood with him but whom he had treated as his own. Sam had worked hard to make himself into Jack's father. Jack could remember the days at the infant and primary schools before Sam had showed up. Other kids' dads helping with school projects, shouting at the sports afternoons, dropping them at school, picking them up. It didn't make sense to Jack that a man who cared so little for his wife and kid that he could walk out on them should keep a watch to satisfy himself that their survival was assured. Jack didn't know a single detail about the man who was his father.

23

He crossed the Strand. The rain ran on his forehead, dribbled into his eyes and his nose and his mouth.

There were six demonstrators outside the South African embassy and eight policemen standing on the steps of the building.

It was obvious enough that he should come here. He knew the embassy. Everybody who travelled through central London knew that the embassy was in Trafalgar Square, huge and powerful in its cleaned colonial yellow stone. He had seen the demonstrators on television the week before, when they started their vigil. The embassy building's solidity mocked the critics of South Africa, the orange and white and blue flag sodden but defiant on the high pole. The policemen, gathered close to the main double doors, were able to take some protection from the rain. The demonstrators had no shelter. Two were coloured, four were white. They were drenched. The rain had run the paint of the slogans on their placards which they held against their knees.

FREEDOM FOR THE PRITCHARD FIVE.

NO RACIST HANGINGS IN SA.

THE ROPE FOR APARTHEID, NOT FOR FREEDOM FIGHTERS.

Before last night Jack would not have given a second glance to men and women who stood in the rain outside the embassy of the Republic of South Africa. Any more than the diplomats inside, in the dry and the warm, gave a shit for them, or their slogans.

He saw the distaste on the police sergeant's face as he walked to speak to the demonstrators. The man he picked out was middle forties, Jack guessed, because the hair that was lank on the back of his neck was streaked grey. The man was shivering in a poplin sports top that was keeping out none of the rain. He wore plastic badges for Anti-Apartheid and the African National Congress and the South West African People's Organization. His jogging shoes were holed and worn, but he stood motionless in the streams of water on the pavement. His placard was

FREEDOM FOR THE PRITCHARD FIVE.

All six looked at him coldly, mirroring the stares of the policemen.

'Good morning. Can you tell me about your protest?'

'Pretty obvious, isn't it? You can read.'

'I thought you'd want to tell me,' Jack said.

'We don't need your kind of interest.'

'What the hell does that mean?'

'Just go up the steps and join the other fascists.'

Jack read the man's supercilious stare. He had his hair cut short, he wore a businessman's raincoat, a charcoal suit, he wore a tie.

He looked hard into the man's eyes.

'Listen, I am not a policeman. I am not a snooper. I am a private citizen, and I want to know something about the Pritchard Five.'

There must have been something in Jack's gaze, and the lash of his voice. The man shrugged.

'You can sign the petition.'

'How many signatures?'

'One hundred and fourteen.'

'That all?'

'This is a racist society.' The man rolled his words, as if they gave him a satisfaction. 'There's not many who care that four heroic freedom fighters will go to their deaths.'

'Who are they?' Jack asked.

'Happy Zikala, Charlie Schoba, Percy Ngoye and Tom Mweshtu. They took the battle into the middle of Johannesburg in broad daylight. It will be a crime against humanity if they hang.'

'Your placard calls them the Pritchard Five.'

'He only drove the car.'

'And he's *white*,' Jack yelled. 'So he doesn't get to be a hero.'

Jack wanted to get the hell away, but the man was tugging at his sleeve.

'The issue is whether the White minority government and the White minority courts will dare to hang four Black freedom fighters. That's what it's about . . .'

Jack wrenched himself clear.

He walked the length of the Strand and on until he came to Fleet Street. Sam and Hilda Perry always took the *Daily Telegraph* at home. The *Daily Telegraph* was as routine as shaving and brushing his teeth in the morning. He asked at the Reception if he could see someone from the library. When the woman came he didn't spin a story, just asked directly if he could see a file. Nine times out of ten he would have been told that visitors were not permitted access to files without prior arrangement, but she looked at the rain-swept young man, and said:

'What file is it you want?'

'Everything on the Pritchard Five.'

'The ones who are condemned to hang in South Africa?'

'Everything you have, please.'

'I can tell you now there's not much. The unrest and the economic crisis and the sanctions issue, that's what has taken up the space.'

But she took him to the library. She sat him at a table and brought him the file of newspaper clippings. She shrugged, she said that it was pretty thin, that there would probably be a long story on the day before the execution. She left him to read the file.

There was a clipping from the day of the bombing that just mentioned the arrest of an unidentified White. Nothing then until the trial, and most of that detailed the prosecution's evidence against Tom Mweshtu, that he'd been trained by the Soviets and had spent time in Kiev. James Carew was described as a white South African taxi driver, aged 53. Two paragraphs on the sentencing, what they were accused of, what their names were, that they showed no emotion when they were told they would hang. Months of a hole in the story and then the dismissal of the appeal, four paragraphs. Jack learned that the five had been in the maximum security compound of Pretoria Central gaol for thirteen months, that the Pope had urged the State President to exercise clemency, that three EEC Foreign Ministers had sent telegrams urging reprieves. Everything that he read had been in the paper pushed through the letter box every day at home – and he hadn't bothered, just as he hadn't stirred himself to take an interest in the shootings in the townships or in the detentions or the bombings.

And then, there it was, the photograph.

In last Tuesday's paper. It was probably still in the cupboard under the stairs. Might be lining a dustbin, or it might have been crumpled up by his mother for cleaning the front room windows. His mother always read the paper, front to back. Jack didn't know how she could not have recognized the photograph of her first husband. He had never before seen a photograph of his father.

It was a mug shot, might have been a police picture, might have been a passport. He peered down at the column-wide photograph, at the man who only managed two paragraphs with four others, who didn't rate as a hero, who was a white South African taxi driver, 53. He saw a gaunt face, staring, ungiving eyes, shadowed hollow cheeks, sparse short hair. The photograph was misting, blurring. Jack's fists were white knuckled, tight. He felt the choking in his chest. He saw the tears fall on the newsprint and be absorbed.

When the woman came back from her desk to look into the corner where the young man had been sitting she found the file neatly piled, but open. She saw the damp on the photograph and wondered what the silly man had managed to spill on it, could have been the rain from his hair. She noticed when she gathered up the file that the final clipping reported that within the next few days the State President would make his decision as to whether the sentences of death should be carried out.

Jack drove to Dorking and made sure of the contract for the removal of the thirty-two elm stumps. He rang his mother and said he'd be late home; then he set off to get himself drunk.

3

The drink hadn't hurt, had been something of a blessing because his stupor sleep didn't let him nightmare.

First thing when he came down the stairs he hunted for the newspaper and his father's photograph. It was one from the top of the pile, next to the firelighters. He tore out the picture and folded it into his wallet.

Breakfast in the kitchen and not a word of his lurching up the stairs a little after midnight. His mother didn't ask him why he had been out so late. Big boy, wasn't he? Twenty-six years old, a grown man. Nothing had ever been said about his moving out, not that Sam would have complained if Jack had announced one Monday morning that he was off to look for a flat. He couldn't have faulted Sam for the way he had taken this other man's son into his household, but kindness and patience couldn't have turned them into father and son. Sometimes they were friends, sometimes he was a generously tolerated lodger. Jack could recognize there was more fault in him than in the attitudes of his stepfather. He was close to himself, rarely gave of his affections, took his pleasures away from home, pubs and squash club friends and the girls who were casually hooked into that scene. He was aware of his own cold streak of independence. Natural enough, for a boy who had never known the companionship of a true father.

And no mention made at the breakfast table of James Carew. Didn't have to be talked about, because he was there with them. Sam too loud, his mother too quiet, and Jack behaving as if he had buried the whole matter, and all of them hurrying through the bacon and the scrambled egg the sooner to escape to their work and the privacy of their thoughts.

Jack didn't even call the office.

He drove into London and parked off the Vauxhall Bridge Road, behind the cathedral, and walked through the park to Whitehall. Yesterday had been wasted, and now there was no more time to waste because time was short for James Carew.

He stood in the courtyard outside the Foreign and Commonwealth Office. He made some rapid calculations and decided to advise Richard Villiers not to accept the contract. It was just two damn four-square big. Almost intimidating.

He watched the civil servants arriving with their uniform EII R briefcases, most of them looking as though they had nothing but a morning paper in them; and the leggy secretaries, and the chauffeurs and the messengers. He went up the steps and into the dark reception area.

There was a commissionaire, blue uniform and medal ribbons, an old regular army man. There was a security man a yard or two back in the shadows. There was a woman with grey hair drawn into a tight knot. She wore a white blouse over what didn't look like regulation underwear. He wasn't asked what his business was. They waited on him to speak. He was an ordinary citizen who was calling by because his father was going to be hanged in South Africa. He wondered how often the ordinary citizen came to announce themselves in the reception area. They were all looking at him, like it was an attempt to make him grovel. Probably not worth pointing out that he and a few other ordinary chaps off the street paid their salaries.

'My name is Curwen. I'd like to see someone, please, who deals with South Africa.'

There was a very slight smile at the commissionaire's mouth. The security man looked as though he hadn't heard.

The woman said, 'Do you have an appointment?'

'If I had an appointment, I'd have said so.'

'You have to have an appointment.'

'I don't have an appointment, but I do insist on seeing someone who deals with South Africa, on a matter of urgency.'

Jack wondered what the word urgency might mean under this roof. He'd used it forcefully enough for her to hesitate.

'What's it in connection with?'

'Are you an expert on South Africa?'

'No.'

'Then it won't help you to know what it's about.'

A flush spilled through the make-up on her cheeks. She turned her back on him and spoke into a telephone, then told him to take a seat.

He sat on a hard chair away from the desk. He reckoned he'd spoiled her day. He was more than half an hour on the chair, and she began to look herself again. He wondered what they would be doing upstairs that meant he had to sit for more than thirty minutes waiting for them. Getting the coffee machine working? Sharing out the sandwiches? Filling in the South African Department's football pool coupon?

'Good morning, Mr Curwen, would you come this way, please.'

The man might have been in his late forties, could have been the early fifties. His suit didn't look good enough for him to be important, but he had a kindly face that seemed worn thin with tiredness. They went down a long and silent corridor, then the man opened a door and waved Jack inside. It was an interview room, four chairs and a table and an ashtray that hadn't been emptied. Of course they weren't going to invite him into the working part of the building. They were in the quarantine area.

'I'm Sandham. I'm on the South Africa desk.'

The man apologized for keeping him waiting. Then he listened as Jack told him about the letter from Pretoria, and of the little that he knew about his father.

'And you want to know what we're doing for him?'

'Yes.'

Sandham asked him please to wait, smiled ruefully, as if Jack knew all about waiting. He was gone five minutes. He came back with a buff file under his arm, and a younger man.

'Mr Sandham explained to me your business with us, Mr

Curwen. I decided to come and see you myself. My name's Furneaux, Assistant Secretary. I read everything that goes across the South Africa desk.'

Furneaux took a chair, Sandham stood.

A short, abrupt, unlikeable little man, not yet out of middle age, with a maroon silk handkerchief flopping from his breast pocket. Furneaux reached for Sandham's file.

'This conversation is not for newspaper consumption,' Furneaux said.

'Of course.'

'I understand that your father left your mother when you were two years old. That makes it easier for me to talk frankly to you. I am assuming you have no emotional attachment to your father because you have no memory of him. But you want to know what we are doing to save your father's life? Publicly we are doing nothing, because it is our belief that by going public we would diminish what influence we have on the government of South Africa. Privately we have done everything possible to urge clemency for the terrorists . . .'

'Terrorists or freedom fighters?' Jack held Furneaux's eye until the Assistant Secretary dropped his face to the file.

'Terrorists, Mr Curwen. Your government does not support the throwing of bombs in central Johannesburg. You've heard the Prime Minister on the subject, I expect. Bombs in Johannesburg are no different to bombs in Belfast or in the West End of London. It is not an area we can be selective over . . . Privately we have requested clemency because we do not feel the execution of these men will ease the present tension in South Africa.'

'What sort of reply have you had?'

'What we'd have expected. Officially and unofficially our request has been ignored. I might add, Mr Curwen, that your father is only a British subject in technical terms. For the last dozen or so years he has chosen to make his home in the Republic.'

'So you've washed your hands of him?'

Furneaux said evenly, 'There's something you should understand. They execute a minimum of a hundred criminals a year there. There's no capital punishment debate in the Republic. From our viewpoint, your father received a fair trial although he declined to co-operate in any way with his defence advisors. The Supreme Court heard his appeal, at length.'

'I'm not interested in what he did, I only care about saving his life.'

'Your father was found guilty of murder. My view is that nothing more can be done to save his life.'

'That's washing your hands.'

'Wrong, that's accepting the reality that in South Africa people convicted of murder are hanged.'

'He's my father,' Jack said.

'His solicitors don't believe he has a chance of a reprieve. I am sorry to have to tell you this.'

'How soon?'

Furneaux scanned the papers in the file, flipped them over. He fastened on a single sheet, read it, then closed the file.

'It may have been discussed by the executive council last night, but it might be next week – they're more preoccupied with the unrest – three weeks, a month maximum.'

Jack stood. He looked at the table, he looked at his hands.

'So what am I supposed to do?'

Furneaux looked to the window. 'Baldly put, Mr Curwen, there's nothing you can do.'

'So you're just going to stand back while they hang my father?' Jack spat the question. He saw his spittle on Furneaux's tie, and on his chin.

Furneaux looped his handkerchief from his pocket, wiped himself. 'Mr Curwen, your father travelled quite voluntarily to South Africa. He chose to involve himself with a terrorist gang, and it is, and from the very beginning was, more or less inevitable that he will pay a high price for his actions.'

The file was gathered against Furneaux's chest.

'I'm sorry for wasting your valuable time . . .' Jack said.

'Mr Sandham, would you show Mr Curwen to the front hall.'

Jack heard Furneaux's heavy tread clatter away down the corridor.

He said, 'I don't understand. My father is a British citizen living in South Africa for years, suddenly turns up in a murder trial, but your man has a pretty ancient looking file on him an inch thick. How's that?'

'Don't know.' Sandham bounced his eyebrows.

Sandham took Jack to the front hall, asked him for a card so that he could contact him if there were developments.

He saw the young fellow walk away, threading between the official cars. He noted the athleticism that couldn't be hidden by the disappointed droop of his shoulders. He went back up the three floors to the South Africa desk. Smoking too damned much, and his chest was heaving when he made it to the open-plan area where he worked.

He thought he knew the answer to the question that Curwen didn't understand. He was old enough, and passed over often enough not to care too much what he said and to whom he said it. He knocked at Furneaux's door, put his head round the corner.

'That chap they're going to hang, Mr Furneaux, is he a bit complicated?'

'Too deep water for you, Jimmy.'

'I really don't want to talk about him.'

'I have to know about him, Mum, everything about him.'

'You should be at work, Jack.'

'He was your husband, he's my father.'

'Sam's right. It's nothing to do with us.'

'Mum, it's killing us, just thinking about him. Talking about him can't hurt worse.'

Hilda Perry couldn't remember the last time that Jack had come home in the middle of a working day. He hadn't told her of his visit to the Foreign Office, nor about the embassy, nor about the visit to the newspaper's library. They were in the kitchen with mugs of instant.

'Mum, he's in a death cell. Can you think of anywhere more alone than that? He's sitting out the last days of his life in a gaol where he's going to hang.'

She said distantly, 'I've hated him for more than twenty years, and since I had his letter I can only think of the good times.'

'There were good times?'

'Don't make me cry, Jack.'

'Tell me.'

He brought her a drink. Two fingers of gin, three cubes of ice, four fingers of tonic. She normally had her first of the day when Sam came back from the office.

She drank deep.

'Your grandfather was stationed in Paderborn, that's in West Germany. He was a sergeant major. I was seventeen, just finished school. I used to nanny for the officers' wives. Jeez was on national service. He was a cut above the rest, not classy, not like an officer, but Jeez was always correct. Treated me like a lady. He always stood in a cinema for the national anthem, stood properly. We didn't go out much, a lot of evenings I was tied with the officers' kids and Jeez was a sort of batman and driver to the colonel. He was well in with the colonel. After we were married we used to get a card from the colonel each Christmas, not after Jeez went. Jeez went back to the UK, demobbed, we used to write a bit, and then Mum and Dad were killed in the car accident, it was in the papers. Jeez wrote by express, gave his address. I was staying with an aunt and he used to come and see me. I suppose I loved him, anyway we were married. There was a cottage right down in the country that Jeez got his hands on, near Alton in Hampshire. It was only a couple of bedrooms, pretty primitive, that's where we lived. He once said the colonel had helped him find it . . . Fill me up again, Jack.'

He took her glass to the drinks cabinet in the living room. Three cubes of ice, six fingers of tonic. She wouldn't notice.

'He was born in 1933 and we married in '57, and I was

35

nineteen. It was lovely down there, cress beds, trout streams, nice pubs, walks. Jeez didn't see much of it. He was up in London when he wasn't away.'

She stopped. Her hands fondled the cut glass tumbler.

'He was very close, didn't talk about his work, only said that he was a clerk up in Whitehall. He called it a souped-up secretary's job.'

She had never before talked calmly to her son about his father.

'Jeez used to take a train up to London, most of the year before it was light and come home in the evenings most of the year when it was dark. I didn't ask him where he went, he didn't tell me. He just said that what he did was pretty boring. He'd be away about half a dozen times a year, most often for about a week, sometimes as long as a month. I never knew where he went because he never brought me anything back from where he'd been, just flowers from Alton on his way home. Lovely flowers. Sometimes he looked as though he'd been in the sun, and it was winter at home. It's hard to explain now, Jack, but Jeez wasn't the sort of man you asked questions of, and I had my own life. I had the village, friends, I had my garden. There wasn't much money, but then nobody else round about had money. Then I had you . . .'

'What did he think about me?'

'Same as with everything else, you never really knew with Jeez. He used to do his turns with you at weekends. He'd change you, feed you, walk your pram. I honestly don't know what he felt.'

'And when I was two years old?'

'You're interrogating me, Jack.'

'In your own time.'

'It's twenty-four years ago this month. He packed, always took the same small suitcase, always took five shirts, five pairs of socks, five sets of underwear, a second pair of trousers and a second jacket, and his washing bag. He went off on a Monday morning, said he'd be gone two weeks. Two weeks was three,

three weeks was four. I was busy with you so until it was four weeks I was reasonably happy. Jeez wasn't the sort of man you chased up on. I can't explain that, but it's the way it was. Then at the end of four weeks there was money lodged in our account, the same amount as he always gave me, and I knew he'd walked out on me, on us. I went through the whole house looking for something about his work, there was nothing. Can you believe that? Not one single thing, not one scrap of paper with so much as a London phone number on it. No address book, no diary, not even a national insurance card. It was so horrible to realize I knew nothing about him. I rang the bank. I asked them where the money had come from. It had come from Liechtenstein, would you believe it? I had them send me the name of the bank. I wrote and I had a two line letter back. Regret not in a position to divulge. Divulge, dear God,' she said and the tears were bright in her eyes. After a time she went on: 'I went to a solicitor, he wrote and had the same answer. Jeez had gone from me . . . The money was the only way I knew he was still alive. Each January the sums he sent would go up as if Jeez was keeping abreast with the prices index. The month I married Sam they stopped. But by then I was long past caring. The only man I knew who knew Jeez at all was his old colonel. I wrote to him through his regiment, and he wrote back to say he was sorry, but he knew nothing of Jeez. There was just a wall, everywhere I turned.'

'So you gave up?'

'You've no right to say that to me.'

'No, I'm sorry.'

'I did not give up. I carried on, trying to be a mother to you, trying to get the shame out of my system. Has it ever crossed your mind what it's like to live in a small community, a village, when you're marked down as the woman whose husband walked out? I did not give up, I was building our new life. I managed to shut Jeez out for two years, close him down. Two years, and then I couldn't stand the ignorance any longer. The solicitor had gone cold on me. I did it myself. One weekend I left you with a neighbour and I took the train to Chippenham, then a taxi to the address that had been on the colonel's letter. It was my last throw . . .' She stared once more into her glass.

'Was he there?'

'Entertaining, for lunch, guests on the patio, smart cars in the drive, uniformed drivers. They all looked at me very puzzled till the colonel came and took me inside to his study where the dogs were. He was obviously embarrassed. I suppose it wasn't easy for him . . . He said that your father had been some sort of clerk up in London in a government office, that his trips away had been couriering documents or working on low-level audits. He said Jeez was a deep, close man, without friends, but the opinion was that he'd just become restless, things too quiet for him, that he'd just upped and away. His advice was that I should try to put your father out of my mind and start again. He asked after you, and I can still see his sad smile when I showed him your photograph. I think he was trying to be kind to me . . . His wife brought me some sandwiches for the journey home. When the colonel brought me out of the house all his guests stopped eating, they were all staring at me. The colonel told one of the drivers to take me to the station. The next week I went to the solicitor and filed for divorce, desertion. That's when I gave up.'

'Did he love you?'

'I thought so,' she said simply.

'Can you believe he'd go along with murder and bombing, or be associated with black South African terrorists?'

'No.'

Jack reached into his pocket, took out his wallet. He laid the newspaper photograph in front of his mother.

'Who's that?'

'That's Jeez today,' he said. 'That's my father.'

Jack was annoyed, stamping about the field, time wasted. And this after he had broken off milking his mother's memories to get there punctually.

A small crowd waited on the blaster. There was the farmer who was selling the field, there were three from the development company which was buying the field. There were the JCB drivers, and the oxyacetaline cutting team, and the lorry men. There was a deputation from the housing estate 300 yards from the pillbox rabbiting on to anyone who would listen about how all their windows would be broken.

The blaster was working quietly with his spade, filling sandbags.

Jack knew the blaster was slow. He knew also that the blaster was good, and he knew there was no use at all in offering to get anyone to help him. It was the blaster's way that he did his own work, himself, because as he'd often told Jack that way there wasn't any other bugger to get things wrong.

D & C used George Hawkins as often as he was available. He was their regular. They put up with the wizened little man's cussedness because the job was always done as it should have been, but every time they had him they cursed the old sod and asked themselves why they went on using him and always had the same answer. George would retire the day after they found another blaster who could do the job better.

A young man from the development company walked brusquely to them. His shoes were caked in mud. He had ripped his raincoat on barbed wire. He had come for an argument. Didn't they know they were running late? George Hawkins ignored him and Jack tried to shut him up with a sharp glance. Time was money, you know. George Hawkins spat to the ground and went on with his work.

'In fact your running late is causing us considerable inconvenience.'

Jack said, 'And unless you get out of this gentleman's way and let him get on with the job that he's damn good at then you'll be running even later.'

The young man's moustache trembled on his lip. Jack thought it was shaved so thin that it might be touched up with eyeshadow.

'What I meant was . . .'

'Just make yourself scarce, and quickly.'

The young man backed away. He'd seen the bloody-minded crack on Jack's face. He decided this wasn't a man to fight with.

The pillbox was part of a line that had been built along the Surrey uplands during the summer of 1940. If the Germans had landed on any of the beaches around the resort towns of Eastbourne or Brighton and if they had broken out of the beachhead then the high ground 30 miles to the north would have been the last defensive barrier before the southern outskirts of London. They might have been chaotic times, but they had known how to build pillboxes. It was squat, hexagonal, walls 2 feet thick with three machine-gun slits giving a wide view down towards the Surrey and Sussex county border. No-one wanted the pillbox as a memento of the war. The farmer was selling his field, the developers were buying it for twelve houses to the acre, and anyway it was a hangout for the local teenagers and their plastic bags and solvent sniffing.

The last sandbag was filled, the top knotted.

'Do I have to carry 'em all myself?'

There was a titter of laughter. He had them all lifting his sandbags, right down to the developers in their shined footwear and styled raincoats.

Jack carried a sandbag beside George who carried two.

'You're running bloody late.'

'It's been there close on fifty years, another fifteen minutes won't hurt.'

They reached the pillbox. George stopped his helpers a dozen yards short.

'What are you going to use?'

'Got time for a lesson, have we?'

'Only asking.'

'Get that shower back and I'll talk you through.'

Jack waved the drivers and the farmer and the developers away.

He watched George work. All the time he worked he talked. A thin nasal voice describing the skills that he loved.

'I've drilled shot holes right through to the reinforcing net of wire, got me? Reinforced concrete, right, so there's wire in the middle. Each wall, I've got six shot holes a foot apart, and I've six more in the roof drilled vertically. For each hole there's three cartridges of PAG, that's Polar Ammon Gelignite to you. All in it's close to twenty pounds that's going to blow. Don't ever force the cartridges, see, don't mistreat the little fellows, just slide them in, like it's a bloody good woman you're with . . .'

Jack enjoyed working with the old man. For more than two years he'd been with George once a week, once every two weeks, and he was always made to feel it was his first time out. There hadn't been anything of a friendship between them until George had one day cried off a job, and Jack had been in his area and called by. He had found him alone with a twisted ankle and an empty larder and gone down the local shops and stocked the cupboard, and ignored all the moaning about not accepting charity. He'd called in a few more times till the old man was mended, but though they marked the binding of an unlikely friendship his visits were never referred to again.

'Bastard stuff this reinforced concrete. Takes double what you need to knock over brickwork . . .'

Jack knew that. He'd known that from the first time he'd worked with the old man. He just nodded, like he'd been given a jewel of new information.

The detonators went in on the end of white Cordtex, linked with safety fuse. Detonator ends crimped to the Cordtex, safety fuse tied to the Cordtex. Every shot hole had its own detonator, and in minutes the pillbox was covered with a web of wire.

'Always run the Cordtex and the safety fuse out carefully. Bastard if you get a kink in the stuff. You get a bloody misfire. What does a misfire mean? Means it's bloody dangerous when you get to dismantling the whole shooting match and starting all over. And another thing, Jack boy. You look a right prick if you've a shower of shit like that lot watching you . . .'

He was wiring his cables into the charger box. George and Jack were more than a hundred yards back, down in a dip in the field's contours.

'Get that lot under cover, and get your hat on. One minute.'

Jack bellowed back to the watchers and heard a police sergeant repeat the instruction by megaphone.

'You're a bloody vandal, Mr Hawkins.'

'Get your nose up, so's you see. Twenty seconds.'

Jack had a hard hat rammed down on the top of his head. He peered across the open ground to the pillbox.

'You all right, Jack? You're quiet today. Ten seconds.'

'Fine.'

He thought that if it had been put to the test the pillbox could have held up an infantry battalion for half a day. Graceless, strong and seemingly indestructible.

'Here we go.'

Jack saw the flashes, then the debris moving upwards and outwards, then the smoke. He heard the echoing rumble of the detonations. He felt the blast of air on his face. He ducked his head.

'Bloody good,' George growled.

Jack looked up. George was hunched beside him. The fortification was a rubble of concrete loosely held together by twisted wire.

There was a long thirty minutes before the blaster would allow the men forward who would cut through the wire with their torches.

When they stood at the edge of the rubble Jack marvelled at what Hawkins had achieved.

'That was pretty professional, Mr Hawkins.'

'Explosives'll get you through anything, Jack boy, if you know how to use them.'

4

On Tuesday and Thursday mornings Frikkie de Kok dressed in the bungalow's living room.

His alarm warbled quietly at three on those mornings. He dressed in the living room so as not to disturb Hermione. On those Tuesday and Thursday mornings he liked to dress well, to be at his best.

His wife knew why Frikkie rose early on those mornings, his sons did not. In a fashion she pretended that she did not know. Where he went and what he did as the dawn was rising on Pretoria, sometimes once a week, sometimes once a month, was never talked about between them. She knew, and in her own way she supported him. There were only small ways that she could help him at those times. She never troubled him with family difficulties or nagged at him to pay bills when she knew he had set the alarm for his early rising. He was sure that the boys, aged seventeen and fifteen, knew nothing of their father's work. The boys were the apples of Frikkie de Kok's eyes, especially Dawie, the elder.

He dressed in a white shirt, a tie that was the darkest blue, shoulder holster, a grey, almost charcoal suit and black shoes. He brushed his teeth brutally to try to erase the taste of yesterday's cigarettes. He took a glass of orange juice from the fridge. His wife wanted a new fridge and he could see from the packed shelves that the present one was inadequately small. Hermione had last mentioned the need for the new fridge on Sunday, she had not mentioned it on Monday. She'd be back again, he thought, tomorrow.

From behind the sofa he picked up his small case. He went to

43

the front window, drew back the curtain and looked out. There were two cars waiting.

He left his home in the Waterkloof suburb of Pretoria at 3.40 on those Tuesday and Thursday mornings. He let the cars wait for two more minutes, then emerged from his porch at 3.39. The cars would be moving off at 3.40. His was an exact science, and he had nurtured exactness in most aspects of his life.

At the front door he paused. He could hear the faint sounds of his sons, asleep. They shouldn't have had to share a room, but all government salaries were falling behind the private sector. Costs were steepling and taxes too, and there was no chance of a larger bungalow so that the boys could each have a room of their own. Great boys, doing well at school, and they'd do well when they went into the army. The boys would be a credit to their father and mother because their parents had scrimped to give them an education that had not been possible for the young Frikkie de Kok. The boys thought that he worked as an instructor in the carpentry shops. Time enough to tell them what he did when they had finished their schooling and perhaps not even then. He closed the door gently behind him. There was no tightness in his legs, no nervousness as he walked. If Frikkie de Kok showed either emotion or hesitation then the effect on the men around him would be catastrophic.

He saw the glow of two cigarettes in the second car. On those mornings he always had an escort of two plain clothes policemen. His work was classified as secret. When he went to the prison before dawn he always had the armed men in support, and he carried his own hand gun in the shoulder holster.

The first car was driven by his assistant. A fine young man, heavily built, bull-necked, hands that could pick up a blown football, one in the right and one in the left. The assistant had been a policeman and had served in the *Koevoet* unit in the Owambo area of South West Africa. The 'Crowbar' men were an elite inside the South African police confronting the SWAPO insurgency campaign. The assistant was equally at home with the FN rifle, the M79 grenade launcher, 60mm mortars, and

44

.50 cal machine guns. There was nothing squeamish about the assistant's attitude to his civilian work. Frikkie de Kok thought him the best of young South Africans. If Frikkie had had a daughter then he'd have been pleased for her to become his assistant's wife.

He climbed in beside his assistant and closed the door noiselessly.

The cars pulled away. Waterkloof was a fine suburb for Hermione to live in. They weren't in one of the better avenues, but it was a good district. They lived alongside good clean-living people. Just hellish expensive for a man who worked with his hands for the government.

The capital city of the Republic slept.

They came fast down Koningin Wilhelminaweg and past the bird sanctuary.

Frikkie loved birds, all of them from the big predators to the little songsters. When he retired he hoped to buy a small farm in the north east of the Transvaal, not that he would do much farming but he would be able to study the birds. All dependent on bastard politics. Farms were already selling cheap if they were up in the north east of the Transvaal because the farmers were quitting, and those that were staying were buying rifles and German Shepherds and spending their thin profits on high wire fences. Just like Rhodesia. But if he bought a farm he'd take some shifting. Take a big, big fire to burn out Frikkie de Kok if he'd put his life savings into a farmhouse and some acres and some stock.

In the centre of the city they came on the first of the corporation's street cleaners. No other sign of life. The city slept, and it didn't know and didn't care that in the state's name Frikkie de Kok and his assistant were going to work.

They drove through the empty streets, past the great buildings of commerce and government power. He had lived 35 years in the capital, he was proud to be a part of it. No way that the communists and the terrorists and the agitators were going to undermine the authority of Pretoria. Over Frikkie de Kok's dead body . . . They turned onto Potgieterstraat. Nearly there. He noticed that the breath came faster from his assistant. He'd learn. Frikkie de Kok had been like that, panting, tightening when he was the assistant to his uncle, and he'd conquered it.

They went under the railway bridge.

The floodlights of Pretoria Central were in front of them.

The assistant was changing down, slipping his clutch, shaking the car before the right turn in front of Local. Frikkie de Kok never criticized his assistant. On from Local and past the high walls of the White politicals gaol. They came to the checkpoint. From his hut the armed prisons man stepped into the middle of the road. The lowered bar was behind him. The assistant dipped his lights. The prisons man cradled an FN. More than a hundred times a year this car and Frikkie de Kok and his assistant came up this side road, Soetdoringstraat, to the roadblock. They held their ID cards up against the windscreen. The prisons man had seen their faces, good enough for him. The car slid under the raised bar, was inside the perimeter of the prison complex.

Left now, past the prison service store on Wimbledon Road, past the prison service swimming pool, past the prison service tennis courts, past the rows of prison service houses and flats, past the old gaol where he had worked his apprenticeship with his uncle.

A long lit wall rose in front of them. They were high on the wooded hillside above the scattered lights of Pretoria.

They were at Beverly Hills. And in Frikkie de Kok's opinion that was a hell of a silly name to be given to a section of a gaol. But maximum security had always been Beverly Hills to both the prison staff who came in and out on their shift pattern and to the inmates on their one-way visit. Beverly Hills, Frikkie had heard, was a flash hotel down in Durban. Frikkie disliked Durban. Too many English down there, too many liberals, not his place for a holiday. But the new gaol, opened eighteen years before, the most modern in the country, and the most secure, was Beverly Hills to all who talked of it. The most modern and the most secure.

The detectives parked the escort car. They would wait outside for Frikkie and his assistant until their work was done.

The assistant drove to the gates. The lights beamed down on them. A television camera jutting from the wall followed them. By a hidden hand the gates glided open. The car drove inside. The gates closed behind. More gates in front. An airlock. Close walls. An iron grille for a roof.

Through a glass panel a warrant officer looked down into the car from his control centre.

The assistant wound down his window, showed their two cards perfunctorily, then passed their hand guns up to the waiting hand. It was two minutes to four o'clock. The gates ahead of them opened and they drove on.

The hangman and the hangman's assistant had reached their place of work. All of the 'condemns' who had been sentenced to death in courts throughout the Republic were brought to Beverly Hills to while away the months before their appeal, before the State President deliberated on the matter of clemency. All of the condemns whose appeal failed, whose plea for clemency was rejected, died on the Republic's single gallows beam in Beverly Hills.

They were in a small parkland. Their headlights caught a startled antelope and a warthog in the white light. Frikkie thought it a good thing that a hanging gaol should harbour a small nature park between the perimeter walls and the cell blocks. He liked to see the animals. If he had been asked he would have said that he thought it unfortunate that the cells of the condemns did not have windows that looked out on to the animals. The windows were set too high for the condemns to see out. But Frikkie was never asked what he thought, and he would not have ventured an opinion of any matter that was not his business.

As soon as he was inside the administration with its cathedral steps he heard the singing. The singing used to upset him when he first came to the old Pretoria Central with his uncle. He had learned through his uncle's indifference to accept it. The whole of A section and B section singing, all of the Black condemns. Not a sound from C section, the White condemns hardly ever sang. Frikkie de Kok was a regular churchgoer, he knew his hymns. He'd never heard singing the like of that in Beverly Hills on the mornings that he worked. Wonderful hymns that the Blacks had learned in the mission schools and their own fine natural rhythm. When the Black condemns sang about Jesus, then they sang with feeling and with love. Best thing. He had many times told his assistant, the singing helped their work.

They were escorted to the duty officer's room. They were given coffee.

The singing helped because it calmed the condemns who were to be handled that morning. The singing gave them strength, seemed to drug them, meant they didn't give any trouble.

Creamy coffee and sugar. Only half a cup. As Frikkie had told his assistant, he didn't want his bladder under strain when he was working.

There hadn't been any trouble for years, but the trouble then had been so bad that Frikkie de Kok would never forget it, so if the singing helped to quieten the boys then that was fine by him. His last assistant had packed it in after that piece of trouble. Four condemns had barricaded themselves in a cell and they couldn't be forced out when the execution detail came for them. They'd sent for the riot gas canisters and the whole block had been screaming, and they'd kept Frikkie de Kok waiting. Once they'd opened the doors the execution detail had moved so fast that they hadn't stopped to get their masks off before they reached the gallows building.

The duty officer passed a remark about the weather. He didn't think it would rain, not from the forecast given the previous evening on the SABC. It hadn't rained for three and a half months in Pretoria so it was a fair bet that it wouldn't rain. Frikkie just acknowledged him. The assistant didn't speak.

Most of them went well. Most of them had a lot of guts. The Whites always went well, especially after the Blacks were gassed to the gallows. The sort of White that he hanged was the sort of guy who wanted to show that he had more guts than a Black.

At three minutes to five Frikkie de Kok levered himself up from the easy chair. He nodded his thanks to the duty officer for the coffee.

They crossed the prison. There was the slither of their shoes, and the crack of the boots of their escort. There were voices that warned of their approach so that doors could be opened ahead of them. The singing was rising to its pitch.

They climbed the steps.

Frikkie de Kok pushed open the heavy double doors. This was his preserve, where his orders were not questioned. He was in the preparation room. A high room, brilliantly lit by a fluorescent strip. There were a dozen men waiting there, all in the uniform of the prison service. He recognized three of them, they were three who were always there. It was a job of work for Frikkie de Kok, but he always marvelled that some made it their business to be present each and every time. The other nine were youngsters, five Black and four White. It was the law of Beverly Hills that every man who served there must attend a hanging. None of these execution virgins caught his eye.

He opened the interior door. He switched on the lights. No official from the prison service would have presumed to go ahead of him. The gallows room was a blaze of light. Along the far wall, where the railed steps went below, lay the shadows of the long beam and four nooses. The four ropes above the nooses were coiled and fastened with cotton thread. It was as he had left it the previous day when he had made his arrangements, tested the lever and the trap, measured each rope for the drop, made his calculations based on height and weight.

The district surgeon came to him. There was the first sheen of dawn in the skylight. The district surgeon told him that the four men were in good shape and none of them had asked for sedation. The district surgeon, a pale-faced gangling young man, was the only person that Frikkie de Kok would speak to at this time. That was privileged and valuable information.

He stood on the trap. Firm.

He wrapped his fist on the lever. Shining and oiled.

He looked at the cotton holding up the nooses to chest height. Correct.

He glanced at his watch. Three minutes before half past five.

He nodded to the duty officer waiting at the door of the preparation room. The duty officer raised his personal radio to his mouth.

Frikkie de Kok knew of the crimes for which the four had been convicted. One had stabbed to death a White housewife after they had disagreed on what he should be paid for sweeping her drive. One had raped a six-year-old girl, White, and strangled her. One had shot to death a petrol station attendant during an armed robbery in East London. One had been sentenced to death for ritual witchcraft murder, the killing of two men and the cutting out of their organs for *muti*. To Frikkie de Kok's mind execution by hanging was the correct penalty for such crimes.

He had stipulated in which order the four should be brought down the corridor and into the preparation room. He had heard once of a mistake, many years ago, before his uncle's time. Two men, one heavy and tall, one slim and small, brought in the wrong order. The small fellow had had the short rope and they'd had to pull on his legs under the trap. The big fellow had been on the long drop and nearly lost his head with his life.

Frikkie de Kok had never made a mistake.

The singing approached him. A tumult of harmony. He liked it when they were brave because that made it easy for him, and if it were easy for him then he could do better by them.

He waved the spectators into the gallows room and over to the far wall. He saw that the governor had arrived in the preparation room. They acknowledged each other. Frikkie straightened his tie.

A good hymn. Not four weeks before that hymn had been sung in his church in Waterkloof. Sung in Afrikaans, of course.

Good theme, good words. He had the four freshly laundered white cotton hoods in his hand.

They came fast into the preparation room. The first man had a prison officer supporting one arm and the chaplain the other, the three that followed had a prison officer on each side of them.

They were wide-eyed, they were shivering. In the preparation room the words of the hymn died in their throats and the chaplain sang on alone, lustily. All the reading of the warrants, all the formalities, had been completed back in the cell block . . . time now just to get the work finished. Frikkie de Kok remembered each face from the view he had had of them in the exercise yard the previous afternoon. They were in the right order. He nodded his head. No man spoke in the hanging shed, only the chaplain sang. The four whimpered and seemed to fight to find their voices. They were moved inside. Moved onto the trap. If it were one man, or even two, then the assistant would have pinioned the legs, but with four it was necessary for the hangman to take two and his assistant to take two. They moved quickly and quietly behind the men, fastening the leather thongs. The chaplain was in front of them. The chaplain knew he was at God's will, otherwise how could he have looked them in the face.

Hoods on.

Two of them were singing. Muffled, indistinct, quavering.

Nooses round the necks. Frikkie did this himself. Tightened the knot under each of the left side jaw bones. He saw the feet in line of the trap. He flicked his hand. The prison officers stepped back, releasing their hold on the condemns.

With both hands he gripped the lever.

The explosion of the trap.

Jeez lay rigid on his bunk.

His breath came in great pants.

The silence.

He had heard the feet stamping and shuffling on their way to the gallows. He had heard the swell of the singing, seeking out new heights of sympathy. Then the crash of the trap.

An awful sorrowing silence. The singing was to support four men, and the men were gone from where singing could boost them. The singing had ceased with the fall of the trap, cut in mid phrase.

The God awful silence around Jeez, like he was alone, like he was the only man in the bloody place.

He always heard the trap go.

He heard it the day before when the hangman was practising his drops with the earth-filled sacks, he heard it go on the morning of a hanging. As the crow flies or the worm crawls, Jeez lay on his bed just 29 yards from the gallows beam. He heard everything in the hanging room, and everything in the workshop and the washhouse underneath. They'd be suspended now, they let them hang for twenty minutes. Then there would be the water running in the washhouse as they cleared up the mess after the district surgeon had completed his post-mortem. Then there would be the hammering in the workshop as the trusties nailed down the coffin lids. Last there would be the sounds of the revving of an engine and the sounds of the van pulling away, running down the hill.

Beverly Hills wasn't a place for seeing what happened. Christ, it was a place for hearing.

Listen to a multiple execution.

Singing, trap, silence, water, silence, hammering, van engine.

Those were the sounds of four men getting to be stiffs. God Almighty, Jeez . . . It was the route they had in mind for Jeez. While he had been at Beverly Hills he had heard the sounds of 121 guys getting stretched. And now 125. Jeez had heard the trap go under each last one of the mothers.

He shouldn't have written the letter all the same.

The letter was weakness. Shouldn't have involved her. But he had heard the trap go so many times. Shit, and he had to call for *someone* . . . he felt so alone.

This was a civilized gaol, not like the one a long time back. There were no beatings here, no malnutrition, no rats, no disease, no forced labour. Here, his cell door wouldn't be thrown open without warning for a kicking and a truncheon whipping. No risk that he would be frogmarched into a yard and kicked down and shot in the nape of the neck. This was five star. So bloody civilized that Jeez had sat in a cell for more than a year, a cell that measured 6 foot by 9 foot, while the lawyers debated his life. Three meals a day here, a good medic here, because they wanted him healthy on the day. He had written his letter because he was losing hope.

What were the bastards doing? Why hadn't the bastards got him out?

He hated himself for believing they'd forgotten him. They'd got him out the last time. Took the bastards long enough, but they'd got him out. They couldn't let a man, one of their own, couldn't let him . . . never finished. Couldn't let him . . . Course they couldn't. He hated himself when the hope went, because that wasn't the Jeez way.

He was one of a team, a bloody good team, a team that didn't forget the men out in the field.

He was fine on the days when he didn't hear the trap fall. It was only on those sodding days that the doubts bit.

He'd done them well. He'd kept his mouth shut through interrogation, bloody weeks of it. He'd kept his mouth shut through the trial. He'd kept his mouth shut when the security police from Johannesburg and the intelligence men from Pretoria had come to talk to him in his cell. He hadn't let the team down.

Jeez heard the spurting of the water hose in the washhouse.

On the high ceiling of the cell the bulb brightened.

Another day. God Almighty, it just wasn't possible that the team had forgotten about Jeez.

In an hour, and after he had eaten his breakfast, he would hear the hammering start.

It was difficult ground for the Minister. Any by-election would be in these days, but the Orange Free State was the heartland of the Afrikaner world. A dozen years before, in Petrusburg and

53

Jacobsdal and Koffiefontein, he'd been cheered to the echo by the White farmers when he talked of the inviolability of the policy of separate development. Today he would have to speak to the same White farmers with the currency collapsed, with further foreign sanctions in the air, with unrest in the townships, with taxes up, with markets disappearing. No easy matter up here to sell the ending of the homelands policy, to uphold the repeal of the Immorality Act, to defend their record in the collapse of law and order. One thing for the State President and his ministers to talk in Pretoria about dismantling separate development, quite another out in the constituencies to explain to the faithful the reasons for the retreat. They had a big enough majority in Parliament, the National Party, but by-elections counted. The most recent by-elections had shown the subsidence of the Party's vote and the increase of the pulling power of the Conservative right. The State President was enjoying the greasepaint and the television lights and his broadcasts via satellite to the American networks where he spoke earnestly of reform. The ministers, the donkeys, they were the ones who legged it down to the grass roots to explain that everything that was traditional and taught from the mother's knee was now subject to revision.

The Minister of Justice had a long day in front of him. Public meetings at breakfast, midday and late afternoon. The by-election was to be held in 27 days' time. The Minister of Justice had been preceded by Water Affairs, Forestry and Environment Conservation, and by Community Development and State Auxiliary Services. In this constituency alone he would be followed before polling day by State Administration and Statistics, by Transport Affairs, and by Minerals and Energy.

The minister had slept in the back of the car for the most of the drive from Bloemfontein to Petrusburg. He woke when they were 3 miles short of the town. His secretary passed him a battery shaver. The secretary sat in the front beside the police driver. In the back of the Mercedes with the minister was the local area Chairman of the Party, a fellow Broeder-bonder.

'What'll they be like?'

'Cool.'

'Which means iced.' The minister strained his chin upwards to get the razor's teeth against the skin of his jowl.

'We all want to know what the future holds.'

'Change.'

'You won't find this audience applauding talk about change. They like the old ways. They want reassurance that *we're* running our country, not American bankers.'

'I'll get them laughing . . .'

'You'd have to get your trousers off to get a laugh.'

'What do they want?'

'To know that our government is not abdicating its responsibilities in the face of overseas pressure, and Black pressure. Persuade them and we might just win.'

'It's rubbish to talk of abdication.'

The Party man shrugged. 'Fine when you say that to me. Tell your audience that and they'll shout you out of the hall, I promise you.'

'What'll satisfy them?'

'You know the name of Prinsloo?'

'Should I?'

'Gerhardt Prinsloo.'

'Don't know him.'

'His parents live in Petrusburg.'

'Don't give me riddles, man,' the minister snapped.

They were coming into the town. One street on a main road, low buildings, a small shopping arcade, a decent church.

'His father runs a hardware store. His mother teaches in the nursery school. You should go to Gerhardt Prinsloo's grave.'

'If I knew who he was.'

'Everyone in Petrusburg knows the name of Gerhardt Prinsloo. He's the nearest thing they have to a genuine South African hero.'

'Tell me, man.'

'If the people here thought that you didn't know who

Gerhardt Prinsloo was and what he did, then I assure you our vote would be halved.'

'What did he do?'

'Warrant officer Gerhardt Prinsloo gave his life to save others. He smothered the terrorist bomb in the Rand Supreme Court . . .'

The minister bit his lip in anger. 'You caught me cold, early in the morning.'

'I've heard it said in this town that our government of today is so preoccupied with foreign opinion, with the shouting of the liberals, with appeasement, that the men who murdered Gerhardt Prinsloo might receive the State President's clemency.'

The minister leaned forward, tapped his secretary's shoulder. 'Give me my speech and your pen.'

Resting the speech on his knee he made a long addition to the back of the first page.

The car came to a stop. There was desultory applause from a small group of the faithful out to greet the minister.

'Straight after my speech I will visit the grave. I will lay some flowers there, and I want a photographer.'

A tiny cramped cell, Jeez's home for thirteen months.

In the top half of the heavy door was an aperture covered by close mesh, too close to get the fingers through. Beside the door, and looking out on to the corridor of C section 2 was a window of reinforced glass. Against the far wall to the door was the flush toilet, and beside that, set in a cavity, was a drinking water fountain. If he sat on his bed, at the far end of the pillow, then his legs fitted comfortably underneath the work surface area that jutted out from the wall. He had brought no personal mementoes with him to Beverly Hills, there were no decorations on the walls, no mementoes of any previous condemns. Eight feet above the floor a heavy metal grille made a false ceiling. The cell was 16 feet high. On the corridor wall, above the grille, were slatted windows, and the guard who patrolled the catwalk above the corridor had a clear view down through these windows into the cell. In the ceiling the light burned, bright by day, dimmed by night, always burning. No daylight could reach the cell. Natural light came from windows above the catwalk, and then by proxy into the windows above Jeez. From his cell he could see no blue sky, could never see the stars. The windows on to the catwalk and into the cell were always open, so the temper of the seasons reached him. Stinking hot in high summer, frosty cold in winter. Now the cool of the autumn was coming. He doubted that he would shiver again in the winter cold.

He had eaten his breakfast, he had shaved under supervision, he had swept out his cell. He waited for his turn in the exercise yard. Other than his turn in the exercise yard, this day would go by without him leaving his cell.

He was the celebrity, the first White political to face death by hanging since John Harris and that was more than twenty years before. No-one who worked in Beverly Hills had ever before handled a White political who was condemned. Many times in each day he would look up from his bed to the corridor window and see the flash of a pale face, the face of a watcher. They might have had a camera on Jeez for all the time they watched him. They watched him while he slept and while he ate and while he read and while he sat on the lavatory. He knew why they watched him, and why his shoes were slip-ons and without laces, and why he had no belt, and why there were adhesive tabs on his prison tunic in place of buttons.

When he had first arrived at Beverly Hills he had been told why they would watch him. One guy, a White, had once stood on his bed and nose-dived onto the concrete floor to try to cheat them out of his appointment. No chance that they would provide Jeez with an opportunity not to show for his appointment.

Because Jeez was a political he was allowed no association with the other two White condemns in C section 2. They were new boys. One had moved in three weeks before, and one had been there for four months, and three had gone because their sentences had been commuted to imprisonment. The other

57

White condemns were permitted to exercise together in the yard leading off C section 2, but Jeez was only taken out when they were back and locked in. Jeez's cell was at the far end of the section corridor. The cells of the other two condemns were opposite each other and beside the door that led to the main C section corridor; there were empty cells separating the White criminals from the White political. He had never seen their faces. He had heard their voices in the corridor. He knew they called him the 'bleddy commie' or the 'bleddy ter'. These two bastards wouldn't be singing for him, not if it came to him keeping his appointment.

Sergeant Oosthuizen was the prison officer who had responsibility most days for Jeez. Most days Sergeant Oosthuizen escorted Jeez to the exercise yard.

Each time he heard the slam of the door that separated the main C section corridor from the C section 2 corridor, and each time he heard the key slot into his cell door he hoped, a short soaring hope, that the governor was coming with the message that would tell Jeez that the team had not abandoned him.

They always slammed the door between the main corridor and C section 2.

The team had been his life. The team was names and faces, clear as photographs, no blurring with time. The captain of the team was Colonel Basil, big and bluff and with thin blue veins surfacing on apple red cheeks. The men in the team were Lennie who had a patter of whip crack jokes, and Adrian who flirted with the fresh new recruits, and Henry who on a Friday evening at the end of the working office week played the piano in the saloon bar of the pub that the Century men used. Colonel Basil and Lennie and Adrian and Henry were his team and his life.

He hadn't let them down, neither a long time ago nor in Johannesburg. Of course they'd be working for him, moving bloody mountains for him. Probably old Colonel Basil would have set up a special task force desk to supervise the prising of Jeez out of the hole he was in.

Sergeant Oosthuizen was smiling at him from the opened cell

door. They were cutting it rather fine. Hell of a good time he'd had on the team, the real friendships, home and away. Being on the team mattered, because membership of the team was the guarantee. Shit, the guarantee was important to a legman. It said that the team would never stop working their balls off for a legman who was in trouble. And Christ, was he in trouble. Jeez Carew, member of the team, was going to hang. And his faith in the team was slipping.

'Nice morning for a walk. Come on, Carew.'

The solicitor had driven that morning from Johannesburg because it was useless to telephone for information, and worse than useless to write letters to the Justice Ministry.

He was not shown in to the civil servant's office until after the lunch hour.

It was a brittle meeting. The elderly Afrikaner South African and the young English heritage South African. The man on government pay and the man on private practice.

The solicitor's questions were blunt enough.

Had the decision been taken by the State President on whether James Carew would hang?

The civil servant had parried. 'The decision has been taken, but the decision is not yet public.'

Could the solicitor's client know of the decision of the State President?

'He'll know when he needs to know.'

Surely, if he was going to get clemency then he should be told immediately?

'If he's not going to get clemency then he's better not knowing.'

Couldn't the solicitor be given an indication of the State President's thinking?

'Look, I'm not going to tell you what is the State President's opinion. The way we do it is this, the deputy sheriff will go to the gaol not more than four or five days before an execution and he will then inform a prisoner that the appeal to the State

59

President has been turned down. I'm not saying for certain that the sentence will stand in the case of your client, but I can tell you that if it does stand you will know at the same time that Carew knows.'

It had been spelled out to him. The young solicitor softened.

'Not for Carew, but for me to know.'

'You're asking me to read the mind of the State President.'

'A bit of guidance.'

'The minister was in Petrusburg this morning. He made an addition to his prepared speech. He said . . . "There are people who say that your government is soft on the matter of law and order. We are not. There are people who say that our legal processes can be influenced by the threats of foreign governments. They can not. There are people who say that terrorists will get away with murder in our fine country. They will not. I warn people who seek to bring down our society that they will face the harshest penalties under our law, whether they be White or Black, whether they be our citizens or jackals from outside" . . . It's not me that's answering your questions, it is my minister.'

'How long?'

'Not long, not a month.'

'It's cut and dried?'

'Listen. At the moment we have a police strength of around forty-five thousand. In ten years we will have a force of more than eighty thousand. Right now we have to fight this unrest with an understrength force. If any South African police line cracks then there is nothing to save us from anarchy. We have to sustain the morale of the police or we go under, and supporting the morale is not best served by reprieving police murderers.'

'I appreciate that you've spoken to me in confidence. What can save my client?'

The civil servant examined the file in front of him. He was a long time turning the pages. He looked up, he gazed steadily at the solicitor.

'If at this late stage your client were to give to the security police every detail of his knowledge of the African National

60

Congress, then there might be grounds for clemency in his case alone.'

'The others would go?'

'We could handle one reprieve, not more. We have never understood why your client ever involved himself in terrorism, and he hasn't helped us. If we had names, safe houses, arms caches, everything he knew, then we could talk about clemency.'

'Guaranteed?'

Fractionally the eyebrows of the civil servant lifted.

'You should tell him to talk to the security police, that's all that can save him.'

Sergeant Oosthuizen stood by the locked door of the exercise yard and talked. He talked of his daughter who was big in wind-surfing down on the Cape, and of his son who owned a liquor store in Louis Trichardt.

Sergeant Oosthuizen had been 38 years in the prison service, the last eleven of them in Beverly Hills. He was to retire in the next month, and then he'd be able to spend time with his daugh-ter and his son. Sergeant Oosthuizen didn't require Jeez to have a conversation with him. He just talked, that was what he was happiest at.

It was more of a garden than an exercise yard. Against the walls was concrete paving. Each wall was 9 paces long. Thirty-six paces for a circuit. Forty-nine circuits was a mile's walk. The centre of the yard was Jeez's garden. The soil was 12 inches deep, then concrete. It was Jeez's garden because none of the other condemns showed any interest in it. The garden had not been looked after since a child killer had gone to the rope the month before Jeez arrived at Beverly Hills. Last spring Oosthuizen had brought Jeez seed. The gerani-ums had done well, the marigolds had threatened to take over, the chrysanthemums had failed. Jeez crouched on his haunches and picked discoloured leaves and old blooms off the geraniums. The sunlight was latticed over the bed and the concrete by the shadow of the grid above him. The garden was a cell. The song birds could manage it through the grid and out again, but nothing as large as a pigeon could have squeezed down to feed from the grubs that he turned up when he weeded his flowers.

In the exercise yard Jeez could see the sky and he could feel a trapped slow breath of wind, but he could see no trees, and no buildings, and no men other than Sergeant Oosthuizen and sometimes the guard at his catwalk window. He could see the wall of C section 2, and the outer wall, and the wall of C section 3, and the wall of the C section corridor. If he stood with his back to the wall of C section 2 and raised himself onto tiptoe he could look over the roof of C section 3 on to the upper brick-work of the hanging room.

He wondered if Sergeant Oosthuizen would have retired before it was his turn, Jeez's turn, to take the early walk. He wondered if the sergeant would walk with him.

That was stupid thinking, because there was no way the team would let it happen. Burning the candle they'd be. Couldn't for the life of him think how the team would pull him out. Thought about it often enough, but couldn't work it. Colonel Basil wasn't the one for ideas, nor Lennie. Adrian was good with ideas, better than Henry. Have to be Adrian who was going to crack it, and then the team would all thrash it round. Wouldn't see their feet for dust once they'd settled on an idea. Clear memories, faces clear in his mind, Colonel Basil, and Lennie who had the limp from the ambush in Cyprus, and Adrian who'd bloody near lost his career in the gentlemen's toilet at Piccadilly underground, and Henry . . . Shit, and wouldn't Henry have been up for retirement, gone to breed the bloody pigeons he always talked of. What if they'd all gone? Couldn't have done . . . All bloody older than Jeez. Colonel Basil was, certain, Henry was. Bloody Lennie *looked* older. Couldn't tell Adrian's age, not with the hair rinse. What if they weren't there at Century . . . ? Stupid thinking. No way the team would let him hang . . .

'Carew, I'm speaking to you.'

Jeez started up. 'Sorry, Sergeant.'

'You weren't listening to me.'

'Sorry, Sergeant, I was far away.'

'You don't want to brood, you know. It's where we're all going. You don't want to think too much.'

'No, Sergeant.'

'Why I was talking to you was that I'd just seen your fingers, first and second on your right hand. How long is it since I've been with you?'

'It's thirteen months, Sergeant.'

'And I've never noticed your fingers before.'

'Just fingers, Sergeant.'

'I've never noticed them before, and my wife says I'm the noticing kind.'

'What didn't you notice, Sergeant?'

'No nails on the first and second fingers of your right hand.'

Jeez looked down. Pink skin had grown over the old scars. 'Someone took them out, Sergeant.'

'Ingrowing, were they? I once had an ingrowing big toenail, when I was serving at the old Johannesburg Fort gaol. That's closed now. They thought they might have to take it off, but they cut it back and it grew again, but not in. Hell's painful.'

'Someone took them out for fun, Sergeant. Can we go inside now, please, Sergeant.'

'Who took them out for fun ... That's a very serious allegation ...'

'Long ago, Sergeant, long before South Africa.'

He could remember the pliers grasping at the nails of the first and second fingers of his right hand. Pain rivers in his whole body. He could remember the smile of the bastard as he jerked the nails off. He hadn't talked to the bastard who had ripped his nails off, just as he hadn't talked to the security police in Johannesburg.

'And you get yourself washed up for the medic.'

They went inside. Jeez going first and Sergeant Oosthuizen following and locking the door to the exercise yard. The doctor

63

saw Jeez once a week, and weighed him. Jeez knew why he was weighed each week.

Sergeant Oosthuizen stood by the door of Jeez's cell.

'That must have hurt when they took them out.'

'A long time ago, Sergeant.'

5

Hilda Perry liked to see her family on its way in the morning.

Sam had taken Will to school, and ten minutes later she was back at the front door holding Jack's raincoat ready for him. He came hurrying down the stairs. If he ever managed to get himself married or get a flat of his own, she'd truly miss him. She always thought it was because of the time they had been together, the abandoned wife and the fatherless son, that they had a special bond . . . He wasn't sleeping properly, she could see the eye bags. She reckoned she looked the same.

Today she hugged her boy. She knew they were both thinking of the man half way round the world from them in a cell, thinking of the man she wouldn't have recognized, her Jack couldn't have remembered. He told her he would be home early, he would have seen her gratitude. They'd keep a sort of vigil in the house, the two of them, for however many days and weeks it took, until Jeez was . . . Just the two of them. Sam didn't know, but she'd started to take Librium three days earlier, just one tablet each night when she was getting into bed, so that she wouldn't dream. She shrugged him into his raincoat. He managed a smile for her, and was away down the front path to his car. The telephone rang behind her. She wanted to see Jack go before answering the telephone, but he had taken a chamois out of his car and was cleaning the windscreen. She went back into the hall and lifted the telephone.

'Could I speak to Mr Curwen, please?'

She could see Jack at the rear window, finishing off.

'Who is it?'

'Name's Jimmy Sandham. He'd want to speak to me.'

She ran awkwardly in her slippers down the path. The engine was starting, coughing. She caught him just in time.

She saw the frown. She heard him say, 'I'll be right with you.'

He put the telephone down.

'Only work, Mum.'

She knew when he lied. She had always known. He was away, running down the path. She thought she was losing him. Could no longer reach him in the way she had before. He had changed when he had broken with that nice Miriam. She knew what had happened from Miriam's mother when a rain squall had driven them off the course into the lounge of the golf club. Something methodical and cheerless about his life. Two nights a week, after work, at the squash courts, working himself out until he was near sick from exhaustion . . . and the same with his studies again, picking up the lost degree course, working late into the nights. She preferred him the way he had been before, when he was with Miriam. She could never understand how he had lost the degree chance, thrown it up four months from his finals, seemed ridiculous to her, and so trivial.

She watched him drive away.

He had been so matter of fact that evening. He had come home from college and told her that his university days were finished. He'd told her the circumstances, like they didn't matter. A single student who was a paid-up member of a Fascist party being heckled by a group of Trotskyites between chemical engineering and applied mathematics. A point of principle, he'd said flatly, didn't like bullies. He'd told the Trots to leave it, they hadn't and they'd jostled the lad and were spitting in his face. Remembered Jack remarking that he'd thrown a punch, broken a boy's jaw. So matter of fact. Jack spelling it out that he had been up before the disciplinary court of the senate that morning, and the provost had asked him for an apology, and his reply that he would do it again, because it was bullying, and being told that he must give the assurance, and refusing, and being told that he'd have to leave, and leaving. Telling it like it wasn't

66

important, telling it just like Jeez would have. And here he was, back at his books.

She closed the door. She was alone with herself. The Librium didn't last into the morning. She worked at speed with the hoover and the dusters and the brush and pan, upstairs round the beds and downstairs through the kitchen.

The front doorbell rang.

It was a cosy and predictable household. It was her home that was being damaged by nightmares and sedation pills and lies. The doorbell rang again. She didn't want to answer it, she didn't even want to go to the door and peer through the spy hole. Another long ringing. The milkman had already been, the post was on the sideboard in the hall beside the telephone, the newspaper was on the kitchen table. She looked through the fish eye spy hole. It was a tall man, still short of middle age she thought, and he wore a light grey suit and his face was tanned and his moustache was clipped short into a crescent over his upper lip. She tightened the belt on her housecoat. The door chain was hanging loose, unfastened.

She opened the door.

The man was smiling.

'Mrs Perry? Mrs Hilda Perry?' A soft casual voice.

'Yes.'

'Did you used to live, Mrs Perry, at 45 Green Walk, Coulsdon, in Surrey?' Another smile. She couldn't place the accent. There was a lilt in his speech that wasn't English.

'Yes.'

'Could I come inside, please, Mrs Perry?'

'I don't buy anything at the front door.'

'It's about a letter you had, Mrs Perry.'

'What letter?'

'You had a letter from a Mr James Carew in Pretoria Central prison. My name's Swart, it would be easier to talk inside.'

She recognized the accent as South African. 'What if I did have such a letter?'

'I'm from the embassy, consular section. The letter Mr Carew wrote to you is the only letter he's written to anyone inside or outside our country. We're trying to help Mr Carew. Sometimes a man's background, his personal history, can help a prisoner in his situation. It would be better if I was inside.'

Because Jack had lied to her that morning she was fine tuned to a lie. She knew this man lied. The man was taller than her even though he stood on the step below the front door.

'If you could help us with Mr Carew's background, his friends and his work and so on, then there might be something you told us that could make a difference to his situation.'

Whatever he said he smiled. She wondered if he had been on a course to learn how to smile. She knew Jeez's letter word by word. Each guarded sentence was in her mind. Jeez didn't want them to know that Hilda Perry was his wife, that Jack was his son.

'I've nothing to say to you.'

'I don't think you understand me, Mrs Perry. James Carew is going to hang. What I'm trying to do is to find out something that might lead to a reprieve.'

His foot was in the doorway. Jeez wouldn't have wanted him in her house, she was sure of that.

'I just want you to go away.'

The smile oiled across his face, and then he was inside the hall.

'Why don't we just sit down and talk, Mrs Perry, with a cup of tea.'

She thought of the good years with Jeez, and the misery without him. She thought of the way she had willed herself to hate him after he had gone. She would have sworn that the man who had pushed himself into her home was Jeez's enemy.

She picked up the telephone. She dialled fast.

'Who are you ringing?'

'Police, please,' she said into the telephone.

'That's a hell of a stupid thing to be doing.'

'Mrs Hilda Perry, I've an intruder in my house – 45 Churchill Close.'

'Are you trying to put a rope round his neck?'

'Please come straightaway.'

She put the telephone down. She turned to face him.

'They're very good round here, very quick. Why don't you come into the kitchen and sit down, and then you can explain to the officer who you are and what you want.'

Cold anger, no smile. 'He'll hang, Mrs Perry.'

He was gone through the door. She saw him trotting down the path. When he was outside the garden he started to run.

Years of placid and sedate domestic life were disintegrating. For a long, long time she had loathed Jeez. For the last few short days she could remember only the times that she had loved him.

By the time the police car turned into Churchill Close, Major Hannes Swart was 2 miles away, going fast and fuming.

It had taken him long enough to track Hilda Perry from the address used by the prisoner, Carew. Some good, honest foot-slogging had translated Green Walk into Churchill Close, and for nothing. Swart had been in the South African police for seventeen years, but he hadn't done footslogging for more than a dozen. Security police officers were too precious to have their time wasted on door-to-door and scene-of-crime.

For some of his work he was a businessman promoting in the United Kingdom the sale of Stellenbosch wines. At other times he was an accredited journalist at the Foreign Press Association specializing in financial affairs. Most often he was a lowly member of the visa section of the embassy's consular staff. He worked for a police brigadier from the fifth floor of the embassy. He was one of the bright stars amongst the detail of security police officers assigned abroad. He had blown what ought to have been a simple task. A dowdy housewife had seen him off.

By the time a bemused police officer was leaving Churchill Close, having been told only that a South African male had tried to force entry into the house, no explanations of why, the temper of Major Swart had matured to controlled fury. They should have jazzed the swine, used the helicopter on him, and the electrics when they had him in John Vorster Square. Too damn correct they had been with him in the interrogation cells.

And a hell of a damn good thing that he had taken the precaution of parking his car out of Churchill Close. At least the cow didn't have the number plate to add to whatever bloody story she hatched to the local force.

Sandham had said that this was an, ah, irregular meeting, if you follow.

He sat with Jack in a tea bar off Victoria Street, some way from the Foreign Office.

'It's irregular because I haven't cleared it with my superiors and because I'm giving you the gist of FO thinking that may turn out to be incorrect. Your father's going to be hanged, and neither the private nor the public shouting of our crowd is going to change that. Your father's solicitor has told our people in South Africa that they'll spare him if he turns state evidence. Up to now he's told them nothing. He doesn't sound to me like a man about to splash through a sea change. That's one pointer, there's another. A few days ago their Justice Minister made a speech that effectively shut out all prospect of clemency. They want to show they're strong. They want blood.'

'What would happen if I went out to see him?'

'You wouldn't get a contact visit. You wouldn't be able to touch him, hold his hand. You'd have a glass plate between you. You'd speak down a voice tube. My opinion, it would be pretty distressing for you and for him.'

What would they talk about? Jack shuddered. The man would be a stranger. God, and small comfort he'd be to his father.

'What's your interest in his case, Mr Sandham?'

Sandham shrugged. 'Something stinks.'

'Meaning what?'

'I'll tell you when I've found out.'

'When my father's dead and buried?'

'I can't say.'

'What stinks?'

'Sorry, Mr Curwen ... but you'll hear from me when I know, I promise you that.'

'I don't know where to go except to you,' Jack said simply. 'That's the hell of it, and time's running out.'

Jack drove back to D & C.

Janice looked at him curiously, then gave him the message that his mother had rung. He telephoned her. He cradled the telephone on his shoulder, his elbows were on his desk top, his hands in front of his mouth. Janice noted his attempt at privacy.

He heard about the visitor and the questions. He told her that he had been to the Foreign Office, that there wasn't any good news. He rang off abruptly. He was sagging over his desk.

'Why don't you go home?'

He looked up. He saw young Villiers staring down at him.

'Why should I go home?'

'Because you look knackered.'

'I'm fine.'

'You're not, and you should go home.'

Jack was shouting. 'If I say I'm fine, then I'm bloody fine. And I don't want anyone bloody tip-toeing round me.'

'Just concerned, old boy.'

'Well, don't be fucking concerned.'

Janice and Lucille studied their typewriters. Villiers flushed, flexed his fingers. His father had told him everything that he needed to know about Jack Curwen, that he had been two years and one term at university and left on a disciplinary matter, that a drop-out added up to a cheap workhorse for D & C Ltd, that Jack Curwen was lucky to have his job however dedicated and able he might be.

'Nice to know that nothing's wrong,' he said evenly.

Because he had a good nose, Jimmy Sandham's diplomatic career had long ago been stunted. He said what he felt it right to say and then managed a quaint look of hurt when his superiors rewarded him with lack of advancement.

As a young man, in Teheran, at a time when British factories were on overtime and weekend shifts to turn out Chieftain tanks for the Shah's army, Sandham had briefed a visiting journalist on the help with direct interrogation methods that British Intelligence were giving to Savak. In Amman he had filed a formal report to the ambassador stating that the representatives of British construction companies were buying their contract to build a hydro plant with backhanders; two of the representatives were at that time putting up at the ambassador's residence.

He couldn't be fired, but he could be disliked, and he could watch his promotion prospects going down the plughole.

It was eight years since the industrious Jimmy Sandham had last been posted abroad. He never complained, never sought explanations as younger men leap-frogged him. But the word was out. If there was a bad smell in a section then keep Sandham's nose at arm's length.

The Carew case was a thoroughly nasty smell to Jimmy Sandham, and the error of Peter Furneaux, assistant secretary, had been to let him within a mile of it.

The friend Sandham had telephoned had been his best man at the English church in Bangkok. The friend thought the day spiced with pleasure because the ambassador had been the guest of honour eleven days after receiving the query from the crown auditors concerning his wife's frequent and private use of the Rolls. Jimmy Sandham's bride had been his friend's secretary.

That had been a long time ago, but they had stayed as close as two men can who meet each other for a couple of meals a year and exchange cards at Christmas. The friend worked from a nondescript tower block on the south side of the Thames, home base of the Secret Intelligence Service. The friend loved Sandham for his pig-headed obstinacy, and made certain they were never seen together.

They sat on a bench in Battersea Park, shielded by a towering shrub from the nearest path. The funfair hadn't opened for the summer season, the kids were at school, it was too short of pick-ings for the tramps, too draughty for the lovers.

'Furneaux's a total arsehole,' the friend said.

'I get this garbage from Furneaux about "deep water", and we have a file with Carew's real name on it. Furneaux didn't put the file back into records, it's locked in his own safe.'

'To keep your prying eyes off it.'

'What would I have seen?'

'Enough to whet your appetite.'

Sandham grinned. 'What about your file?'

'Enough for you to choke on.'

Sandham stared into his friend's face. 'Is James Carew one of ours?'

'Fighting talk, Jimmy. You should know, there's a D-notice.'

'What else?'

'I reckon there'd be Official Secrets Act, Section 1. Closed court. Ten years minimum, could be fifteen . . . You want cream on your raspberries? There's a fair bit of bad blood in the Service over Carew. Desk men say it's entirely his own fault, legmen say that once a man's on the team then it's marriage vows, for ever. Trouble is that the Service has changed since Carew started out. Desk men count, legmen are dinosaurs. Evaluation and interpretation is the name of the game, and you need an Oxbridge degree for that. Running around on the ground's out of fashion.'

'And the desk men'll let him hang?'

'He had a fairy godmother, but that's over. They got him out the last time, second time's one too many. The leg men say that Carew wasn't asked to do what he did.'

'So you bastards are going to write him off.'

'Come off it, Jimmy . . . Are we going to go to Pretoria and tell them that a staffer, a wallah on the pension scheme, is driv-ing the scoot car from a daylight bombing? He was there to infiltrate, provide the raw intelligence for assessments. He wasn't there to lead the bloody charge down the Johannesburg High Street. I tell you what we think happened. We think he had

73

infiltrated the ANC, just inserted himself under the skin. We think the ANC learned to trust him and one day, bad luck for Carew, they trusted him enough to do a little job for them. We think the poor creep probably didn't know what he was into.'

Sandham said bitterly, 'I thought it was holy writ that you lot looked after your own.'

The friend laughed out loud. 'That's gone with the ark.'

'What sort of chap is Carew?'

'Brilliant. You want to know what he said when he was lifted? "Let's have a bit of dignity, boys." That's what he said to the four guys with him, and they'd just knocked half Jo'burg over. He'll keep his secret. Our secret.' The friend looked at Sandham keenly. 'You won't forget the ten years minimum and the D-notice, Jimmy?'

'It's the nastiest story I've ever heard.'

'It's *realpolitik*.'

'The politicians have backed this, leaving him to hang?'

'Who needs to tell them about the big bad world?'

'When he left his wife . . .'

'We got him back, without ten years of his life, four stones, two fingernails, and he never told them anything. But he had the old godmother working for him then. Right now, he's no-one rooting for him.'

'Why not?'

'March of time, Jimmy, comes to us all. The godmother got retired, a bit before Jeez was lifted. There was Lennie Abrams, he's posted to Djakarta for expenses trouble. There was Adrian Mountjoy, fairy, he's in an open prison in the Midlands, groped a vice-squadder in a gay club, once too often. There was Henry Willcox, took an early out and skipped with one of the library girls. Jeez's problem is that no-one's shouting in his corner.'

Sandham shook his head, as if the smell was suffocating him.

'Where was he, the first time, those ten years?'

'Try a happy little holiday home called Spac. A stint of Albanian hospitality.'

'It's disgraceful.'

'Keep in touch, Jimmy.'

'For what?'

'So's I know whether I'm going to have to traipse down to Parkhurst for the next ten years of visit days.'

A West Indian woman pushed a pram past him and gave him a long sneering look, like she'd spied out a flasher or an addict. His friend was gone, vanished into the trees and shrubs. For more than a quarter of an hour Sandham sat bowed on the bench. Finally he stood, and tried to pull the creases out of his raincoat. On his way back to the Foreign Office he found a telephone kiosk, rang Jack, and fixed to meet him the following day.

He was a man heavy with anxiety.

Jack knew from Sandham's voice that he was to be told something that was worse than he had been told before.

They met in a pub south of Westminster Bridge. Sandham found them a corner where neither could be seen from the door, where he could not be seen from the bar.

Jack told Sandham that a South African had been to see his mother. Sandham said that the man would be either from security police or intelligence. He'd check it. Sandham said that they had to have been working on tracing Hilda Perry ever since Jeez's letter had given them her previous address.

Sandham said there was a civil war being fought in South Africa . . .

'. . . And they'll play dirty if they have to.'

'How dirty?'

'Four Blacks from Port Elizabeth, big guys in the opposition United Democratic Front, get a telephone call from what calls itself the British embassy asking for a meeting. They set off, and they disappear on the road. When they're found they've been burned and hacked to death. We never made the call. That was last year. I'll give you another one. Victoria Mxenge, a Black lawyer representing some of the accused in the treason trial. She was coming home after dark to her township outside Durban. Shot dead on her doorstep. No arrests.'

'This isn't bloody South Africa,' Jack said.

'They have a keen idea of national security. They're a serious *volk*, and they couldn't be caring too much about international frontiers.'

'These people in South Africa, the government murdered them?'

'I didn't say that. I said they were opponents of government, and they're dead. There *might* be a difference. Do you know what a D-notice is?'

Jack shrugged. 'It's when the government tells the newspapers they shouldn't print something.'

'Do you know about the Official Secrets Act, Section 1?'

'The charge that's brought against foreign spies and our traitors.'

'What I'm going to tell you is covered by a D-notice and the Official Secrets Act, Section 1.'

'We're going in up to our necks, aren't we?'

Sandham told Jack what he knew.

He knew that James 'Jeez' Carew was on the payroll of the Secret Intelligence Service, had been for a quarter of a century. He knew that Jeez had been in South Africa for the last dozen years with the job of infiltrating the military wing of the African National Congress. He speculated that Jeez had overstepped his brief and become involved in a guerrilla attack. He knew that Her Majesty's Government were not prepared to go to Pretoria and cough up that a White under sentence of death was in fact a legman in deep cover for SIS and therefore should be spared the rope.

A gasp from Jack. 'I can't believe it.'

'You're on the horizon of a tough, rough old world.'

'They always get their people back, that's what you always read.'

'It might have been true once, but isn't true any more, and your father wasn't acting under orders and that's government's let out. There's more to it. Technically South Africa is a major trading partner. We've billions invested there. We may have as many as a quarter of a million jobs dependent on South African purchasing power and South African mineral resources. Government's dislike of apartheid comes a poor second to economics. I'm just telling you what I know.'

Jack flared. 'I'm going to blow this off the roof tops.'

'Don't even try it. The papers won't print it and telly won't broadcast it. That's the D-notice. You'd be charged under the Official Secrets Act, and when you get to court it'll be long after your father's been executed. And then it'll be *in camera*, the court'll be cleared, the doors locked, the Press out.'

'So who's lifting a finger for him?'

Sandham picked up their glasses, went to the bar. Jack sat slumped on the upholstered seat. He was drained. He could not absorb that this was happening to Hilda Perry and Jack Curwen. Worse than a nightmare. Sandham put two large Scotches on the table and sat down.

Jack asked, 'If I blew it would you go to prison with me?'

'Worse than that. Breach of official trust.'

'You've taken a chance on me.'

'It was the only decent course to take.'

Jack gripped Sandham's hand, held it tight. His face was screwed into lines, as if he agonized over the question.

'Is Jeez Carew worth crying over?'

'You know the answer.'

'You have to tell me.'

Gently Sandham released Jack's hand. 'You're his son, you don't have a choice. And from what I've discovered I'd say that your father is a man you should be very, very proud of.'

Sandham said he had set up a meeting at the Foreign Office for the following morning that was to discuss Jeez. He didn't elaborate. He left Jack, grim and drawn.

He walked back to his car.

Waves of outrage lapped over him, outrage against the forces

77

that had intruded into his life, his mother's life. His tongue twisted round obscenities, sometimes silent in the spring evening wind, sometimes out loud. Terrorism, prisons, and the sentence that a man should hang by the neck until he was dead had never before owned a corner of Jack Curwen's mind. Many targets for his hatred. He hated White South Africa. He hated the security policemen who had arrested Jeez. He hated their prisons and their gallows. He hated the Secret Intelligence Service of his own country. He hated the men who had washed their hands of responsibility for Jeez's life.

A long, bitter walk, a mile beyond his car.

When his mind was made up, when a certainty had slashed through the rage and bafflement, he retraced his steps.

South Africa was a place on a map. He had no thoughts on the future of that country, it was of no interest to him. He had no Black friends. In a year he could have counted on his fingers the times he had spoken to Black men and Black women.

Jack knew nothing of Black Britain or Black South Africa. He knew nothing of the Black dream of freedom, and he cared less.

But his mind was made.

He went in search of Duggie Arkwright.

Duggie Arkwright was the best start Jack could think of. Each new year, Jack transferred from his old diary to his new one the addresses and telephone numbers that he had consolidated over the years. The previous New Year, when he had determined on retaking his degree as an external student, he had searched out Duggie to beg and borrow the library books from college that he knew Duggie had squirrelled away. He had an address that was a squat off Camden High Street. He thought they were all Marxists, or they might have been Stalinists, and there was a Revolutionary Socialist Workers Party poster sellotaped to the wallpaper in the hall. He was given a second address.

Duggie had nearly been a friend in the little more than two years they had shared at London University. They had known each other first when they had adjoining rooms in the hall of residence, when they shared coffee, or were short of sugar, or needed to borrow a book. Duggie was an idealist. In his first term he had joined DebSoc, LabSoc, AASoc, and DramSoc. Jack hadn't joined the Debating Society nor the Labour Society nor the Anti-Apartheid Society nor the Dramatic Society. He had joined the rugby club. Jack would have been satisfied to end up with a 2nd (Lower) in Modern History, he knew Duggie had kicked himself for ending up with that grade. Jack had dogged application, Duggie had brains. He'd gone to Duggie for the books because he was damned if he was going to go back to college and request library facilities.

He went gingerly down the dark basement steps in Paddington. When he rang, a woman shouted at him from a window above. She gave him a third address. She said she'd been chasing the bastard herself for his unpaid rent. She may have been misled by Jack's suit to supposing him another creditor, because she wished him well.

They had drifted apart during the second year. But it would not have been possible for Jack to lose sight of Duggie. Duggie Arkwright was the darling of the Left's societies, the regular lambaster of government and institutions. He wrote in the student paper under a photograph and a by-line. He made principal speeches at debates. He had twice been arrested in Trafalgar Square, once on the Anti-Apartheid ticket and once on a CND demonstration.

He ended up in Dalston, quite a long way east over the tracks from tarted-up Islington. It was the doorway beside a newsagent. The newsagent was open. He went inside and asked if next door was right for Duggie Arkwright. He got a cold nod from the young Pakistani at the cash till.

Last year Jack had seen Duggie's photograph, second row in a demonstration in Liverpool. He couldn't think of anywhere else to start.

Jack had rung the bell and a girl had opened the street door and led him upstairs. It wasn't really a flat. It was a room with a table and some chairs, a baby asleep in one of them, and a line of washing and a paraffin stove and a collapsible cot and an electric cooker. For a bed there was a mattress on the floor with rumpled sheets and blankets. Posters on the wall, and Jack fancied they hid the damp.

They looked at each other and Duggie beamed.

'Bloody hell, it's priggy Curwen, the refugee from Modern History. What in God's name . . . ?'

'Nice to see you, Duggie.'

'I suppose you want my notes now, and my essays.'

'No.'

'Ditched it all, have you? Come to tell me you've chucked it?'

'I'll take my degree the year after next, and pass.'

'God, what a crass prig. Do I have to wait till then for my books back?'

'When I've finished with your books I'll be sending them back to the library.'

Duggie was laughing out loud, Jack was grinning. The student that Jack had hit had been standing in front of Duggie Arkwright. Duggie had said at the time that it didn't matter, the student having his jaw broken, because he was unsound, a revisionist.

'Come on in, sit yourself down.'

But there wasn't anywhere to sit down. The baby was in the one comfortable chair, and of the two chairs at the table one was deep in washing bags and the other was a book store.

'Bloody good to see you, Jack bloody Curwen. Jack, this is Anthea.'

The girl stared coldly at Jack. He could measure her dislike. His suit and his raincoat, wasn't it? His hair that was cut every fortnight. She turned away from him, as if she was a bank manager's daughter, as if she detested a reminder of where she had once been.

'That's Joshua Lenin Arkwright, sleeping thank God . . . Don't just stand there, get your bloody coat off. You look like a bloody bailiff.'

Jack grinned. 'Your last landlady spoke well of you.'

'Remember that cow, Anthea? Should have had the rent

tribunal on her, and the Health and Sanitary . . . You're bloody welcome, if you're not after a loan.'

'I do need some help,' Jack said simply.

Duggie's laughter pealed through the room. His smile was huge and his teeth were awful.

'You must be in desperate shit if you need my help.'

Anthea snapped that he'd wake the baby.

Duggie pulled a face. 'Come on, if you've the price of two pints.'

They went down the stairs, and were in the street before Jack realized that neither of them had said goodbye to the girl. 'One glorious night behind a hedge when we'd gone up to help the miners picket some hideous power station. Her daddy said he'd cut her out of his will if we didn't marry. High price to pay for coal, if you ask me, but he's seventy-one next birthday.'

Jack plunged. 'Are you still involved in South Africa?'

'You don't just lose interest because you've left college.'

'It's important to you?'

'Course it is. Most days I'm at Anti-Apartheid.'

'Do you know people at the ANC?'

'Conscience hasn't stricken priggy Curwen, has it? You going to make a donation?'

'It's not a joke, Duggie.'

'I have dealings with the ANC, I've been on liaison committees. I know people there.'

'They have a military wing, right?'

'They've Umkhonto we Sizwe – Spear of the Nation – that's the military wing.'

Jack stopped him outside the pub.

'I want an introduction.'

'You're not a bloody spook are you? I mean, you wanting that, it's ridiculous . . .' He tailed away. He saw the seriousness on Jack's face.

'You have to trust me, Duggie. Trust me when I tell you that I intend nothing that will harm that organization. I have to have an introduction to this Spear of the Nation. I have to know the man I am meeting is able to get things done.'

'They'd kill you if they found you were bent.'

'That's not what they'll find.'

'You didn't tell me what work you were in.'

Jack cracked a thin smile. His mind was made. He was on his road.

'I'm to do with explosives.'

Duggie pulled an old envelope out of his pocket. On it Jack wrote his home number and his office number.

In the pub they had three pints each, paid for by Jack, and they talked about college days and laughed too much. They laughed too loud because Jack had said he worked with explosives and Duggie had heard him.

6

'I see the world's looking up on you.'

Nicholas Villiers noted the change in Jack.

'Sorry about the snap. I was a bit under the weather. The problem's sorted out.'

'Glad to hear it.'

Janice and Lucille heard the satisfaction in Villiers' voice. The girls liked Jack for his apology.

Jack told Villiers that he was going straight out to do his elms, that he'd be back in after lunch. He asked Lucille to mind his telephone. He said that a Mr Arkwright might phone him, and to be sure to get the message exactly.

He drove down to Dorking, then came off the main road and took a winding tree-lined route to Ockley. He reached a remote farm, far up a lane, with post and rail fencing for the hunters. Hell of a backwoods place for 30 miles from London. The owner had looked as though he'd had a death in the family when he'd first had Jack down, when the elms were toppled on their sides, felled but waiting to be cut up and carted away. Taking out the stumps was small business to Jack, but he'd had to work for the contract because the owner seemed hesitant to uproot his final memories of the elm avenue.

For once George had beaten Jack to the site. Just the two of them. The JCBs and the lorries would come in the owner's own time. Jack had asked that the horses be kept well clear and there was no sign of them. Some beef bullocks watched them. They'd take plenty to be frightened.

George had already dug neat holes at the side of each of the stumps.

By his small unmarked van was the wooden crate that held the nitroglycerine, ammonium nitrate based dynamite, and also the metal box in which he carried his no. 6 detonators, and also a drum of Cordtex and a drum of safety fuse.

'Are you going to sit on your arse, or are you going to help?'

'I'd like to help, Mr Hawkins.'

They worked together, Jack at George's shoulder as the old blaster stowed the 4 oz cartridges of explosive down under the arches of the roots. Jack didn't speak, didn't interrupt. He watched as George slid the aluminium tubed detonators into the cartridges. He saw him crimp the Cordtex to the open ends of the detonators. He was learning. He was watching a master at work.

'Set 'em off all together,' George muttered. 'Cordtex and safety fuse are cheaper than my time.'

Jack had many times witnessed the routine. He had seen the laying of the explosive, the insertion of the detonators, the crimping in of the Cordtex, the linking of the Cordtex to the safety fuse, the unwinding of the safety fuse back to the van and the charger box.

'You're bloody quiet this morning, Jack boy.'

Jack didn't answer, just watched. A long job with thirty-two stumps to be taken out.

If Sandham was nervous then he was good at hiding it.

A secretary had come up to the South Africa desk to collect him.

Furneaux had been in the open-plan area, he had seen Sandham summoned, and known who the secretary worked for, and wondered what in hell's name was going on. Sandham, Grade 2, having an audience without it going through the Assistant Secretary running his desk.

Sandham came into the hush of the outer office, where the girls' fingers whispered over the electric typewriters. He thought a funeral parlour might have been more cheerful. The Permanent Under Secretary was waiting in front of the closed inner door, ill at ease. Sandham understood. When a Grade 2 man requests a personal meeting with the Foreign Secretary on a matter concerning national security then the fat cats would be wetting themselves, one and all. There had been some exquisite moments in Jimmy Sandham's life. He reckoned this would knock spots off *les affaires* Bangkok, Teheran and Amman.

The PUS opened the inner door, waved Sandham inside.

It was the first time that he had been inside the Foreign Secretary's office. He was too far down the ladder to take part in the South Africa policy meetings, where strategy was hammered over. He thought the Foreign Secretary's wife must have had a hand in the decor. It was seven years since his own wife had left him, shouting from the pile of suitcases at the front door that she couldn't endure one more day with a man so pompous and self-opinionated. And nor had she. But he still recognized a woman's hand. The Foreign Secretary, tepid and small, wouldn't have had the wit to choose the colours and the fabrics and the gentle hidden lighting.

The Foreign Secretary had his nose into a paper-covered desk.

There was a second man in the room. He sat in a low chair with his back to the door, the bald crown of his head just visible over the chair's back.

The PUS announced Sandham. He pointed to a plain, upright chair and Sandham went to it, and sat. Sandham wondered if they had any inkling of what was about to drop into their laps.

The Foreign Secretary raised his head. He had pale skin and owl spectacles.

'Ah, Sandham. Thank you for coming. You wanted to alert us to a matter of national security, I think. I have asked the Director General to sit in. You know the PUS, of course, who will make any notes that may be required . . . The floor is yours.'

The Foreign Secretary had his elbows on his papers, his chin in his hands. The PUS lounged back on a short settee, a pad on his knee. The Director General gazed with frank hostility into

Sandham's face because he had read the wretch's file. J. Sandham, Grade 2 man, given the moment could be mischievous or impertinent, but he needed a deep breath. He had expected that the PUS would sit in with the Foreign Secretary. He had not expected that the Director General would have been summoned across the Thames from his Century tower. The Director General as the man in place in the Secret Intelligence Service had responsibility for Jack's father. The Director General was the employer of Jeez Carew, alias James Curwen. A hell of a deep breath before launching into his accusation.

'Thank you for seeing me, sir. I thought there was a matter that you should be aware of. It is a question of life and death and that is why I have requested this personal meeting with you . . .'

The PUS's propelling pencil was poised.

'In South Africa, in about three weeks' time, a man called James Curwen, but who goes under the name of James Carew in that country, is going to hang . . .'

Sandham saw the muscles tighten under the pug dog chin of the Director General.

'I'll call him Carew because that's the only name that the South Africans have for him. Carew was convicted of driving the getaway car used by African National Congress guerrillas in their escape from the Supreme Court bombing in Johannesburg fourteen months ago. At the time that Carew drove the vehicle he was a full-time operative of the Secret Intelligence Service . . .'

He saw the eyebrows of the PUS flicker upwards, he saw him begin to write.

'A situation has arisen where a man working for his country is going to hang because the British government has not chosen to exercise its influence, first to secure clemency and second to win Mr Carew's release . . .'

There was a cloud of surprise on the Foreign Secretary's face. Sandham wondered what had surprised him. The allegation, or the fact that a Grade 2 man knew the history.

'If you'll forgive me, sir, I think it's unacceptable that a man doing his job should be abandoned . . .'

The PUS closed his notepad, pocketed his gold pencil.

'What's your source?' The Director General beaded Sandham with his eyes.

'I saw a file that I was not entitled by rank to see, sir.'

'Have you passed on this allegation to any other person?' The Foreign Secretary spoke through closed teeth.

'No, sir.' It was Sandham's second instinctive lie. With it clear of his tongue he thought of the earnest, sincere, concerned face of young Jack Curwen.

'And that's all that you wanted to tell the Foreign Secretary?' The PUS seemed to make a trifle of Sandham's statement.

'Yes, sir.'

The PUS shone Sandham an affectionate smile. 'We're very grateful to you for drawing this matter to our attention. If it's not inconvenient for you, would you mind waiting a few minutes in my office?'

The Foreign Secretary had twisted in his chair to look down from his window and into the park. The Director General stared at the tapestry screen that masked the open fireplace. The PUS ushered Sandham towards the door. They wanted him out. They wanted to thrash it round. It had been bloody good entertainment. He would have liked to dance a bit, and shout.

'No problem, sir,' Sandham said easily.

'I'll get someone to take you down to my room. You won't be kept long.'

They watched him leave. They waited for the door to close behind him.

The Foreign Secretary spoke with a squeaking, nervous voice. 'You knew about this, Director General?'

'I did not.'

'Your department, your man.'

'I'll be making it my business to find out, Foreign Secretary.'

'If this Sandham is to be believed . . .'

The PUS swirled his head above his knee, cut the Foreign Secretary short. 'He's to be believed. Our Mr Sandham is always

87

to be believed. More important, he's a difficult man, that's his history.'

'What's to be done with him?'

The Director General looked up. 'He should go home, Foreign Secretary, that's best. He should be at home where he can commit no damage. I'll have a man take him home.'

'If this allegation were to become public property . . .'

'It won't,' the Director General said quietly.

'You can guarantee that?'

'Foreign Secretary, leave it in my hands. You give me that authority?'

'Whatever authority you want.'

'Thank you, Foreign Secretary, just the authority to isolate him.'

They had the hard hats on, and they were crouched 150 yards from the nearest stump, and they were sheltered by the van. George always crouched, didn't matter what protection he had. They'd done the checks together.

Jack had watched each step. He reckoned he could have gone through all the procedures himself.

'Well, don't hang about all day, lad.'

Jack thought he'd die old waiting for a bit of politeness from George.

'What's so bloody funny?'

'Nothing's funny, Mr Hawkins.'

'Get on with it.'

Jack rested the palm of his hand over the bar of the plunger.

'Don't stab it, ease it.'

He closed his fist on the bar. He looked at George, warts and wrinkles and thinned out hair protruding from under the garish orange rim of his helmet. George winked. Jack pressed the charger bar slowly, steadily down.

There was the clap thunder of the detonations. There was the rich loam soil spurting up, the shuddering climb of the tree stumps, the thumping patter of earth and roots landing, the furious croaking of rooks.

Jack gazed fascinated at what they had achieved. Away beyond the line of uprooted stumps the bullocks were in flight.

George studied the scene. His face was closed. Jack looked into George's face. One thing to know a man and work with him, another thing to trust him. He thought he could trust George Hawkins, but what he thought didn't really matter because he had to trust the man.

'Get on with it, Jack,' George said tersely.

'Was it that obvious?'

'Say what you've got to say.'

He told George that his father had disappeared from his life when he was two years old, before he could remember. He told him that he had been brought up to believe that his father was cruelty incarnate. He told him that there was not even a photograph of his father that had been kept by his mother when she had cleared out her husband's possessions. He told George of the letter, how the missing James Curwen had been resurrected as James Carew, under sentence of death. He told him that his father had been working for the government, an agent in place, that his life was not going to be pleaded for.

'That's the history, Mr Hawkins.'

George's was a low gravel voice. 'You could have spoken to your MP, a journalist, one of those lads on television. Why didn't you cry on their shoulders? Why do you talk to me, a blaster?'

'Had to be you.'

'You didn't have to come today and watch me lift a few bloody tree stumps.'

'Right.'

'You want some know-how?'

Jack nodded.

George said softly, 'Where are the targets?'

'Not here, waste of time in London. I know where the target is, I don't know what it'll take.'

'Explosives?'

'Has to be.'

George was striding fast to his van.

'Hope you're not asking me for explosives. Every last cartridge of mine has to be accounted for. You're going to South Africa? Even if you could get them here you can't just put them in your bloody suitcase and fly out of London. Don't think the x-rays and the sniffers would miss it. You wouldn't get as far as the 'plane.'

'I'll get the explosives there.'

'You got the right friends?'

'I'm finding them.' There was the obstinate thrust to Jack's chin.

God, he was racing ahead. He hadn't the targets, he hadn't the explosives, he hadn't the friends. So bloody innocent, and talking as though he could just snap his fingers and achieve them.

George cuffed him. 'Come back to me when you've some answers.'

Major Swart resented having any more of his time taken up with the Carew affair. The file was hardly worth the effort of couriering it from Pretoria on the overnight 747 of South African Airways. Carew was a home desk problem, and following up stray ends was unrewarding work for a major of security police. The woman had seen him off. He'd have thought she'd have spilled her heart out given the chance to save a man from the rope. A week earlier he thought he had placed her in the game. All my leg work and tracking back in the files of Somerset House. Before her divorce Mrs Hilda Perry had been Mrs Hilda Curwen. She had been married to a James Curwen. James Curwen was his man, until he had driven down to the Hampshire village which was listed as the woman's address at the time of her marriage. He'd had a photograph from Pretoria, taken in the gaol but especially so as not to look like a police shot. He had found three men who remembered James Curwen in a pub by the cress beds. A retired postman, the man who kept the village grocery store, and the vicar. He had said he was the London representative of a South African based legal firm. He had said he was trying to trace this James Curwen because there was money left to him. He showed them all the photograph, and he had seen each one of them shake his head and heard each one of them say the photograph was not that of James Curwen. Wrong face, wrong physique.

So, he hadn't linked Hilda Perry to James Carew, and it didn't have a high priority from Pretoria, and there was a limit on his time.

A higher priority was the man who had come in from Lusaka.

If there was a matter that could make Major Swart emotionally ill, it was that the United Kingdom, on top of all its cant about the suppression of terrorism, could allow African National Congress murderers free rein to visit their chummies in the London office.

He thought he might get to see the bastard from Lusaka that evening, not certain, but a good chance.

In the late afternoon Jack came into the office.

Janice was making up her face over the typewriter, her mirror propped against the ribbon. She waved to indicate the paper she had left on his desk, too busy to speak. Nicholas Villiers had gone home, so had Lucille.

He recognized most of the names and numbers that he was to call back. The people with the chimney in Streatham, a good one for George and he'd get his photo in the local rag. The brewery who were pulling down the Bunch of Grapes in Addington, a ball and chain job. The clearance of a small council house development at Earlsfield where the precast concrete units were disintegrating and it was cheaper for the local authority to demolish than to repair ... Duggie Arkwright and a number were halfway down the list, and again at the bottom of the list.

It was Duggie's girl who picked up the phone, Anthea. She sounded high. She dropped the telephone, and he heard Duggie Arkwright curse her. Jack introduced himself.

'You meant what you said?'

'Yes, I want to . . .'

'Open phone, priggy.'

Jack swallowed hard. And this was London. He felt juvenile, naked.

'Same place as we had a drink, same time – we'll go on.'

Jack wanted to ask who they would meet, where they would be going, but the line was dead.

He rang his mother. He wouldn't be in for supper. He'd be back late. The habit was catching, no explanations.

Next he called Sandham's number at the Foreign Office. He wanted to hear about Sandham's meeting, what the new information was.

He was told Mr Sandham had gone home.

There was no reply at the home number.

'I'm dying for a drink,' Janice told him. 'They're open now.'

Jack said, 'It's the nice thing about pubs these days, that a girl can go in and have a drink on her own.'

He settled back to his list, the people with the spare chimney and the brewery and the local authority. The chimney people had gone home, so had the local authority, but he had a good talk with the brewery.

The Prime Minister was obsessive about 'banana skins', and over the years the Secret Intelligence Service and the Security Service had had more than their share of disasters. It had been only too often the Prime Minister's misfortune to get to the despatch box in a gloating House of Commons and wriggle in the mess. With this Director General the Prime Minister felt secure. The confidence was reciprocated with an all-consuming loyalty.

The Director General was 'clean' in the matter of James Carew. He had been transferred from a diplomatic career the previous year. He had come in after Carew's arrest and trial.

The file on Carew revealed ample evidence of an approach to intelligence gathering that was provenly dangerous.

The man's career was a joke, a pathetic confidence trick.

Colonel Fordham should have been put up against a wall and shot for what he had done for Carew. At the very least Carew should have been wound in the morning after Fordham's retirement. The file was horrifying reading.

Colonel Fordham had transferred from the regular army to the Service. He had recruited his batman for leg work, a man without higher education. In due course a small operation had been run into Albania. Albania was the most irrelevant corner of mountains on the European continent. Colonel Fordham had sent this devoted but second-rate individual into Albania on a mission based on rotten information. The Soviet Union scowling at Yugoslavia *might* do a Hungary or a Czechoslovakia, and then NATO *might* deploy troops and armour in North West Greece, and if NATO were up on the Greek Albanian border then they just *might* need to know what was on the far side of this most closed and guarded frontier. Colonel Fordham had sent this man into Albania for a bit of map reading and reconnaissance, and to see which bridges would carry 55-ton tanks. As if he had never heard of satellite photography.

In the file were the minutes of the meeting where the mission was agreed. It wouldn't have happened in the Director General's day. There was a brief paper on the aims of the mission. There was a telex, decoded, from the mission's forward headquarters in Corfu reporting that radio contact had been lost. And the poor bugger sat in prison there for ten years.

No record of a minute to Downing Street. Alec Douglas-Home, Wilson, Heath, none of them ever heard a whisper of it. And of course the Albanians had never known who they had, right to the end, because Curwen had never confessed anything in ten years. It had ended shabbily with the payment of £100,000 from the Service contingency fund, into a Venezuelan bank account.

Colonel Basil had brought his man home, and about bloody time.

The Director General came to four sheets of lined paper that might have been extracted from the centre of a school exercise book. The writing was close, joined up, in ball point. At the top, in capitals and underlined, was SPAC LABOUR CAMP 303. In the ruled margin, written with a different pen but in the same handwriting, he read, 'Col Fordham, I thought this might be important to you in case anyone else of our team ends up in the place, Respectfully, Jeez'.

It was a factual account of life in the Spac labour camp. It was compiled without a trace of self pity. It described the work of the camp – the mining of pyrites from which copper is taken – eight hours a day and six days a week, and a seventh day if the week's target had not been reached. He read of 10 foot high barbed-wire fences and guards with searchlights and attack dogs. Unheated concrete barrack blocks where more than three hundred inmates would sleep on straw mattresses on three-tier bunks. Of a diet that hardly ever included protein, fresh vegetables or fruit. Of the beatings and the punishment cells. Of fingernails ripped off with plumbing pliers. He read of strikes, riots, reprisal executions.

And every day of the ten years this poor bastard had nurtured the assumption that the Secret Intelligence Service was working for his release. It was a disgrace. He tidied the faded sheets of paper.

Anon, the legman had been brought home, privately fêted as a hero.

But he'd lost his wife, lost his son, lost the best ten years of his life, so the agent had been given a warm berth in South Africa. Controlled from London, working for Colonel Fordham.

The telephone rang.

He thought the man who had done ten years of his life in Spac was indeed second rate. He thought also that the man must have a near limitless well of courage.

He picked up the telephone. He said to send them in.

He put the Curwen/Carew file to the side of his desk.

Perhaps Duggie believed him. Extraordinary that priggy Curwen should have sought him out to set up a meeting with the African National Congress, not just any old Joe there but the military wing, and should have said he worked in the explosives racket. Explosives weren't a joke. Explosives and detonators and time delay fuses were serious business.

They left the pub. Then went in Jack's car, north up the Essex Road. It was dark and raining.

'You scared?'

'No,' Jack said. 'Not now.'

'Perhaps you should be.'

'This isn't South Africa yet.'

'It's a war. We're fighting to destroy them and they're fighting to survive. Point is, we're winning, but that doesn't mean they'll stop fighting. What's at stake is whether South Africa is governed by the representatives of nearly thirty million people, or whether it's run by nearly five million who happen by accident of birth and breeding to have a different pigmentation of skin . . . Jack, if you're getting into South African resistance politics, if you're into explosives then, my opinion, you ought to be a bit scared.'

Jack said curtly, 'I've my own reasons for getting involved, they're good enough for me.'

'Learn first that you don't talk on open phones. Learn fast that they can get a hell of a lot rougher than phone taps. There's bombs in London and Paris and Zimbabwe and Botswana and Swazi and Maputo. Big bombs down to letter bombs. They've got infiltrators. They pay burglars to turn over resistance offices right here in safe old London.'

'Got it.' Even as his father had. He had known what was for real.

'These people you're going to meet don't piss about, not the sort of man you're going to meet. Fighting repression in South Africa is their whole lives.'

'They'll trust me.'

Duggie noticed the assurance. He gave the instructions. Right turn, then a left, then straight on over the lights, another right.

They walked across the poorly-lit playground of a junior school.

There were posters up on the playground fences to advertise the meeting. Big deal . . . It wasn't the Albert Hall, nor the Royal Festival Hall. It was a junior school in Stoke Newington.

There was music beating out through the open doors of the gymnasium. Through the door Jack could see the lines of chairs. They stopped at the door. Duggie turned, hand out, and Jack gave him two pound coins. It bought them admission and a photocopied sheet detailing the evening's programme.

'I'll start you off, then you're on your own.'

Jack looked around him. There were posters and flags fastened to the wall bars. There were pictures of Mandela and Tambo. There were the slogans of the Anti-Apartheid campaign. There were 100 people. He thought he must stand out, a fly in a tea cup. There were eyes watching him. The uniform was jeans and sweaters and shawls and long skirts.

'You said it,' Duggie chuckled. 'You said you knew what you were getting into. Now you find out.'

The apple of Major Swart's attention was Jacob Thiroko.

The Black lounged at the back of the hall away from the low stage and out of sight of the door. He leaned against the gymnasium's vaulting horse. His eyes drooped, as if he was still exhausted from the long flight out of Lusaka. Of course he would be cold after the Central African heat. Around him were a clutch of his European-based comrades.

Swart wore patched denim trousers. He had not shaved that day, his cheeks were rough below the tinted glasses. His hair was brushed up. Before coming he had rubbed his hands in the earth of his office pot plants, getting the stains into his palm and under his fingernails. He sat in the last-but-one row, unremarkable and unobserved.

There was a young man at the doorway, in a suit, staring round him. He saw the man who was with him. He recognized him. Douglas William Arkwright, 27 years old, unemployed, unpaid worker at Anti-Apartheid, verbose and useless. He saw Arkwright speak in the young man's ear and then lead him the length of the hall to stand respectfully on the fringe of the group surrounding Thiroko.

Swart was interested. He couldn't hear what was said, but he saw the young man in the suit shake hands with Jacob Thiroko.

It was for Jack to start. There was casual amusement in Thiroko's expression. Jack saw a handsome man, soft chocolate skinned, mahogany eyed. He couldn't tell the age, anything between middle thirties and late forties.

He was Jack Curwen and he lived in Churchill Close, and he paid into a private medical scheme, and he voted to maintain the status quo. He was Jack Curwen standing in a run down school, shaking hands with a member of a revolutionary movement committed to the overthrow of a government half the world away. Preposterous enough to make him laugh, but his father had three weeks to live.

'I was brought here to meet someone from the African National Congress.'

'There are many of us here, Comrade.' A soft, swaying voice.

'I wanted to meet someone from the military wing of the ANC.'

'Then you should be in South Africa where they are fighting the freedom war.'

'I was told that if I came here I would meet someone from the Umkhonto we Sizwe wing of the ANC.'

'There is no war in London. The war is in our homeland.'

Jack moved close to Thiroko.

'My name is Jack Curwen. I am an expert in explosives. I have to meet, and urgently, someone from the military wing.'

'Perhaps in a month such a person . . .'

'I don't have until next month. I've two days at most to meet someone from the military wing.'

'What sort of person?' Thiroko's face was a mask.

'Someone who can make decisions and see them through.'

97

'I doubt I am that person. There is no-one from the military wing at a meeting such as this.'

'I have to talk to you.'

'You said that you wanted the military . . .'

Jack cut in. 'I told you I don't have time to be pissed about. I can tell you how you are different from these creeps round you. Different face, different eyes, different hands.'

'How different?'

'Different because they are a soldier's.'

'Perhaps you are mistaken.'

From behind Jack there was a burst of applause. He turned to see the stage filling.

'In this room you are the only man who is a soldier.'

'Who are you, Mr Jack Curwen?'

'My father is going to hang in South Africa in three weeks. My father is an activist of the ANC.'

The mask fell. Astonishment flooded Thiroko's face.

'Jeez Carew is my father.'

The applause grew. The audience stamped their feet as they stood and clapped the principal speakers of the evening as they climbed onto the stage. Major Swart could no longer look behind him. He had seen the young man and Thiroko deep in talk. He had to stand with the rest and beat his palms together. He heard the chairwoman of the meeting coo her gratitude that their meeting was honoured by the presence of a distinguished guest from the ANC headquarters whose name for security reasons could not be given out. He saw Thiroko going forward. The bastard didn't look a fit man. When the audience settled down, Swart looked behind him.

There was no sign of the young stranger.

His eyes darted to the door. He saw the back of Douglas Arkwright's duffel coat disappearing.

He sat with his mother in the living room. Sam was upstairs, in bed before Jack had returned. He held cupped in his two hands the mug of coffee she had made for him. His hands were rock still.

'My mind's made up. I'm going to South Africa.'

'To see your Dad?'

'Yes.'

'I've told you, Sam'll help you with the airfare.'

'Not his business, it's mine.'

'What does he mean to you?'

'As much as if I'd known him all my life.'

His mother held a square of lace, dabbed it into her eyes. 'Will you have the strength when you go to see him, when you have to say goodbye to him?'

'It's not just to see him, Mum. I'm going there to bring my father home.'

7

Janice and Lucille stared at the open office door.

Jack was on the phone. He had spun his chair round so that he could rummage into his filing cabinet as he talked. He didn't see Duggie Arkwright. He was a disaster, wearing his oldest patched jeans and a scarlet T-shirt under a skimpy denim top. He saw Jack, and whistled. Jack spun, saw who it was, and with a brisk apology finished his phone call.

Jack stood and muttered something to the girls about being out for most of the day. He took his coat. He felt their questions on his back and ignored them.

They went out of the office and into the mild morning air.

When Jack looked back from the pavement at the office window he saw that Nicholas Villiers and the girls had their noses pressed to the panes.

'You said you were going to ring,' Jack said.

'The kiddie was crying in the night. I got up, I was holding the kiddie near the window and I saw this guy on the far side of the road, covering our place. The kiddie had a bad night. I was up again a couple of hours later, he was still there. I didn't go back to bed, I just stayed in a chair. Each time I went to the window he was there.'

'Have you ever been under surveillance before?'

'Not that I've known . . .' Duggie had a brittle, nervy laugh. 'I went on the tube this morning, travelled a few stops. There was another guy in the carriage, he got up when I got up. I came right across London, did two changes, he was always in the same carriage. I fixed him with the old "on-off". Stay on till the doors are closing, then you squeeze off. He went on down the line, he looked pretty pissed off. He must have been a South African . . .'

Jack was sombre, chewing at his thumbnail. 'Why not our police?'

'They don't have an underground railway in Johannesburg. "On-off" is the oldest one in the book, any London copper would know that one. Have to be a Boer not to know that one.'

Jack felt sick. 'Why follow you?'

'Perhaps they were there last night, saw us with the big fellow. Perhaps they're wondering who you are, perhaps they want a line into Thiroko. I don't know.'

They were still watched from the window. Jack would have loved to have turned on his heel, walked back into the offices of D & C. He would have loved to have remarked easily to Nicholas Villiers that the distractions of the last days were a thing of the past.

The sneer came to Duggie's mouth. 'Don't bloody whine. You were the one whispering about explosives, you were the one wanting to meet the military wing of the ANC.'

'Sorry.'

'I couldn't ring you. I couldn't be sure you weren't tapped here.'

'Thanks.'

Duggie looked exhausted. 'Let's go meet the big boy.'

They drove into London.

Thiroko had come early. He was not a frequent visitor to London, but he was familiar enough with the British capital to be able to select his own rendezvous. He had chosen Lincoln's Inn Fields, a square of lawns and shrubs and tennis courts and flower beds and netball courts. He liked open air meeting places where there were exits at all corners.

He was intrigued by the young man he had met the previous evening. And the young man was a distraction for his mind from the physician's message. He was sufficiently interested in the young man's brief explanation to him to have agreed to the meeting. And he knew, of course, of James Carew. He knew of the taxi driver who carried messages between dead letter drops, transported weapons between arms caches, could take photographs and draw maps. A White had access to many target areas where it was not safe for a Black to go. He knew of the usefulness of the quiet-tongued taxi man.

Thiroko was 48 years old.

He had been out of South Africa since the military wing was formed, since the banned African National Congress had gone underground. He had never been back. His homes had been in Moscow and Dar in Tanzania and Luanda and Maputo and Gaberone and now Lusaka. Some months he dreamed of a triumphant return with the war won and the apartheid regime humbled and beaten. Most years he doggedly refused himself horizons of hope and struggled on, organizing the infiltration of men and munitions into his former country.

Thiroko straddled two generations of the Movement. He was neither a part of the old political hierarchy who wanted the military wing to attack only hard targets where the gesture mattered more than the mayhem, nor was he among the ranks of the young hawks who demanded the right to hit the soft targets of the White supermarkets and railway carriages and resort hotels. To his colleagues he was dedicated, humourless and reliable. To the South African police he was a murderous enemy, one they would dearly love to have trapped when the Recce Commando went into Maputo and Maseru in Lesotho and Gaberone. He had been out of Maseru less than twenty-four hours when the Recce Commando stormed the ANC base houses. He hated the White war machine. He knew of no sacrifice too great if the regime could be brought down.

He saw Jack come into the square. He watched him pass the office girls playing netball in their morning break. He saw him look around and pass the gardener laying out the first trays of the year's bedding plants. He knew of the boy's father. The Movement was peopled with men and women who could not keep their mouths tight shut. Carew had never been suspected of leaking information. A dozen years was a long, long time to have survived the resistance war in Johannesburg.

It had been Thiroko, from his office in Lusaka, who had suggested that Carew should drive the getaway.

He owed it to Carew that he should meet his son.

He watched Arkwright settle onto a bench close to the netball pitch. He disliked the foreign Whites who lionized the Movement from the comfort of their European cities.

He watched to satisfy himself that there was no tail on the young man. The young man saw him, and Thiroko recognized the relief on Jack's face. The relief told him of the strain. The strain told him of the genuineness of Carew's boy. He presumed he was to be offered explosives, that he would have to explain gently that the Movement had all the explosives it could handle. He would do it in a kindly fashion.

'I am sympathetic to you, as I am sympathetic to the families of Happy Zikala and Charlie Schoba and Percy Ngoye and Tom Mweshtu. To all of the families goes the very sincere sympathy of the Movement.'

'And what should those families do about it?' A harshness in Jack's voice.

'They will pray, they will attend protest meetings, in South Africa they are going to make video cassettes that will be sent to every head of state represented at the General Assembly of the United Nations . . .'

'Prayers and protests and petitions, Mr Thiroko, are a great waste of time.'

'Tell me what is not a waste of time.'

'I am going to go to South Africa. To the gaol where my father is held. I am going to blow a hole in the wall, and I am going to take my father out.'

'Should I laugh because you are so stupid, should I cry because you are so sincere?'

'It's not a joke to me.'

Thiroko was hissing back at him. 'You know what the gaol is,

103

boy? The gaol is the peak of a security system. From every other gaol in the country men are escaping, and no man has escaped from that gaol for ten years. They are desperate men, they are going to hang, they are sitting in their cells for more than a year, most of them. They are *thinking* of escape, and for more than ten years none of them has managed it.'

Jack on the offensive. He had the man arguing, not laughing. That was good.

'Anywhere that's maximum security is vulnerable. Maximum security breeds complacency.'

'The gaol isn't up against the street. The gaol is in the middle of a complex. You would be shot hundreds of yards short of the walls. If you are shot dead, how does that help your father?'

'How does it help him if I sit on my arse, and pray and shout outside their embassy and ask politicians to watch a video? That's doing fuck all to help him.'

'You would be killed.'

'He's my father,' Jack said flatly. 'So be it.'

Thiroko leaned back against the arm of the bench. He was trying to read Jack.

'You are a good boy. You work here, you have a family. You have to exist through the next weeks, then you have to resume your life. After it has happened you have to forget your father.'

'I'm going to South Africa.'

'Do you listen to anybody?'

Jack couldn't help himself, a snap grin. 'Hardly ever.'

'It is not my intention to help you to kill yourself.'

'I'm going to bring my father home.'

'Impossible, you understand that word?'

'Give me the chance.'

'Your failure would hurt us, and it is *impossible* that you could succeed.'

'Not if you helped me.'

Thiroko shook his head, as if he did not believe what he learned in the slate grey eyes of Jack Curwen.

'I can't do it.'

Jack's hand covered Thiroko's fist, a hard unyielding grip. 'Where were you when the Court bomb went off? Where will you be when five men hang? Sitting on your arse and comfortable?'

'You take a chance with me, young man.' The anger was brilliant on Thiroko's face.

'Lying in your pit and snoring?'

'I care about my men,' Thiroko spat the answer.

'Your Movement took a chance with the lives of five men. You owe it to them to help me.'

'No-one tells me my duty.'

'Your duty is to help them, not to sit on your bloody hands.'

Thiroko softened. He had never been in combat in South Africa. He had never fired a Kalashnikov assault rifle at the Boer police or the Boer troops. He had never carried a bomb to a target and known the fear sweat in the fold of his stomach. He thought of what the physician had told him.

'What do you want?'

Jack felt the glow of success. 'I can't take explosives with me, I can't get them through the airport. I want access to explosives in South Africa – and I want a team.'

'Why should I trust you with a team?'

'When I get to Johannesburg, give me explosives, that's all. Sit on your hands, on your arse, and wait, and listen to the radio. You'll hear what your explosives have done, the radio'll tell you, what I've done on my own, and when you're satisfied then you'll give me a team.'

'What is it you want exactly?'

'When I arrive I want a minimum of twenty pounds of explosive. I want detonators and Cordtex and safety fuse. I will hit the target of my choice. Then you'll know I'm worth the team.'

'All for your father.'

'To bring him back.'

Thiroko took a notepad from his pocket. He wrote out an address. He showed the address to Jack, told him to memorize it, let his eyes linger on it, then folded the paper and tore it into 100 pieces that he threw to float away and disperse over the grass. He told Jack to meet him at the address the following morning.

'You're going to help me?'

'I am going to think about helping you.'

'Time's very short.'

'I too learned to count. I know how many days are available.'

Thiroko walked away from the bench. He was soon gone from sight. Jack was trembling. God, the assurance and the bombast had fled him. God, and was he frightened.

He was an age finding a phone box that worked.

He rang Jimmy Sandham at work. He wanted to meet with him, had to talk to someone.

A brisk voice answering, stating that he was through to the Foreign Office. Jack gave the extension number. Sandham had started him on his road. Jack wanted to meet him for a drink, to listen to his quiet control.

'Could I speak to Mr Sandham, please – a personal call.'

A woman's voice, 'Not here I'm afraid.'

'Will I get him later, this afternoon?'

'He's taken a few days' leave.'

'Since when?'

'He left yesterday.'

'How long is he away?'

'Who is it asking for him, please?'

Jack put the phone down. He tried the home number. No reply.

He rang George Hawkins and invited himself over. He rang D & C and said he wouldn't be back that day.

It hit him. He had forgotten Duggie Arkwright. After leaving Lincoln's Inn Fields, he had walked into the West End, and then he had spent another ten minutes looking for a phone that wasn't broken or occupied. Duggie had sat down at the entrance to the square when Jack had gone forward to meet Thiroko. He hadn't been there when Jack had left. Duggie had done the introduction and had himself a tail, and Jack had put him out of his mind. He'd ring him when he could. He'd ring him when he came back.

He looked into a shop window. There were three layers of television sets: cash, sale, and credit. They all carried the same picture. Of high armoured personnel carriers driving through a South African township of tin roofs and brick walls, and of gas plumes, and of the blue uniforms blasting with their shotguns, of running crowds, of police chasing with the long whips held back to strike in anger. The caption said they were old pictures, had to be because the camera crews were banned from the riot areas.

He wasn't going there to take a side in a civil war. He was going there to bring his father home. And it wasn't real. It was only old pictures on a bank of television screens. He knew what was bloody real. It was that his father was going to hang in three weeks, that Duggie had a tail that morning, that a woman had said Sandham had gone on leave.

He went to find his car, then to George's to talk about explosives.

He was the moth, the file was the lamp.

The Director General had read, word by word, every page in the Curwen/Carew file. He had started to imagine that he knew the man.

There was a photograph in uniform, early twenties from its date. There was a portrait shot before the fiasco in Albania. There was another shot taken during the debrief and after the hospital check-up. There was a blow-up of a Johannesburg newspaper photograph of Carew being brought out of court. The change was Albania. The flesh had been stripped off the man. But he couldn't mistake the defiance in the features, especially in those taken after the decade in Spac.

He had read Carew's South African reports. They were poorly written, but they were dense with names and gossip. There was no analysis, no interpretation, all as raw as sewage in a down flow. It crossed his mind to wonder whether the security police in Pretoria often had access to such quality information.

In the Alexandra township, three doors down Fifteenth Avenue from the north side junction with Hofmeyer there were stored under the back room floorboards, two RPG-7 anti-tank rocket launchers, and eight missiles for the launchers were in waste ground beside the church wall on Second Avenue.

A 49-year-old street cleaner, who lived on Key in the Jabulani district of Soweto, had for two years been Umkhonto we Sizwe commander of the whole township.

Seven Kalashnikov rifles were buried in protective grease wrapping in Dobsonville in the park that was bordered by Mahlangati and Matomela.

At a house, number given, on Mhlaba in the Chiawelo district, military planning meetings were held, when security conditions allowed movement in the night of the first Tuesday of each month. The fall back rendezvous was on Pilane in the Molapo district.

There was the house number in the Mamelodi township of Pretoria where a press printed ANC literature. There was the name of the school from which that literature was dispersed, the identity of the schoolmaster who wrote the broadsheets.

Lists of officials in South African Laundry, Dry Cleaning and Dyeing Workers Union, and in Textile Workers Union (Transvaal), and in South African Chemical Workers Union, who were either politically or militarily active in ANC.

The names of couriers, African names, who carried low-level messages around the townships. One White named. J. van Niekerk, aged 19, disabled, student. And a White girl, named. Both addresses.

Careful maps showing infiltration routes into South Africa from Botswana.

The numbers of bank accounts, and the addresses of those banks. Accounts and banks where the ANC's money was lodged.

The Director General read through lists of intended targets. Police stations, power lines, railway track, a sewage filtration plant, a military recruiting office. A long list ... There was a sketch plan of the approach route to be used for the rocket attack on the Sasolburg fuel storage tanks. There were the operational orders for the strike on the Voortrekkerhoogte army base. There were verbatim arguments between cadre cells on the priorities of attacks. Damned hard material to come by, no mistake.

The reports from years back had been worked over, he could see the pencil and ink ticks and underlinings that showed him that once these reports had been valued. Not the reports of the year before Carew's arrest. They were unmarked, and he thought they had gone unread into the file.

He was fitting together his picture of his man. He read that the SIS officer attached to the British embassy in Pretoria used to come once a month to Johannesburg and go to a certain taxi rank at the South African Airways terminal and take a certain licensed taxi and pay for his fare and receive the latest Carew report with his change. All as amateurish as if his service had been playing boy scout pranks.

Carew had never come home. An addendum note stated 'Gone native'. A note in Fordham's handwriting to the effect that Curwen wouldn't trust himself too close to his former wife and his grown-up son should he ever return to London.

All the time the poor devil was being paid. Last Friday of every month a pay cheque rolling into a bank account in Liechtenstein. Signatories to the account: James Curwen, Col. B. Fordham. Statements from accounts at Century concerning the amounts deducted from his salary to make allowance for monies earned from his taxi driving.

He had misjudged his man, but he still believed he was past saving. He rose from his desk.

Silently he paced his carpet.

Past saving?

He pondered the options.

He extended the forefinger of his right hand. They could come clean to the South African government and make an apology and plead for clemency. Second finger. They could scuffle around for sufficient leverage to ensure that Pretoria would respond to negotiation and spare his man and hold silence. Third finger. They could break the legman out from the hanging gaol.

He snapped his fist shut. Absolutely not on. Inconceivable in the time, and fantasy.

Past saving.

He had a meeting scheduled with the Permanent Under Secretary for the late afternoon. The PUS outranked the Director General for all that the Director General was in a position to control the flow of information available to the PUS. In the matter of James Sandham, the flow would be dammed at once. He had set aside 45 minutes directly after lunch, for himself and his principal officials to discuss the Carew case. It was a gesture, the setting aside of senior men's time, and unless someone came up with something right out of the ordinary it was the last gesture the Service would and could make.

Major Swart had fretted through the morning. He had sat in his office at the end of a corridor behind an automatic locking steel-barred door, willing the telephone to shout for him.

The two warrant officers who did most of the footwork in his small empire had called earlier to report that they had lost Arkwright, been tricked by him on the underground. Their second call had told Swart that they had picked him up again when he returned to his flat. Swart wanted badly to know the identity of the young man in the well-cut suit who had been huddled at the meeting with Thiroko. That young man was probably worth opening up, and Arkwright should have been the way to him.

There was a third call. Arkwright had just drawn the curtains to his room. From his state of undress it was to be assumed he was taking his slut to bed.

They sat in the kitchen. The sink and the stove needed three hours' work from a strong-willed woman. Jack doubted there had ever been a woman in George Hawkins' life, certainly no kids. The blaster never talked about a woman, talked mostly about his three cats. Big, confident brutes they seemed to Jack, sleeping on the kitchen table or striding over the stove or licking at used plates in the sink bowl. Jack sat on an old explosives box, upturned and covered by a grimed cushion. George was scooping cat food from a tin. Jack thought the cats ate better than the old blaster.

'Was it just kiddie's bullshit?'

Jack said, 'I've found the right man, probably.'

'For trusting?'

'I have to.'

'Genuine guy?'

'He's on the military side.'

The cats were chewing fiercely. George put a page of newspaper over the tin, left it on the window ledge above the sink.

'The targets are in South Africa?'

'Yes.'

'Do you have a bloody conscience?'

'I don't.'

'It's explosives, lad. It's not just a firework show where everyone has a good laugh and hears a big bang. Explosives get to hurt people.'

'I don't want to hurt people. I just want to get my father out of that place.'

'That's a piss poor answer.'

'I don't know where yet, the first target will be in Johannesburg.'

'Good and big, where the whole city sees it. I'll rot in hell, certain. You're talking about an act of war. It's bloody Harrods, lad; it's the Grand Hotel, it's the bandstand in Regent's Park, it's the Household effing Cavalry you're talking about. Have you got the guts for that?'

'I have to, or he's going to hang.'

'There was a bomb in Northern Ireland, the La Mon House hotel . . .'

George went to a drawer. He excavated among cartridge boxes and pamphlets and books and old newspapers and older bills. He took out a nearly clean sheet of blank paper. He flicked his fingers for Jack to pass him a pen. He started to draw the diagram.

Firm and bold strokes of the pen.

'If they ever knew George Hawkins drew this for you then I'd be bloody lucky, Jack boy, if they just shot me.'

'My father hasn't told them anything, I'm not intending to start.'

'You take that away with you, and you learn it by heart, and you flush it away. Don't take that on your bloody aeroplane . . . What's the gaol?'

The marmalade cat had eaten too fast. It vomited on the linoleum. George seemed not to notice. Jack told him that Pretoria Central was a complex of five gaols. In the centre was the hanging gaol. He didn't know the layout, didn't know where his father's cell was, didn't know the guard patterns. He didn't know any bloody thing.

'If I told you it was just daft.'

'I'd say you should mind your own business, Mr Hawkins.'

'By helping you, am I just getting you killed?'

'Without you, I'd help myself.'

George turned over the sheet of paper.

'Is it an old gaol or a new one?'

'I think it's newish.'

'It'll have a wall round it. If it were old it would be brick or stone. If it's less than twenty years then it'll be reinforced concrete . . . You'd be better off just getting pissed every night 'til they hang him . . .'

'How do I knock a hole in reinforced concrete?'

'We're not even talking about how you're going to get into a security area, up against the bloody wall . . . You're not going to be able to drill holes and use cartridges. You're not going to be able to use lay-on charges, because you'd need a dumper load of earth to cover them or you'd have to shift a ton of sandbags.'

'Don't tell me what I can't do.'

'Easy, lad . . . Professor Charles Monroe, Columbia University, way back before we were born. It's what's called the Monroe Effect. It's the principle of armour piercing, what they use against tanks. Shaped or hollow charge, it's what it's called. Jack, they'll shoot you dead . . .'

'Draw me the shaped charge.'

It was dusk when Jack left. He was in his car, the window wound down. George was bent to talk to him.

'I'll miss you, lad.'

Jack grinned. 'I won't be gone more than three weeks.'

'I'm a bloody fool to have talked to you.'

'Could it work, Mr Hawkins?'

''Course it can work. If you remember everything I've told you, and if you remember everything you've seen over the last two years, and *if* you do everything like you've seen me do it, then it'll work. Forget one thing, a little small thing, and you're gone.'

'I'll come on down and tell you how it worked.'

George snorted. He turned away quickly, so Jack shouldn't see his face. He went back through his front door. He didn't look over his shoulder as Jack drove away.

When he was clear of the lane, out of sight of the bungalow, he stabbed the engine into life. The excitement gripped him. The same excitement as when his final school exam results had come through, and his university admission, and his first girl, and his winning of the job at D & C Ltd. Brilliant flowing excitement, like the first time George had let him do a blast. If he remembered every last little thing, then he could do it. He could take his father out.

'We're to meet tomorrow with the Prime Minister to talk damage limitation.'

'I don't think there'll be damage,' the Director General said. 'I have learnt many things from our man's records. One of them is his tried and tested loyalty to the Service. He won't talk.'

'Then he'll hang with his secrets.' The PUS rocked his glass slowly, willing the juice from the slice of lemon into further circulation.

'*Our* secrets.'

'The Prime Minister would look unkindly on the least embarrassment.'

'It won't come to that. I'd bet money on Carew's silence.' He paused. 'The fact is, I should like very much to save this man. I quite accept that it is politically unacceptable to go cap in hand and ask for his freedom, tell them who he is. We have looked at the odds against a team of men lifting him out of this gaol, and they are high.'

'Too high, I don't doubt, and the Prime Minister wouldn't countenance the risk of failure. For heaven's sake don't let's have any old-fashioned stunts. The saving of Mr Carew's life just doesn't warrant the risking of anyone else's, not when you add the political risk.'

Neither in London nor Lusaka did Jacob Thiroko have to consult with colleagues.

That night, alone, he would take the decision on whether the military wing of the African National Congress would back the venture proposed by Jack Curwen.

Amongst the senior officers of the Umkhonto we Sizwe there were some who saw Whites, even if they were prepared to make the same sacrifices, as having no place in the Movement. Those Blacks of the military wing treated all Whites associating themselves with the ANC with suspicion. They believed all of those Whites were communists first, true to the South African Communist Party, and loyal to the African National Congress, second.

Thiroko was not a communist. He had been to Moscow. He believed the Soviets, for all their aid in weapons and money, to be more racist than the Italians or the English or the Dutch or the Swedes.

If he were to have admitted to those senior officers of the military wing that a White had come to him with a plan of action and that he had supported him without consulting them then there would be questions circulated about his fitness to lead. Nevertheless, it would be his decision alone.

He sat in his room in the 'safe house' in a quiet road in North Finchley. He drank coffee.

Better to have tried and failed than never to have tried at all.

Sentimental rubbish.

Revolutionary warfare was about victory. He was no advocate of glorious failure martyrdom. If a cadre of the Umkhonto we Sizwe were to attack the maximum security section of Pretoria Central then they must succeed, they must free their condemned comrades. The agony of the decision lay in a particular area. It was the area that had stuck with him, caused him to drink his fourth and fifth and sixth cups of coffee, stayed with him through half a packet of cigarettes. The physician had told him to smoke as much as pleased him. The pain was more frequent. Was the Movement better served by saving Happy Zikala and Charlie Schoba and Percy Ngoye and Tom Mweshtu and James Carew from the gallows? Did the Movement gain more from the martyrdom of the Pritchard Five?

Which?

Better for the Movement to have at freedom five men who had bungled an attack, or better to have five heroes buried while the world screamed anger at Pretoria?

Which?

8

'Have you made your decision?'

Jack had come early to the 'safe house'. When the door had been opened to his ring he had smelled the aroma of sweet spices from the kitchen. She had been a tall woman with the dark skin of the Bengali and had two children clinging to her sari. She had shown no surprise, only taken him to the foot of the stairs and pointed upwards to the closed door.

'So direct. Should you not give me time to offer you coffee, to ask you to sit?'

He thought Jacob Thiroko had slept less than he had. The coffee mug stood amongst stain rings on the table. Beside it was an ashtray and the empty matchbox that had been used when the ashtray had spilled over. Thiroko sat at the table. The haze of smoke filled a strata of the room, morning mist over a damp meadow. Thiroko sat at the table. There was no other chair, only the unmade bed for Jack.

'I just need your decision. I want explosives, I want to prove myself to you, then I want help.'

Jack saw the sadness on Thiroko's face. He knew it was the sadness of a military commander who sent young men onto the dirty battleground of revolutionary warfare.

'I'm going, Mr Thiroko, with your help or without it. With your help I'll make a better job of it.'

Thiroko stood and pulled out his shirt from his trousers. He lifted the back shirt tail, and then his vest up to his shoulders. Jack saw the thin welt of the scar, pink on the dark skin, running diagonally across the length of his back.

'*Sjambok*, rhino hide whip. It is the way the police break up demonstrations. They use the *sjambok* when they do not think it necessary to shoot. I was a politician before they whipped me, I was a soldier afterwards . . .'

Jack had his answer, his elation shone.

'I take a gamble on you, a small gamble. A few pounds of explosive. Nothing more until you have proved yourself.'

They clasped hands.

Jack said he would fly within two days. Thiroko told him where he should stay, to wait for a contact, and thereafter, since he would be travelling in his own name, to keep on the move.

'Where will you be, Mr Thiroko?'

'I will be in Lusaka.'

'You won't have long to wait.' Jack was smiling.

Thiroko's face clouded with anger. 'You are all children. You think it is a game. Last night I shamed myself with my thoughts. I thought whether it was better for our Movement if those five should hang. I considered whether five men dead was of more advantage to us than those five men free. I know the answer and I prayed for forgiveness on my knees . . . What will be your target for your explosives?'

Jack could smell the sweat on the sheets. 'I don't know.'

Thiroko laughed with amusement. 'You are clever to be cautious.'

'I don't know what the target will be, honestly.'

Thiroko seemed not to have heard him. 'We say that we trust each other, and we are strangers. There are men and women whom I have worked with for many years, and I do not know whether I can trust them. It was sensible of you not to have gone to our offices.'

'I trust you, Mr Thiroko.'

'It is a small building. Always full of people hurrying, busy, greeting each other, telling each other of their commitment to the Movement. But there are worms there rotting our cause. They may have been purchased by the Boers, they may have been compromised by threats against their family still in South Africa. No way of knowing. But you

117

have my word that only those who *must* know will know of your journey.'

'Thank you.'

'You will be foolish if you underestimate the forces you are up against. If you are caught, you will wish that you could die to escape the pain the Boers will inflict on you. They will put electric shocks on you, keep you from sleeping, they will spin the chambers of a service revolver beside your head, they will starve you, they will hang you upside down from the ceiling with a broomstick under your knees and spin you, they will parade you naked in front of the men and women who work in the security police offices in John Vorster Square. It is where your father was, John Vorster Square . . . Trust nobody, trust only yourself.'

'Do you know my father?'

'I know of him. He would know of me.'

'I'll tell him about you.'

Thiroko asked quietly, 'If it were not your father . . . ?'

'I wouldn't have known who the Pritchard Five were.'

'I like honesty, Mr Curwen, but honesty will not help you in South Africa. Be the cheat. Cheat the Boers out of the satisfaction of five hangings.'

Jack saw a fast grimace of pain on Thiroko's face, momentary, then wiped away. 'Perhaps we won't ever meet again, but I'll tell Jeez that you're a good man.'

Jack was lucky to have caught Dickie Villiers in the afternoon, a miracle that he wasn't hacking his way down the fairways. Villiers was at his desk. A quizzical look upwards from his boss. Nicholas would have briefed him, that in a bit over a week Jack was a changed man. Out of the office without explanation, effing and blinding in front of the girls, hangovers, an extraordinary creature coming in to collect him. Villiers had been steeling himself to call the lad in.

'I gather there are some problems, Jack.' Villiers fondled his polka dot bow tie, chaffing at the awkwardness. He thought Jack Curwen was one of the best, one worth keeping.

'I have to go away, Mr Villiers,' Jack said.

'You're not leaving us . . . ?' The blurted question. 'I'm sure we could find more money.'

'No, it's for three weeks only. I'm going tomorrow.'

'That's damned short notice.' Dickie Villiers leaned forward, his avuncular manner. 'Are you in some kind of trouble?'

'I've a problem, I've three weeks to beat it.'

'It's often better to talk something through.'

'I am afraid I can't do that.'

'Where are you going?'

'Sorry . . .'

Villiers' patience was failing. 'That's just impertinence.'

'I hope my job stays open to me, Mr Villiers, and I hope to be back in three weeks.'

'Are you involved in anything criminal?'

Jack smiled at him, shook his head.

'Let's not beat around, you're very fortunate to have this job.' Villiers recovered quickly. 'There're enough graduates looking for work, not to count those who never made it through. We gave you a real break. I made it my business to find out why you were sent down from university, and I've never held it against you. This is no way to be repaying my kindness.'

'I've worked hard for you, Mr Villiers, but I'm not begging any favours. I'm going to be away because I've no choice. If you've given my job to someone else when I get back, I'll just have to find another one. Goodbye, Mr Villiers.'

And before the older man could answer him, he was gone.

Jack went to his desk and picked up the contracts pending file and took it to Nicholas Villiers' desk, dumped it. He put on his coat. He waved a kiss to Janice and winked at Lucille. He went out of the door. He walked out of the building.

He had turned his back on the world he knew.

Jack heard it on the car radio. He was driving across Leatherhead towards Churchill Close. He had just bought his ticket, open return, to Johannesburg, for the following evening.

'. . . The soldier who has not yet been named was a member of a foot patrol in the strongly Republican Creggan district of Londonderry.

'A junior diplomat has been found dead below the summit of Carnedd Llewelyn in the Snowdonia range. It is believed that he fell more than four hundred feet onto a ledge where his body was found by a mountain rescue team. He has been named as James Sandham. Mr Sandham, aged 52, was on a walking holiday in North Wales. It is thought that he lost his way last night and fell to his death while trying in darkness to make his way down from the 3,400 foot summit of the mountain which is described by local experts as treacherous for the inexperienced.

'The Chancellor of the Exchequer said this morning at a news conference before leaving for . . .'

Numbly he switched off the radio.

He was living in Britain. He was living in the oldest democracy and he was frightened. He was living where the government's agencies existed through the will of the people. Crap . . . Jimmy Sandham didn't look like a man who would have climbed two flights of stairs if there was a lift. He had taken Jack into his confidence, into the area of the Official Secrets Act, Section 1, and into the area of the D-notice. Jimmy Sandham hadn't died on a walking holiday, for Christ's sake, he had died because he thought he'd found something rotten at the core of his country's government and had had the guts to say so.

In deep, controlled anger, Jack drove home.

Since Peter Furneaux had made the announcement of Sandham's death to the staff of South Africa desk, that office had been a sombre, lack-lustre place. The staff had packed up, gone home, on the stroke of half-past four, turning their backs on the empty table beside the radiator and the window.

Only Peter Furneaux stayed. He knew Sandham could be a cursed nuisance. He had seen him called to a meeting by the secretary of the PUS; he had no idea what the meeting was about and he hadn't seen him again. He had received a memorandum from personnel informing him that the Grade 2 officer was going on immediate and indefinite leave. Sandham hated physical exercise, despised joggers, sneered at the lunchtime keep fit fanatics. With a straight face, with a stolid voice, he had told his colleagues that Jimmy Sandham had died in an accident while walking in Snowdonia.

Furneaux remembered the meeting when he and Sandham had faced the son of a man who was to hang in South Africa. He knew a little of the history of James 'Jeez' Carew, enough to realize the sensitivity surrounding the man. He deliberated and he decided. He would make no mention to his superiors of the meeting with Jack Curwen. He would not report it. He had not put a minute of the encounter on the file and he wouldn't do so now. To have reported the meeting would have been to involve himself, to have put a spotlight on . . . Well, the odds were that the meeting with the PUS had nothing to do with Carew. Furneaux's decision ensured that the operatives of the Secret Intelligence Service, the men of Century, had no line on James Curwen's son during the twenty-five hours that remained before the departure of his flight to South Africa.

He had come by the back route into 10 Downing Street. The Director General always came through the Cabinet Office entrance in Whitehall, and the underground tunnel to the Prime Minister's office. The PUS had taken the same route.

The Prime Minister said, 'Director General, you were appointed to suppress the type of clandestine nonsense you are now telling me about.'

The PUS said, 'In fairness to the Director General, Prime Minister, Carew was sent to South Africa long before his time.'

The Prime Minister said, 'I want to know exactly what was Carew's brief.'

The PUS nodded to the Director General. For him to answer.

'Carew was sent to South Africa with the job of fastening himself to protest and terrorist organizations operating in that country. The job was created by a Colonel Basil Fordham for whom Carew had previously worked. It was the assumption of the Service that in the years ahead it would be important to know the planning and capabilities of the revolutionary factions.' The Director General paused, relit his pipe. He had the Prime Minister's attention. He fancied the PUS thought him a windbag. 'Some statistics, Prime Minister. South Africa is our twelfth biggest export market. We are the principal exporter into South Africa. We have the largest capital investment there. We have the most to lose if the place goes down in anarchy. We have 70,000 jobs directly linked to South Africa, another 180,000 indirectly dependent in that they are supplied by raw materials mined in South Africa. Should the present regime collapse, then we have to be sufficiently well-informed to ensure that any administration born out of revolution would be friendly to our interests.'

'All of that seems to fall within the scope of conventional diplomatic observation.'

The Director General puffed his disagreement.

'With respect, Prime Minister. In recent years South Africa has attempted to shield itself from guerrilla incursions by agreements with Mozambique, Angola, Botswana and Zimbabwe. This had led to the formation of cells, cadres, of ANC activists inside the country. They act autonomously. General orders are given from outside, specific actions are usually initiated from inside. Conventional diplomacy can monitor outside, Lusaka headquarters of the ANC. Carew's brief was to infiltrate and report on the men inside . . .'

'To report . . .' the PUS mouthed softly.

'Not to take part.' The Prime Minister was hunched forward.

'Indeed not.' The Director General stabbed his pipe stem for emphasis.

'Without being instructed to do so he engaged in terrorism?'

'So far as we know, Prime Minister, Carew's role was strictly on the periphery.'

'An act of quite shocking violence?'

'I don't think we can assume that Carew, who was only the driver of a getaway vehicle, knew of the intended violence.'

'But in which a courthouse was bombed and a policeman was killed?'

'Correct, Prime Minister.'

The Prime Minister leaned back. 'Then, periphery or no, he deserves the gallows.'

'What if he talks?' the PUS asked mildly.

'He won't.' A rasp in the Director General's voice.

'Should he make a confession from the death cell then our position will be that this was a freelancer who supplied occasional and trivial information . . .' The Prime Minister shrugged. 'A private individual, whose terrorist actions we totally and unreservedly condemn . . . I have to be back in the House.'

They were in the corridor outside. It was an after-thought from the Prime Minister.

'This fellow, what sort of man is he?'

'A very brave man and intensely loyal to our country . . .'

The Director General saw the Prime Minister turn towards him, puzzled.

'. . . who will die the victim of one horrendous mistake.'

A spark of annoyance, and then the Prime Minister no longer listened. The meeting had run a little late. The black car was waiting for the drive to the House of Commons.

The Director General and the PUS were left in the corridor, abandoned, because the circus was on the move.

'Why didn't you say that during the meeting?' the PUS asked.

'No point, Carew's beyond our reach.'

The PUS touched the Director General's arm. There was a rare uncertainty in his eyes.

'That fellow we met, Sandham?'

'Happens to people who climb without the proper equipment. A very silly man.'

Sam Perry stood by the window. He looked out over his tended garden. His wife sat in her usual chair, where she would have

123

done her sewing or her knitting, where she would have watched television.

Jack paced. He couldn't have been still. He owed it to his mother, to talk to her. Couldn't have avoided the talk.

She stared all the time at the airline ticket that was on the arm of her chair. She said that she had thought it was just stupid talk when he had told her he was going to South Africa to bring his father home. She said that she had thought that he was just being emotional.

Sam hadn't spoken. Jack couldn't remember a time when Sam Perry had had nothing to say.

'You can't bring him home, can you?'

No reason to tell his mother about the man who was a military commander of the Umkhonto we Sizwe wing of the African National Congress, nor about the man who was expert in his knowledge of shaped and hollow charges, nor about the man who had fallen to his death down a mountain in Snowdonia.

'It's just silliness, tell me it is.'

And no reason to tell her about the man who lived in a cramped bedsit in North London, who had a tail on him, and who had to play the 'on-off' game on the underground to throw the tail.

'I'll see him.'

'You'll give Jeez my love?'

Sam strode to the dark wood cabinet. He poured Hilda's sherry into a whisky tumbler. He poured Jack a beer.

'It'll be all right, Mum, I promise you that,' Jack said.

He doubted she believed him. She had no reason to. She liked to say that her Jack was a bad liar. She muttered about Sam's and Jack's dinner. They watched her go towards the kitchen, nursing her drink.

'Is there a chance?'

'I've no choice but to try,' Jack said.

'It'll break your mother's heart if anything happens to you.'

'I can't leave him there for them to hang.'

The proxy father gazed at him. In many ways he regarded

Jack as his own achievement. He thought his influence had given the young man his work ethic, his straightness, and his honesty. He thought he had the right to be proud of the way his stepson had grown. But the quiet authority and the bloody-minded determination, they weren't Sam's. Since he had met Hilda, when she was a bitter, introverted young woman, he had thought of Jeez Curwen as a right bastard. The authority and the determination weren't Sam's and they weren't Hilda's. They could only be Jeez Curwen's hand down to his son. The man could not be a right bastard, not if this was his boy. He understood that he and Hilda could douse the boy with affection, love, he understood that Jack must go to find his true father. He was ashamed, because he felt envy.

'Come home safe,' Sam said hoarsely.

They'd picked up the scum when he left the flat to go for his drink.

Piet used the pay telephone in the lounge bar, Erik stayed in the public bar to watch. They wouldn't be thrown again. The business in the underground still smarted with Erik, and the yelling he'd had from the major. No chances taken when the scum had gone to the pub, Erik walking behind the scum and Piet on the far side of the road in case the subject spotted the tail and dived into the traffic for a quick jump on a bus.

The scum had been two hours in the pub, sitting on his own, nursing his drinks to make them last. Near to closing time when Piet had gone to the telephone. The warrant officers did as their major told them. Independent action was not their right.

Erik watched Duggie Arkwright. Scum was a good word for the subject. What did the scum know of South Africa? What did he know of the melting pot of the ethnic minorities that made up the Republic's population? Scum, Arkwright, would think of all non-Whites as being the same. The scum wouldn't consider that there were Asian Muslims and Asian Hindus, and Coloureds, and then the groupings of Africans – Tswana and Xhosa and Tsonga and Swazi and Zulu, all the others. Chuck power at these groupings and there would be anarchy. If the Zulu had power over the Xhosa, or the Swazi over the Tswana . . . the State President knew what he was at when he kept the brakes on, which was more than the morons knew who shouted in London about oppression.

Erik was at the bar, leaning back, naturally, overlooking the scum. He could never read Piet's face, had to wait to be told what were the major's instructions.

'Shake the creature a bit. Says he has to know who the creature took to meet Thiroko.'

Erik looked down at Arkwright. All skin and bone and wind. Erik had played open side flanker for Transvaal B. The scum would have no muscle and no balls. If they shook the scum he'd rattle.

Arkwright walked home.

He had drunk four pints of Worthington, it was social security day. He was feeling low, feeling used. He'd put his bloody best bloody foot forward for priggy Curwen, and priggy Curwen had gone off into the wind. No thanks, no call. No bloody decency from priggy Curwen. And Anthea was pregnant again. First vomiting that morning. He was thinking of priggy Curwen and of Anthea heaving in the john, and with the beer inside him it was hard thinking. He never looked behind.

They took him 50 yards from his door. One from the front, one from behind. He thought he was being mugged, which was a laugh, last bloody penny for the last bloody pint . . . Down an alley. No lights. He smelled day old aftershave and day old body lotion, and he knew he wasn't being mugged. A punch in the solar plexus to double him, an uppercut to straighten him. He went down.

For a moment he saw them. He knew they were South Africans. Knew they were Boer pigs. Something of the width of the shoulders, the breadth of the hips. The hands were coming down out of the blackness to pull him up. He saw the pale blur of the faces, grinning. They reckoned he was insufficiently shaken. He was never asked to say who was the young man that he had introduced to Thiroko. It was Piet's hand that groped for Duggie's beard, to pull him up, to hit him again. The fingers found the beard. Duggie bit him. Closed his jaw on the hand and bit and shook his head as a terrier will with a rat. Bit and chewed at the hand, and heard the Boer pig scream, and felt the fingers loose his beard, and clung on while his teeth were half wrenched from his head. Piet heaved backwards and blocked Erik's chance to get his boot into the scum's rib cage.

Duggie staggered and ran.

He ran towards the lights and safety of the main road. He thought only of flight. He heard the pounding feet behind him. He ran up the alley, across the pavement, and into the path of a 38 London Transport double decker bus.

At the end of the alley Erik gripped Piet's arm, stopped him from going forward. He held him back in the shadow. Erik could see the white-shock face of the conductor of the bus as he knelt beside his front wheel. He could hear the screams of a woman who had bent to look under the bus.

'You should get some medication for that hand, the scum might have rabies,' Erik said.

Jack's flight was delayed for fifty minutes.

Because of the late departure, sitting in the lounge, he read the evening paper front to back. He read of the death of Douglas Arkwright. It was said that Douglas Arkwright, 27, married and one child, had been drinking, that he had walked under a bus. The story made the paper because the traffic jam that followed the fatal accident had held up a royal princess on her way to open an art exhibition in Hertfordshire.

When the flight was called, Jack dropped the newspaper into a rubbish bin and walked briskly towards the boarding gate and his aircraft.

9

Jeez sat on the end of his bed.

He had eaten his porridge breakfast and given back his bowl and kept his mug. He was allowed to keep his mug and use it for drinking water during the day. He had washed and shaved under supervision. He had swept out his cell, not that there was much to sweep away because he had swept the cell floor every morning for the thirteen months that he had been in Beverly Hills. After he had swept the floor he had scrubbed it with a stiff brush and the bar of rock solid green soap that was for the floor and for his body. Sweeping the floor and scrubbing it were the only workloads demanded of him. No other work was compulsory for the condemns.

There was no singing that morning.

He sat on his bed because it was the only place he could sit when the floor was damp. Later in the day he sometimes sat on the floor and leaned his back against the wall that faced the cell door, beside the lavatory pedestal, but only for variety. Most of the day he sat or lay on his bed. He read sporadically, books from the library. He had never been a big reader. At Spac he had learned to be without books. If he was not reading then there was nothing but the time for thinking to disturb the events of his day which were his meals and his exercise session.

The thinking was hell.

Difficult ever to stop thinking. Thinking when his eyes were open and when they were closed, and when he was washing, and when he was eating, and thinking through dreams when he was asleep.

He hadn't had much of an education, but there was no

stupidity in him, not until he'd been hooked into driving the getaway out of Pritchard. Jeez knew the days were sliding. He knew the legal processes had been exhausted. He knew his life rested on the State President's decision. He knew that the State President refused commutation of the death penalty to the cadres convicted of murder. He knew that in these days of unrest the State President would hardly waive the penalty just because Jeez was White . . . Here we go, alto-bloody-together we go . . . Jeez didn't have to have a university degree to know.

He wondered how much notice they would give him. He wondered whether it would be the governor who would tell him.

He wondered how he'd be.

Some thoughts took charge in the night, some in the day. The overwhelming thought was the fear of fear. The fear of buckling knees, the fear of his bowels and his bladder emptying, the fear of screaming or crying.

His thoughts of the team were increasingly rare. When he had first come to Beverly Hills he had thought every day of the team he had been a part of. Then there had been the favourite thought, an indulgent memory. He had been flown back from Greece after the exchange, with two guards down the steps of one military aircraft, marched across 80 paces, head back, elbows stiff, outpaced the guards, somebody signing something, the rest lost in a blur, up the steps into the RAF transport, mugs of hot tea laced with something by Lennie and then what seemed like two days' sleep before he had been met at Northolt by Colonel Basil. He'd had his hand pumped and he'd been whisked into the big black car. He'd expected that he would be booked straight into a medical examination. Hadn't reckoned with bloody good old Colonel Basil. Directly into London. Over the bridge, down the ramp to the underground car park. Up the lift. Onto the 7th floor of Century. Into East European (Balkan). All of the team there, all of them sliding up from their chairs, and then Henry clapping his hands over his head, getting Adrian going, and Lennie following. And all of them giving Jeez the big hand, and Adrian kissing him on both cheeks and then on the lips, and the back slapping so hard that they half blew him away. And Colonel Basil smirking by the door and saying in his Brigade of Guards whisper, 'The team never forgets a man in the field. The team always gets its men back.' One of the girls scurrying off for beakers, and the champagne corks rocketing into the ceiling, and Jeez grinning like a Cheshire cat. And much later the car to a private clinic . . . His favourite thought. The good thoughts had faded with the months. The thought of how the team would be working for him came only infrequently now, usually when he was dreaming, and when he woke and felt the cold dawn air then the thoughts of the team were bloody smashed. It wasn't that he doubted that the team was working for him, he doubted now that the team had the power to take him out from Pretoria Central.

He yearned for quiet outside his cell. But the C section corridor, and the small corridor through C section 2 were never quiet in the daylight hours. There were always the voices of the prison officers as they told stories, laughed, talked about the papers and the television. There was always the shout of a duty officer approaching a locked door, and the door clattering open, and the smack of it closing. Those were the noises that were on top of the singing. No singing that morning, and that meant no hammer of the trap being tested in the afternoon. Each time he heard the shout for the doors to be opened, and then the clatter, and then the smack, he stiffened, and the sweat sprang to his forehead and his armpits and his groin. There would be a shout and a clatter and a smack when they came to tell Jeez that it was commutation, or when they came to tell Jeez which day it would be, which dawn for the short walk.

He often thought of the others.

He hadn't seen the others for thirteen months, not since the passing of the sentence and the drive in the meshed police wagon across Pretoria and up the hill to the gaol. He hadn't seen them since the apartheid of the reception area at Beverly Hills. They had gone right to B section, he had gone left to C section. That was 'separate development' for you. Four for B section because they were Black, Jeez for C section because he was White. They'd been laughing that day thirteen months before, walking loosely, easily in their leg irons and handcuffs. He wondered how they'd be now, waiting to learn if they'd all go. A bastard, that, if one or two of them were reprieved, and the others were taken to the hanging room . . . Wouldn't be a bastard, they'd all five go, because it had been a policeman. He'd meet them again in the preparation room. There they'd be together, apartheid waived, 'separate development' non-operable . . .

There was a shout. There was the clatter of a door opening. There was the smack of a door closing.

Still and upright on his bed, Jeez waited.

He knew all the distances that sound carried through the unseen parts of the gaol. He had heard the door that was the entrance to the C section corridor. There was a murmur of voices. Another door opening. The door into C section 2. The unchanging ritual. He wondered why they always shouted their approach to a locked door, why the door was invariably slammed behind them.

He felt the wetness on his skin. He saw the flash of a face at the grille.

He stood at attention. He stood every time a prison officer entered his cell. A key turned in the oiled lock.

Sergeant Oosthuizen, smiling benignly.

'Morning, Carew. You slept well, did you, man? Your room's a picture. Wish my lady kept our house like you keep your room. You're going to have your exercise early, straight after your lunch . . .'

Jeez closed his eyes. All the shouting, all the clattering of the doors, all the slamming, to tell him that he was to be exercised an hour earlier than was routine.

'Yes, Sergeant.'

'There's a nice afternoon for you, you've a visit.'

He was very slight. With his crash helmet on, Jan van Niekerk seemed almost misshapen. There was something grotesque about such small shoulders capped by the gleaming bulge of the helmet.

The Suzuki 50cc was his pride and joy. For insurance purposes it was a moped, but in Jan's mind it was a fully-powered scrambler/road machine. He passed only cyclists and joggers, he was forever being buffeted in the slipstream of overtaking lorries and cars, but the Suzuki was his freedom.

In term time he came each morning from his parents' home in Rosebank down the long straight Oxford, onto Victoria and Empire, and then along Jan Smuts to the University of Witwatersrand.

He loved the moped, whatever its lack of speed, because the under-powered Suzuki provided him with the first real independence of his 21-year-old life. His club foot, his right foot, was a deformity from birth. He had endured a childhood of splints and physiotherapy. He had had to be ferried in his mother's car to and from school, he had never played rugby or cricket. The wedge that was built into the raised heel of his leather ankle boot gave him a rolling limp and prevented him from walking any great distance. Before the moped he had been dependent on others. Along with the moped came a black leather two-piece riding suit. The combination of his stunted physique and his taste for biker's gear made Jan a student apart. In the huge university he was virtually friendless, and that bothered him not at all.

His friends were far divorced from the Wits campus. His own comrades. He had his own contact codes. He enjoyed a secret area of life that was undreamed of by his colleagues on the Social Sciences course. In this society, dominated by muscle power and sports skills where he could play no part, his Suzuki and his comrades gave him the purpose he craved.

His parents marvelled at the difference in their son's attitude since they had bought him the moped. They thought of him as a good serious boy, and one who showed no inclination towards the radicalism that they detested and that seemed so rife on the campus. At home, Jan gave no sign of interest in politics. They knew from their circle of friends who had kids at Wits that their Jan had no links with the students, mostly Jewish, who led the university demonstrations and protests, who were whipped by the police, savaged by the security staff dogs. Jan had described those activists to his parents as ridiculous middle class kids with a guilt complex. They knew Jan had left the campus early on the day that Dr Piet Koornhof, Minister of Co-operation and Development, had been pelted and heckled. On another day he had walked away from the burning of the Republic's flag and the waving of that rag of the African National Congress. His parents thought the making of Jan had been his moped and his studies.

There was a White girl doing ten years in the women's prison at Pretoria Central. She had been active in radical politics before devoting herself to the collecting of information for the ANC. Impossible to make the switch from overt to covert work. Jan had always been covert. Anyone who knew him, his parents, his sister, his lecturers, the students he sat with in lectures, would have been thunderstruck to have discovered that Jan van Niekerk was a courier for the Umkhonto we Sizwe.

A harmless little figure on his bumblebee of a moped, Jan pulled into the campus, parked behind the Senate House.

He limped past the portico and columns at the front of the building, across the wide paved walkway and down over the lawns. He preferred to walk on grass, easier and less jarring on his right foot. He walked around the amphitheatre, ignored the swimming pool and slogged his way up the steps to the modern concrete of the Students' Union. He saw the posters advertising the evening meeting to protest against police brutality on the Eastern Cape, went right past them. His greatest contempt was for the students who shouted against the government from the safety of the campus. He believed that when those students had graduated they would turn their backs on decency and honour, that they would buy their homes in the White suburbs and live out their lives with privilege stowed in their hip pockets.

Crippled and forever awkward, Jan van Niekerk would be

there on the day of reckoning. He believed that absolutely. A day of reckoning, a day of fire. His struggle with his disability had tempered his steel strength of purpose. That purpose was the cause of Umkhonto we Sizwe.

On the first floor of the Students' Union he had a metal locker, opened by his personal key. He had depressed the top of the door at the centre, where it was weakest, a full quarter of an inch. The locker was where he kept his biking leathers and it was his dead letter drop. Four other men only in the sprawling mass of the city of Johannesburg knew of Jan van Niekerk's locker. In these days of the state of emergency, of the regulations justifying widened police power, to be cautious was to stay free, to be exceedingly careful was to avoid the interrogation cells of John Vorster Square.

He stripped off his leathers. He unlocked the door.

The note was a tiny, folded, scrap of paper. The corridor holding the bank of lockers was always crowded, a concourse for students and lecturers and administration personnel and cleaning staff. Good and secure for a dead letter drop. Hidden by the open door he read the note as he packed his leathers into the locker.

About once every two weeks he was contacted.

A small link in a long chain, there was much that Jan van Niekerk was unaware of. A message from Thiroko had been telephoned from London in numbered code to Lusaka. Part of that message had been relayed on from Lusaka to Gaberone in Botswana. A smaller part of the message had been handcarried towards the international frontier and on by bus to Lichtenburg. From Lichtenburg that smaller part had been telephoned to Johannesburg.

He read the message. He had the paper in the palm of his hand as he closed the locker's door. He went to a lavatory and flushed the message away.

He had to hurry. He was late for the morning's first lecture.

The aircraft lurched, the engine pitch changed. The captain announced the start of the descent.

Around Jack the South African nationals were crowding to the windows to look down, excited. God's own country was unfolding below them. Jack's mind was a blank. Too tired to think. The stewardess was collecting the blankets and the headsets. He felt as a small boy does, sent alone for the first time on a train journey. The fear of the unknown. The stewardess took his earphones that he hadn't used, and his blanket that he hadn't unfolded.

He drew his seatbelt tighter round his waist. The fear was new to him. He did not know how it should be conquered.

Frikkie de Kok had slept in.

He'd hardly heard Hermione leave her bed when she'd gone to get the boys up and dressed and fed for school. He was allowed his peace. She was in a fine mood, fine enough for her to have allowed Frikkie, in the night, out of his own bed and into hers. Fine enough for her to bring him his breakfast once he had grunted, coughed a bit, cleared his throat. He thought she was in so fine a mood that she wouldn't bother him if he smeared his marmalade on his sheets. Well, he had capitulated to her, he had promised that she would have her new refrigerator. Imported, of course. And since the rand had gone down and the foreign bankers had sold the South African currency short, the refrigerator would cost him a small fortune, not so small because his mind was working better, because he was waking, counting the cost and the tax. But she was a good woman, and she needed the new refrigerator.

With his breakfast of juice and coffee and thick-sliced toast, there was his mail. Frikkie de Kok always opened all the family post himself. A postcard from his sister, and a bill from the electricity, and there was a familiar brown envelope carrying the official stamp of the Ministry of Justice, and there was a letter bearing the crest of the boys' school. He read the postcard, snarled at the bill. He opened the school's envelope.

Brilliant . . . The principal writing to say that Dawie's progress was excellent, he was working hard, and could well be university material . . . Hell, there had never been a graduate in Frikkie's family.

Calculations in his mind. Could he afford the weights that Dawie hankered for? If he could afford the weights as well as the refrigerator then he would be helping Dawie towards a place on the fifteen, and a boy on the school fifteen with good marks would be more likely for a scholarship when the university time came. But if he bought Dawie the weights, if he could afford them, would that make young Erasmus jealous? No, no problem, because Erasmus could share the weights.

He would have to work harder. Work harder, that was good . . .

He opened the letter from the Ministry of Justice. The Ministry always posted first and then telephoned two days later to confirm the notification of another early rising.

The judder as the undercarriage was lowered.

Jack could see the ground below as the Boeing banked for final approach. Row upon row of small squares reflecting back the sun. The tower blocks of Johannesburg were on the horizon. He realized the squares were the tin roofs of tiny homes. Endless straight lines of light flashes, and then the patch of yellow dried-out veld between the townships and the city. The chief steward was hurrying along the aisle, steadying himself against the seat-backs, checking that the seatbelts had been fastened and the cigarettes extinguished. Jack read through his answers on the blue foolscap sheet for immigration. Questions in English on one side, Afrikaans on the reverse. OCCUPATION – Manager. PURPOSE OF VISIT – Holiday. LENGTH OF STAY – 3 weeks.

If he hadn't managed it in three weeks then he might as well have stayed at home.

They liked her in the office. They thought Ros van Niekerk was one of the most conscientious girls that they employed. They thought her sensible, level-headed, and able to take the limited responsibility that could be pushed her way in the Insurance high rise tower on Commissioner.

She was 24 years old. She was plain because she didn't care to be otherwise. She worked in the property insurance department. On most household policies there was reassessment as the policy became renewable at the end of a year's cover. Ros van Niekerk could have told the Minister of Finance where the economics of South Africa were going. It was in front of her from 8.30 in the morning to 4.30 in the afternoon five days a week. Three years earlier when she had gone into the property department, a good bungalow in the better Johannesburg suburbs would have fetched 350,000 rand and been insured for that value. The market had gone from bad to worse. A year ago that same property might have changed hands for 200,000 rand and now it might fetch 120,000 rand, it was that great a change. The home owner wasn't going to renew a 350,000 rand policy if his home would only fetch 120,000 rand. But the rates of insurance were going up. The political uncertainty, the unrest, the quagmire of Black and White relations guaranteed that insurance rates would rise. For very nearly every policy that Ros renewed there was a correspondence. She was busy. She rarely took more than twenty minutes of her lunch hour. She alone knew her way through the hillocks of files that covered her desk-top.

She used no lipstick, no eye shadow. She washed her auburn hair herself, combed and brushed it from a central parting. She dressed functionally and without ambition. The men in the office, the married and the unmarried, had long ago lost interest in her. She was not taken out. She had been asked, when she was a new girl, and she had invariably declined, and the invitations were no longer offered. The salesmen and the junior managers were polite to her but distant. If her social isolation in the company disturbed her then she was successful at disguising the disappointment. To those who worked alongside her she seemed happily self-sufficient. They knew she came from a good home, that her father was a professional man. They knew she had a younger brother at Wits. They knew very little else about her. In truth, there was very little else they might have known. At the end of each day she went directly home in her Beetle VW, she had her dinner with her mother and father, and her brother if he was back from the campus, she listened to music and she read. They might have thought of her as a boring girl who was on the road to end up an old maid. The young men in the office had decided she wasn't worth the trouble, there was easier game.

Her telephone warbled. A pay box call. A frown of irritation at the interruption.

Her brother on the telephone. The irritation was gone. Her young kid, her Jan, her crippled brother. Always so close, brother and sister. Since he was little more than a baby she had loved the young kid. Perhaps a reaction to time long ago when she had seen the poorly-disguised dismay of her father that his only son was handicapped.

Could Ros tell her mother that Jan would not be home for dinner. Jan couldn't call his mother direct, of course, their mother was out at whist.

To Ros, her brother was a more precious part of her life than anything she thought she would find in the hands of the young men in the office.

A radio news bulletin on the hour. The correct English diction of the South African Broadcasting Corporation.

'One person was killed in unrest at a Black township on the Western Cape. A spokesman at the Police Directorate in Pretoria said the Black teenager was shot dead when a policeman's relative fired into a crowd that was trying to set light to a policeman's home.

'A total of 107 Blacks were arrested during unrest in the East Rand following incidents during which administration board vehicles and municipal buses were stoned.

'In another incident of unrest in the East Rand a White woman driving an administration board car fired in self-defence on a mob that had stoned her. No injuries were reported.'

A pretty quiet night.

But since the state of emergency had been declared by the State President, and since the curbs had been slapped on Press reporting, fewer details of attacks and incidents and deaths were furnished by the Police Directorate.

A quiet night, and the unrest was far down the order of the bulletin. The unrest came after a speech by the Foreign Minister, ahead of the results of the Springbok men's gymnastic team on tour in Europe.

The message of the bulletin to its White audience was polished clear. Difficulties, of course there were difficulties. Crisis, of course there was no crisis. Inside the laager of the old wagons the Republic was holding firm. Holding firm, and holding tight.

That was the message of the SABC as the Boeing from far away Europe taxied on the long Jan Smuts runway.

Jack came down the steep open steps onto the tarmac.

Around him the passengers blinked in the crisp sunlight. Jack was tired, nervy. Had to be nervous because he was going to walk up to immigration and make the pretence that he was a tourist with his head full of sea and sunshine and safaris. He was part of a shuffling crocodile that moved past four Black policemen, immaculate and starched, and into the terminal.

A young White policeman was seated by the doorway. He was lounging back on a tilted straight chair. He wore short drill trousers, long socks to the knee, shoes to see his face in, a tunic and a Sam Browne belt onto which was hooked a shined brown leather revolver holster. Jack caught his eye, looked away. He thought there was an arrogance about the bastard, a contempt for these unshaven, crumpled flotsam spilling in from Europe.

He took his place in the FOREIGNERS line.

It was brief and it was correct.

All that anxiety had been for nothing. Passport examined, immigration form looked over, the belt of the stamp on the slip of paper that was stapled into his passport, his passport returned.

They had given him six weeks.

He had to grin.

He would be out in three weeks or he would be dead, or he would be staying as a guest for twenty years.

He collected his bag, was waved through customs, and took a taxi. He was driven away on a sweeping multi-lane highway. He flopped in the back seat. The tiredness was aching in his shoulders and legs. The driver was middle-aged, White, overweight. Beside his speedometer there was sellotaped a photograph of his family, an obese woman and two plump children.

'You're from England, eh? What brings you to South Africa, eh?'

The driver ignored Jack's silence.

'Don't get me wrong, man, I've nothing against you, but that's where our problem is, foreigners, specially English foreigners. People telling us what to do. People who don't live here, don't know a thing about South Africa, and all they can think of is telling us how to get on with our lives. The English tell us . . . That's rich, that's a real joke. The English tell us how to treat our Blacks, and they've riots in Birmingham and London . . . What more do I have to say?'

On either side of the road Jack could see the effects of the months of drought, high dried out grass. Then modern industrial estates, sprinkled with the For Sale and To Let signs.

'Eh, man, we know our Blacks a sight better than they do. We've had years of them. You know that. What a Black man respects is strength. If you pussy-foot to the Black man then he'll cut your throat. If you're firm with him, then he behaves himself. You have to be firm with the Black man and you have to remember not to trust him, not an inch. What I say about the Black man is this – if he can't steal it or screw it, then he'll break it. My sister, she's on a farm up in the North East Transvaal. She's got a neighbour who's come from Rhodesia, started again, started from nothing, building up a new farm. You know what her neighbour told her, as God's my witness? He said, "Winnie, if there's trouble, just a hint of trouble, first thing to do is to slot the nanny." Good advice, because you can't trust the Blacks.'

The road was lined now with small concrete bungalows. White homes. Perhaps the homes of taxi drivers. Higher up on the hill, on sites that were scraped from the ochre-red soil were the speculators' town houses.

'What they don't understand, those people in England, preaching to us, is that the violence isn't about Blacks and Whites, it's Black against Black. You didn't know that, I'll bet. You should see what they do to each other. They're savages, they chop each other, burn each other. And people in England say we should give them the vote. Most of them can't read . . . They don't want the vote. Most of them just want to live quietly, have their beer, work on a farm. They don't want politics and they don't want violence. The blame's with the agitators and the commies, winding them up. All the encouragement they're getting from liberal places, England, America, it's doing nothing for the Blacks. I've a nephew in the police, great young man, in the anti-terrorist unit, uniformed, he tells me it's all the fault of agitators and commies. They're too soft on those ANC people, that's my criticism of the State President. They should hang the lot of them. Shouldn't just hang those they get for murder, like those swine that did the court, they should hang any of them they find with guns and bombs.'

'Are they going to hang them?' Jack asked.

'You know about them, do you? In your newspapers, was it? It was on the radio last night. No clemency, not for any of them. All the liberals in England will be shouting when we hang them, but we're a long way from England and we don't hear the shouting . . . You a rugby man, eh? That's the Ellis Stadium . . .'

Jack saw the huge terraces of concrete, the rows of red seating.

'My idea of heaven. Up in the West Stand with a few beers and the Boks in their green jerseys, and even that those radicals have managed to spoil. I had tickets for the All Blacks last year, I thought they had more guts in New Zealand, I didn't think they'd cancel on us. Here you are, man, your hotel.'

Jack slid out of the taxi. He was bathed in sweat. He paid the driver, gave him a tip before he realized how much he loathed the man.

'Thank you, very kind. I've really enjoyed our conversation. You have a good holiday, sir. And you take my advice, get yourself to the Ellis Park when the Transvaal are playing.'

There were grinning faces around him, smiling faces of the Black doorman and the suitcase boy. He was led across the ornate hotel lobby, past the jewellery and curio shops, to the front desk. He wondered what they would have to say about the supreme penalty and the Pritchard Five. He filled in the registration form. He reckoned that he was 30 miles from Pretoria Central prison.

As soon as he walked into the room Jeez recognized the colonel.

Sergeant Oosthuizen had brought Jeez from his cell to the visit. He had known there was something extraordinary when they had walked on past the line of doors for C section's visit rooms, and on into the administration block. He had not been back in that block since his first day at Beverly Hills.

Jeez stared from the door into the colonel's face.

Jeez had been through the Spac labour camp and before that through the investigation centre in Tirana. Only the thought of being hanged frightened him. The sight of the colonel did not make him afraid.

The colonel's empire was the interrogation floor of John Vorster Square police station in Johannesburg.

On the tenth floor where he ruled, the gaze of the colonel was reckoned to buckle a man's knees, a Black man's or a White man's, to make water of his bowels. The colonel never hit a prisoner, he was always out of the room by the time that a prisoner was stripped, was gasping, was screaming. The colonel ordered what happened to the prisoners. The servants of his empire were the captains and the lieutenants and the warrant officers of the security police.

Jeez knew the colonel. An old acquaintance.

Jeez had never given him anything. Each time that the colonel had come back into the interrogation rooms of John Vorster Square after the beating, when the torturers were panting from their work, Jeez had stayed silent.

'I hate you, all you White bastard commies. I want to kill

you White filth. I want to shoot you with my own gun.' Jeez could remember the straining red blotched face as the colonel had shouted at him, early in the days of John Vorster Square. The colonel, with his retinue of phone-tappers, searchers, tailers, letter openers, frighteners, had screamed at him through the spittle. Jeez reckoned he'd given up early. Jeez reckoned the colonel had given up on this one prisoner when he had realized he was fighting a losing battle, and he hated to be close to failure.

The colonel was Jeez's 'visit'.

The colonel and his warrant officer. Jeez knew the WO. He had done time on Jeez at John Vorster Square, hand slaps and punches, and twice the boot. He had started in on Jeez as soon as the colonel had gone back to his office. Jeez had heard in the basement cells of the Pretoria court house, when he was locked in with Happy and Charlie and Percy and Tom, that it was the WO who had got Percy talking first, and Tom second, and then Charlie and Happy. They had all been softened by the WO and then made their voluntary statements to the colonel.

They were in a senior officer's room. There was a glass-topped desk and comfortable chairs and a vase of flowers on a shelf over the radiator and a photograph of the State President on the wall and curtains. Jeez hadn't known that such a room existed inside Beverly Hills. The door closed behind him. Jeez looked round. Oosthuizen had gone. He was alone with the colonel in his slacks and his blazer, and the WO in his lightweight suit. Both sitting, relaxed, as if they'd enjoyed a good lunch.

'I am a convicted prisoner, sir,' Jeez said firmly. 'I do not have to submit to further police interrogation.'

The colonel smiled, bending the line of his snipped brush moustache. 'Who said anything about interrogation, Carew?'

'Sir, I would like to go back to my cell.'

'You're jumping the gun, man. I'm not here to ask questions.'

He would have seemed a slight, frail figure to them. Jeez thought that the WO would have dearly liked him to raise a fist to the colonel, would have enjoyed beating the hell out of him.

'We wanted to have a talk with you, Carew. We wanted to see if we could be of help to you.'

An old trick that Jeez had taught himself in Spac, with the real bastards among the interrogators. Take away the uniform, strip off the shirt and vest and socks and boots. See them only in their underpants. See a menacing man in his underwear, see his hanging white belly and his spindly legs, see him without the uniform that makes for fear, creates authority. His mind gave him the picture of the colonel in his underpants. He stared back at the colonel.

Eyes meeting, neither man turning away.

'Has the governor seen you today, Carew?'

'No, sir.'

'You haven't been told of the State President's decision regarding clemency for you?'

'No, sir.'

The colonel turned slowly to his warrant officer. 'You'd have thought Carew would have been told, with it on the radio and all that.'

'Too right, Colonel.'

They were winding him up, Jeez knew that, turning the screw. He stood his ground. He listened to the silence in the room. There would have been a conspiracy between the colonel and the governor, news to be kept from Carew in order that the condemned man might prove more pliable to the colonel of security police.

'I'm very surprised that you haven't been told, Carew.'

He bit on his lip.

'When a man's been here thirteen months, waiting to know whether he's going to hang, you'd have thought he'd be told which way it's going for him.'

'You'd have thought that, Colonel.' The echo from the warrant officer.

Jeez imagined the hot sweating hair on the gut of the colonel, and the pig-bladder bulge of his belly, the milk white matchstick legs.

144

'You want to know what the State President has decided, Carew?'

There was an ache of pain in Jeez's lips. He thought the skin must be near to breaking. The colonel's voice hardened.

'You are an impertinent little swine, Carew, and not for much longer. You are going to hang, Carew. That's the State President's decision . . .'

Jeez felt the skin open. There was the warmth of the trickle of blood heading for the point of his chin.

'You're going to hang, Carew, hang by the neck until you are dead. You are going to hang through the due process of law. You can be impertinent for two more weeks, and then you hang.'

He tried to see the men at Century, the men on his team. He tried to find the image in his mind of when he had come back from the clinic and they had taken him down to the pub behind Victoria railway station and made him pie-eyed, and made him talk about the conditions in Spac. They couldn't have acted the way they hung on his words, Lennie, and Adrian and Henry, the way the eyes of the youngsters they'd brought along shone with admiration. What was the length of Century's bloody arm? Couldn't be true, that the team couldn't reach him.

'You have been an enigma to me, Carew. I'll admit to you that we know very little about you, but look at the way you're standing, man. You're standing like a soldier. I don't know which army, I don't know when, but you've been a soldier and served your country. Look at you today, man, you stand your ground because you've got guts. But where is having guts taking you? To the rope, and an unmarked grave.

'Carew, there is nothing about you, that I know of, that gives me an idea of why you should be associated with Black terrorism, but it is that association that is going to hang you. Do you think those Blacks of the ANC care about you? They care shit all for you. They used you and they dropped you right in it. You know, Carew, there have been some protests in Europe about these death sentences, pretty pitiful protests, and your name's not mentioned. You know that? All the talk is of Zikala and Schoba and Ngoye and Mweshtu. You'll hang and nobody'll care.'

'Can I go back to my cell, sir?'

Whatever the torment, misery, always address the interrogators with courtesy. Courtesy brought a small victory over the bastards. The bigger victory was never to plead. He wanted the loneliness of his cell, he wanted the anguish to be private. He wanted to cry alone within the walls of his cell for help from his team.

'I don't want to see you hang, Carew. It would give me no pleasure to have you hanged by the neck until you are dead. I come here today with the offer that can save you from the executioner. Are you listening, Carew? Don't play the "Mister" with me, man.'

The blood rolled from his chin onto his buttonless tunic.

'On your behalf, Carew, I had a meeting with the Minister of Justice this morning. I have made a bargain with him.'

It was the colonel's moment. He took a sheet of headed paper from his pocket. He unfolded it, he waved it at Jeez. He laid it on his knee.

'If, even at this late stage, you agree to co-operate fully with me, to make a detailed and verifiable statement concerning every dealing you have had with the ANC, then the minister will go to the State President and get an order of clemency for you . . .'

He heard the singing, and then the trap, and then the spurt of water, and then the hammering, and then the cough of the van engine.

'A detailed statement, Carew. Personalities, safe houses, arms caches. Give us those and you get clemency, that is the bargain, here in writing.'

Jeez was rocking on the balls of his feet. Swaying as a sapling in light wind. Moisture bursting all over his body. Tickling fear at the nape of his neck.

'Make it easy for yourself, Carew, help us to help you. There's a good chap. The ANC doesn't give a damn for you. It's martyrs they want, photographs of martyrs to drape round Europe and

America. You owe them nothing, man. You owe it to yourself to co-operate with me. Are you going to be a good chap?'

He was burdened with his secret. He had never reneged on that secret, not during the years in Spac, nor during the weeks in John Vorster Square, nor during the months in Pretoria Central. To renege on the secret was to believe that the team had abandoned him. Better to hang than to believe Century had ditched him. Still the small kernel of hope, whittled down, the kernel said the team at Century would never believe that Jeez Carew would betray his secret.

He turned on his heel. It was a parade ground swivel. He was facing the door.

'You're putting the rope round your neck, Carew,' the colonel snarled.

The warrant officer shouted for Oosthuizen.

Still in his clothes, his shoes kicked off onto the carpet, Jack slept. Beside him on the wide bed was a copy of *Star*, open at the page that reported the decision of the State President that five convicted terrorists should hang.

IO

From his eighth floor window in the Landdrost Hotel Jack Curwen stared out over the city and beyond to the open ground. He looked past the office towers and away across the pale yellow pyramids of goldmine waste. He saw a modern city where less than a century before there had been only flat veld. He had read the books in his hotel room, and had to smile. An Australian, one George Harrison, had come here in search of gold, and stumbled on the main seam, and been given his discoverer's certificate – and sold it for £10. It was all down to George Harrison from Oz, all the towers, all the wealth, all the unrest. And poor George Harrison had disappeared with his £10 into the Eastern Transvaal, never to be heard of again. All that Jack saw was built upon the discovery of George Harrison, poor sod, loser. Waste heaps stretching to the south into the early morning haze mist, the towers to the east and north, the concrete streets to the west. Wherever he was, George Harrison, he must be crying in his box.

He took the lift down to the lobby. He had wondered if he would be contacted on his first afternoon, first evening, in the hotel. He had lain on his bed, sometimes reading, sometimes asleep, and waited. He hadn't taken breakfast, couldn't face a meal.

Time to find the target on which he would prove himself.

He was crossing the lobby. He heard his name called. The Indian day porter was coming from behind his counter.

'You want a taxi, Mr Curwen?'

'No, thank you.'

He saw the frown pucker the Indian's plump forehead.

'I'm going to walk,' Jack said.

'Be careful where you walk, Mr Curwen. Some very bad things happen to tourists. Definitely, no walking after four o'clock, Mr Curwen. Please not, sir.'

'I'm just going to walk around the main streets.'

'Anywhere, sir, it is better by taxi.'

He had seen the printed slip on the desk in his room. 'You are warned pickpockets have been known to assault tourists in Central Johannesburg.' He walked outside into a bright sunshine.

Once he had turned the corner from the front of the hotel he lost the sun. Buildings too tall for the width of their streets. Into shadow. Into the grey of concrete buildings and cracked litter-strewn pavings where the grass sprouted. A dirty city. He passed two paint-peeling, dowdy-fronted escort agencies, then on to Bree Street. Clothes shops and dismal coffee shops. The few Whites went on their way and hesitated not at all, and the Blacks leaned in the doorways, tilted themselves against the lamp posts. A beggar pleaded to him, Black, squatting over a crippled left leg, and Jack flushed and hurried on. The Blacks seemed to watch him, size him, weigh him.

Back into the sunlight.

He had come off Jeppe and onto Van Brandis. A square opened in front of him. He felt the warmth of the sunlight. Safety from the loiterers. He came past a high tower that gave way to a mock Gothic front, to a building of tall rectangular windows, and entrance steps leading to a wide portico. He saw the street sign ahead of him. Pritchard. He looked back across open lawns to the doorway and saw the spider web of scaffolding obscuring the black scorched stonework.

He gazed at the Rand Supreme Court.

He thought there must be a terrorist trial at the court. Too many police, too many yellow police wagons parked on Pritchard. He looked at the policemen, White and Black, some in denim blue overalls and forage caps, some in trousers and tunics and caps. He saw the way their holsters were slung from their webbing belts, slapping their thighs. There were high fire stains around the doorway. He wondered where his father had sat in the van. He wondered from which direction the four had approached with their bomb. He saw some flowers lying at the side of the steps leading up to the court. He wondered who in South Africa would want to put out flowers all those months later for his father, if he hanged . . .

Bullshit. Bullshit, because Jeez Curwen wasn't going to hang.

. . . He was standing on the pavement beside the path to the front entrance. A Mercedes pulled up beside him. A policeman saluted. The chauffeur sprang out to open the passenger's door. Jack watched the small and unremarkable man go slowly up the path between the lawns. Shrunken by age, his suit now a size too large for him, a judge going to work. A judge like another judge. A judge like the judge who had sentenced his father.

Not enough of a target.

He heard a faraway siren. He saw the police stiffen to alert, then move to cordon the pavement, to shepherd the drifting Blacks back from the kerb. A policeman standing in the junction of Van Brandis and Pritchard, beside his motorcycle, had his arm raised to halt the oncoming vehicles, leaving the road clear for the siren. Two cars, coming fast, and sandwiched between them a yellow van with tight mesh over the side window. Jack saw the blur of a Black face. He thought he saw the momentary image of a clenched fist, couldn't be sure.

A Black, a dozen yards from Jack, roared out loud the one word.

'*Amandla.*'

Jack thought he heard an answer shout from the speeding van. The convoy turned along the front of the court, down the far side of the building. A policeman, Black, truncheon drawn, stalked the man who had shouted.

He walked away. He had said that maximum security was the breeding place for complacency, but there was no complacency at the Rand Supreme Court. Strong enough for a target, but not Jack's because he would fail.

He looked at his map. He cut across Pritchard and President and Market. He had gone from the sunlight. He had returned to the gaudy world of fashion clothes and patent shoes. A Black man at a bus stop eyed him, head to toe, then turned his head and spat into the rubbish-filled gutter.

He walked onto Commissioner.

He stopped to stare into a gun shop window. In the window were targets. Not rabbits, nor squirrels, nor pheasants, nor duck. The silhouettes were of men. The size of men. Black men. White background. Jack could buy himself a life-size target of a Black man to pump away at, and it would cost him 50 cents. There was a poster on the outside of the shop door. Omar or Yousuf or Moosa Latib offered the Dunduff Shooting Range along with the slogan 'Defence with an unknown Firearm is Meaningless'. Nothing about game. Learn how to shoot a Black man. He went inside. He had no reason to explore this shop, but it fascinated him. He had never used a firearm, not even an air pistol on an empty tin. He went down into the basement. The customers were two deep and stretched the length of a long counter. Men and women, all Whites, were handling pistols and revolvers in the front rank, while those behind waited for them to make their choice, pay their money, get the hell out of the way. There were two young men behind the counter. No big deal for them that men and women, all Whites, were crowded in their shop to buy pistols and revolvers for personal protection, to blow away Blacks. Such difficult choices to make, between Smith & Wesson and Browning and Beretta and Colt and Heckler & Koch and Steyr and Walther. The men wanted to know about range, and the women wanted to see whether it would slip in their handbag. The men argued about cost, because up to 1,000 rand was a hell of a sum to pay for stopping a Black man. The women wanted to be shown mother of pearl in the weapon's handle. The counter men said the supplies were short, that they didn't know when they'd be topping up on stock, that was what they had. Jack saw they wore waist holsters, filled, strapped in their trouser belts. He saw that no customer wanted more time to think about a purchase. Everyone ended up producing a firearms licence and writing a cheque.

Jack spoke to the man standing in front of him, queuing.

'Is it easy to get a licence?'

'Not the year before last. Pretty simple last year. Dead easy this year.' He was a soft spoken man, could have been a schoolmaster. 'Just a formality now. You a visitor here? If you've got a good property, if you're a city centre trader, if you're living on your own, if you have to put your takings in a bank night safe, if you have to go home regularly after dark – that's just about everyone. You're English?'

'Yes.'

'I came out eleven years ago, from Weston-super-Mare. You know that place? I'm getting a gun for my wife, she's nervous on her own. We've a Doberman, but my wife says it's too easy on Blacks . . .'

'Perhaps you should have stayed in Weston-super-Mare,' Jack said mildly.

'I pay my taxes, every last rand of them, I pay for the police, but the police are all out in the townships . . .'

He was still talking as Jack turned away.

He went out of the shop. He pocketed his map. He went west down Commissioner.

He saw the building ahead of him. It seemed to block his path, far ahead. He was going towards John Vorster Square.

He had read in the first clipping in the newspaper office library that his father had been taken to John Vorster Square. Thiroko had told him about John Vorster Square.

Not really a square, a wedge of ground between Commissioner and Main, curtailed at the far end by the raised De Villiers Graaf motor link.

John Vorster Square was nothing more than a police station. Jack grinned to himself. The toughest, most feared police station in the country named after a Prime Minister and State President.

John Vorster Square was their power. Where the guns were,

152

where the uniforms were, where the interrogation rooms were, where the cells were, where Jeez had been held.

He couldn't know what had been done to his father in John Vorster Square. He could remember what Thiroko had told him. Rivers of pain. The helicopter. The screams. If his father had been there why should it have been different for him?

John Vorster Square was the place for the proving target. It was out of sight of the offices of the multinational corporations. It was far from the tourist routes. He thought it was where the real business of the State was done.

There was a central block of brilliant sky blue panels topped by layers of plate-glass windows. There were three wings. He walked past the door that led into the charge office, and then past the security check and the heavy metal turnstile. He saw the armed police guard, languid, bored. He walked round the back of the buildings where there were tended gardens and the wide sweep of a driveway for staff cars. He saw the 10 foot high railing fence, and at the Commissioner Street end a long brick wall set with small barred windows. He retraced his steps, went around the building again, seeming to have lost his way. He would come back in the afternoon. When he came back in the afternoon he would wear different clothes.

Jan van Niekerk carried out his instructions to the letter.

It was his way. It was why he was useful to the Umkhonto we Sizwe. He had been given those instructions the previous evening.

He disliked being given jobs for the daytime. Daytime jobs broke the routine of his studies and he believed that his routine at Wits was his best defence against suspicion. In common with most White comrades he found it hard to consider the possibility of arrest. Arrest was what happened to Black comrades. The Whites, graduates, were too bright to be caught out by the Boer security police.

He rode his Suzuki towards the Alexandra township, but before reaching it he turned north into the industrial estates of

Wynberg. He found the rubbish heap where he had been told it would be, close to the corner of 6th Street and 2nd Avenue. There was a dirty plastic bag on the edge of the rubbish heap. No-one was in sight. He picked it up, twenty pounds, more. It was an effort for Jan van Niekerk. He carried it to his moped. He put his face close to look into the bag and sneezed. The irritation welled in his nostrils, the sneezing convulsed him. He knew then that he carried explosives. Pepper was always strewn over explosives and between the wrappings of foil and plastic to throw the police dogs. He put the package into two new shopping bags from the Checkers store group, first one, tied it with string, and then into the second. He strapped it to the back seat of his moped.

He rode carefully, avoiding the potholes. He knew nothing of the volatility of explosives, and he presumed that if there were explosives then there would also be detonators.

He came back into Johannesburg, making for the Landdrost Hotel.

Jack lay on his bed.

It was the smartest hotel he'd ever booked into. Overnighting for D & C would never be the same.

A soft knock at his door. He sat up.

'Come in.' He thought it might be the maid to turn down his bed.

There was a second knock. He padded across the room in his socks. He recognized the bellboy.

'Your shopping, sir. Very heavy, sir.'

He had it on his tongue to say there was no shopping to be delivered. The heavy parcel was bending the kid's shoulder. He bit off the denial. He gave the bellboy a tip. He closed the door. He carried the Checkers bag to his bed, laid it down. He lifted out the second bag that was inside, that stank. He carried a chair to the door and lodged it under the doorknob. He opened the window wider.

He opened the second bag.

He sneezed.

His head rocked back, couldn't help himself. He lifted the shopping bag into the bathroom and spread out yesterday's *Star* on the floor, and gently opened the black plastic. He stripped off a cooking foil wrap.

The explosive was in three piles, layer upon layer of ½ inch thick ¼ pound slabs. He could tell it was fresh, the greasepaper on each slab was firm. He thought it would be plaster gelatine, couldn't tell from the print on the wraps. The writing was in Cyrillic . . .

He had liked Thiroko, but he hadn't known how much he trusted him. I love you, Jacob Thiroko. Listen to your radio. Wherever you are, keep your finger on the tuner button, keep following the news bulletins. Keep your ear to the seat, Mr Thiroko.

. . . There was a small jiffy bag, cut off and the top stapled down to half size. Gently, he pulled it open. He found four small pinched bundles of cotton wool with Sellotape binding. He prised one open. He extracted the gleaming detonator. There were lengths of wire. One roll would be the Russian-made equivalent of Cordtex, and the other their own safety fuse. From the thickness he thought he could tell which.

He could smell the explosive. The sickly scent of almond sweets. Like the marzipan under the icing on his mother's Christmas cake, and on the cakes she made for his birthdays, when there was just the two of them, when she had been without a husband and he without a father. He replaced each layer of wrapping as neatly as he could, then brought out his underarm deodorant canister. He sprayed over the package, then opened the bathroom windows to let in the sounds of the traffic below, to let out the scent of his spray and the scent of almonds. He put the package into his suitcase, locked it, returned it to the bottom of the hanging cupboard.

Jack sat on his bed and drew up a shopping list.

A grip bag, a 10-litre can, a roll of heavy adhesive tape, a pair of washing-up gloves, a packet of 1.5 volt torch batteries, electrical flex, a watch, a litre of two-stroke oil, 9 litres of petrol.

He had tidied his room. He had sprayed again with his deodorant.

He had made up his mind. He was on the road, far on the road.

Jack Curwen went shopping on a sunny Johannesburg afternoon.

An everyday afternoon at John Vorster Square.

The army of prisoners whiled away the hours in the half basement cells of the east wing, some under investigation, some in detention, some criminal and some political.

The hard everyday afternoon were reserved for the politicals. The criminals were just *tsotsis*, the hooligans, the thieves of the townships. The criminals made only a slight impact on the smooth running of the state's apparatus. The politicals needed breaking, putting in court, locking away. The politicals threatened the state's apparatus.

Bars dominated the east wing cell blocks. Bars across the windows, bars across the corridors, bars across the light wells. A filthy place where the prisoner is dehumanized, where he cannot believe that anyone cares about his fate. A place where the grime of years coats the cell floors and walls. Where the graffiti is of despair. Since the state of emergency on the East Rand the prisoners had been brought in their hundreds to John Vorster Square. Many Blacks and a few Whites. The elderly and the schoolchildren, the community workers and the trade unionists, the revolutionaries and those registered by computer error or an informer's malice on the police records. Better to be a robber of banks than to have publicly denounced as 'mere tinkering with apartheid' the State President's package of reforms. Better to have mugged the migrant workers in the shadows outside their township hostels when they have wages and are drunk, than to have protested on the streets the right to vote.

The politicals were the targets of the security police working on the upper floors of the south wing of John Vorster Square. Pleasant offices, airy and light behind the plate-glass windows, but in their interrogation rooms the air and the light could be cut with the dropping of blinds.

The security police at John Vorster Square were good at their work. A White Methodist priest once held in John Vorster Square had written afterwards of the 'decrepit docility of despair' that cowed the Blacks in the townships. The policemen exploited that despair in the interrogation rooms, they found little resilience in those they questioned. Even the comrades of the Umkhonto we Sizwe condemned themselves in their statements given on the tenth floor. Happy Zikala and Charlie Schoba and Percy Ngoye and Tom Mweshtu had made their statements here, gathered the noose closer to their necks here. All the Whites, those who talked and those who stayed silent, those with the privilege of third level education, those who were active in the cadres, would speak of the expertise of the security police on the tenth floor. Most cracked.

Jeez hadn't. He was a rare exception.

And Jeez was now little more than a faded statistic in the hand-written ledgers of John Vorster Square, remembered only by a very few.

The colonel was principal amongst the few.

The instruments of his power were the Terrorism Act, No. 83 (1967) with a minimum sentence of five years and a maximum of death – the General Law Amendment Act, No. 76 (1962) Section 21, also five years to death – the Internal Security Act, No. 79 (1976) giving the power of preventive detention and banning orders. There were not many prisoners, politicals, who did not feel the sliding bowel weakness and the tickle of terror when they stood in the presence of the colonel.

He would have described himself as a patriot. He would have said that every action he undertook in John Vorster Square was for the benefit of his beloved South Africa. He would have said that he stood in the front line of the battle against the contagion of communism and the drift to anarchy.

On that everyday afternoon, the colonel watched with grudging satisfaction as a full time clerk of FOSATU made a voluntary statement. Small beer, a Coloured, an insignificant creature, admitting to handing out leaflets demanding the release of political prisoners. With the vermin's own guilt tied down, the work might begin of extracting information from him on more senior members of the Federation of South African Trade Unions. He would be charged under the Terrorism Act. They could do for the clerk under 'activities likely to endanger the maintenance of law and order', or they could do for him under 'activities likely to cause embarrassment to the administration of the affairs of state'. They had him by the throat, they had his confession, and now they could bargain the length of his sentence against the incrimination of the leaders of FOSATU. It was the leaders that the colonel wanted, not this rodent.

The clerk sat at the table and dictated a stuttering statement to a White corporal. He was watched by the colonel who stood in the doorway.

The journey to Pretoria was a sore in the colonel's mind. He did not comprehend how a White preferred to hang rather than to come clean about the Blacks with whom he had collaborated. The visit to Beverly Hills had been a failure. He would happily have hanged James Carew himself to have expurgated that failure. He was no fool, he could rationalize his failure. He supposed that he had failed with Carew because he was unaccustomed to interrogating White politicals. One or two a year came into his domain on the top floors of John Vorster Square. Some he categorized as dedicated communists, some were gripped with the martyr wish, some he regarded as mentally deranged, some were all three. All of them he thought stupid. To suffer in the cause of Black freedom was idiotic. Carew was outside his categories, a mystery. He thought he hated the man which was why in this same room he had lost his temper, shouted.

There was no further reason for the colonel to stay and watch the clerk. He went back to his own office.

The sun was dipping between the mine waste mountains to the west. Far below him were the gaudy street lights and the ribbons of the headlamps of the homegoing traffic.

There was a sheaf of telex messages on his desk. There was a photocopy of a report from Major Swart in London.

The colonel thought that Pretoria overrated Swart.

Darkness was falling on the city.

He gutted Swart's telex. More failure. Buck passing and excuses. Failure to make the connection between Mrs Hilda Perry and James Carew. Failure to link one Douglas Arkwright, deceased, on a contact between a White male, unidentified, and Jacob Thiroko. Failure to maintain a tail on Jacob Thiroko.

Categorized totally incompetent, that Swart. The one and only link to Carew's earlier life and Swart had failed to make anything of it. The report was soon pushed aside, categorized not useful, back in the tray beneath less intractable problems.

The piece of paper that had failed, that he had reckoned a guarantee of success, the piece of paper that carried the minister's signature, lay in the colonel's personal safe. He would shred it on the morning of the execution. That failure would die with Carew.

But failure it was. At the heart of the failure was the void that was Carew's past, exacerbated by the man's refusal to talk. The bachelor apartment in Hillbrow had been searched and searched again and revealed not a clue to the past. The drivers on the taxi ranks had been quizzed, interrogated even, and found to know nothing significant about the man at all. The bombing team had all said in their statements that they had never seen the man before he drove them away from Pritchard. The void spirited up the colonel's suspicions. No man could so effectively hide his past, unless he had deliberately hidden it, had a very good reason for hiding it . . .

He consumed the paperwork on his desk. He had promised his wife that he would not be late home.

He had waited until the bus load of tourists filled the hotel lobby with their stacks of suitcases.

He had taken the lift down twice before, holding the grip bag sagging close against his knee, and each time the lobby had been

159

almost empty and he would have been noticed by the night porter and the bellboy and the luggage boys and the doorman. Twice he had gone back to his room to while away the minutes before trying again. Very tense, close in his thoughts. All his concentration was on the hulk that was John Vorster Square, and the fence around it, and the lights, and the armed police sentries, and on his father and on suppressing his fear. The plan called for him to expose himself to challenge and gunfire. He knew of no other way.

He stepped into the lobby. The lift doors shut behind him. The bellboys and the luggage boys were marshalling a huge pile of suitcases, the doorman was loudly supervising their distribution. The reception was lost in a half moon of argument because there was a double booking problem. The night porter was doling out keys to those who had been checked in and who had allocated rooms. They were Americans, fresh from safari.

Jack crossed the lobby unnoticed. Unseen, he went out through the swing doors. Behind him rose a tumult of angry voices.

Dark streets. Streets given up by the Whites. The Whites were powering home to the suburbs in their BMWs and Jaguars. Jack walked with a brisk purpose. He stayed far out on the pavement, close to the kerb and the cars' lights, avoiding the shadowed shop entrances from which spurted the flash of a match, the glow of a drawn cigarette. There was no reason that he should have attracted attention. He was a young White who was late, hurrying with a bag that might contain his sports kit, whose weight he struggled to disguise.

He took the route that he knew, down Van Brandis, right onto Commissioner. Above him the lights were flickering out in the towers, the last workers leaving. The security guards with their polished staves patrolled the wide entrances.

Jack saw the lights in John Vorster Square, an oasis of work as the rest of the city shut down for the night. He took from the bag a rough stone, picked from a street building site on Commissioner. The stone gripped in his left hand, the size of a cricket ball. At school, in the team, they'd played him for his fielding. He could certainly throw. The stone was now his weapon and his protection.

There was a constable guarding the back gate.

A presentable young man, straight-backed, clean-shaven, and he wore his uniform and his Sam Browne well. He was often given the 6 p.m. to 10 p.m. shift on the rear entrance because his sergeant thought him the right sort of constable to open and close the gates on the comings and goings of the top brass. The constable sat in his box. His service revolver was holstered, the flap buttoned down because that was tidier. In the box was a loaded FN rifle, safety on, a gas mask, a telephone link to the operations room inside, and his personal radio.

He saw the car approach. He saw the lights flash and the indicator wink to him. He saw the uniform of the driver, and the uniforms of the passengers.

Behind him he heard the revving of an engine outside the gates, and he heard the shout for the gates to be opened.

The constable had a car to let in and a car to let out.

He went forward. He slipped the bolt that was accessible only from the inside. He swung the near gate back towards him, pushed away the further gate. He had to step back smartly to avoid the car coming from the outside, from Main Street.

There was a moment when he was back at the edge of the driveway, readying himself to salute, and the gates were fully opened, and the cars were jockeying to pass through.

There was a moment when he did not think to study the shadows across the road.

He only saw the blur of a man running. He saw the figure coming fast across the road. He saw the low-slung bag trailing from the figure's arm. He stepped forward, picking at the flap of his holster. He hesitated. He turned back for his rifle. Whichever way he looked he was dazzled by the headlights. The figure ran past him on the far side of the incoming car. The constable was rooted to the concrete floor of his sentry box. The figure charged to the main doorway, pushed it, swung the bag inside. The constable saw the bag sailing into the rectangle of light, and lost sight of it.

He was spinning, trying to get the lights from his eyes. He saw the figure for a moment more, seeming to fill the doorway into the hallway area. He reached again for his holster, then for his rifle, then for his radio, then for his telephone link. The constable had never before confronted an emergency, and nothing had ever happened at the back gates of John Vorster Square. And the bastards in the car hadn't reacted.

He saw the shadowy shape of the figure turn and run back from the doorway. He hadn't the flap off his holster, nor the rifle in his hand, nor was he reaching for his radio, nor had he lifted his telephone.

Everything too fast for the constable. The figure running to get by the car that was coming out. The driver of the car that was entering seeing a figure, no longer in shadow, bright in the headlights, swung the wheel to block the figure, run the figure down. The figure stumbling to a stop, backing away, into the courtyard, trapped. An anorak hood over the figure's upper head and a handkerchief knotted over the figure's lower face, and a dark slash where the eyes would be. So fast, too fast. The arm of the figure swinging back, whipping forward. The crack of the windscreen, like a bullet snap. The constable saw the windscreen freeze, shatter to opaque. The incoming car swerving. The outgoing car turning away from collision.

He yelled, not into his radio, not into his telephone, out into the night air.

'BOMB!'

The presentable young constable ran from his box. The outgoing car careered from a side-on collision towards him. He was blinded by the lights. He ran for his life, and behind him his sentry box was taken down by the impact of the outgoing car's radiator and engine weight, squashed away through the shrubs, flattened against the low wall and the high railings.

There was the thud of running feet. He saw the figure come down the driveway, skip past the incoming car.

He had the flap off his holster now. He had the pistol butt in his hand, lifting. The figure gone, out into the street. The pistol was in his hand, his thumb had taken across the safety. He had the running figure, seen between the railings, over the end of his barrel. Steady, squeeze . . .

The constable was bowled over by the blast that erupted from behind the plate glass of the hallway area. And with the driven wind came the glass shards, and then the crimson and orange billowing of the flames. Before he lost consciousness he was aware of the glass splinters fragmenting around him, and of the heat of the spreading fire.

Jack ran 200 yards. He had pulled the handkerchief off his face, tugged the anorak hood down from his head. Up Main, cars overtaking him, up Market, into the narrow side street off Becker, no-one in sight, off with the anorak, dump it, a distant siren, along the lanes off Diagonal, two men sitting, their backs against the wall, neither moved, past the closed Stock Exchange, onto Bree. He was walking when he reached Bree. He controlled his speed, harder to control his breathing. He tried to window shop, to appear to be strolling away the evening.

Two police trucks racing, sirens wailing, and the whine in the streets around him of approaching fire engines.

From the far side of Bree he looked back towards John Vorster Square . . . a bloody lunatic plan . . . He saw the orange glow reaching for the night sky. He saw the dark climbing column of smoke. Can you see that, Mr Thiroko?

He walked along Bree towards the Landdrost Hotel. He straightened his tie in a window, he casually wiped the sweat off his forehead. He knelt to wipe the earth from the gardens of John Vorster Square off his shoes. The last 100 yards, forcing himself not to look back. He steadied himself, and went inside. He stood in the lift with his back to a cluster of tourists. He went down his corridor, into his room. He went first to the cupboard. He saw that the packaged pile of explosives was undisturbed. Of

163

the three slabs that had been delivered in the Checkers bags, two were still inside his suitcase. He might have failed. But now he thought he had enough dynamite still to blow his way into the hanging gaol.

Jack dived onto his bed. His face was buried in his pillow, his legs shook without control.

God, what had he done? For his father, what had he done?

11

Just before eight o'clock, Jack joined the office workers and the labourers and the vagrants at the junction of Market and Main and Commissioner to see the damage. Police with dogs and soldiers in full combat kit kept the watchers far back from the fire darkened building. There was little to see, but that was no discouragement to the crowd.

Jack had already seen his morning *Citizen* with the special colour front page. The main photograph showed the orange flame ball alive inside the ground and first floor, billowing up the stairwell. He had read of the 'miraculous escape' of the policeman on desk duty inside the door, how the heavy steel-panelled furniture had protected him from the immediate force of the fire and explosive blast. He had read that the offices above the hallway had been unoccupied, that had they not been the officers who worked there would have been killed when the floor above the hallway caved in. He had read that the steel and concrete construction of the block had prevented the spread of the fire, and that within 48 minutes the fire service had brought the blaze under control. He had read that a single man was believed responsible, that there were reports that the man was a White, that the police were 'keeping an open mind'. The smell of a water-soaked fire is unlike any other. It was a familiar odour for Jack to sniff at as he stood with the crowd, and he thought of George Hawkins, pictured him beside him, remembered the demolition of a fire wrecked office in Guildford, and seemed to hear George's growl of approval. The newspaper said it had been the most dramatic attack against the country's security system since the car bombing of the Air Force headquarters in

Pretoria and the rocket firing at the Voortrekkerhoogte base of the South African Defence Forces. All down to you, Mr Hawkins.

He listened to the talk around him, mostly in English, a little in the Afrikaans language that he could not understand, all of it angry.

He took a last look at his work, and at the fire engines far up the street, and the police wagons. It was the controlled anger on the policemen's faces that would stay with him.

'You know what I heard?' A man with a loud voice and a florid face and a butcher's apron. 'I heard that last night the *bandiete* in the cells over there were shouting and singing, all the bastard politicals, cheering they were. Pity the scum didn't roast.'

John Vorster Square still stood, foursquare. But he had shown them, he had singed its beard.

He walked down Commissioner to the junction of Harrison. Another thought as he walked. There had been Blacks among the sightseers, and he had not heard them speak above a whisper. He had heard the vengeful fury of the Whites, but he knew nothing of the Blacks, whether they cheered his attack, whether they feared the reprisals that would follow the violence he had directed against the principal police station in the city. He thought that in the world of Jack Curwen the Black man's opinion was irrelevant. Their fight was not his fight. His fight was family.

He took a taxi to the railway station.

The colonel sat in on the conference. He was not himself responsible for the direct gathering of intelligence. Many times Intelligence knew of an impending attack. Not the exact location, nor the timing, but Intelligence generally knew of a major infiltration, of the movement of explosives, of an order from Gaberone or Lusaka. Intelligence had many sources. There were covert watchers, small teams of Recce Commando operating deep inside Angola, observing the Umkhonto we Sizwe camps, listening to their radios, hooked into remote telephone lines that served those camps. There were deep sleepers in the overseas offices of the African National Congress. There were traitors, arrested in great secrecy, interrogated, frightened, turned, released. There were men and women inside South Africa who were under constant surveillance, their names having been first revealed to Intelligence by the SADF capture of documents from ANC offices in Gaberone. A treasure chest.

Intelligence had this time had no word.

The conference was boring the colonel.

For a while he endured in silence, then intervened.

'Was it a White or was it not a White?'

He could not be given an answer. The vehicle drivers had said they had seen the shape of a man, momentarily in the lights, nothing else. The gate sentry had been the only continuous eye-witness to the attack. The gate sentry had been concussed, was still sedated. The colonel was told that the gate sentry had rambled a description between reviving from concussion and being given sedation. A hood, a mask, eyes in shadow, always moving too fast.

'I think he was a White,' the colonel said. 'If he had been Black then there would have been a fire support team. I think it was a White working alone. He ran away. There is no report of a pick-up vehicle. If this had been ANC then there would most certainly have been a pick-up. This one man, one White man, is at best no more than on the fringe of the ANC. It is now more than thirteen hours since the explosion, and Lusaka has said nothing. How many times do they wait thirteen hours? By the news agencies they would have known of the explosion within thirteen minutes, and they have still said nothing. I believe they have made no claim because they do not know who is responsible. I suggest this is the work of an individual, not of a cadre of Umkhonto we Sizwe. Gentlemen, we have a White, we have a male. He ran forward fast, he threw a bag or sack weighing perhaps five kilos, he threw a fist-sized stone accurately through a windscreen. In my submission, we have a White male who is athletic, reasonable to assume that he is aged between eighteen years and thirty years. We should meet again when we have the forensics.'

The fire service had moved back from the hallway of the building.

Detectives and scientists moved amongst the sodden debris searching and picking. What they had collected in this initial examination was placed in metal bins to be sifted and then carried to the laboratories. A slow process, one that no detective experienced in this work, nor any scientist, would rush.

Jack went to the Whites Only ticket office.

He bought a day return ticket to Pretoria.

He went down the Whites Only entrance to the Whites Only section of the platform, alongside which would stop the Whites Only carriages.

Once the train had cleared the industrial and mining areas of Germiston and Edenvale and Kempton Park, it should have been a pleasant and picturesque journey. Past the factories and the gold waste mountains the train ran by the dry farm lands of the Witwatersrand. But Jack Curwen was not a tourist. He was an unidentified terrorist. He was on a journey to the city where his father was held, condemned to die. He thought it better to travel by train. No driving licence to be produced, no forms to be filled in at Avis or Hertz. In a train he was a lone microbe swimming in the vein of the state. He was in the heart kingdom of the Afrikaner regime. He was passing through the pretty satellite towns of Irene and Doornkloof and Verwoerdburg, rolling by the Johannesburg highway and the Fountain Valley Nature Reserve and the massive modern University of South Africa. He was coming to Pretoria, he was coming to his father.

A moment of confusion when he stepped down from the train. Which way to go? Streams of men and women, White and Black, crossing the platform around him. Confusion until he realized that the Blacks went left, the Whites went straight ahead. 'Separate development' for leaving a railway station. He went through the Whites Only exit, and out into the Whites Only hall-way of the station. His ticket had been clipped by a White official. He knew the cause of his confusion. His was a fear of going through the wrong exit, sitting on the wrong seat, urinating in the wrong lavatory, and being shouted at, called back, by a man in uniform.

There were uniforms all around him in the hallway. Soldiers with the berets of the Parabats, and of Armour, and of Artillery, and of the Medics. Scrubbed clean conscripts who were serving out their army time in administration in the capital city. Haggard young men changing trains on their way home for leave from the operational areas of South West Africa and the fearsome close quarters of guerrilla war. The airforce technicians of the Mirage squadron at Hoedspruit. The bearded and confident elite of the Recce Commando.

Jack eased his way through them. He was so very close to his destination. He went into the station magazine and sweet shop. He bought a map of Pretoria.

His fingernail searched for and found Potgieterstraat. He memorized the turns, the roads he would follow. He folded the map, stowed it away in his hip pocket. He would not be seen on Potgieterstraat studying a map.

He went out of the station. Pretoria was higher on the veld than Johannesburg, cooler, and the first frosts were not long away. He ignored the taxis. He would walk. He could see more by walking. He went past the booths where Blacks could buy their railway tickets, then out of the station yard. He went past the Combi vans that ferried Blacks between the station and the townships of Mamelodi or Atteridgeville, by the small street market where fruit and milk was sold, and vegetables. He could sense the difference to Johannesburg. He felt a little at ease walking here, because there seemed no threat, no scowling eyes gazing at him. He walked past the big dairy, and there the pavement ended, as if Whites' territory was bounded by pave-ments. He crossed coarse open ground. Potgieterstraat was ahead of him.

So very close to the road he had taken when his mind was made.

Under the old railway bridge of darkened steel and cut stone. Potgieterstraat stretched away up the hill.

Far in front of him, across the road, was a high slag yellow brick wall. He was within sight of Pretoria Central, of the Local gaol of the Pretoria Central complex.

Hell, and his gut was tight, and his legs were jellied.

He was the insect brought to a night light.

The wall was the colour of the mine mountains in Johannesburg. Pristine, dirty yellow and new. He walked up the hill. He was again on a pavement. Sometimes he looked to his left where there was nothing for him to see, sometimes he looked straight ahead at the tilt of Potgieterstraat. He pleaded with himself for naturalness. He was on foot, alone, and approaching one of the most security conscious square miles of the State. If he were to be challenged he had no story. Jack Curwen had sneered at Jacob Thiroko, he had told his mother that he was going to bring his father home, and he had planned bomb making with George Hawkins, and because of his hot headed nature and his arrogance Sandham was dead and Duggie Arkwright was dead. Lunacy and arrogance had carried him on the wing to Potgieterstraat. And thank God that Sandham and Duggie couldn't see him with jelly legs and his tight gut as he flickered his eyes forward to the high yellow brick walls of Local.

He looked right. He had seen on the map that he would pass what was labelled as DHQ . . .

Couldn't believe it . . . DHQ. He was walking past the Defence Headquarters of the Republic. The bastards had built Pretoria Central up the hill, same side of the road, spitting distance, rifle range distance, from the Defence Headquarters of South Africa. Throwback to the days of Empire, stone pillars holding the portico, weathered red brick, barred windows, creeper-draped railings topped with coils of barbed wire.

Eyes moving. From the nothingness of scrub and railway sidings to his left, on to Potgieterstraat and the walls that grew in height as he came closer, on back to the formal gardens of Defence Headquarters where the sentries patrolled with magazines fitted to their assault rifles. Duggie and Sandham were dead, and Jack hadn't even known that DHQ was right alongside his target. All the sentries, and all the back-up that would be out of sight but there in support of Defence Headquarters.

The excitement seeped from him.

The building next to Defence Headquarters, sandwiched between DHQ and Local, was that of the South African Air Force. More wire, more sentries.

Thiroko had said it was impossible.

Across the road from him was Local. He stopped, and bent down to flick his shoe lace undone. It took him several seconds to retie the lace. He looked down the side street that ran under the wall of Local, he stared down Soetdoringstraat while his fingers fumbled to make the knot. Immediately across Potgieterstraat, at the top of the angle of the Local walls, was a jutting fire position. There were dark slits, Jack couldn't know whether he was observed. The main gatehouse of Local was down Soetdoringstraat, covered by another fire position. At the end of the Local wall on Soetdoringstraat he saw the lowered barrier of a checkpoint. The walls of Local were 30 feet high. Local was covered by enfilading gun positions, and Local was only the gaol for the short-term Black criminals. Further down Soetdoringstraat, past the checkpoint, was the gaol for White politicals, and away and hidden from the road were the old Pretoria Central and the women's gaol, and further away and further hidden was Pretoria Maximum Security. At that moment Jack Curwen would have believed Jacob Thiroko.

He stood. He tried to resume a casual walk, and the walk was dragged and slow.

He went on up Potgieterstraat.

Over the height of the Local wall he could see the top floor cell windows of five blocks. There were clothes hanging from some of the windows, underpants and socks and shirts, and once he saw the face of a Black who gazed out into the bright

171

morning light. A terrible quiet about the place. Difficult for him to realize that hundreds of men were held behind that wall, that they made no sound. At the end of the Local wall the brickwork gave way to a mesh wire fence that stood between the road and tropical gardens, and then the wildness of high trees climbing over a steep hillside. He knew from his map that the hill was Magasyn Kopje. He knew that Beverly Hills was set back on the slopes of Magazine Hill.

Behind the trees, out of sight, were the walls of Beverly Hills.

A daft fantasy in Jack's mind. If he yelled his father would hear him. He reckoned he must be within eight hundred yards of the cell blocks of Beverly Hills. And he had seen high walls and gun positions and sentries with assault rifles. The fantasy slumped. He was 800 yards from his father, but he might as well have been in Churchill Close and five and a half thousand miles away. Despair, hurrying after the fantasy. He thought there was nothing more for him to see on Potgieterstraat. Despair, because he thought the bomb in John Vorster Square was for nothing.

Jack retraced his steps. He came briskly down the hill. He snatched one glance down Soetdoringstraat. He saw the check-point barrier rising, and a car coming out, leaving the cocoon of wire and walls and fields of fire. He looked away. On down the hill, back towards the ordinariness of Pretoria. The car that had come through the checkpoint sped past him. He went back towards the railway bridge. He felt he had turned his back on his father because he had been intimidated by the walls of Local that he had seen, and the walls of Beverly Hills that the trees obscured.

He took the first train back to Johannesburg.

Jacob Thiroko had heard the news of the John Vorster Square bomb on the radio in the morning.

He was astounded. He had thought in terms of an unguarded civil administration building, a noisy gesture simply.

John Vorster Square was something else . . . He had heard on the radio that the attacker had picked his moment to charge through an opened gate, hurl his bomb, and then escape under the nose of an armed sentry. An attack with the spontaneity of passion, nothing that was cold and predetermined. Thiroko recognized the extent of the danger. The most feared soldier was the man who was prepared to make the ultimate sacrifice.

Thiroko thought that he had gambled hugely on Carew's son, and the boy had repaid him by throwing a bomb into the most hated institution on the whole of the East Transvaal. The radio had said that long into the night there had been crowds on the streets of Soweto cheering the success of the attack, jeering at the police in their Casspirs who had come to disperse them with gas and bird shot.

The Indian owner of the safe house had long since gone about his business of selling motor car accessories when Thiroko came downstairs. In the kitchen he ate a slice of toast and drank strong coffee prepared for him by the Indian's wife. He ate increasingly little. Easier not to eat. His suitcase was packed, his room ready for another guest. He said his goodbyes to the Indian's wife, and left her home, and walked slowly with his suitcase to the Finchley Central underground station.

For the first time since he had arrived in London he journeyed to the offices of the African National Congress.

A terraced house in a side street off the Pentonville Road. A heavy green door beside windows covered with close mesh that was proof against fire bombs.

He endured the backslapping greeting of the London comrades – Blacks and Indians and Whites. He elbowed his way with little grace through the earnest congratulations of those who fought the regime from trenches that were separated from the battlefield by thirteen hours' flying. A small few he trusted. A great many he regarded with contempt. Thiroko was a military man. These were the pamphleteers and the speakers at fringe meetings, and the dreamers who said that the total revolution was at hand and that power was at the corner to be grasped. Thiroko was at home in the training camps of northern Angola, or with the young people of the Solomon Mahlangu school in

Tanzania, or with the fighters when they retired across the Botswana border to rest up in Black Africa. He thought they were all communists in the London office. They were the men and women with whom he hardly cared to pass the day. There was one man in the terraced house with whom he would have entrusted his life. A man who was old, a skinny tent pole with a pebble rolling accent of Hungary, a man they all called Magyar and who had spent fourteen years in the regime's gaols, and served his time to the last day without an hour of his sentence remitted before travelling to London and exile. A pale, pinch-faced man with a whispered voice who had never been heard to boast of his commitment to the Movement, a man who had made his sacrifice and expected no praise for himself. This one man he would trust.

Thiroko handed his plane ticket to Lusaka to a young White who he thought was at heart a Boer because he wore jogging shoes and a tracksuit and cut his hair as if he were a conscript in the SADF. He asked to be booked on the evening's flight home.

He took Magyar to a small room, and when they had sat down amongst the cardboard cartons of ANC literature that were expensively printed but not distributed, he turned up the volume of a cassette radio. Thiroko took few chances. He had no right to take chances, not with the safety of a young man who was prepared to run inside the John Vorster Square perimeter with a home-made bomb.

Magyar wouldn't ask him, so Thiroko gave the information.

The Hungarian had been in the Movement from the early days of the dive underground at the time of the banning of the African National Congress. He had stood in the same dock six years after it had held Nelson Mandela and Sisulu and Mbeki and Mhlaba and Motsoaledi and Kathrada and Denis Goldberg and Mlangeni. And now, in his sixty-seventh year, he was hardly listened to by the members of the London office. He pushed paper and he drafted press releases that would be rewritten. He was the one for Thiroko to talk with.

Thiroko told Magyar that the attack on John Vorster Square

174

was the work of a single committed individual supplied by the agencies of Umkhonto we Sizwe. He saw the quiet pleasure on the wrinkled face. Thiroko knew what the security police had inflicted on the old man.

Their voices were low against the barrage of the music.

'You were in the maximum security section of Pretoria Central?'

'What we called Beverly Hills, the hanging gaol. Yes.'

'For how long were you there?'

'There was a group of us, White politicals, we were there for two years and eight months. From 1980 to 1983 we were there. It was after Jenkin and Lee and Moumbaris escaped from the White political section that all of the rest of us were taken up the hill while they rebuilt our former place.'

'Such an escape is only possible once?'

'Of course. From the new gaol for politicals it would not be possible.'

'From Beverly Hills?'

Magyar smiled sadly. His mind was taken far back.

'Nothing is possible from Beverly Hills. Before our time, a White condemn, Franz von Staden, escaped. He was at exercise and the wall of the exercise yard was not as high as it is now, and in those days it had no grille. He saw his chance, took it, and then he went to the station and a policeman who was not on duty saw him and remembered his face. They took him back and they hanged him. Now nothing is possible from Beverly Hills.'

'From the outside?'

Magyar shrugged. 'What is on the outside, Comrade Jacob? What do I know of the outside? I was brought to the gaol in a closed van with slit windows. I saw some trees, I saw some houses for the prison staff, I saw their self-service store, but I have no detail. It is the same inside. I lived in the gaol for thirty-two months, I was in C section 1. I can tell you about each inch of the floor of C section 1, not of C section 2, not of C section 3. I would have to imagine that C section 2 and C section 3 are the same as our section. I can tell you nothing of B section, nor of A section, where the Blacks are. There are gardens inside the outer wall that come up to the sections. I saw those gardens when I went inside and when I left. You are there a long time and you know very little. It was the same for all of us who were there . . . It is not a place that I care to remember.'

Thiroko was hunched towards him.

'For me, I want you to try to remember.'

For more than an hour the radio played light music, and a disc jockey doodled away his time in a London studio. The old man covered a dozen sheets of foolscap paper with his drawings. At the moment of his arrest he had been an architect's draughtsman in Cape Town.

He drew a plan, as best he knew it, of the square mile to the west of Potgieterstraat, a square mile that encompassed Defence Headquarters to Pretoria Central to Magazine Hill. He drew a plan of the whole of Beverly Hills, cursing the gaps in his knowledge.

He drew C section. He drew C section 1. He drew an individual cell. He drew a cell in relation to the catwalk above the linking corridor. He drew the corridor of C section 1 and the catwalk. He drew the exercise yard of C section 1, and after that he drew a top view plan to show the positioning of the metal grid over the yard and of the supporting beams. He drew the visit rooms. He drew the gallows shed as it had been described to him. Last he drew the airlock entry through the outer wall.

He said drily, 'Under the Prisons Act, I could get ten years for drawing you such plans . . . should I be returning to South Africa.'

Thiroko accepted no time for banter.

'Firearms?'

'There is an armoury in the administration block where they keep hand guns, machine guns, grenade launchers. There are guns available at all times in the gatehouse and at the reception at the entrance to administration. There are guns on the watchtower that is set onto the highest wall on the hillside where the sentry can overlook the whole of the compound. The men on the catwalks have FNs or Lee Enfields, they are issued with six rounds for a duty. No-one carries a gun if they are in contact with prisoners.'

'What is the closest guard to the condemns?'

'I cannot tell you about B section and A section. Over C section there is the armed guard on the catwalk. Through the windows he can look down into each cell. In addition there is one guard, not armed, who is locked for the night into the individual corridors of C section 1, and 2 and 3. Each of those men has a telephone line to the Control in the gatehouse.'

Magyar looked up to see the fighting concentration in Thiroko's eyes.

'Comrade, I do not think you can go to any of the others of us who were there and find more. One man's experience is the same as every man's. I have forgotten nothing that I knew. You cannot break out. You *cannot* break in.'

Thiroko said, 'Last night a man broke into John Vorster Square.'

Again the sad smile, as if it was a disappointment to the old man that he played the bearer of bad news.

'John Vorster Square has public roads on all sides. Go east from Beverly Hills, you have half a mile before you get to Potgieterstraat, all a control area. Go south, and you are climbing Magazine Hill which is within the prison complex. Go west, you have a rifle range for the military, and then you have the police training college, and then you have the police dog centre. Go north, you are into Defence Headquarters and the Air Force command bunker. There is not just a high railing. You cannot break in nor out of Beverly Hills . . . Is it because five comrades will hang?'

A defiance in Thiroko, an echo in his words from a park bench. 'It is not right that we should do nothing.'

'Sentiment from you, Comrade Jacob? There was one amongst the White politicals serving with me, serving longer than I. He used to say, "Why don't they hurry up with their bloody revolution, get us out of here?" I tell you, every man in Beverly Hills, political or criminal, yearns by the candle of hope for freedom, that is what I know. Comrade, there are five of our men in there who are going to hang and they have no hope.'

Thiroko put the drawings into his briefcase.

'If you hold the candle of hope for them then that is wonderful,' the old man said.

Their farewells were curtly made. Thiroko switched off the radio. He went out of the room. He was given his ticket. It had been taken to the Zambian airlines office in Piccadilly, and endorsed for that night's flight.

He was photographed when he left the green painted front door, as he had been when he had entered. The cameraman freelanced for the Special Branch and operated from the Metropolitan Police offices on the opposite side of the street. Thiroko would have expected to be photographed. He didn't care. He had curtailed his visit to London. He was going home with the pain in his stomach. And when he got there he was going to provide the support that an extraordinary young man had asked of him.

Jeez knew of the bomb.

The sentries changing duty on the catwalk would have been disciplined, up before the governor, if it had been known that they had let slip such a nugget of information.

Jeez had heard them talking.

It seemed a small matter. What seemed a big matter was that Sergeant Oosthuizen had informed him that his solicitor was driving from Johannesburg the next day to see him.

He thought the days were sliding fast, each day shorter. He thought his time was bloody racing.

George Hawkins was driving to inspect a chimney when he heard the one o'clock news.

He was preoccupied with the chimney because he was certain it would be difficult. The chimney was 112 feet high, and to bring it down he required an additional 28 feet of clearance on the fall line. It was a built-up area of Hackney, and the oaf who had telephoned him hadn't known whether there was 140 feet clear. He was going to see for himself and he was going to charge them for his time whether or not he agreed to do the demolition.

Johannesburg's central police station? Stone the bleeding crows.

He knew it was his boy. The fire told him that the blue print for the bomb had been his own diagram of the La Mon Hotel device.

Christ, and he hadn't told the kid much. Hadn't told him much because he hadn't thought the kid was getting far beyond having his arse shot off. He'd given the boy nothing but the barest and the briefest. The boy must have followed to the letter what he had been told, must have memorized every bloody word. And what he'd told him for the hotel job was sweet bugger all of what he'd need to know to blow a hollow charge job against a prison wall. Hadn't even told him of the safety procedures to go through in the loading of a hollow charge job with Polar Ammon.

He thought that if Jack Curwen died that he, George Hawkins, would never forgive his bloody old miserable self for allowing the boy to stuff such nonsense in his head.

Hard for the student to concentrate on his afternoon lecture.

The subject matter was The Role of the State in Support of the Single Parent Family. Hard for Jan van Niekerk to concentrate on anything. All the talk in the cafeteria, and over the whole campus was of the bomb in John Vorster Square.

He had read that there was a theory that the bomber was White. Jan van Niekerk had carried a package to the Landdrost Hotel. A few Blacks got to stay at the Landdrost, token Blacks, but he thought that the Mr Curwen to whom the package had been carried on by the bellboy must be White, a White name. He was involved, certain of that. He was guilty under the terms of the

Sabotage Act, five years to death. Always, since he had begun, they could have manufactured a case against him. There would be no need to manufacture anything when he had carried explosives, when those explosives had been used in something so super fucking fantastic as the bomb *inside* John Vorster Square.

After the lecture, managing almost a bounce in his crippled stride, he made for his locker. There was no message for him.

Frikkie de Kok liked a drink, and he liked to talk. There were few men he could drink with because his working life was his secret, a matter that put him apart from other men. His assistant was his natural drinking partner, on Wednesdays in the late afternoon and early evening, if they did not have to be out of their beds while it was still dark on the following morning. Frikkie de Kok liked the Harlequin Club for his drinking and the chance to watch a rugby match from the old dark wood long bar. He had a small circle of acquaintances amongst the solicitors and barristers and government servants and accountants who patronized the bar on their way home from work.

His place was a corner table against the wall and the window, where he could talk to the man who would succeed him on his retirement. Where, also, he could watch the match.

He gave all he knew to his assistant.

He thought that was the least he could do for this young man who was so keen to learn. He had decided when the time would be, very soon, that he would allow his assistant to take over the full role of judging the length of the rope to be used, of fitting the pinions and the hood, of handling the lever. He reckoned that an assistant had to be given a chance to learn for himself. Not for a multiple of course, but for a single execution, and as long as they had no reason to think that the man would not go quietly . . . probably be best if it were a Coloured, that's what he thought, because in Frikkie de Kok's experience, the Coloureds were usually no trouble . . .

Frikkie de Kok checked his watch. The players should have been out of the dressing room by now.

He carried on talking.

'You see, there's a great irony about the method of execution, hanging. We now support the method of hanging over firing squad or gas chamber or electrocution because we say it is the most effective and the most humane. It didn't start like that. Look where it started, hanging. They wanted the most degrading way of death, and they wanted it to be slow and painful because that was good deterrent. What they were looking for was something that shocked and terrified the people who came to watch a public execution. The slower the better, because that way the spectators were most frightened. That's the irony. We have taken the most inefficient method and changed it into the most efficient. I like to think that in Pretoria we have the very most efficient and the very most humane system. You can go anywhere in the world, you won't find anything that is better organized than our situation. It's something that we in South Africa can feel genuinely proud of ... I think they're stupid not coming out earlier, that's the way you get to pull a hamstring, when you're not properly loosened ...'

There was a ripple of applause from the touchline, and shouts from members in the bar. The players ran onto the pitch.

'There was one thing that concerned me the first time I was an assistant, that was the heart of the man. The heart kept beating for a full twenty minutes after he'd dropped. I'd been told all the things that I told you when you first started. Fracture dislocation of the cervical vertebrae with crushing of the spinal cord. Immediate unconsciousness, no possibility of recovering consciousness because there is no chance of breathing. But that heart was still going. I put my ear against his chest, while he was hanging, and I could hear the heart. It took me several minutes to get accustomed to that heart keeping going ... They want to watch the new boy at out half. Fine boy, off last year's high school side. He could go all the way. I'd like to think my boy could get to play for Harlequins.'

'He's on the school team, Mr de Kok.'

'But the school's filling his head with university, not with rugby. He's in his books, that's why he's not on the line watching.'

There was the question that the assistant had waited two years to ask, the question that fascinated him. For two years he had waited for the opportunity to appear. He thought it was the moment.

'Does he know?'

'Know what?'

There was the roar as the Harlequins kicked off.

'Know what his father does.'

He wished he hadn't asked. He saw Frikkie de Kok hesitate.

'I've never told them, not Dawie, not Erasmus. You could say it's like telling them about the sexual functions. There's never a right time, and anyway they'll learn it all at school. There's never been a right time to tell Dawie what I do, and if I tell him then do I tell Erasmus, and he's two years younger. I suppose I'll wait until they're adults. They might not understand, funny things are young boys' minds. He thinks I run the carpentry courses at Central.'

'If my Poppa had done such work, I'd have been proud of him.'

'Who knows what they might think . . .'

The assistant was hunched forward. 'Mr de Kok, what would happen to us if the political situation were to change?'

'Change how?' Frikkie de Kok was entranced by the game, nose close to the glass.

'If the present government were to fall.'

Frikkie de Kok chuckled. 'No chance. And we'll survive, our job isn't political. Every government needs us . . . Let me tell you an anecdote from history. There was an executioner down in the Cape, and he hanged and he quartered and he severed limbs, and he was paid by each item, then the British came. We're nearly two hundred years back. The British said that he should just do hanging. The poor man saw his livelihood going, so what did he do? He went and hanged himself . . .'

They were both laughing.

'. . . A little bit of change never hurts anyone. I won't be hanging myself, not even if they abolish maximum security. Too damned fast I'll be off to buy a farm. You won't see me for dust . . . That man, he's offside.'

'Me too, Mr de Kok, I would have said he was offside.'

Frikkie de Kok said from the side of his mouth, casual, 'Next Thursday, tomorrow week, that's the Pritchard Five.'

'All together?'

'They killed together, they were convicted together . . . Look at that.'

'That referee's a disgrace, Mr de Kok.'

Jack, still dressed, slept on his bed. Exhausted. Harrowed by the high walls he had seen.

He had turned his back on Magazine Hill, he had walked away from the green tree slopes where his father was held.

12

The minibus driver kept the stops short. Just enough time for the tourists to take their photographs, and for the guide to give her spiel to a German couple, four Americans, and Jack.

The guide was an attractive girl, might have been thirty years old but she wore her hair young in the blonde Diana style. She had sensible shoes, and perhaps that was the giveaway that the girl who had the job of introducing tourists to Soweto was not a child. She talked well. She had to talk well because the material for her to talk about was pathetic in the uniform dreariness of the streets and the homes.

They had come through the Orlando area of the township city. They were on high ground and looking down over the corrugated roofing and the straight roads and across the railway yards and away over further hills that were blistered with roofs.

The guide said, 'We don't really know what the population of Soweto is. It's very difficult to get these people to fill in a census form, and they have their relations come to stay with them. They aren't the sort of people who are good with forms. So, it could be anything between one and two million people, we really don't know . . .'

The first reason for Jack to come to Soweto was that he must behave as a tourist. Yesterday he had gone to Pretoria. Today he was waiting for his contact. And he needed desperately to be out of the hotel, was fearful of every footfall in the corridor, dreaded having to go back, wondering whether his room would be staked out, the explosives discovered.

The day porter had made the telephone call, placed the

booking. The Rand Development Board tour was back on schedule, he said, because Soweto had been quiet for a week.

'You can see with your own eyes that this is a community into which a great deal of government money has been placed, millions of rand have been spent on making the living conditions of our Black people more acceptable. Most of Soweto now has electricity, most of it has running water. All of the main roads now have tarmac, and later you will see that we have started to build shops, the supermarket type of shops. The amount of money that we are spending is a very great drain on the country's resources, but we are spending it . . .'

The second reason for Jack to have made the journey into Soweto was vaguer. He felt that he had joined a war, that he had become a part of the armed struggle of the people who lived in this and other vagabond townships. He wondered how many of the one or two millions who eked out an existence in Soweto acknowledged the legitimacy of the tactic of bombs and bullets to change the conditions of their existence, how many of them knew the name of Jacob Thiroko. Not one of them would have heard of Duggie Arkwright. He thought of his journey into Soweto in part as a tribute to Duggie. He had thought that he might learn something of the people in whose cause Duggie had laboured. Driving past the stunning repetition of the homes of one million, or two million, people gave him not an iota of an idea of what their notion of a political future might be.

'Why are there high lights in the middle of open ground, illuminating nothing?'

The German man waved airily in the direction of hugely tall arc light stands that were dispersed over an open area of rubbish and building debris and raw earth. The German woman looked at her husband sheepishly as if she thought it impolite to ask a question.

The ready answer. 'They are there to make it safer for the residents. Unfortunately, Soweto is a very lawless place. On average, every weekend, there are thirty murders in the township boundaries. The gangsters prey on the wage earners, rob them and kill them when they are coming back from the beer halls. We call the gangsters *tsotsis*, they are just hoodlums, sometimes they are ordinary criminals, sometimes they are agitators trying to intimidate the peace loving people . . .'

'I was told,' the German said, 'that they put the electricity in so that the Africans would buy televisions and radios and all the electrical appliances that are sold in the White owned shops. I was told it was just to expand the market that they put the electricity in.'

'Whoever told you that was lying.' The guide withered the German.

She had a fixed smile when she was talking to the tourists. But in the front seat beside the driver her smile dropped. When the tourists were muttering amongst themselves or trying to photograph from the moving bus, then Jack saw the reality of her face. He saw the frowns on her neat forehead as she talked with the driver, discussed where it was safe to go. The driver would pause at each crossroads, and the White guide and the Black driver would stare and hesitate. Jack couldn't help but see the reasons for the hesitation. Slogans aerosoled on walls.

KILL ALL WHITES. Be Kind to Animals, Adopt a Policeman. Death to Traitors and Informers and Collaborators. Children of the African Heroes Do Not be Afraid of Whites.

Jack thought it was lunatic to be running a scenic drive round friendly Soweto. The Germans and the Americans didn't seem concerned. The Germans were preoccupied with their focal lengths. The Americans were so busy in a denunciation of their own media, and Edward Kennedy and all the liberal East Coasters who gave them the picture of South Africa in flames, that Jack wondered if they had even seen the armoured personnel carriers parked at the side of the petrol station, and the second group that were parked close to the big school complex. He wondered if the Black police were local, what it was like for them to be on law enforcement in their own community. He kept his peace. Jack thought the rows of small brick homes, matchboxes, and the pitted streets and the piled rubbish and the pitifully few shops were pathetic. He couldn't understand how the authorities could put a bus on, with a pretty girl as guide to boast about how much had been achieved, and drive tourists round so that they could see with their own eyes how bloody awful the place was.

'The impression you get back home, back in the State of Washington, is that the whole place is aflame. Looks pretty peaceful to me.'

'What I reckon is that all these folks want is work and to be left in peace.'

The bus jerked to the right. Jack saw the guide pointing to a group of young Blacks standing on waste ground 100 yards ahead. The driver had turned down a holed track. They went fast past a fire-blackened house. He saw the driver's face when he turned to the guide for instructions. There was a sweat sheen on the driver's skin. Jack wondered how it would be to go back to the township each night when your job was driving White tourists round your backyard by day. They came back onto a main road. There was no commentary from the guide. He could sense the mood between the driver and the guide, that they had been around too long. There were schoolchildren streaming along the sides of the road.

An American woman said that the kids looked cute in their white shirts and black trousers or skirts. The German woman was complaining that the minibus was going too fast for her to take photographs through the window. They went along two streets where the houses were larger. Black middle-class homes. The guide started to talk about the owner of a taxi fleet, and the owner of a Black football team. Jack thought the houses belonged to White clones, because there were leaping German Shepherds in the front gardens. There was smoke rising ahead.

The German man was tapping the guide's back, then pointing to a bungalow that was larger than the others, once the queen of the street. A smoke charred bungalow, with fire scorched beams littering a front lawn.

'What happened there?'

The guide turned to speak to the German, wasn't looking ahead, hadn't seen the smoke rising from tyres in the road.

'That was the home of the Mayor of Soweto. That is the work of the agitators. His home was burned down. It was an attempt by the agitators to intimidate those who are trying to better the life of the Blacks in Soweto . . .'

The driver was slowing, but he was Black. He couldn't tell the guide to shut her mouth and concentrate on what was going on in front of them and tell him what the hell to do. Over the guide's shoulder, Jack saw the schoolchildren, cute, running forward from the tyre barricade towards the bus.

'It would be quite wrong to think that the majority of Blacks are hostile to the reforms that we are making, only a very few try to sabotage the sincere efforts that the State President is making to involve Blacks in local government . . .'

Cut off in her speech the guide looked irritably at the driver. The bus was stopped. He was wrenching through his gears, looking for reverse and panicking, spinning his wheel. She was about to snap her impatience at the driver, when she saw the sprinting children.

Jack saw the fury on their faces.

The faces were blurred in the dust-dirty windows of the bus, but the rage was unmistakable. Ecstatic loathing. Arms raised, stones held up. Boys and girls running together, shouting together.

The bus was across the road, the engine racing.

The guide was shouting high-pitched at the driver, and covering her face with her arm. She shouldn't have screamed at him, she should have let him get on with taking them clear.

He stalled the engine.

Stones rained on the minibus. The windscreen cascaded into the driver's face, across the guide's lap was a shower of diamond glass. Jack was rigid in fear, couldn't move, didn't know how to help himself. Everyone inside the bus shouting, and one of the Americans starting a prayer, and the German pulling his wife back from the side window and replacing her head with his wide-angle lens.

Black faces against the window. A hand with a knife, fists with stones. Muscles to rock the bus. Almost a darkness inside, because the window light was blocked by the Black faces, Black bodies, Black fists.

It was over very suddenly.

Jack hadn't heard the crack of the gas grenade guns, nor the patter of the shotguns, nor the roaring power of the Casspir APC.

When he was aware of the silence he lifted his head. The screaming had stopped. There was a whimpering from one of the American women, the one whose husband had said that the Blacks just wanted work and to be left in peace. The guide was shivering, but upright, and was painstakingly starting to pick the windscreen fragments from her sweater. The Casspir had gone past them. The schoolchildren had scattered.

The Casspir bumped on the body of a kid who had been shot in the legs and was writhing, and who was still when he emerged to view again from under the wide heavy tread of the tyres.

A police jeep pulled up alongside the minibus.

Jack saw the savage expression on the officer's face as he climbed out. He couldn't follow the detail of the language as the officer tongue-lashed the guide in Afrikaans. The message was clear enough, they were bloody fools to have been there, they should get the hell out.

Subdued, they drove back to Johannesburg.

The German had damaged his wide-angled lens but by God he'd have a picture or two. The American, from Washington State, announced that he'd be making a donation to the South African police. The guide looked straight ahead, hugging herself against the wind through the jagged edges of the windscreen. Jack had learned something of the war. He had seen twenty kids who would have stoned him to death because he was White. He had seen a kid, minutes out of the classroom, become a statistic in death because he was Black.

At the Carlton Hotel where the bus dropped them off there were no goodbyes, no tips for the driver. The guide had nothing to say to them, not even about communists and agitators.

He went back towards the Landdrost. He approached it as calmly as he could from three angles. No sign of a police presence. And eventually just a friendly greeting from the day porter. Infinite regrets that sir had not had the best impression from his tour.

There was no message.

The solicitor looked again at his watch. In four and a half minutes it was the third time he had looked at the gold face on his wrist.

The prison officer stood behind him, ignoring him.

He sat on the hard wooden chair and looked through the plate glass at the mirror of the room that was opposite him. The room he looked into was the same in each detail to the one in which he sat. There were no decorations in the visit rooms. A room divided by a wall and a window of plate glass. An identically placed door in each section. Identical tables below the plate glass. A single chair on each side of the glass, and a voice pipe that was like an inverted elephant's trunk for speaking into and for listening through.

He hated this little room, had hated it each time that he had come to visit his client. His one aim was to get his work done, to get back to his car, to drive with his escort to the airlock gate in the outer wall, to get himself through the identity checkpoint on Soetdoringstraat, to get himself out onto Potgieterstraat, as soon as it was marginally decent for him to do so. They had treated him like dirt when he had come in through the checks and searches and delays. They seemed to despise him as they had walked him across the lawn to the visit room. No small talk, as if the presence of a solicitor, a man trying to cheat them from their work, was an irrelevance to their way of work. He had the job because he had once represented James Carew in a case involving a minor traffic accident. In John Vorster Square Carew had given the name of the young solicitor, and a damned black day that had been. He wished to God he had never been involved.

Because he was frightened being so close to the hanging shed, and to the man who was to walk into that shed, he felt resentment against Carew.

He had been telephoned by the colonel of the security police. He had endured a lecture from the Boer policeman.

He knew what had happened. He was a lawyer and he was a citizen of the Republic of South Africa. He had done his damned best to represent Carew at committal, at trial, and since sentence. He had not considered it possible that his client would reject the colonel's deal, not when the rope was the irrevocable alternative. He had done his best for his client, and he had hoped to God that his client would do the best thing for himself and talk to the security police about the ANC. The solicitor's parents lived in Durban; that city had been the target of a bomb at Christmas of all times; the ANC were foul murderers. From all he had seen of his client he could not place him in the same category. But then Carew, for all the sessions they had had together, remained an enigma to the young solicitor. The man had a past, he was certain. The nature of the past, his ignorance of it, burned as resentment.

He had done as much as he could for Carew and Carew had done nothing for him, nothing for himself.

He was quite justified in his resentment.

He heard the approach of footsteps down the corridor, sounds distorted through the tube that was the link between his outside world and Carew's inside world in the hanging place.

He had prepared what he would say to Carew. He would tell Carew that he had done all that was possible to save his life. He would tell his client that rejecting the colonel's offer had been an act of egregious folly. He was going to tell his client that it would be a waste of time to attempt another clemency petition. That in his view it was so damned unnecessary.

The door was opened.

Jeez was led in.

Through the glass the solicitor stared at Jeez. He thought his man was frailer than when he had last seen him, as if he had lost weight, as if the skin on his cheeks had been peeled back and the flesh underneath scalpelled away and then the skin rolled back again to sag over the hollowness.

Jeez sat down opposite him.

God, how to be sharp with a man who was going to walk to the gallows.

There was a small smile on Jeez's face. The solicitor understood. The bastard knew. The obstinate bastard had known what he had done when he had walked out on the colonel. The solicitor could not consider how a man voluntarily turned his back on life, not when the choice was his.

'Good of you to call round, young man. Did you have a pleasant drive over?'

The solicitor swallowed hard. The resentment died in him. In a torrent flow he told Jeez that the legal options were exhausted.

It was all because of a series of coincidences.

Because an assessor had been called back into the army for reserve service, and another assessor had been at home with his wife and newly-born baby, and her supervisor had thought it would be good experience for her to be out of the office, Ros van Niekerk had gone to a fire damaged home in Sandton. The cook/maid had left the electric chip frier on all night. The chip frier had finally caught fire in the small hours, gutting an expensive kitchen. She had gone to work that morning in a pure white skirt, and that skirt had been dirtied as she had moved about the kitchen assessing the damage and agreeing the size of the claim. Ros went home to change after the call.

Because her father was at work and her mother was at morning bridge, she let herself into the house that she expected to be deserted except for their maid. The maid had been a young nanny once, but with Ros and Jan grown up the nanny's role was gone. She could hear the maid in the back washhouse. Ros didn't announce herself, went up the stairs to her room.

Because the radio was playing in Jan's room she went to the slightly opened door. It surprised her to hear the radio. She thought her brother must have left it on when he had gone to Wits – always late. She eased the door open. The room was empty. The bed was made. The radio was playing. There was a sprawl of papers on the small teak wood desk where he did his studying.

Because Ros sometimes wished that she had gone to university and not straight to work when she had left school, because she always took an interest in what Jan read and what he wrote in his essays, she glanced down at the papers on the table.

Because of that short series of coincidences Ros van Niekerk found herself staring down at the drawn plans made by the old Hungarian for Jacob Thiroko.

She was no fool. She understood immediately the content of the map drawn on the uppermost sheet of paper. The broad strokes of the roads were marked. Potgieterstraat, Soetdoringstraat, Wimbledonstraat. There were rectangular blocks drawn beside the roads. Local, White Political, Pretoria (Old) Central, New Women's, Beverly Hills. She knew what she looked at.

Mechanically, as if she sleepwalked, she lifted the piece of paper. The second sheet was drawn to a larger scale. A rectangular block enclosing another block, and a part of the inner block was drawn in detail. She read. Gate house and radio control, wooden gates, steps, light, watchtower. She read measurements. The longest of the outer lines was marked at 200 metres, what she took to be an inner wall was marked at 100 metres.

She heard the toilet flush down the landing. Her eyes didn't leave the detail. She read. Corridor, C section 1, exercise yard, visit room . . . She heard Jan's trailing footstep shuffle towards his room . . . She read. Workshop, washhouse, preparation room. She read the one word . . . She heard him stumbling from the door towards her . . . She read. Gallows . . . Jan's hand caught at her, spun her away from the papers.

'What the hell are you doing?'

She faced up to him. He was the boy but he was no taller than her. She could look straight into his eyes.

'You bloody ask yourself what you're doing.'

She had never before seen such violence on Jan's face.

She said, 'This is bloody treason.'

He shouldered past her, he was snatching at the papers. She caught his arm.

She said, 'You can't undo what I've seen. I've read the word. Gallows. That map's treason.'

He shook her hand off him. There was a high livid flush on his face. He was vulnerable, in her eyes always had been.

'You shouldn't have come snooping in here . . .'

'I come in here, I find a map of Pretoria prison. I find a map of the place where they hang people. You have to do better than tell me I'm snooping.'

He thrust the papers into his desk drawer. He locked the drawer with the key on his waist chain. He turned to her, defiant, cornered.

'So what are you going to do?'

'What the hell does that mean?'

'Are you going to inform on me?'

'I'm your sister, Jan. Your bloody sister. Where did you learn that sort of bloody talk? Sister, got it.'

'Are you going to Father, are you going to the security police?'

'For God's sake, I'm your sister. I love you, you're my brother.'

They clung to each other.

Ros said softly, 'How long have you been living a lie, Jan?'

'I swore an oath of secrecy.'

'I'm your sister, I'm not your enemy.'

'It was an oath, Ros.'

'We never had secrets.'

'You wouldn't understand.'

'That my brother is involved in treason, perhaps I wouldn't understand that.'

'Treason is their word. It isn't mine.'

'Jan, I love you, but you are involved in something that is *against* the law.'

'That's important?' He shouted at her. 'It's only important because it's against the law? Don't play the bourgeois cretin, Ros. The evil in this country is ending, it's time's up. We're on the march, going forward. It's over for the Boers and the racists . . .'

'The Boers make the laws.' Her voice raised against his. 'If you go against the law then you go to prison.'

'I swore the oath, Ros.'

'For what?' A snap of contempt.

'To be able to look in the eye the men and women of our country. To have my pride. You have to fight something that is wrong. Not like those bastard businessmen fight it, mealy statements about "concern", plane trips to Lusaka to plead with the Freedom Movement not to give all their shares and their stocks to the people when the revolution comes. Not like those crappy Liberals at Wits, all piss, all wind. I fight the evil with the language the system understands.'

She snorted at him. 'What do you do?'

'I do my part.'

She couldn't help herself, there was the sneer of the elder sister. 'What's your part? Running messages on your little moped?'

'My part.'

'How can little Jan van Niekerk *hurry* the revolution?'

'I do my part.'

'The Blacks wouldn't trust you.'

'They trust me.'

'How do they trust you?'

He turned away from her. He went to his bed, flopped down. His head was in his hands.

'I swore an oath of secrecy.'

'How do they trust you?'

She knew he would tell her. She had always had the power to take anything from him, even the things that were most precious. He was always weak in her hands.

'Is it the terrorists of the African National Congress? How do they trust you?'

He spoke through his fingers. She had to lean forward to hear him.

'The bomb in John Vorster Square. I delivered it to the man who placed it.'

'What?' Incredulity widening her mouth.

'They trust me that much. I moved that bomb.'

'You could go to prison for the rest of your life.'

'That's a God-awful reason for backing off the fight against evil.'

'Rubbish.'

He looked up at her, clear faced. 'You go to the police, Ros.'

She hissed, 'Say that again.'

'Just go to the police, Ros, turn me in.'

She took the step towards him. She raised her hand. He didn't flinch. She slapped his face. His head rocked. She saw the smile that was beaming up at her.

'What are you going to do?'

She stared out of the window. She saw the maid hanging the washing on the rope line. She saw her father's good quality shirts, and her mother's good quality underwear, and she saw Jan's T-shirts and her blouses. She saw neat gardens ablaze with shrubs and flowers. She saw a Black man collecting grass cuttings. She saw their world that was comfortable and familiar, and now threatened.

'I'm going to fight to keep you out of prison.'

'What does that mean?'

'It means that on your own you'll rot the rest of your life in prison.'

The words were music to Jan van Niekerk.

Quietly he told her that he was under instruction to go to a certain place and deliver a message for a man to make a rendez-vous. He knew the name of the man. He said it was the man who had taken the bomb into John Vorster Square police station. He told her that he had to meet the man and give him the plans of the Pretoria Central prison complex.

'Left to yourself, little brother, you'll rot for the rest of your life,' Ros said.

The man was White.

He had been born in Latvia. He was a colonel in the KGB. He was marked for assassination by the security police and National Intelligence Service in Pretoria. He was the chief planner of Umkoto we Sizwe operations inside South Africa. More than a year before he had authorized the fire bomb attack on the Rand Supreme Court. That attack was one of a long list of projects that had crossed his desk. He had approved the bombing of the Air Force headquarters in Pretoria, and the attacks on the Sasol synthetic petrol refinery and on the Koeburg nuclear power plant and on the Voortrekkerhoogte military base. More recently he had sanctioned the laying of mines in the far north east of the Transvaal on roads that would be used by civilians, and the detonating of a shrapnel bomb in a Durban shopping mall crowded with Christmas custom. The long retaliatory arm of the security police and NIS had swiped close to him. His former wife had died, mutilated by a letter bomb in her office at the Centre for African Studies in the Mozambique capital.

The meeting was in a small air-conditioned office at the back of the ANC compound on the outskirts of Lusaka.

Jacob Thiroko was not interrupted.

He stated his plan. Five men, Kalashnikovs, grenades, 100 kilos of explosives, four cars for the run to the Botswana frontier, the skill of the White explosives expert now loose in South Africa. Thiroko had spoken of John Vorster Square, he had sung of the pedigree of the expert. He had been heard out. He kept his high card for the end.

'I will lead the cadre.'

Nothing astonished this White man. His eyebrows flickered a trace of surprise. He stayed silent.

'I will go back myself into South Africa, into my motherland. I have not been there since I was a young man. Perhaps it is a hallucination. Perhaps it is my duty to the men who otherwise will hang. I have a responsibility for them, five times of responsibility. You gave the authorization, I prepared the plan. I cannot escape my responsibility ... The young man in Johannesburg is the son of James Carew, the driver. The son taught me about sacrifice, when I thought I had nothing to learn. For his father he is prepared to sacrifice his life. I should be prepared to make the same sacrifice. They are sons to me, Happy, Charlie, Percy and Tom. What did we do when Benjamin Moloise walked to the gallows? We issued statements ... I don't want to issue a statement this time!'

'Tell me about London, Comrade.'

'In London I went to see a physician.'

'What were you told, Comrade Jacob?'

'To live each day of my life to the full, to enjoy each minute of each day.'

'Is there pain?'

'The pain will be nothing to the joy if I can give life to my children.'

'Is it possible, to bring them out?'

'I would have said it was impossible for a stranger to carry a bomb into John Vorster Square. I no longer know what is impossible.'

The pain was deep in the lower bowel of Thiroko's stomach. He winced as he stood, as he shook hands with the man from Riga. He had chosen the four men who would go with him, who would return with him to South Africa.

The physician had not been specific, he had spoken only of the few months that remained.

Jack came back into his room, closed the door behind him, slipped on the security chain, checked the suitcase.

In the afternoon, after the experience in Soweto, he had had to force himself to go out into the city, to walk on the streets amongst Blacks, be a tourist. Be a tourist and also make some enquiries.

He had gone to a small engineering firm in the back streets down from Marshall. He had asked about the availability of a short length of 8 inch iron piping.

When he crossed the room he saw, lying on his dressing table, left there by the bellboy, a sealed envelope.

He saw the bold handwriting. He thought the envelope had been addressed by a girl.

When the colonel left the meeting he brought back to his office a copy of the initial forensic report.

Embedded in the walls of the hallway of John Vorster Square had been found the synthetic fibres of a cheap bag. Blown clear through the doorway and into a flower-bed had been a piece of a metal can. This first examination stated that the fibres came from a little-used bag, and the 50 cent sized piece of metal from a clean painted can without corrosion or rust.

The colonel had given it as his opinion that both items had been bought specifically for the bombing, for the making up of the explosive device, for carrying it.

'I'm truly sorry, Carew.'

'Thank you, sir.'

'There's not a decent man I know who can get pleasure out of this moment.'

'I'm sure there isn't, sir.'

'For what we do in life . . . we have to take the consequences of our actions.'

'Just so, sir.'

'I take no delight in seeing a man go to his punishment, whatever he's done.'

'I appreciate that, sir.'

The governor stood ramrod straight in the doorway of the cell. Behind him, his message read, the deputy sheriff of Pretoria waited, his arms hanging, his hands clasped in front of his trouser flies. Jeez had the centre of the floor space, he was at attention, his thumbs on the seams of his trousers. He thought the sympathy was genuine.

He thought the governor was an honest man. The governor didn't frighten Jeez, not so that he had to imagine him out of his tailored uniform, shorn of his medal ribbons, stripped to his underpants. The governor was nothing like the bastard who had run Spac, who had been Jeez's gaoler way back for so many long years.

'I like a man to go proudly. I like a man to behave like a man. I can tell you this, Carew, go like a man and it will be easier for you. A prisoner who makes difficulties hurts himself, not us.'

'Thank you, sir.'

'I'd bet money on you, Carew, that you'll go like a man who is proud.'

'Yes, sir.'

'I always tell a man at this time that he should think through his life, think about his affairs, and stay with the good times. We don't want any melancholy.'

'No, sir.'

'Carew, you wrote a letter a few weeks ago, I checked with Records and you've had no letter back. I'm sorry. Of course, you are permitted to write as many letters as you wish.'

'There won't be any more letters, sir.'

'Is there anyone we should contact, anyone you would like to be offered facilities for a visit?'

'No, sir. There's no-one who should visit.'

'I tell you frankly, I've never met a man who has been here, White, who has been as private as you. Nor of your bearing, if I may say so.'

'Yes, sir.'

'There's a point I would like to make to you, Carew. The State President has refused you clemency, he has named the date of your execution. There have come from abroad several representations to the State President urging him to think again. From His Holiness the Pope, the Secretary-General of the United Nations, many others. Carew, you should know that in these matters the State President will not alter his decision. I tell you that, man to man, because it is better that you prepare yourself without the distraction of false hope.'

'Yes, sir.'

'The decision that you hang next Thursday is irreversible.'

'I know that, sir.'

'The colonel from the security police, he will come back and see you, Carew, if you care to reconsider his proposal.'

'I have nothing to say to the colonel, sir.'

13

He took a taxi from the hotel to the zoo gardens.

Jack had memorized his instructions and flushed the sheet of paper away down the lavatory.

The driver hissed against the wooden toothpick that was clamped in his teeth through each detail of the bland police statement of unrest overnight in the Cape and the East Rand on the early morning news. Two shot dead by the police in the Cape, and a Black woman burned to death in an East Rand township.

'Seems to be getting worse,' Jack said.

The taxi driver looked over his shoulder. 'You'd need to be smiling from your cheeks to your backside to think it's getting better.'

'What has to happen for it to get better?'

The taxi driver settled comfortably in his seat, like the question was a box of chocolates, to be enjoyed.

'My opinion, take a tougher line with the Blacks. That's not what we're doing at the moment. Right, the State President's put the military and the police into the townships. Wrong, each time he makes a speech he's talking about reform. Result, they think they're winning, they reckon if they keep up the murder and the arson that they're on their way to government. On the one hand the State President is trying to intimidate the Blacks into ending the violence, on the other hand he's trying to buy them off with promises. The two don't sleep in the same bed . . .'

Jack slid out of reach of the driver's eyes in the rear-view mirror, took a fast, deep breath, and asked: 'Did you know the taxi man, the one they're going to hang?'

'Carew, that bastard?'

'Did you know him?'

'I didn't myself. I've a friend who did.'

'What sort of fellow was he?'

'Mystery man, that's what my friend says. When the name was in the papers he just didn't believe it, says he was a very private fellow.'

A recklessness in Jack. 'Where did he live?'

'He had a flat, behind Berea, furnished, that's what my friend says. When he was arrested he gave instructions to his lawyer man that everything in the flat should be sold, went to a children's home charity. My friend says there wasn't much, bits and pieces and his clothes, but they've all gone, like he knew he was never coming out. My friend says that he used to talk quite a bit with this Carew, but he never knew anything about him. I mean, they didn't talk about family, just used to talk about the motor, that sort of thing. Long time ago, he wrote to ask whether Carew would like a visit, and the letter came back from the authorities that Carew didn't want any visit . . . What's your interest?'

Jack said, 'I read about it in the English papers.'

He was dropped at the main entrance.

He must have been one of the first customers that morning because the wide sloping grounds with the autumn in the trees were near-deserted. He walked over the dun yellow parched lawns. He did exactly as he had been instructed. He went to the cafeteria where they were still putting out the tables, and he ordered a cup of coffee. When he had drunk it he walked away past the big wingspan vulture in a tall cage, and past the compound where a young gorilla gambolled, and past the green water pool of the sea lions. He understood why the instructions had demanded that he followed a set route. He was being watched and checked to see that he had no tail. He climbed the hill and strolled slowly past the big cat enclosures. Well before the heat of the day and the leopards and the jaguar and the lions were pacing. He sat on a bench in front of the Bengali tigers. He didn't look around, he made no attempt to identify the people he assumed to be watching him. Up again and past the stink of the elephant and the rhino, past a bee swarm of tiny Black children out with their teacher, past a party of shambling mencaps with their nurses. He followed the instructions.

He went up the long hill towards a huge memorial, to British victory in the Boer War of nearly a century ago. He drifted into the military museum. More schoolchildren, but middle teens and White, and with a pretty young teacher who had a strident voice as she quizzed her pupils on Bren gun carriers, Churchill tanks, 25 pounders, an 88 mm recoilless anti-tank. They'd be needing that knowledge, the little sods. Their country was going into automatic rifles and armoured personnel carriers and White conscripts in the townships, and by the time these kids were fattened up then it might have come down to tanks and artillery. It was a bad image for Jack. His thoughts ran fast to Potgieterstraat and Defence Headquarters and the guns of the sentries and the fire slits on the walls of Local. A bad awful bloody express train of thought because he had never believed that Beverly Hills could be so well protected . . .

If he had known it would be *that* well protected then Jimmy Sandham would be alive, and Duggie would be alive, and Jack Curwen would be in his office, at his desk, on the north side of Leatherhead.

Bit bloody late, Jack.

He sat on a bench. He waited.

Jan and Ros had argued half the night away. They had argued in the car on the way to the zoo. The argument had continued as they tracked the Englishman.

'Violence doesn't change anything.'

'The Boers listen to violence, they don't listen to debate.'

'Blowing people up, killing and maiming people, won't change the government.'

'Change will only come when control of the townships is lost.'

'The state is committed to real change, all that's needed is a breathing space for the moderates on all sides to come forward and negotiate.'

'The *moderates*? What do they want to talk about? About opening up Whites beaches for non-segregated bathing? Do you think they care in the townships, where they're queuing up for charity food parcels, about a nice little swim on a Whites Only beach? The moderates aren't relevant, might have been twenty years ago, not now. It's about power, not about which beach you're allowed to swim on. Anyone who has power will never hand it over voluntarily. The Boers'll have to be burned out of power.'

'Your way, Jan, only slows the pace of change.'

'They're *playing* with reform, Ros. They want to get the Americans off their backs, so they can go back to living the way they've always lived, the White boot on the Black throat.'

'Are you ashamed of being White?'

'I've no shame, because I'm fighting against a White evil. I didn't ask you to spy in my room. You can get out of my life.'

'I'm stuck with your bloody life. I'm your sister. On your own you're dead or you're locked up. I won't turn away from you. I wish I could, and I can't.'

For half an hour they watched the Englishman move through the zoo's gardens. At the sea lions and the compound for the big cats they had split and gone in opposite ways so that each of them could be sure they were free of a tail. Jan thought that his sister learned fast. If there had been a tail he believed they would have seen it.

For Jan there was the fascination of seeing the clean shouldered back of the man who had achieved the remarkable, and carried a bomb into John Vorster Square. For Ros there was the fascination of seeing the man who had come as an activist to their country, who was capable of murder. For what he had achieved, Jan thought the stranger was a hero. For involving her brother, Ros thought him an enemy.

They came into the military museum.

Through the heads and shoulders of the schoolchildren, between the snub barrels of the artillery pieces, they saw him.

They were a boy and a girl out walking, there was nothing about them to excite suspicion. They looked at the man who sat hunched on the bench.

Ros said, 'Once you've spoken to him then you're more deeply involved than ever before. You could turn round, you could go home. Father would get you a ticket, you could fly out of the country tonight. You could be safe.'

Jan said, 'I don't run away.'

'You don't run away because you can't run . . .' She hated herself.

'They don't listen to reason. Last year when they hanged Ben Moloise they had petitions from all over the world. They didn't give a shit. They strung him up because what the rest of the world says doesn't count . . .'

'He was convicted of killing a policeman.'

'Now they're going to hang five men, and again the rest of the world's pleading for mercy. They don't give a shit. This man knows it, fight force with force. Fight the force of John Vorster Square with the force of a fire bomb.'

'And Pretoria Central?'

'I don't know,' Jan said.

He had the diagrams of the gaol in the inner pocket of his windcheater jacket.

'You're getting to be a real creep, Jan.'

They went forward, Jan limping and ahead, and Ros trailing him.

He turned when he heard the voice. The voice spoke his name.

Jack saw the boy. He saw the shallow body and the thin face. He saw the way the shoulder drooped. He saw that the boy was crippled. The boy was behind the bench, trying to smile a greeting.

He looked the other way. The girl was standing back two more paces than the boy. A nice looking girl, and older than the boy, and she wore a summer skirt and a blouse buttoned to the throat. He could see the lines at her mouth, tension lines.

'I'm Jack Curwen.'

'I was ordered to contact you. You followed the instructions, thank you.'

They stared at each other. As if neither had quite believed the ordinariness of the other.

Jack smiled, the boy grinned. Jack wondered why the girl didn't smile.

'I'm Jan, this is my sister. You don't need any more names.'

Strangely formal. Jack shook hands with them.

A shyness in Jan's voice. 'What you did at John Vorster Square was incredible.'

Again the silence. None of them knowing what to say. Out of earshot the schoolchildren were spidering over the hulk of the museum's largest tank.

Jan drew the envelope from his pocket. He passed it to Jack. Jack ripped open the fold. He saw the diagrams. He leafed quickly through the sheets of paper, the frown settling sharp cut on his forehead. He knew the girl's eyes never left his. The school teacher's voice carried gently to him. She had raised her voice because she was describing to her class the cyclic rate of fire of a heavy machine gun from the Great War. He saw that the diagrams were details of Pretoria Central. He saw the positioning of Beverly Hills, he understood why he had not seen the walls when he had walked on Potgieterstraat.

'What happens now?'

Jan said, 'I have to take you into the north of the Transvaal. There is a rendezvous there for you, close to a town called Warmbaths. It is a spa town about a hundred kilometres from Pretoria. You should go back to your hotel, and you should check out of your hotel, then we drive to Warmbaths.'

'Do you know why I have come to South Africa?'

'No.'

Ros snapped, 'And he doesn't need to know.'

Jack saw the anger on the boy's face.

Jan said, 'I'm just a courier. I am ordered to deliver you to a rendezvous. I do what I am told, just as I brought you the envelope today, just as I brought you the package of explosives.'

'You don't know why we are hitting the gaol?'

'As he said, he's just a courier.'

Ros twisted away, swirled her skirt. Jack stood up and walked behind her and Jan hobbled after them. Jack caught up with her.

'You're not a part of it,' she said bitterly.

Her eyes were on her sandals, striding out.

Jack bored on. 'I'm not a part of it, it's true. In England, my home, I'm not an activist, I'm not political. I don't give a damn for this war. I have to be here, probably like you have to be here.'

She tossed her head back, rippled her hair, gestured at her brother behind her. She said, 'It's lunatic for him to be involved.'

'Lunatic for all of us.'

'So why did you honour us with your presence?'

'A week today they're going to hang my father.'

She looked away. He saw her close her eyes, squeeze them tight shut. They stood together and waited for Jan to catch them.

There were eighteen detectives from the plain clothes branch of the security police who had taken the desks and tables in the large room set aside for the investigation. The detectives worked with their telephones and notebooks eight floors above the back hall of John Vorster Square.

Ten of the detectives worked on tracing the grip bag.

Eight worked on finding the source of the petrol can.

In front of each man was a commercial telephone directory of the greater Johannesburg area. By the middle of the morning it was believed that a manufacturer had been identified for the bag, a factory employing similar synthetic fibres to those retrieved by forensic. The detectives then took sections of the directories to ring each and every number where the bag could have been sold. The information given to the detectives pointed towards a White attacker. It was therefore probable that the bag and the petrol can, if bought in Johannesburg, had been bought either in the city centre or in a White suburb. The outlets through which the bag might have been sold were fewer than the outlets for petrol cans. It was thought that the bag, rather than the can, would prove decisive.

Twice that morning the colonel had come down the two flights of stairs to the incident room.

He was not directly involved, not yet. His involvement was two stages away in the process of the investigation. First the source of the sales must be identified, second the purchaser must be described.

Jacob Thiroko and his group travelled apart, but on the same aircraft.

He carried a Tanzanian passport. He had never used that passport before. It described him as an engineer. He carried letters of introduction from the Botswana Enterprises Development Unit, and also from the Botswana Meat Corporation for whom, he could tell immigration, he was designing a new abattoir. The younger men were on a variety of Black African passports, and each was equipped with the cover to talk his way through immigration at the international airport at Gaberone.

With more time for planning and for taking advice, he might have attempted to travel overland from Angola, or overland from Mozambique, both difficult but both possible. The fast way to South Africa was through Gaberone, not the safe way.

It was eighteen months since the Recce Commando squads had been helicoptered into Gaberone at night to kill twelve of Thiroko's comrades, to blow up their offices, to bring home what was described as a treasure trove of intelligence material. Since the raid, the Botswana government had ceded areas of their sovereign independence to permit covert members of the National Intelligence Service to operate in various guises from their territory.

Thiroko walked from the aircraft across the tarmac towards the single-storey building housing lounges and offices. He walked almost in the shadow of the squat, square built, air traffic control tower. He was concerned with the immigration officers. He should have been concerned with a White air traffic control supervisor. His photograph was taken. It would not be a good likeness, but it would serve as confirmation of this supervisor's opinion, made instantly; that he had sighted Jacob Thiroko.

By the time that Thiroko and his four men had collected their baggage, queued for immigration, gathered together to be met by their contact driver, there were two vehicles waiting to follow them out of the airport car park. There was a Land Rover with the markings of a locally based safari holiday company driven by a White with a Black passenger, and there was a Peugeot 504 estate carrying three Blacks.

Inside the car, when it was speeding on the Palapye road, Thiroko told his companions that they would cross the border that night in the wide area between Martin's Drift and Oranjefontein, that they would be moved south by lorry, that they would meet with a sixth man at a place where weapons and explosives were stored. He saw they were cool to what he said. Not excited. They were all in their middle twenties. They had all left South Africa as children, they were coming home as men.

The Peugeot 504 was 800 metres behind. It did not have to be closer. If the car ahead turned off the metalled road it would have to give up tarmac for dirt. A billowing grit storm would telegraph a detour from the Palapye road.

Jack paid cash for the two lengths of steel tube.

Hell's expensive for just a metre in length apiece, but the steel was as thick as the width of nail on his little finger, and the diameter was 9 inches. It was what he wanted.

A White in the front hall of the engineering works tried to strike up a conversation with Jack while a Black was sent to the rear yard to bring out the tubing. Jack didn't respond, gave no explanation for buying the tubing.

He refused the White's offer that the Black carry the tubing to his car. If he had been a South African, if he'd stopped to think, he would have allowed the Black to take it to the car. But he didn't want anyone to be able to link him to Jan who sat in the back seat of the Beetle, nor to Ros who was behind the wheel.

Two blocks away, down on Anderson, Jack again paid cash for a set of heavy wire cutters.

The tubing was on the back seat of the car. Jack's case was in the boot.

They took the Pretoria road. They would bypass the capital on their way to Warmbaths.

The chaplain could have sat on the lavatory seat, or on the bed beside Jeez, or on the table that might have come away from the wall under his 16 stones. He said he spent too much time sitting, and he stood.

Jeez sat on the bed. The chaplain wore uniform, identical to the other officers' but for the purple shoulder flashes. A big man with a big gut and mane of white hair, and a voice that barked even when he tried to be kind.

'Are you a child of Christ, Carew?'

Jeez hardly knew the chaplain. He didn't go to the chaplain's Sunday services. Religion was not compulsory at Beverly Hills. When you were a condemn you could take God or you could leave Him. Religion, like work and exercise, was voluntary. Jeez took only exercise.

'I'm not a praying man, sir.'

Many times the chaplain brought his chess set or his draughts board into a condemn's cell, and talked and whiled away afternoon hours. He had never played chess or draughts with Jeez. Duty had brought him that day to C section 2, and the prodding of the governor.

'You don't help yourself, Carew.'

'My problem, sir.'

'You should place yourself before God in a state of humble repentance.'

In daylight hours there were fifteen prison officers administering the White condemns, all bored out of their skulls and reading picture magazines and polishing their kit, and kicking footballs in the exercise yard, and laughing too loud and joking too much. Jeez wondered if, for variety, they'd come on their toes to the door of his cell to listen to the chaplain.

'You know, Carew, many of the Blacks that go, they thank me

just before. They thank me because they say they have found repentance, they say they are at peace with God. They say I have guided them to God . . .'

Jeez said, 'I reckon you *enjoy* working here.'

'You're a hard man, Carew, without contrition.'

'My life's going to end the hard way, sir.'

The chaplain smiled, avuncular. 'I'll be with you when you go.'

'Wouldn't miss it, would you, sir?'

'To offer you comfort.'

'Do you go and have your breakfast afterwards?'

'I don't get provoked that easily, Carew.'

'We've not much to talk about, sir.'

Jeez thought the chaplain loathed him. In the eyes of the man there was a watery gleam, as though the chaplain thought this man would crack at the last, cry for help. He thought the chaplain wanted nothing more in life than to walk the corridors of Beverly Hills with young Blacks on their way to their Maker with mission hymns in their throats.

'Do you want me to ask the surgeon to give you a sedative?'

'What for?'

'We sometimes give a White a sedative.'

'I want nothing from you, sir.'

'Others, they ask for a drink, a big whisky or a brandy.'

'I want nothing, sir.'

'Carew, the Blacks sing for each other, you know that. When you go then you will have the men with you, those that were arrested with you, and they will be singing the penny rhymes of the African National Congress. I cannot believe you want that. I could get in a church choir to sing for you. It has been done before.'

'Why should I want that?'

'Damn you, to give you comfort, man.'

Jeez thought the man might have been organizing a confirmation service. And did he want some flowers, and did he want his hair cut, and did he want a clean shirt? And if he said that he wanted a choir then they could settle down for a cosy chat to decide what the choir should sing, and then whether the choice would be suitable for bass voices as they might be a bit short on contralto and soprano.

'I'm not dragging anyone else in here. I'm not dirtying anyone else's day.'

The chaplain sighed.

'You can always send for me. I am always available.'

The chaplain rapped on the closed door of the cell.

'Thank you, sir.'

The door clattered shut on the chaplain's back. Jeez lay on his bed. He was dry eyed. For ten years in Spac he had believed, known, that the team was working for him. And after ten years in Spac there had been the fêting and the restaurant meals and the debriefs for the Balkan desk and the weekends down at Colonel Basil's home. He had to believe in the team, or his cheeks would have been wetted.

Facing another shortening day.

Jack talked softly.

Ros drove well. She kept her attention on the road, but she listened.

In the back, curled round the metal tubes, Jan was quiet.

'. . . Right through the time when I was a kid my father was held up to me as being just about the most rotten man that ever lived. Had to be rotten because he walked out on his wife and son, left them for dead with an impersonal financial arrangement to make sure they didn't starve. But I found out why he'd gone missing, and who was responsible for him, and how he'd been ditched, but that was only confirmation material for me. I'd have come here anyway, whatever he'd done when he left my mother. I have to see him and talk to him and bring him through, nothing else seems important. He's the fall guy, he's the expendable legman . . . You know what I want to do? More than anything else I just want to walk him through Whitehall, that's where all our government sits on its backsides, and I want to walk him into the fat cats' rooms, and I want to say that I did what none of them had the guts to do. And after that I'm not going to give a shit about their security and their Official Secrets Act. I'm going to blow it all open. I don't care who the bloody casualties are, and I don't care if I'm one of them. There are people in London who are going to pay a bloody great price for what's happened. They'll have to kill me to keep me quiet.

'You know, since I started out on this I've never even thought that it might not work. Right, there are times when I don't know what the next stage is, how we're going to crack the next barricade, but it's going to happen. When I went up to Pretoria, then it looked impossible, like everyone had told me it would be. After I'd seen Local and Defence HQ I could have packed it in, gone off for the airport. I sorted myself out. Doesn't matter how difficult it is, it has to be done. I mean, there isn't any way out of it, not for me. My father's going to hang, that's the beginning and the middle and the end of it, and something has to be done . . .'

'Even if it is, actually, impossible?' Her gaze was straight ahead.

'Has to be tried, because he's my father.'

Jan shouted. 'Roadblock.'

Jack hadn't seen it, nor Ros.

They were on the N1, a little past the turn off for Randjiesfontein.

There were two police vans, primrose yellow, drawn across the road. There was a short queue of cars. Ros was going down through her gears. Jack winced. Only he knew of the explosives in his suitcase. Hadn't told Jan, nor his sister, that he had squirrelled away 15 pounds of explosives. And the prison plans . . . The pain was immediate, and then gone. None of the cars was being searched. They were the seventh car in the line. A police sergeant came towards them, stopping by each driver. He wondered how Ros would be, couldn't tell. No-one spoke in the car as the sergeant approached. Beyond the vans was parked a high armoured personnel carrier, off the road. Jack saw policemen standing and sitting in the open top, displaying automatic shotguns and FN rifles.

'We're running escorted convoys down the next ten kilometres, Miss.'

'What's happened?' Ros asked, small voice.

'A gang of Blacks stoned a car, a kilometre down. White woman, elderly. Car went off the road. The bastards got to her, dragged her out. They had rocks and knives, Miss. They set light to her, she was an old lady. We've a big search op in there, but it's a wilderness. Supposed to be a helicopter coming. She wouldn't have had a chance.'

Jack saw the pallor on Ros's face.

There was a klaxon blast from the APC and exhaust fumes fanned from its tail. More cars were behind them, the sergeant had moved on. The APC set off down the road, they followed in a twenty mile an hour crawl.

Ros didn't speak. Jack didn't have to scratch his mind to remember the crowd coming down the shabby street in Soweto, and the din of the stones on the coachwork and the rocking of the vehicle and the screaming of the woman from Washington state. Not hard to imagine the last moments in an elderly woman's life as the stones started to fly and the windows were caving in, and the mob was materializing out of the long grass that flanked the road. Not hard to see the fingers ripping at the doors of a crashed car, and the fists raised and the clawing nails and the knives and the sharp edged rocks. He shuddered. He prayed that she had been unconscious when they had poured the petrol on her, thrown the match. They passed the burned car. There were skid marks on the tarmac, then the wheel tracks through the grass and then the blackened surround where the earth had been scorched near the car and under the body of the woman.

Ros retched. Jack looked away. Jan was breathing hard.

She snarled, 'Great bloody day for the freedom fighters.'

Jan rose to her. 'Of course they're brutalized. What else could they be, given the regime they live under?'

'That's the work of the people you're so bloody fond of.'

'I don't condone that, and the ANC doesn't condone that, but when you treat people like filth then they'll behave like filth.'

'Pathetic excuses.'

'It's the price the Whites are going to have to pay for half a century of naked racism.'

'Childish slogans.'

'Think of all the Black children that have been shot by the police.'

She let him have the last word. Ros drove on towards Pretoria. All her life she had let her brother have the last word. It was why she was driving her car north, it was why she had entered a state of madness. The tie of family had captured her. She understood the young man sitting bowed in the front seat beside her. She believed herself to be as captured by her brother as he was by his father.

The White from the safari Land Rover watched as the Blacks kicked the resistance out of the driver of the pick-up car.

They had tracked the pick-up car after it had turned off the Palapye road, when it had headed south towards the border hamlets of Sherwood Ranch and Selika. Through field glasses they had watched Jacob Thiroko and the four other men get out and unload their bags. When the car had come back up the road it had been blocked.

The driver was a loyal member of the Movement, but the beating and the kicking were ferocious. The driver told his captors that the older man in his car had been addressed as Comrade Jacob. He told them that this Comrade Jacob had spoken of striking a great blow for the Movement. He told them that the old man had spoken of Warmbaths.

When he had nothing more that he could tell them, the driver was kicked to death. Boots in the stomach and the head killed him. The kicking was without mercy. When he was dead he was dragged to his own car and thrown inside. It was intended that he should be found.

It surprised the White that the Blacks under his command

kicked the victim of their own colour with such enthusiasm. The White worked to trail out 50 feet of radio aerial from the short wave transmitter in the Land Rover to a branch high in a thorn tree.

His coded broadcast was picked up in the offices of the security police at Potgietersrus 160 kilometres away.

Jacob Thiroko and his cadre were to hike across country to a road junction outside Monte Christo, ten kilometres. At midnight they were to be met at the road junction and driven by lorry to a rendezvous north of Warmbaths. He believed they could cover that distance before the breaking of the morning light. At the rendezvous they would find a cache of weapons and explosives, buried there more than two years before.

They moved by compass bearing.

It was difficult for Thiroko to keep his attention on the animal track in front of him, and on the dried grass that cracked under foot, and on the wind scattered branches that snapped under his tread. He had come home, he was back in his own place. The scent of the scrub as familiar to him as his mother's body had been when he was a child. The smells of home, and the whirr of the insects, and the fear of snakes, and the bright light of a clear sun shining on his homeland. Nowhere else in Africa had he tasted the same smells, sounds, shining sun as he found on the hike towards Monte Christo, going back inside his country, his fighting ground.

Inside the operations room at the Hoedspruit base, home of 31 Squadron (helicopters), they followed a familiar routine. The Puma was tasked to take off in the late afternoon, and to reach the point of the border incursion before dusk. The quarry was to be given time to move away from the frontier and so to be unaware of the military movement behind them. The Puma was a good old workhorse, with improvised replacement parts it had flown for eighteen years in South Africa's colours.

In the thrash of the rotors it took off into the low slanted

217

sun. Behind the two pilots were eight. White soldiers of the Recce Commando, a dog handler with his golden labrador, and a skeletal Bushman. The Bushman wore only shorts, his shock of black hair was ringed by a green tennis sweat band. He spoke his own language only, that of the Kavango region of South West Africa.

The officer commanding the hunting team had been given an exact reference for the border incursion.

As they were coming in to land, as they looked ahead into Botswana, the pilots could see a car parked on a dirt track, and pulling away from it were a Land Rover and an estate car.

It took the Bushman only a few minutes to be sure of his starting point. When it became too dark for him the dog would take over the tracking.

It was not a difficult trail to follow.

Ros drove into the poorly lit one street of Warmbaths.

They checked into a hotel. They took single rooms.

At the reception desk, as they wrote false names and false addresses in the book, Ros remarked to the owner that they were breaking the journey north west to the Ebenezer Dam where her brother and his friend would be fishing.

14

'If they knew what Jan was into, my Mom and my Dad, they'd die.'

'I told my mother that I was coming here to bring my father home – it must have sounded so daft that she didn't bother to argue with me.'

'Being daft isn't being a traitor.'

'You have to live your own life, for yourself, you can't live your life for your parents.'

'Try telling them . . .' Ros laughed.

Jan was at the hotel.

Jack and Ros walked along the pavement of the street that sliced through Warmbaths. A desultory conversation, and blotted out when the big lorries and their trailers passed. The road through Warmbaths was the principal route from Johannesburg and Pretoria to Potgietersrus and Pietersburg and Louis Trichardt and on to the Zimbabwe border. The road rumbled under the lorries. Jack liked this small town, it was an escape from the threat of the cities. Agricultural country.

He had met the farmers the previous evening.

With Jan and Ros he had eaten a quiet meal in the hotel's dining room. He'd gone for a stringy T-bone and shared what he couldn't eat with the hotel cat. It had been a quiet meal because the brother and sister had been arguing in her room, and they hadn't anything to say to each other in front of Jack. He thought she might have been crying before she'd come down to dinner. Her eyes had been reddened and her upper cheeks puffed out. It could have just been the strain of the drive, but he thought she'd been crying. He'd left them after the meal and gone into the bar. One of those God awful entrances. The talking had stopped. A warble of noise when he had opened the door, silence when he had come forward to be served, as he was looked at and stripped for information. They would have known he was English from the moment he opened his mouth to ask for a Castle. He'd been lucky because the old soak who propped himself in the corner of the bar had a grandson in England, at an agricultural college in the West. Jack had listened and laughed aloud at the alcoholic's jokes, and he'd been included in a round, and stood his own for half the bar. They were huge lads, the young farmers. He knew they thought he was all right because each one of them through the long evening had come to him to try out their English. There wasn't much politics talked, a bit towards the end. Jack had thought they were all as confused as hell. What the hell was their government doing? What was all this crap talk about reform? Was the State President in the business of giving the country over to the *kaffirs*? Funny for Jack, because back home the State President was seen as the high priest of conservatism. In the bar at Brown's, the State President was the missionary of liberalism. He quite liked the young farmers, and it was a good evening, and it cost him three visits to the lavatory along the open veranda from his room.

Jack and Ros turned off the main road.

Ros pointed out to him the weather-worn red stones of trekkers' nineteenth century graves. They walked into a network of straight avenues bounded by bungalows and glorious gardens. Flowering shrubs, cut lawns, beds in bloom, and the drone of mowers and the hiss of standpipes.

'Jan's right,' Jack said. 'He's taken sides and he's right, because it can't last.'

'What's he right about?'

'That it can't last, that it's going to collapse. It's beautiful and it's doomed because nobody outside White South Africa cares a damn for you. Not the Europeans, not the Americans, not the Australians. Nobody's going to lift a finger for you when it all goes wrong.'

She looked at him. She had a small and pretty mouth. A strand of hair was across her face.

'I don't want a lecture, Jack, and I know what I want from my country. But my way of getting there doesn't include old ladies being pulled out of their cars and being knifed and being burned.'

He thought she walked beautifully. He thought there was a sweet loose swing in her hips. She had her arms folded across her chest, her breasts were lifted to push hard against the crumpled cotton of her blouse. She wore the same clothes as the day before.

'Do people care about hanging here?' Jack asked.

He saw a frown puckering and her eyebrows rising. They were a couple walking in a flower filled suburb, with a blue mountain ridge in distant sight, and he had asked her to talk about a court sentence that a man should hang by the neck until he was dead.

'It's not an issue. It's accepted that the penalty for murder is death by hanging. You've seen what they're like, our Blacks. Hanging protects us, the Whites. There's overwhelming support for hanging.'

'If it wasn't my father . . .'

'And if it wasn't my brother.'

'. . . then I'd probably think the same.'

'If it wasn't my brother that's involved then I wouldn't cross the road for you, not if you were bleeding in the gutter.'

He ducked his head. He walked faster. As surely as he had involved her brother, he had involved her. Just as he had involved Sandham and Duggie.

'What would you do for your brother, Ros?'

'I'd do for him what you're doing for your father.'

'And after today?'

'We drop you this afternoon, we turn round, we drive like hell back to Johannesburg. I give Jan my ultimatum, big word for a big speech, I tell him that he quits or I inform on him. I don't have to go to the security police, I tell my father. He'll do as my

221

father tells him, or my father will turn him in. That's what's happening today and after today. I'm not going to spend the next weeks and months wondering how close some pig-eyed policeman is inching to Jan, and I'm damned if I'm going to spend the next few years traipsing to White Political at Pretoria Central.'

They turned back. He couldn't think of anything to say to her. He ought to have been able to talk to her because she wasn't an activist, neither was he. They were near to the hotel when she stopped, dead, swung to face him. They were in the glare of the sun, on a wide pavement, they were dusted by the lorries passing on the road.

'Please, if you're trapped then get yourself killed.'

Jack squinted at her. 'Great.'

'If you're held they'll make you talk. If you talk, Jan's implicated.'

'And you're implicated, if I talk.'

'So just get yourself killed.' She was angry because he laughed. 'I'm in deadly earnest. The decent thing for you to do if you're trapped is to get yourself killed.'

Jack straightened. There was a mock solemnity in his voice. 'Goodbye, Miss van Niekerk, it has been a most pleasurable acquaintance.'

'You're pretty ordinary, you know that?'

'Meaning what?'

'So ordinary that you're quite interesting . . . If you were a mercenary or if you had some political hang-up about fighting racism, God you'd be boring. You're an ordinary person, ordinary attitudes, ordinary life. As I read you, there's nothing that ever happened in your life that wasn't just ordinary. Then you took a plane, then you burned the back off a police station, then you planned to explode your way into a hanging gaol. But that doesn't change you, doesn't stop you being just ordinary.'

He took her hand. She didn't try to pull away.

'Thank you for what you have done for me.'

'God damn you if you get yourself captured.'

They went into the hotel. They went upstairs to pack their bags.

Later they would pay the bill, check out, and drive together to the rendezvous that Jan had been given. Jack could picture it. The car would stop. He would get out. The car would drive away. He would be met at the rendezvous. He would never see the car again, nor the boy with the crippled foot, nor the pretty girl who couldn't be bothered to make herself beautiful. In his room, before throwing yesterday's socks and yesterday's shirt into his case, he looked over the plans of Pretoria Central. By the time they met, later that day, he would have the germ of a strategy to put to Thiroko.

The Bushman and the dog had led the troops to the road junction outside Monte Christo.

Through night binoculars they had observed the five men who waited for their pick up. They had seen them eat and urinate. They had heard the murmur of their voices. They had called in by radio for the necessary support. It had been a fine moonlit night. An ideal night for the operation. They had seen the collection of Thiroko and his comrades. Over the radio link had been passed a description of the vehicle and its registration plate.

A motorcycle, travelling without lights, had picked up the vehicle at Ellisras, south of Monte Christo. It was the only route the vehicle could have taken. Moving behind the motorcycle was an unmarked saloon car carrying four more members of Recce Commando. The vehicle had been trailed through the night as it came south through the Waterberge mountains towards Warmbaths.

The Puma had come again and made a night landing in the play area of the school at Monte Christo, and roused the village as it picked up the troops. By a relayed radio link the pilot was able to keep in contact with the car that followed the motorcycle that followed Thiroko's vehicle. The Puma, with its range of 570 kilometres, had had no difficulty in holding the contact before the last message was passed to the cockpit from some four kilometres north of Warmbaths.

A morning of rare excitement for the colonel.

The fire bomb investigation in the hallway ten floors below

was no longer priority. His plan personally to interrogate the Methodist priest, White and elderly and stitched for subversion, was shelved. Set aside, too, was the case file that would convict two and possibly three of the FOSATU leadership.

One file on the colonel's desk. The heavily stencilled title was JACOB THIROKO. At the top of the file was a wire print of the photograph taken at Gaberone airport. The picture showed a slight, insignificant man walking on the tarmac, and there was something in his expression that told the colonel of pain, as if the wind were caught in his bowels.

The file was ¾ of an inch thick. Intelligence material collected over the years from Gaberone, Maputo, Luanda, Lusaka and London, and for embellishment there were the statements of the men from the 'suicide-squads' who had allowed themselves to be captured . . . It always amused the colonel that the ANC cadres liked to call themselves 'suicide squads' and then chuck away their weapons and emerge from their bolt-holes with their hands held high . . . He knew Jacob Thiroko well, as well as he knew an old friend. He thought he had evidence enough to put him away for twenty-five years. He was less certain that he would be able to stick upon Thiroko a charge of murder without extenuating circumstances.

It would be good to hang the man, it would be a disappointment only to lock him away. Whether Thiroko hanged, or whether he was imprisoned, would depend on what information the bastard gave his interrogators. If he talked he would hang. Clear cut. The colonel would be responsible for the interrogation, responsible for making him talk. The photograph pleased the colonel. If Thiroko was in pain, if he had pain in his gut, then that would make easier the job of lifting the bastard onto the gallows trap.

The latest report was that Thiroko and four other Black males had crossed the border and were now resting up, that his resting place was surrounded by the Recce Commando. The soldiers were ordered to hold off until it was clear whether a further rendezvous was to take place. He had been told that the military would move in by mid-afternoon, that directly after his arrest Thiroko would be flown by helicopter to Johannesburg.

The colonel was wondering at the risk of it, why a man of Thiroko's prominence in Umkhonto we Sizwe would dare to travel back inside South Africa, when his telephone rang.

It was the direct line, with the unlisted number. He reached for it. He heard his wife's voice.

Had he read the morning paper? About Aunt Annie?

No, my dear, he had not.

So he did not know that yesterday afternoon Aunt Annie, his brother-in-law's sister, had been killed by a Black mob on the Pretoria road?

To his wife and himself she was always Aunt Annie, though only a few years older than they were. A dour old lady, and she had given them, as a wedding present, a silver teapot which they always used in the afternoons when he was at home.

He consoled his sobbing wife. He said he would not be able to come home before the small hours, persuaded her to go at once and spend the day with her brother, probably best to stay overnight too. He rang off.

Land mines, bombs, murders, riots, and the hacking and burning of Aunt Annie. And the statistics of revolt spiralling. As if a roof had sprung leaks, and as fast as a leak was blocked there were more water springs soaking through. It was the bastards like Thiroko who pick-axed the roof, made the leaks, slaughtered old Aunt Annie who came to tea on each of their wedding anniversaries, and who poured from the silver pot.

Thiroko lay on his back. His bed was loose straw, wrenched from a string-tied bale. He was the only one awake. The boys were sleeping, snoring at the roof of the cow shed.

They had arrived in the dark, and stumbled from the road across rough ground to the cow shed. The place stank of the animals. The shed was used by the farmer for storage and for when he had a difficult calving and the cow needed attention. They had dug against the back wall of the shed to uncover the weapons cache. Each of the AK 47 assault rifles was well sealed in plastic bags, each was dry and oiled. They had taken five of the rifles stored in the shed. They had taken also 50 kilos of plastic explosive, and detonators and firing wire. What they had not needed they had buried again under the soil and manure.

When it was first light he had crawled to a place where the overlapping metal walls of the shed had been prised apart by the winter storms. The cow shed was on rising ground. He could see where the road ran close by, where they had been dropped after the drive down from Monte Christo, and he could see in the far distance the grain silos of Warmbaths.

He had tried to sleep. The pain ate inside him. It might have been the long flight from London, and then the flight from Lusaka to Gaberone that had welled the pain. It might have been the bone-shaking drive from Monte Christo. It might have been the twenty-four hours without food. It might have been fear. The pain was sharp in his stomach.

Travelling with the boys, he had learned much. Each of them had looked good enough in the training camps, and the instructors from the German Democratic Republic had said they were as good as any, and Thiroko had thought they were good until he had walked with them. Now he thought they were crap, because they had talked rubbish to him of a welcoming uprising. No inkling of the danger of coming as a stranger into their own land. They were going to have to shape up and learn fast and much between here and the gaol.

He lay on his back, in his pain, and he thought of the Englishman. An anxiety simmered in him, of business not yet talked through. Happy and Charlie and Percy and Tom were held in cells on the opposite side of Beverly Hills to Jeez Carew, and they would have to be reached before the assault on C section . . . He thought Jack Curwen would understand that four men must come before one.

Thiroko pushed himself awkwardly to his feet. The motion hurt him. He went out through the open door. He breathed in the cool clean air of his mother country. Down from this height

226

was the sprawled town and beyond it the hazed flat veld. It was right that he should have come back, that before he died he should smell the air of his home.

He squatted beside a bush. His bowels were water, and he had no paper to wipe himself. When he stood and pulled up his trousers he saw that there was blood mucous in his mess.

He saw no movement except the birds skimming the long grass, he heard no sounds except their shrill calling.

The soldiers who watched the cow shed were the élite of the South African Defence Force. They were used to sterner tasks than this. In total and motionless silence they lay up in cover, at the nearest point 100 metres from the rusted metal building, watching the four walls from behind machine guns and automatic rifles. They had seen Thiroko come out of the shed. It had been noted that he had no paper.

Six hundred metres away, where the road curved, hidden by a coppice of eucalyptus and scrub, was parked the car that had travelled after Thiroko from Ellisras. The four men who sat in the car, or squatted outside it, wore civilian clothes, slacks and sweaters. Their hair was not cut short in the style of the military, two were bearded. They were unremarkable.

Crouched down in the coppice were the dog handler, his labrador, and the Bushman.

All watching until mid-afternoon to see if there would be a contact.

Ros drove away from the hotel. It was just past one o'clock, but they hadn't bothered to eat. They were not hungry, and Jan cracked a thin joke about Jack wanting to wait till he could have maize porridge with his friends.

Jack said that Brown's was like something from the cowboy pictures. The open veranda, the swing slat doors from the street into the bar, posters for Saturday night live music and dancing, the carving in the dining room that was an FN rifle in relief. Jack said that as long as he lived he'd remember the springs in his bed. Ros didn't speak. They went right down the main road, then turned off towards the mountains. Past the huge modern angles of the roof of the Dutch Reformed Church, up along the straight tarmac strips that bisected the bungalow land, past the White school where the small boys were having rugby coaching and the girls were playing hockey. Jack thought Warmbaths was an oasis. Abruptly they were out of the town's limits, lawns and residences giving way to grazing lands. There was another 3 kilometres to go before the pale dust road ahead began to climb for the foothills and then the mountains. The high ground was grey hazed, cool and without threat.

Jan spoke to Ros in Afrikaans. She nodded. Jack sensed they were close to the drop point.

Jan switched to English.

'We're hardly stopping for you. You can see the place from the road, that's what my message said. It's a place where they can keep cattle if the weather's bad. You'll have to carry it all yourself, your bag and the tube things.'

'That's fine.'

The sun was high. The light bathed them through the car windows. Ros wound her window down; Jack followed her. There was the rush of air on his face, her hair streamed across her cheeks and nose and mouth.

'There it is.'

Jan was leaning forward between their shoulders. He pointed ahead, through the windscreen, under the central mirror. For a moment the sun had caught the roof of a building that was set back from the road. Beyond the place was a clump of tall trees. For only a moment the light hit at that particular angle and reflected from the tin roof.

'We'll put you down by those trees. Wait until we are gone ten minutes before you move.'

'Goodbye, and again, thank you,' Jack said softly.

'Good luck, Jack. I hope you pull it off,' a fierceness from Jan.

'I'll put you down in those trees,' Ros said.

Jack grinned. 'Not a chance that we won't.'

The last of the big boasts. They had lost sight of the shed. The big boasts were all right for his mother and fine for George Hawkins, great for Duggie, brilliant for these kids. Ros was braking. The big boasts would stop when he joined Thiroko's men. Jack thought they were familiar trees, peeled bark trunks, but he couldn't put a name to them.

There was a car parked off the road and in the shade of the trees.

Jack saw two in the front and two in the back of the saloon car.

'I can't put you down next to them,' Ros said.

They were passing the car.

As a flash, Jack saw the front seat passenger hunched forward, something in his hand, and his hand close to his ear. As a flash, Jack heard the distorted snatch of a radio transmission. Just a flash . . .

He had heard a radio transmission.

He swung to Ros.

His voice was a whisper. 'Just keep going.'

She turned to him, mouth sagging open.

'No sudden movements. Don't slow, don't accelerate.'

Her face was washed with questions.

'Just drive as if it's normal, like nothing's important to us here.'

Jack could hear her breath spurting.

'Don't turn round, don't look back.'

God, and he wanted to look back. He wanted to look back and into the parked green saloon car and see whether the attention of the men inside was on the Beetle that had sidled past.

'Just drive on, as if it's natural.'

Past the trees, he saw a cattle track leading from an iron gate away across a crudely fenced field, uphill towards a cow shed. He could see no movement at the shed. Above the engine were the crisp calls of the birds. He felt Jan's fingers on his shoulder.

'Don't stop, drive on,' Jack snapped at Ros.

Christ, the girl was good, didn't argue, didn't talk back.

'Keep driving,' a rasp in Jack's voice.

They went on up the slow incline. Jack pulled the map from the glove compartment. He unfolded it over his knees. His finger was searching for Warmbaths.

The girl was great, the girl was driving with her eyes on the road like it was a Sunday outing.

'When we went past the parked car, as we passed it, did you hear anything?'

'I hardly saw the car.'

'It was taking a radio message.'

'So what?' Jan spoke before he had thought.

'There's not going to be a taxi out here. It was taking a radio message which means it's a police car. Cop on, kid.'

'Christ . . .'

'Which means that the drop is under observation.'

'Shit . . .'

Ros was expressionless. Jan sagged back into his narrow space alongside the metal tubes. Jack went back to the map. He was a long time poring over it. He traced a route on to Mabula, and then a secondary road to Rooiberg, and then on until the turn off to Rankin's Pass through the mountains, and a crossing of the Mogol river and back to Nylstroom that was thirty kilometres north of Warmbaths. Without measuring the distance with his finger, he thought that the whole journey was more than a hundred and fifty kilometres, and that was the most direct route to Warmbaths without going again down the road past the cow shed and past the parked green saloon car.

'If they're there, in the shed, and the police move in on them, what would they do with them?' Jack asked.

A dulled response from Jan. 'They'd take them to the police station at Warmbaths. From there they'd probably helicopter them out to Pretoria or Johannesburg.'

'I have to know, what happens to them.'

Jan flared. 'It wasn't us that was followed.'

'Pretty bloody irrelevant right now.'

'I have to see what happens.'

He gave Ros the route that he wanted her to take. She nodded, she was impassive.

'Is that all right?' Jack asked.

'I'm just your chauffeur,' Ros said.

'You know what's there, Carew, and you know it's something that I never thought you'd let me see, too right.'

'What's there, Sergeant Oosthuizen?'

'Can't you see what's there for yourself, Carew?'

Sergeant Oosthuizen liked a little game. He liked a child's riddle. Mostly Jeez humoured him. Most times in the last thirteen months Jeez had played along with him. Buggered if he wanted a joke that afternoon.

'I can't see that anything's there, Sergeant.'

Jeez was pacing the concrete of the exercise yard. Sometimes the yard seemed large enough for him to stroll in. That afternoon he was constricted within the walls, caged by the roof grille shadows on the ground. Oosthuizen stood beside the locked door that led into the corridor and Jeez's cell. His arms were folded. The great jowls of his chin were spread with his smile.

'Now, come on, Carew. You're not trying for me.'

Jeez thought Oosthuizen so thick-skinned, and yet so innately kind, that he could rarely be sharp with the man. Truthfully, Jeez thought it would be cheap to squash Oosthuizen. Nothing to do with the disciplinary measures that queued up behind Oosthuizen, not many privileges they could take away from a man when they were scheduled to take away his life within a week. He would hate himself if he put down Sergeant Oosthuizen. But buggered if that day he wanted to play a game, and buggered if he knew how to tell the old fool to shut his mouth.

Perhaps Oosthuizen knew of Jeez's wish for quiet. Perhaps he was determined to deny it.

'You've got to try for me, Carew, like a good man.'

Jeez surrendered, as he usually did. 'Where am I supposed to be looking, Sergeant?'

'I'm giving you a good hint, you're supposed to be looking at the flower bed, Carew.'

Jeez stared down at the flower bed. Most of the geranium blooms were over, should have been pinched off. The lobelia was straggling, should have been pulled.

'I'm looking at the flower bed, Sergeant.'

'And there's something in the flower bed that I never thought you'd let me see.'

'I don't know what it is, Sergeant.'

'You're not trying for me, Carew.'

'Please, Sergeant, what is it that's in the flower bed?'

Oosthuizen tugged at his moustache. He stood at his full height and dragged in his belly so that his belt buckle sagged. He was hugely satisfied.

'There's a *weed*.'

'A fucking *what*?'

'Watch your language, Carew . . . You've allowed a dandelion to grow in your flower bed.'

Jeez saw the dandelion. It had no flower. It was half concealed by a geranium plant.

'Yes, you can see it now, but you hadn't noticed it before. I'd never have thought you would let me find a weed in your garden, Carew.'

Jeez wondered what would happen if he smashed Oosthuizen with his fist. He thought the man might burst.

Jeez knelt on the concrete.

The concrete was not warmed by the sun, the grilled shadows kept the heat off the concrete. He hadn't noticed the weed because he hadn't watered his garden for two days. He could see that the geranium leaves were dropping and that the lobelia was parched. He pushed his fingers into the earth, he tugged at the dandelion root. He felt the root snap under the earth. The weed would grow again. He smoothed the earth over. The weed would grow again, but not surface before the following Thursday morning. He carried the dandelion to the plastic bag in the corner of the yard, where the dirt sweepings were left for a trustie to take away.

'Doesn't do to let it get the better of you, Carew,' Oosthuizen said quietly.

'No, Sergeant.'

'Believe me, man, you have to keep your standards up from the first day you come here, right up to the last day.'

'Thank you, Sergeant.'

'That's solid advice. You have to find something to think about. Whatever's going to happen to you, you have to keep going, keep those standards . . . Have you got no visits coming?'

'No.'

'All those other fellows you were with, they've all got their families coming.'

'No-one's coming.'

'I never saw a man who was so really alone, Carew.'

'No-one.'

Oosthuizen looked once, almost furtively, over his shoulder and up to the empty catwalk window. He dropped his voice. 'I'm only supposed to make little talk with you. I'm out of order, but there's something I should like you to know, Carew. I'm retiring next week. Wednesday's my birthday. I should have retired on the coming Tuesday evening. They have a party all lined for me . . .'

'Will they give you a gold watch?'

'I don't think so, I think it'll be a decanter and some crystal glasses . . . But I've said to the governor that I don't want the party on Tuesday, nor on Wednesday. Our governor's a real gentleman, he said I could have the party on Thursday. You understand me, Carew?'

'You're going to be here on Thursday morning. Thank you, Sergeant.'

Jeez looked up. He followed the flight of a grey wagtail to the catwalk window.

Oosthuizen said simply, 'It's because you don't have any visits, Carew.'

He saw the wagtail start away from the narrow ledge below the window.

There was a face at the window, a pale face against the darkness behind. He saw the collar of a suit jacket and the brilliance of a white shirt. He knew who he had seen. He knew who would wish to look over him while he was at exercise.

Their nerves were raw because the rendezvous had not been kept.

It was two hours past the time of the rendezvous.

Thiroko had started to ponder what he should do if Jack Curwen had not arrived within an hour, when the next transport was due to pick them up. He could think of many reasons why Jack should be delayed, but as the minutes slipped to hours each reason had grown less credible. He knew the boys were on edge, strained, because they talked more, because it was harder for him each time to quiet them.

'JACOB THIROKO, YOU ARE SURROUNDED BY UNITS OF THE SOUTH AFRICAN DEFENCE FORCE . . .'

It came as an amplified bellow. The noise of the magnified voice swept through the half opened door of the shed and coursed round the four walls. They were all frozen. They were all rigid. They were held in their postures of sitting, lying, squatting, crouching, standing.

'YOU SHOULD SURRENDER IMMEDIATELY. YOU SHOULD THROW YOUR WEAPONS OUT THROUGH THE DOOR, THEN YOU SHOULD COME OUT WITH YOUR HANDS ON YOUR HEADS . . .'

Movements now. Each man's hand moving stutteringly towards the stock of his Kalashnikov. Frightened little movements, as if the voice that overwhelmed them had an eye to see them.

'. . . YOU HAVE ONE MINUTE TO COME OUT. IF YOU COME OUT WITHIN THE ONE MINUTE THEN YOU WILL NOT BE HARMED IN ANY WAY . . .'

The four boys looking at him, broken hope in their faces. He saw the accusation of betrayal. He could have cried. They all looked to him. He was their commander. He had told them of a great strike against the Boer regime, and they were in a cow shed and amongst cow dirt and they were surrounded by their enemy.

'...WE ARE STARTING THE ONE MINUTE, FROM NOW...'

Thiroko crawled to the doorway. He hugged the shadow. He looked out. He could hear the drone of insects and the cry of birds and the whispering of the afternoon wind in the dry loose grass. He could not see his enemy.

'Are we the heroes of our revolution, or are we the frightened children that the Boers think us?'

None of the boys had voices in their throats. They nodded dumbly to Thiroko.

'Their promise of no harm is twenty years in their gaols.'

One boy cocked his rifle. The chain was started. The rattling of the weapons being armed rung inside the shed.

'I have to win time, time for a young friend who is braver than I.'

He saw the chins jut, and the eyes blaze, and the hands were steady on the rifles. He saw the trembling pass.

'...THIRTY SECONDS. YOU THROW YOUR WEAPONS OUT. YOU COME OUT WITH YOUR HANDS ON YOUR HEADS. YOU HAVE A GUARANTEE OF SAFETY...'

They shouted together, the four boys and Jacob Thiroko. The word in their shout was *Amandla*, the word ballooned inside the tin walls.

He waved them to the sides of the shed, each to a firing position. He stripped from his rucksack a khaki pouch. He tore a wad of papers from the pouch and ripped at them and made a cairn of them. He lit the heap of papers. His boys began to shoot. The smoke eddied through the shed, and with the smell of the burning paper was the stench of the cordite. Incoming fire, punching, ricocheting, into the shed. He lay on the straw and the manure and he drew the air down into his lungs and breathed so that he could fan the small flames licking into the

235

papers. He saw his notes curling. He saw names blackening, the coded plans flaking.

So little time, and the boy against the back wall was whimpering, hit in the buttocks and the stomach. He blew again on the papers and prayed in anger for the fire to be fiercer. The boy close to the front door was coughing mouthfuls of blood onto his chest. He shouted for the two boys at the side walls to keep firing. No reply. He could see the clumsy postures in which they had died. The boy at the back wall no longer whimpered. The boy at the door toppled suddenly out of the door frame into the sunlight, and was hit and hit before he fell into the dry hard dirt.

Jacob Thiroko summoned a prayer for the comrades around him and reached for his rifle.

They stood in the crowd outside the police station in Warmbaths.

The men of the Recce Commando had come and gone. They had come by police truck, and then run to a helicopter with their arms held over their faces to save their features from snapping cameras. The crowd could hardly have seen them but had cheered their every stride. It was an all White crowd outside the single storey brick police station, a crowd grimly satisfied.

Ros never showed her emotions. Jack didn't know what she felt.

They stood and they watched as the bodies were lifted from a van and laid out in the forecourt, between two low sand-bagged emplacements, for the police photographer.

There were four young Blacks. They were laid on the dirt, their clothing and the bodies torn, shredded. Last to come was the corpse of Jacob Thiroko. His face was intact, recognizable to Jack. He blinked, felt a sickness in his gut. The back of Thiroko's head was gone, a mushy wet crater. He thought Thiroko must have put the barrel of his weapon into his mouth. His talk had brought Thiroko back to South Africa, and killed him. They dropped the body, like it was a meat carcass.

Jan was cold faced. Jack short punched him in the kidneys. Jan had tried to look as though he enjoyed what he saw, and made a piss poor job of it.

The green saloon car drove to the police station steps. Jack half remembered the front passenger of the car, who had worn a red shirt when he was parked off the road against the trees. A man in a red shirt carried from the car five AK 47 rifles, each sealed in a separate Cellophane bag.

He watched a detective wash his stained hands in a fire bucket. He saw the driver of the green saloon car walk to the doorway, tight in his fist was a clear plastic sack. Jack saw that it was filled with charred paper. He felt the weakness sinking through his knees, into his legs.

The light was going over Johannesburg.

The colonel hadn't lowered his blinds, hadn't switched on his strip light. He had sat unmoving, nursing his frustration, since the news had been relayed to him from Warmbaths.

His aides had abandoned him. Now, in the outer office, they warned the detective of his mood. The detective had shrugged, knocked and gone in.

'I thought you should know, sir, of the developments in connection with the bomb investigation. A youngish man, English accent, purchased a similar bag and a similar can of petrol in the city centre on the day of the bomb. The description given by the two sales points is pretty much the same. We're working on a photo-fit likeness, sir. I'll have a copy of the full statements for you first thing.'

15

R os took charge.

Someone had to. Her brother couldn't speak, was utterly drained. Jack was black in his mood, brooding. While her brother and Jack floundered, Ros assumed the decision taking. Into the car. Away down the long road and back towards Pretoria and Johannesburg. She wondered whether they were already compromised, all three of them. She anticipated that the security police would be waiting for the van Niekerk kids when they reached their home city, the Beetle having been traced. She didn't air her fears.

She asked clipped questions of Jack. She ignored her brother.

'Do you want to fly out tonight?'

'No.'

'There's a British Airways every night after the SAA flight, there's Lufthansa and Alitalia. What's the point in staying?'

'I'm not flying.'

'You don't have a group, you're one person. Do you have any other contacts to get help?'

'I don't.'

'It's idiocy to think of anything but getting yourself out. Don't you see that?'

'I've no choice.'

'Then you've got a death wish.'

He told her about Sandham. He told her about Duggie. 'I've debts that have to be paid off. They helped me and they were both killed. They were murdered because I involved them. Do you think, because it's getting hot, I can just pack up and go home? "Sorry you got chopped, chaps, but it's getting too difficult for me, I'm not going to risk *my* skin . . ." Ros, it can't be done.'

'Suicide.'

'I'll tell you about suicide. The old one amongst the bodies was called Jacob Thiroko. I don't know what was in his mind about coming here, but he hadn't been in South Africa for more than twenty years. And inside his own country the last thing he did was to blow his own brains away. That was suicide. That was so he couldn't be made to talk. And before he blew his mind out he burned his papers. He stayed alive long enough to burn his papers and then he killed himself. He can't tell them my name, or any name, or what was the target. That's a hell of a debt to be paid off. I can't walk away, not from them, and not from my father.'

'On your own you won't even get to see the gaol.'

'Then in Beverly Hills they'll all hear the gunfire. The plans told me that they'll hear it. They have high windows into the catwalks, and up in the catwalk space there are more windows that look down into the cells. Those windows are always open. My father will hear the gunfire. Everyone in that bastard place will know that someone came, someone tried.'

She couldn't look at him. She didn't dare to see his face.

'It's madness.'

'If I walked away I'd have to live with next Thursday morning. I could be back in London. I could be sitting and filling my gut with booze, and I could take all the tablets that get you to sleep. Wouldn't matter. I'd be in that cell, wondering whether he was scared, what he was thinking. I'd hear them come for him. I'd see them walk him along the corridors. What do you want me to bloody well do, Ros, go to sleep, set the alarm for five in the morning, wake up to know that my father's being pitched off a trap? What do I do then? Turn over and go back to sleep?'

Jan had leaned forward. Pushing his head between the high seat backs.

'It's to break out one person?'

Jack said, 'Yes.'

'It is to save *one* of them?'

'Yes.'

'There are five that are going to hang.'

'The one is my father.'

'And you don't give a shit for the other four?'

Jack dropped his head. 'Jan, believe me, I'm not interested in five, I'm going to break out one.'

'He's like every other White,' Jan shouted. 'He's a racist.'

Ros snapped, 'Grow up, for Christ's sake, he doesn't give a fuck for your grubby little Movement.'

'To leave four Blacks to hang, and to try to save one White, that's racism.'

'They're killers, those four murdering swine.'

'You're a racist, too, Ros.'

They were both yelling. Jack's hands went up, palms open, on either side of his head.

'I'm not proud of what I've decided but it's my decision, alone.'

'It's all horseshit about you being alone,' Jan said.

'If you were alone you wouldn't be in my bloody car,' Ros said.

Jack leaned across and kissed her on the cheek, and she didn't pull away. He took Jan's hand and shook it fervently.

Christ, what a bloody awful army.

Ros said she was going to Hillbrow. She said there was a studio flat there that belonged to a friend from school. Her friend always gave her the keys when she took her small son back to Durban and her parents. Ros said that there wasn't a husband, nor a live-in man. Ros said that her friend liked to know that someone came to keep an eye on the flat when she was away. Ros said that Hillbrow was the home of the drifters in Johannesburg, where Blacks and Asians and Coloureds and Whites lived alongside each other in tower blocks without being constantly harassed by the police for violating the residential codes. Ros said he wouldn't be noticed in Hillbrow.

It was dark when they reached Johannesburg.

And he needed to think, because the days were slipping away, Thursday was rushing to him.

The studio flat, fifth floor, was an untidy mess.

They'd come in the back way. The car parked at the rear, so that they could all climb the five flights of the concrete steps of the fire escape. Heavy going for Jan, and Ros and Jack had their hands full. Ros had the key, took a bit of finding in her handbag.

Just one dismal room for living. All there. Bed, cooker, shelves, cupboards, prints on the wall of views of the English Lakes.

He went to the one window. He reckoned he was less than a mile from the Landdrost, but this was a different world. A crowded pavement below him. He could see Blacks and Whites strolling, and there was a café opposite with chairs and tables in the open where he could see the colour mix. Music from radio stations and records merged, deafening, from the street, from alongside, from above. A prefabricated block, and he thought he heard the bed springs going upstairs and he didn't like to look at Ros. A fight below, same side of the street as the block, and he had to crane to see two guys, White, kicking hell out of a third guy, White, and a girl watching, Black or Coloured or some mix. People walking round them, letting them get on with it.

Jan told him that they had to go home, Ros nodding. Jack understood the risks they took. He had the airport, they had nowhere to run for. Ros had her mouth clenched as Jan said that he would ring at eight and at ten and at midnight. Jack should let the phone ring, but not pick it up. If there were a trace on their home telephone then it would only operate when the phone was lifted at the receiver's end. The ringing phone would tell Jack that all was well with Jan and Ros . . . Jack didn't ask what he should do if the phone didn't ring. It was for Jack Curwen to make decisions, not to ask what he should do. His responsibility, all on his shoulders. Jan said he would come back to the flat in the morning. Ros didn't say when she might see him again. He thought he was alone because he could not imagine how a crippled student and an insurance office desk worker could help him work the break out from the maximum security cells of Beverly Hills. Hard put to see how he could help himself.

He hadn't eaten since breakfast.

He looked in the fridge. There was yoghurt, and some cream cheese, and the remains of a bowl of salad, and some salami slices. He reckoned the girl who lived in the studio flat must be a virtual skeleton. He cleaned out the fridge. He quartered the large room. It was a compulsion, to see how the single parent lived, what she read, what she wore. He couldn't have answered for this violation of her privacy other than by saying it was a symptom of his aloneness.

He found the building bricks.

They were the same as he had had when he was a kid. They were the same as Will had back at Churchill Close. Lego bricks, product of Denmark, there was a bread bin of them.

Jack sat on the floor and laid out his plans of Beverly Hills, and built the gaol in plastic bricks of blue and red and yellow and white. He built technicolor perimeter walls.

He made C section from red bricks, and administration in yellow, and A and B sections in white. He made the exercise yard of C section 2 in blue. He made a watchtower behind the gallows block, and he built towers where the floodlight stanchions were set.

He was a child at play.

There were no roofs for his buildings. He could look down into each cubicle he made, into the cells, into the corridors, into the exercise yards. He put a door between C section's corridor and C section 2's corridor. He put a door on a cell. He could count the number of the doors, he could count the number of the walls.

With the bricks that remained he located Pretoria Local and Pretoria Central and the White Politicals and the Women's. He scattered the prison staff homes, and the self service store, and the recreation and swimming areas, all on the north slope below Beverly Hills. Level with the gaol, on the west side, he put the Commissioner of Prison's residence. He laid out a sheet of paper for the rifle range on the east side. He made a broken line with the last of the bricks to make the outer ring of wire fences on Magazine Hill to the south.

He sat cross-legged, his back against the bed, and gazed down at the gaol. A long time he sat, unmoving, searching for the plan, worrying for the route. He sat in the half light, only the light beside the bed on. Searching and worrying.

Jack stood. He went to the kitchenette area of the room and rifled the drawers and cupboards until he found a set of cooking scales. From his suitcase he lifted out the package of explosives. He didn't think the wrapping would weigh much, not enough to confuse his calculations. He weighed the explosives.

He had 15 pounds and 4 ounces of plaster gelignite.

He replaced the gelignite in the suitcase, laid it beside the wrapped detonators and the firing wire.

There was a telephone beside the bed.

It was an impulse, born of aloneness. It was eight minutes to three in the morning, Sunday morning.

Below the flat, Hillbrow slept. The streets had at last quietened.

He wondered if his father slept.

Jack knew that if he did not make the call then he might just as well take a taxi to the airport in a dozen hours' time and book a flight and fly out.

He found a book with the code and dialled. He had made up his mind.

The ringing of the telephone scattered the cats.

The bell drove them from the newspaper covering the kitchen table, and from the cushioned chair beside the stove, sent them scurrying to the dark corners.

George Hawkins blundered into the kitchen, groping for the light switch, reaching for the telephone. He heard the distant voice. No rambling small talk, no crap about the weather, nor about the time in the morning.

The wall was 20 feet high, it was 18 inches thick. What was

the minimum explosive required with a conical shaped charge of 9 inches in diameter to knock a man-sized hole at ground level?

'Bugger . . .'

George needed paper and pencil. Couldn't find them. Didn't know where he'd last put them. Had to do the calculation in his head. And he was half asleep.

'Shit . . .'

And the boy was talking about minimums. If he was on about minimums, then the boy was in trouble, deep bloody trouble.

'Twelve pounds is absolute bloody minimum. Problem with the minimum is that the concrete on the far side of the reinforcing mesh may not be broken clear. Ideal would be fifteen to eighteen.'

The minimum?

'That's twelve pounds.'

How could the reverse end of the firing tube be blocked?

'Concrete mix.'

Could the conical shaping be lightweight, aluminium?

'Not important that it's heavy. It's good if it's lightweight.'

How much stand off should there be from the firing end of the metal tubing to the wall?

'For a man-sized hole you should have six to nine inches . . . Twelve pounds of explosive, that's the absolute bloody bottom line . . .'

The telephone purred in his ear.

For a full minute George Hawkins held the receiver against his face, shivered in his pyjamas. He put the telephone down and went and sat in his chair and he called for the cats and rubbed the warmth into his bare skinny feet. George Hawkins shook his head, slowly, sadly. He had been asked for the minimum. He had answered the question. Twelve pounds was the bloody border line. The boy was in trouble.

He sat for an hour with his cats on his lap before he eased them off and went back to his cold bed.

* * *

As the city slept late on Sunday the colonel worked at his desk.

He had excused himself from taking tea with Aunt Annie's relations after church. He had told his wife to offer his apologies to the minister.

He read the reports that had come in late the previous evening. He couldn't have waited for them the previous evening, because the loss of Thiroko had been too great a blow. It should never have been left in the hands of Recce Commando, that he was certain of. He had been sure of it all through the late hours at home as he had listened to his wife, sniffling and talking of Aunt Annie.

Another day, another opportunity.

He gutted the reports.

A White male. Age between middle twenties and thirty years. Grey trousers and a green sports shirt and a mauve sweater. Common to both sales.

An English accent.

The reports were specific. Not an English accent that was South African. Not the accent of a long term English immigrant . . . and they were pigs who should never have been let into the country, hanging on to their British passports, shovelling money out of the country, sending their kids away to avoid army service, sneering at the Afrikaners who had made the country . . . The accent of an *English* Englishman.

The purchases had been made within one hour of each other on the day the bomb exploded.

Under the reports he had two photo-fit portraits. They had been built as mosaics from the descriptions of the two shop-keepers. The hair style, the deep set eyes, the strong nose, the jutting chin.

It was the colonel's belief that he stared at the two faces of one man. They were the faces of the man who had destroyed the back hallway of John Vorster Square. And his mind could wander. If he had been consulted he would have argued strongly against the use of Recce Commando in the tracking and failed capture of Jacob Thiroko. He had not been consulted and as a result he had been denied the chance of extracting information from one of the best sources he'd ever been close to. He had scarcely slept for rage.

He went down the stairs to the incident room. He let it be known, that in his opinion, from the weight of his experience, the bomb was not the work of Umkhonto we Sizwe.

'I believe it was thrown by an individual who arrived recently from England, otherwise more care would have been taken in the purchase of the materials. It should be assumed that he came to South Africa very shortly before the attack. The airports should be checked. You should look for a flight from Europe because the shop men have given him a pale complexion, he hasn't been in the sun. You should also check every one of the city's hotels. That is my suggestion.'

He knew his suggestion would be taken as an order.

'You slept on it?' Jan asked.

'My decision, yes.'

'No flight?'

'No,' Jack said.

A pointless question. Jan could see beside the unmade bed the toy building that was Pretoria Central.

'I don't want to . . .'

Jack cut in. 'You don't want to get shot.'

'I don't want to start something that is impossible.'

'It's an over-used word.'

'You don't have explosives and you don't have weapons.'

Jack waved him quiet. He told Jan about the 15 pounds of gelignite, saved from the John Vorster Square bomb. He told him about the detonators and the firing fuse. He saw the surprise growing on the boy's face.

'Didn't you trust us?'

'Nor myself.'

'Each one of us, the activists of Umkhonto we Sizwe, each of us has an implicit trust in our Movement.'

'It was sensible to be careful, it's nothing to do with trust. Jan,

I have to have more explosives or grenades, and I have to have firearms. I have to have them.'

'I'm just a courier,' the boy said, and the nerves showed.

'I have to have them, Jan.'

'By when?'

'Tonight.'

'That's impossible.'

'Over-used word, Jan.'

Jack started to make the bed. Jan paced the floor, there was the rhythm of the shuffle and the thud of his feet. Jack smoothed down the coverlet. He thought he would never understand this boy. He could understand a man such as Thiroko, and the young men who had died with Thiroko. Blacks fighting for what Blacks thought was theirs. Couldn't place this crippled boy in the game, a White fighting for what Blacks thought was theirs. He thought it was all to do with the foot. He thought the misshapen foot had alienated the boy from the White society around him. He thought the boy must find a satisfaction from his hidden betrayal of his own people.

The boy stopped, turned. He faced Jack squarely.

'I'll be back in an hour for you.'

After Jan had gone, Jack sat again on the floor beside the model. He was drawn to an approach to Beverly Hills from the south side, over Magazine Hill. He knew why that approach appealed to him. Defence HQ was to the north. The east approach was through Pretoria Local and Pretoria Central. From the west he would have to cross beside the police dog training school, and the secure mental hospital. He did not know what was on Magazine Hill, and ignorance was a comfort, his only ally.

'You're not usually here on a Sunday morning, Sergeant.'

'Overtime, Carew. I get time and a half on a Sunday morning. I need the money, what with retirement coming. You can always get overtime on a Sunday. The young fellows don't want it. They want to be with their families, get outside the city, get away from here.'

Jeez had eaten his breakfast. His breakfast on a Sunday morning was the same as on any other morning. Jeez had eaten porridge made from maize, with milk. And two slices of brown bread, with thinly smeared margarine and jam. The same as on every morning that he had been in Beverly Hills. He had three more breakfasts to eat. He would be gone before breakfast was served on Thursday. He had drunk his mug of coffee. He knew that he would get one meal that was different to all the other meals inside Beverly Hills. On Wednesday afternoon he would have a whole chicken for his dinner, cooked by the chef in the staff canteen. For the last meals there was always a whole chicken for the condemns who were White. He couldn't remember where he had heard that, whether it had been from way back when he was on remand, or whether he had read it in the newspapers before his arrest. It was a part of the lore of the condemns that they were given a whole chicken the dinner before they were hanged, just as it was part of the lore that the Blacks only had half a chicken. Jeez couldn't believe that, that the pigmentation of the skin made the difference between two legs and two wings and two breasts, and one leg and one wing and one chicken breast. And he wouldn't get to know, because he was buggered if he was going to beg an answer from Sergeant Oosthuizen.

Jeez wasn't sharp that Sunday morning.

So dull that he didn't even question Oosthuizen's claim that he was only at work to get time and a half for his nest egg. There was a weakness in Jeez's legs and in his belly. It was with him more frequently, as if he had a cold coming on, and the microbe was fear. Couldn't rid himself of the fear, not when he was locked in his cell, not when he was alone, particularly not when the high ceiling light above the wire grille was dimmed, when he was alone with his thoughts of Thursday morning and the rambling night sounds of the gaol.

The sounds carried into the upper areas of the cells and through the open windows to the catwalks, and from the catwalks they eddied to the next window and floated down from there to the next cell, and the cell beyond that.

The young White, the one who hadn't been there for more than a few weeks, always cried on a Sunday morning, in the small hours. Oosthuizen had told Jeez that he had been an altar boy, was a Roman Catholic, and cried because when he had been a teenager he was out of bed early on a Sunday morning and away to his local church for first Mass. Oosthuizen had confided that the young White was getting to be a pain with his crying. The old White, charged with killing his wife for the insurance, he coughed and spat each morning to clear the nicotine mucus from his throat. Oosthuizen said that the old White smoked sixty cigarettes a day. Oosthuizen had once said, in his innocence, that the old White would kill himself by so much smoking.

There was the crying and the coughing and the slither tread of the guard on the catwalk, and there was the sound of a lavatory flushing. There was laughter from out in the corridor, where the prison officers played cards to pass away the day.

Faintly he heard the singing.

Just a murmur at first.

The edges and clarity were knocked off the singing by the many windows and the yards of the catwalk that it passed through. The singing was from right across the far side of Beverly Hills, from A section or B section. Jeez saw Oosthuizen fidget.

'Who's it for?'

'I'm not allowed to tell you that.'

'Sergeant . . .' Jeez held Oosthuizen with his eyes.

Oosthuizen pulled at his moustache, then shrugged, and dropped his voice. 'For the boy who's going on Tuesday.'

'Who is he, Sergeant?'

'Just a Coloured.'

The whole place was mad. There was a worry that a man smoked too much and might harm his health before it was time for him to have his neck stretched, which might just do his health a bit more harm. There was worry that a prison officer who was retiring on Thursday might get into trouble for a quiet conversation on his last Sunday morning.

'What's he like, the fellow who does it?'

'You trying to get me on a charge sheet, Carew?'

'What's he like?'

The voice was a whisper. 'He's damned good . . . Doesn't help you to think about it, forget what I told you . . . He's as good as anywhere in the whole world. He's fast and he's kind, a real professional.'

He won't hurt you, Jeez. So get a grip on it, Jeez, because old Sergeant Oosthuizen says the executioner's a hell of a good operator. Great news, Jeez . . .

'I'll walk with you on Thursday morning, Carew. I'll hold your arm.'

Jeez nodded. He couldn't speak. He didn't think Oosthuizen had attended a hanging in years. He thought that Oosthuizen had made him a bloody great gesture of love.

'I'm going to do the rosters so's I get Monday in here for the day shift, and then I'll have Tuesday off, and then I'll come on again for Tuesday night, and then I'll have Wednesday off and I'll be back on again for Wednesday night, and I'll stay on through . . .'

'Why, Sergeant?'

The words came in a flood flow. 'Because you aren't the same as the others. Because you're here by some sort of accident, I don't know what the accident is. Because you're covering for something, I don't know what it is. Because you shouldn't be here. Because you're not a terrorist, whatever you've done. Because you had the way to save yourself, I don't know why you didn't take it . . . It's not my place to say that, but it's what I think.'

Jeez smiled. 'Not your place, Sergeant.'

He watched the cell door close on Oosthuizen.

A hell of a week to look forward to. Clean clothes on Monday, and fresh sheets. Library on Wednesday. Early call on Thursday . . .

Jan had been home, spoken to her, and gone.

Ros waited for her father to leave for his Sunday morning round of golf.

He played every Sunday morning, then came home for his cold lunch. In the afternoon he would do the household bills and write letters. Her father didn't take a drink on Sundays, not even at the golf club. She waited for her father to leave the house, then went to their bedroom.

Her father always brought her mother breakfast before he left to play golf. The maid had all of Sunday off. The family fended for itself without her for one day a week. Every Saturday night and every Sunday night the maid took the long train journey to and from Mabopane in Bophuthatswana where her husband was out of work and where her mother looked after her five children. The maid was her family's breadwinner. And when she was away the van Niekerks let the dust accumulate and filled the sink with dishes and were content in the knowledge that it would all be taken care of on the Monday morning.

Ros told her mother a little of the truth, a fraction.

Ros said that she and her brother had met a pleasant young Englishman. She said that she was sorry that she had stayed out for a whole night the previous week, and offered no explanation. She said that she was owed time from work, and she was going away with the Englishman and her brother for Monday and Monday night and all of Tuesday. She'd laughed, and said she'd be chaperoned by Jan.

When she was her daughter's age, her mother had used to drive with her father through the night to Cape Town, for the weekend, more than one thousand four hundred kilometres each way, and sleep together in a fleapit, before they were even engaged.

She wondered why her daughter bothered to tell her what she was doing, and couldn't for the life of her fathom why the girl was taking that awkward, intense brother with her.

She thought it would do her daughter the world of good to be bedded by a strong young man. Half the daughters of her friends were married at Ros's age, and some of them already divorced. She thought there was something peculiar about her own girl's plain dressing and shunning of make-up.

She slipped out of bed. She slung a cotton dressing gown across her shoulders.

She took Ros to her dressing table and sat her on the stool. She did what she had not been allowed to do for ten years. She took the girl in charge. She changed Ros's hair, lifted it, swept it back and gathered it into a red ribbon. She put on for Ros her own eye make-up and cheek highlight and a gentle pink lipstick. She didn't dare to stop. She could hardly believe she was permitted to make the transformation. She let Ros gaze at herself in the mirror above the dressing table.

She said, 'This young man, he's an immigrant?'

'Just a visitor. He's hoping to go back to England on Wednesday or Thursday.'

Ros saw the flush of her mother's disappointment.

Later, when her mother had gone back to bed, Ros went to her father's desk and took from the bottom drawer the key to the gun cabinet that was bolted to the wall of the spare bedroom. Gingerly she took out a pump action shotgun, a box of cartridges, and her father's two revolvers along with a second box of .38 ammunition. She returned the key before hiding the weapons and ammunition in her bed.

The road was straight and the ground on either side of it was barren waste.

Jan talked, too bloody much. He turned his head and shouted through the visor of his crash helmet, and Jack had to lean towards him to hear anything through the thickness of his own helmet. For Jack it was little short of a miracle that the Suzuki moped was able to carry the two of them. He felt a complete, conspicuous idiot perched on the pillion, squashed into Jan's spare helmet, towering above the kid as they dribbled along at 35 miles an hour.

They were heading for Duduza, some fifty kilometres south-east of Johannesburg.

Staccato bursts of explanation from Jan.

Past mine workings, through small industrial towns, past a

row of empty bungalows deserted because the White staff had left when the mine was exhausted and the homes had been left to the weather and to disintegrate alongside a shanty town for Blacks.

They were on a straight stretch. High grass beside the road. Jan leaned back to shout.

'A White woman was driving past here, couple of years back, before the state of emergency, she was pulled out of her car, killed. It was kids from Duduza did it. Just about here . . .'

Jack remembered what he had seen on the Pretoria road. The picture was clear in his mind.

'At that time the Whites had killed hundreds of Blacks, and Blacks had killed two Whites, but the Fascist law and order lobby went to work. It was vicious what the army and police did in Duduza. Most of the mothers tried to get their boys out, in girl's clothes, get them away and over the border. Just like the class of '76 in Soweto, there is a class of '85 out of Duduza. Those kids, now, they're in ANC schools in Zambia or Tanzania. They'll come back when they're trained. There's no escape for the Boers . . .'

'I don't want a bloody debate,' Jack yelled.

'You'll be in a debate when we get to Duduza.'

'Then it'll keep until we get there.'

Why should anyone help Jack Curwen? Why should anyone in Duduza lift a finger for Jack Curwen? He didn't give a damn for any of their slogans. His only commitment was to his father.

'You know that racism is endemic among Whites?'

'Not my business, Jan.'

Warm air blowing past Jan's helmet, dust skimming from the tinted screen of Jack's visor.

'Take the courts. Take the difference between what they do for ANC fighters, and what they do for the right wing scum of the Kappiecommando or the Afrikaner Weerstand Beweging, that's AWB, pigs. Are you listening, Jack?'

'Jan, shut up, for Christ's sake.'

Jack heard Jan laugh out loud, like he was high.

'Jack, listen . . . If a Black throws a petrol bomb it's terrorism, if it's the White backlash then it's arson. A Black explosion is treason, a White explosion is a damage to property charge. A Black arms cache is plotting to overthrow the state, but if he's White he's done for possession of unlicensed weapons . . . Isn't that racism?'

'I'm not listening to you, Jan.'

'You better make the right noises when we get to Duduza, if you don't want a necklace.'

Jack wondered what the hell the kid was shouting of. He didn't ask. Right now he thought the kid was a pain. He thought that if he hadn't needed the kid he would happily have jumped, walked away from him . . . But he *had* involved Jan van Niekerk, and he *had* involved Ros van Niekerk. He was leading the crippled boy and the office worker girl towards the walls and the guns of Pretoria Central.

'I'm sorry, Jan. You have to forgive me.'

Jan turned his head. Jack saw the wide grin behind the visor screen, and the moped swerved and they nearly went off the road.

'Nothing to forgive. You're giving me the best damned time of my life. You're kicking the Boers in their nuts, and that's nothing to forgive . . .'

The shouting died.

Over Jan's shoulder Jack saw the dark line of the edge of the township. Red and black brick walls behind a fence of rusting cattle wire. Low smudges of dull colour, nothing for the sun to brighten.

Jan had told Jack, before they had started out, that Duduza was the only place where they had the smallest chance of raising his munitions. He was too junior in the Movement to be able to contact senior men at short notice. Part of the protective cover screen, in place to maintain the command chain's security, meant that a junior, a Jan van Niekerk, only responded to anonymous orders in his dead letter drop. Jan had said there was a Black he had once met, at a meeting in Kwa Thema township, a

254

lively happy faced young man with a soft chocolate au lait complexion who had said his name and said where he lived, and been too relaxed and too confident to stay with the ritual of numbered code identifications. Jan had said that the young Black's name was Henry Kenge.

They saw the block on the road into the township.

Four hundred metres ahead of them. Two Casspirs and a yellow police van.

Jan had been very definite, that he hadn't any way of promising that he would find Henry Kenge. Couldn't say whether he was one of the thousand detainees, whether he had fled the country, whether he was dead. Jan had said that trying to trace the man was the only chance he knew of getting weapons by that evening. He had told Jack that it would be many days until he was contacted through the dead letter drop. The Movement would wait with extreme caution to see whether the death of Jacob Thiroko had compromised that part of the Johannesburg structure that had known of the incursion towards Warmbaths. Jan had said that every person who had known of the incursion would be isolated for their own safety, for the safety of those who dealt with them. And they would all sit very tight for a while anyway until it was discovered how Thiroko was betrayed. Jan said he would have to be under suspicion himself, having known of the rendezvous.

The moped slowed. Not for Jack to give advice. For the boy to make up his own mind. Jack's frustration that he was a stranger, without experience, unable to contribute.

The jerk off the tarmac. Jan revved all the power he could drag from the engine. They surged and bumped away across the dirt, away from the road and the police block.

Jack clung to Jan's waist.

The boy shouted, 'Carry yourself well, and for God's sake don't look scared. Scared is guilt to these people. If you see me move, follow me. If we have to get out it'll happen fast. The mood changes, like bloody lightning . . . and this is a hell of a scary place we're going into.'

Jack punched the boy in the ribs.

Away to the right there was the bellow of a loudspeaker from the police block. Jack couldn't hear the words. He thought they were beyond rifle range as they slipped the cordon.

There were holes in the fence. Jan searched for one that was wide enough for the Suzuki and jolted through it.

Jan cut the engine.

A terrible quiet around them, and then a dog barking. No people. Jan pushed his moped. Jack was close behind him. They went forward down a wide street of beaten dirt. Jack thought that Soweto was chic in comparison. He saw overturned and burned cars. He saw a fire-gutted house. He saw the dog, tied by string to a doorpost, angry and straining to get at them.

'Straight roads make it easier for the police and military to dominate. They haven't electricity here, the water's off street taps, but they've good straight roads for the Casspirs.'

Jack hissed, as if frightened of his own voice, 'Where the hell is everybody?'

'A funeral's the only thing that gets everyone out. They've had enough funerals here in the last eighteen months. It's a tough place, it's hot. There's not a Black policeman can live here any more, and the Black quisling councillors are gone. Shit . . .'

Jan pointed. It was a small thing and without having it pointed to him Jack wouldn't have noticed. Jan was pointing to a galvanized bucket, filled with water, in front of a house. Jack thought of it as a house but it was more of a brick and tin shack. He saw the bucket. When he looked up the street he saw there were buckets filled with water in front of each house, each shack, in the wide street.

'Means bad trouble. The water is for the kids to wash the gas out of their faces. If there's going to be trouble everybody leaves water on the street.'

'If you don't put the water out?' Jack asked.

'Then they would be thought of as collaborators and they get the necklace. Hands tied behind their backs, a tyre hung on their shoulders, that's the necklace. They set light to the tyre.'

'Bloody nice revolution you've started.'

'It's hard for these people to touch the police, they haven't a cat in hell's chance of hurting the state. What are they left with, just the chance to hurt the Black servants of the state.'

'So what do we do? Scratch our backsides, then what?'

'We just have to wait.'

It was a huge funeral.

The gathering was illegal. Under the amendment regulations following the state of emergency it was prohibited that mourners should march in formation to open air funeral services. It would have required a battalion of infantry to have prevented the column reaching the grave that had been prepared for the body of a thirteen-year-old girl, knocked over ten days before by a speeding Casspir.

Sometimes the regulations were enforced, sometimes not. Enforcement depended on the will of the senior police officer for the area, and the size of the forces available to him.

On this Sunday the military were not present. The police seemed to have stayed back and watched from a distance as the migrant ant mass of men and women and children took the small white wood coffin to the cemetery.

An orderly march to the grave. Hating faces, but controlled. The young men who had charge let the priest have his say, and they allowed the bereaved family to get clear in an old Morris car, and they gave time for the old men and the women and the small children to start back towards the township.

There was organization of a sort in what happened afterwards.

A single police jeep was out in front of the main force, there to overlook and photograph. A shambling charge at the jeep, and the driver had lost his gears, and lost time, and the men who guarded the photographer and his long lens had fired volleys of bird shot and gas to keep the running, stoning crowd at a distance.

The driver of the jeep never found his gears. The crowd surged on, vengeance within reach. The police ditched the jeep, left it with the engine howling, ran for their lives. Good and fit, the policemen, and running hard because they knew the alternative to running fast, knew what happened to policemen who were caught by a funeral mob. The photographer didn't run fast, not as fast as he had to run. The lens bouncing awkwardly from his stomach, and the camera bag on his shoulder, and none of the policemen with guns taking the time to cover him.

The officers commanding the police were still shouting their orders when the fleetest of the mob caught up with the photographer. The photographer was White and a year and a half short of his fiftieth birthday. A growl in the mob, the breath intake of a mad dog.

The hacking crack of rifle fire, aimed at random into the crowd at 400 metres. The crowd of youths not caring because the photographer was caught.

The Casspirs came forward, and the kids fled before them, back towards the township.

The photographer was naked but for one shoe and his socks and the camera with the long lens that lay on his belly. His clothes had been taken from him as vultures take meat from bones. He was dead. An autopsy would in due course state how many knife wounds he had received, how many stone bruises.

The start of a routine township battle. An hour of unrest.

Shotguns and rifles and tear gas grenades from behind the armour plate of the high built Casspirs. Petrol bombs and rocks from the kids. Pretty unremarkable happenings for the East Rand.

The police saw the kids back into the warren streets of Duduza and left them to their destruction. Eighteen months after the start of the petrol bombing and the rock throwing against the Black policemen's homes and councillors' homes there was little left for the crowd that was worth burning.

Two shops were destroyed by fire. The days were long since gone when the elderly would try to prevent the kids burning a shop out. To have tried to have saved a shop from the fire was to have invited the accusation of collaborator. Two shops burned.

Four kids died. Eighteen kids were treated for buck shot injuries in Duduza's unregistered clinic. No chance of them going to hospital.

A thirteen-year-old girl had been successfully buried.

Sunday afternoon in Duduza, and time to bring the buckets indoors.

His eyes were red rimmed.

He sat on a wooden chair in a small room.

Faces peered at him through the cracked glass of the window. Jack looked straight ahead, looked all the time at the man who had been introduced as Henry Kenge, and at Jan.

He dabbed his eyes with his water-soaked handkerchief, and each time he did it he heard the pitter patter of laughter from all around him.

He had made his speech. He had asked for help. He had been heard out. He had been vague and unspecific until Jan had waved him quiet, taken over and whispered urgently a statement of intent in the ear of the one identified as Kenge.

He was filthy from the ditch he had lain in as the Casspirs had rumbled down the main street. With Jan in the bottom of a ditch that doubled as a street sewer.

He thought that if the youngsters he had seen that afternoon had been Black kids on the streets of London or Birmingham or Liverpool then he would have rated them as mindless and vicious hooligans. He thought the kids of Duduza were the bravest he had ever known. So what was the morality of that? Fuck the morality, Jack thought.

Kenge brought Jan a holdall. Jan passed the bag to Jack. He counted five RG-42 grenades.

Jack tugged at Jan's sleeve. 'This shouldn't be in bloody public.'

'The necklace has made ashes of informers, they're scrubbed out of Duduza. The eyes of the security police have been put out with fire, that's why they're losing . . . They have a song about you. They don't know who you are, but they have a song in praise of you. They made a song about the man who carried the bomb into John Vorster Square.'

Jack shook his head, like he'd been slapped. 'You told them about that?'

'You've been given half of this township's armoury. You grovel your thanks to them.'

When they left they could see the lights of the roadblock vehicles. Jan kept his own headlight off and drove cross-country in a loop taking them well clear of the block. For a short time a searchlight tried to find the source of the engine sound in the darkness, and they stopped in shadow until it lit upon some other threat, and then rode on.

Jack thought he was pretty damn fortunate to have the grenades. He appreciated that after Thiroko was killed Jan would be isolated from the Movement. That's what any Movement would do. He pounded Jan's back, in gratitude, in relief to be out of Duduza.

Ros was at the flat in Hillbrow. She showed Jack what she had brought. Only after he had seen and handled the pump action shotgun and the two revolvers and the ammunition did Jack realize that she had changed herself.

He thought Ros van Niekerk was quite lovely.

He had 15 pounds of explosives and detonators and firing fuse and five grenades and a shotgun and two revolvers. And he had a crippled student to help him, and a girl who worked in an insurance office and who was lovely.

No going back, but then there had never been a time for going back.

16

A crisp, bright, autumn morning over the flat veld, the diamond frost going with the sunlight.

Monday morning. Another week. One more used up.

Jack had dismantled the model. He had returned the pieces to
the bread bin.

In a corner of the yard at the back of the block of flats he
discarded one of the two metal tubes. He had explosive
enough for one tube only. He had to go out the way that he
went in.

Jan carried the suitcase to the car. Ros had the shotgun,
broken and carried under an overcoat, and the two revolvers.
Jack brought the tube.

Jack had told them he needed a stop on the way for a bag of
readymix concrete. He said that he would sit in the back of the
car, that he needed to think. He sat in the back of the car and
concentrated on an approach from the south side over Magazine
Hill, and diversions on the north side near the guarded perim-
eters of Defence Headquarters.

They could rent a service flat in Pretoria, Ros said. It wouldn't
be difficult to find one, but it would be expensive. Jack passed
her a wad of rand notes. He slipped back to his thinking.

How much could he ask of them, of Jan and Ros?

The principal hotels were tried first.

Two detectives, with the two original photo-fits and also with
a third photo-fit that was an amalgam of the shopkeepers' opin-
ions, were briefed to visit the city's four and five star hotels.
Other teams were directed towards the two and three star hotels,

the booking offices of South African Airways, of the European airlines, and to Jan Smuts.

Every one of them worked from John Vorster Square, had been violated by the bomb. The two with the four and five star list appreciated that the hotels worked shift systems of reception and porter staff. They knew that if they drew blanks with this visit that they must come back to interview those staff who were not on duty that Monday morning.

At the Landdrost, first visit, the detective found the Indian day porter on duty. He left his colleague with the brunette on reception, poring over the composite photo-fit. She had known the face. The detective showed the day porter the photo-fits.

The day porter recalled the features. He had quite liked the man. He'd had a good tip for arranging the visit to Soweto, and another tip when the man had checked out. He nodded his head. He understood that the detective was from the security police. And if it was the security police then it was not pilfering or the fraudulent use of a credit card, it was sedition or terrorism. Heavily, the day porter nodded. He wrote a room number on a slip of paper and pushed it across his desk to the detective. He was asked whether he knew the man's name.

'His name was Mr Curwen.'

'*Was?*'

'The middle of last week he left, sir.'

The day porter was in work. Not big pay but the tips were good. He'd remembered this man, for courtesy and for a warm word of thanks when the man had gone, carrying his own suitcase out, he hadn't forgotten that. It hurt the day porter to implicate the young Englishman.

The detective went to the cashier's desk. With the name and the room number it took only half a minute for him to be given a copy of the bill, and the dates of the guest's stay.

Soon afterwards a watch salesman from Port Elizabeth, sleeping in late with a Coloured call girl, was disturbed in his room. They were given two minutes to get their clothes on.

The salesman was in the corridor zipping his trousers, his

100 rand companion was beside him buttoning her blouse, as the dog was unleashed in the room. The salesman, in increasing desperation, tried without success to discover why his room was being searched. The detectives stayed in the corridor and gave him no satisfaction. Just the handler and his small black labrador dog in the room.

The dog explored the bed, and the drawers of the bedside tables, no reaction. It covered the desk beside the window, and the drawers there. It went past the television set. The cold nose flitted over the dressing table. The dog and the handler had made a slow circuit of the room when they reached the wardrobe in the corner opposite the bathroom door.

The dog snorted.

It had been trained over months to recognize the scent of minute traces of explosive. The dog had no skill at tracking a man, nor at finding hard or soft drugs in luggage. It was an explosive sniffer dog. The dog pawed at the wardrobe door, scratched at the varnish finish. The handler slid open the door. The dog sniffed hard into the bottom corner of the wardrobe, then up to the inside of the door. The dog barked, the tail going, then came out of the wardrobe and sat, and the handler gave it a biscuit.

'There were explosives in this cupboard,' the handler told the detectives. 'My guess would be that the suspect had traces on his hands from handling the explosives when he closed the cupboard door. The dog has found the traces inside only, but the outside would have been cleaned by the maid staff. But there's no doubt, there were explosives very recently in this room.'

He had the name of Jack Curwen. He had an address in the Surrey town of Leatherhead. He had a date of arrival in South Africa.

The colonel dictated his telex.

He had forensic confirmation that the explosive traces found on the inside of the wardrobe door matched the types of plaster gelignite most generally issued by the Soviets to the military wing of the ANC.

By choice he was an overworked man. He drew to his own desk as many strands of investigation as it was possible for him to gather in.

He missed a link.

He did not marry the information he now possessed with the report sent from London by Major Swart before the John Vorster Square bomb, which had been circulated to the colonel by Pretoria.

The colonel had so much to concern himself with, it was understandable, only human, that he missed the link.

The telex had been transformed from a jumble of numbers to a demand for immediate information. The telex lay on the desk of Major Swart.

Major Swart's office was deserted. The telex was placed on the untenanted desk.

Halfway through that Monday morning.

There had been a short hail shower. The forecast was for rain later.

Major Swart thought it a dismal occasion. A burial service without dignity. But then Arkwright had been a pathetic creature.

It was an hour's drive out of London for Major Swart. Piet had brought him down the M4 to the village beyond Reading.

They were dressed for the part, the major and his warrant officer.

The major was unshaven and in jeans with an old donkey coat on his shoulders. The warrant officer had chosen denims with a Campaign for Nuclear Disarmament logo on the back of his jacket. The major had thought there would be a better turn-out. It was the last chance perhaps to get a tail on the young man introduced by Arkwright to Jacob Thiroko. And the bastard hadn't shown. He could have saved his time.

He recognized faces from Anti-Apartheid. No-one that was special. A few kids out of the secretaries' pool, a man who made

264

speeches at the really bum meetings when the seniors didn't want to know. He saw Arkwright's parents, country people, and they looked as embarrassed at the contingent from London as they were by the attendance of Arkwright's wife's people whose Jaguar was a flashy intrusion in the lane outside the church.

The group was around the open grave. He could hear the vicar's voice, as sonorous as the clouds. He and Piet were standing back, amongst the old headstones.

'Pleasant surprise to see you here, Major Swart.'

He turned fast. He didn't know the man who had come silently over the wet grass to stand behind him. A big man, wearing a good overcoat.

'Detective Inspector Cooper, Major Swart. Didn't expect you'd be out and about to offer your condolences at the death of an Anti-Apartheid activist.'

The anger was crimson on the major's cheeks.

'I'd have thought the embassy could have done better on the clothing allowance, Major Swart.'

Swart saw the amusement on the detective inspector's face. 'There is no regulation restricting the travel of South African diplomats inside the United Kingdom.'

The detective inspector looked him over, with mocking enjoyment. 'None at all, Major. Going on afterwards to the family for a drink and a sandwich, are we?'

'Go and fuck yourself,' Major Swart said.

'Nice language for a cemetery, Major, very choice. I doubt you'll tell me why you're here, but I'll tell you why I'm here. Our investigations tell us that Douglas Arkwright was followed out of a public house on the night of his death. It is our belief that he was attacked as he walked home. Some of his injuries were consistent with a kicking. Stroke of luck for us, really, but when he went under the bus only his head and shoulders were hit by the tyres, that's how we can say for sure what were other injuries he had very recently sustained. It is our belief that Arkwright was running away from his assailants when he fell under the bus. Wouldn't be murder, of course, manslaughter would be the charge. You'd know about that, Major Swart, you being a policeman back home. Any ideas on who would be interested in roughing up a creep like Douglas Arkwright?'

'Any time you want advice on how to police your inner cities, just telephone me, Inspector.'

'The National Theatre could give you a hand with your costume, Major. And you, Warrant Officer. It is Warrant Officer Piet Kaiser, isn't it? I thought so. Ask for the wardrobe mistress at the stage door. Very helpful folk.'

The major walked away, his warrant officer close behind him. He didn't look back. He presumed the man was Special Branch.

They drove off, crashing through the gears, causing the vicar to pause in mid flow.

Major Swart and Warrant Officer Kaiser stopped at a pub on the Thames and didn't leave before closing time.

It would be late afternoon before he found the telex on his desk that required immediate attention.

The funeral of James Sandham, held by coincidence that same Monday morning, was an altogether grander affair. The Foreign and Commonwealth Office saw to the arrangements. The Personnel Department had booked a chapel of rest, and the official fleet of cars, and the crematorium, and enough flowers to make Sandham seem to have been a loved and respected colleague.

His former wife had married again, and successfully, and was able to afford a clinging black frock that set her off well against the men from the FCO. She was allocated the front row in the crematorium chapel, never whimpered, never produced a handkerchief. The PUS was behind her, and sitting alongside him was Peter Furneaux, head of the late Jimmy Sandham's section.

They didn't speak, the PUS and Peter Furneaux, until after the curtains had closed on the coffin, and the taped organ music had come to a stop. As the mourners scraped to their feet and followed the former Mrs Sandham to the door and into a light shower of rain, Furneaux said, 'I wonder if I could have a word with you, sir.'

'I've lunch out of town, I am afraid, then the Cabinet Office, so I haven't a lot of time.'

'It's quite pressing, sir.'

'Let's walk a bit.'

There was a garden around the crematorium, trimmed lawns with staked trees and ordered borders.

'Well, Peter, let's have it.'

'This fellow, Carew, sir, that's going to hang in South Africa . . .'

'Thursday, right?'

'I know that Carew is an alias. I know that his true name is Curwen . . .'

'Classified, Peter, in the interests of national security.'

'Shortly before James Sandham died, a young man came to FCO. His name was Jack Curwen. He said that James Carew was his father. I saw him, and Jimmy Sandham was with me . . .'

'Was he now?' the PUS mouthed softly.

'Then Sandham disappeared, then he was dead. So we move on . . . I have regular reports coming in from Pretoria, the run-of-the-mill embassy material, and I have a note on Carew. Last Friday I get a confirmation that Carew will definitely hang this Thursday. No more speculation. Finish. He's going to hang . . . This Jack Curwen, he was a stroppy fellow but he was decent. He told me to my face that I was washing my hands of his father and I wasn't pleased at being told that, but in his position I reckon I'd have said the same, so I thought he deserved a call. He'd left his numbers. On Friday evening I rang the home number . . .'

Furneaux saw a thoughtful, concerned face, he saw a gathering frown. Behind them the cars were pulling away. Another line of vehicles waited at the gates for the next cremation.

'I rang the home number. I think the phone was answered by Curwen's mother, who was first married to Carew. I told her what I knew, delicately, and then asked for her son. She put the phone down on me. I wanted to speak to the boy himself so this morning, before coming down here, I rang the office number that he'd left with us. He wasn't there. Young Curwen had taken abrupt leave. I spoke to his employer, I was told it was a very sudden departure.'

'You're taking, Peter, a long time getting to the point.'

'I asked the nature of young Curwen's employment. The firm he works for is called Demolition and Clearance. Curwen drums up business for the sort of work that required demolition by explosives . . .'

'The point, please, Peter.'

'It's conjecture, of course . . . I would hazard that Curwen has flown to South Africa. That blast at police headquarters in Johannesburg, our people report that the rumour in security circles is that a White with an English accent planted the bomb. I would further hazard that Curwen, having launched one attack, is going to make something of a noise at around the time his father hangs . . .'

'Thank you, Peter. You're going by train, I'll drop you at the station.'

They walked to the PUS's official car, the doors were opened for them by the chauffeur.

'There wasn't anything strange about Sandham's death, was there, sir?'

'What sort of strange, Peter?'

'He'd no more go mountain climbing than I would, sir.'

'You never can tell, can you, with people?'

The PUS asked the chauffeur to find the nearest underground station. They drove away.

'It's my duty to tell you, sir . . .' Furneaux was muttering, difficult ground. '. . . there's been a fair amount of disquiet on the desk. So far out of character that he should be mountain climbing. He spoke to no-one about taking leave. It's caused quite a bit of anxiety on the desk, and I thought you should know that, sir.'

'As head of department, you'll want to discourage idle speculation.'

'Yes, sir.'

Lighting a cigarette, the PUS said, 'Thank you, Peter, for your guessing game about Carew's boy. If it needs to be taken further I'll handle it. You don't have to concern yourself with the matter. By the by, Peter, you probably heard that there's going to be a gap in Nairobi. Needs a most responsible and sensitive man to fill it. Quite a posting for a youngish man, don't you think, eh, Peter?'

They shook hands, the PUS smiled a watery smile. Furneaux went down into the underground and bought a ticket. He shrugged. Every man had a price. And he was not much of a mountaineer himself.

The Director General scraped with a match at the mess in the stem of his pipe, and listened.

'Let me give you a scenario. Young Curwen has gone to South Africa, unconfirmed, but possible, and you will check it at once. Through his work he is familiar with explosives, that we know. A bomb goes off in Johannesburg and is rumoured to have been planted by a White. For the sake of our scenario let us assume that James Carew is to hang on Thursday, at the moment intending to take his secret to his grave, and let us assume that young Curwen is arrested in the hours remaining before the execution. What chance *then*, if they put the screws on him, so to say, that Carew would remain silent?'

The PUS had cut short his lunch and driven to Century House for the meeting. Still the Director General said nothing.

'Or the related scenario: Carew hangs and Curwen is subsequently arrested. How much does the boy know? He met Sandham; Sandham knew only so much and probably hadn't told him. Would the boy talk?'

'Probably.'

'I believe it is back to Downing Street, Director General.'

'For what earthly reason?'

The Director General filled his pipe. It was a mechanical action. His eyes were never on the bowl, but none of the tobacco fibres fell to the polished surface of his desk.

'I don't intend to finish *my* career in an exposé on the front page of Sunday's newspapers. Never forget, Director General, our job is to advise and to execute. The politicians are paid to make decisions, whatever a ham-fisted job they make of it. Keep this one in the dark and I reckon we'll get swamped by home-flying chickens. Lay it all before them and we safeguard ourselves and possibly them too. I'll fix an appointment for early evening.'

'If the Prime Minister's schedule permits.'

'No problem. Any Prime Minister I've worked with would meet one in a dressing gown at four in the morning if the matter under consideration involves an intelligence foul-up.'

When the PUS had gone, the Director General called in his personal assistant and named a man who was to be called to his office immediately.

Major Swart read the telex.

They'd had to stop once at a service station on the way back to London. Heavy stuff, English beer. He read the telex, then went back to his private lavatory, and back again to the telex.

Shit, and he was half-cut. He was never at his best after he had drunk at lunchtime.

He knew the name of Curwen. Checked it out, hadn't he, days before. Checked and found that Mrs Hilda Perry had been married to a James Curwen. Thought he'd cracked the connection between James Carew and Hilda Perry. Had it all sewn up until he had taken the photograph of James Carew to the village in Hampshire and been told four times that the photograph was not that of James Curwen. From Somerset House he knew there was a son of the marriage between Hilda Perry and James Curwen, he knew from those same records that the son had been christened Jack.

Johannesburg wanted information on a Jack Curwen. They wanted background, and they wanted confirmation of a photo-fit likeness.

Major Swart could have sent off an answer straightaway . . . But he wanted to piss again . . . He reckoned he could have established the link between Jack Curwen and Hilda Perry and a letter written from Pretoria Central by James Carew.

With too much beer inside him, and a foul temper still from the encounter at the funeral, he chose a different course.

He would first stitch the matter, then he would send his message.

He would stitch it so tight that there were no call backs, no demands for follow-up information.

He rang Erik. Yes, the bloody man had replaced his bloody television set. Yes, Erik would be at the embassy within forty-five minutes. He shouted down the corridor to Piet that if he had plans, life or death, for the late evening then he should bloody well forget them.

And then hastily back to his private lavatory, fumbling with his private key, to leak.

He came heavily down the staircase. A beautiful staircase, oak, probably Jacobean, he thought.

The hostility swarmed from the short, slight woman. The hostility was in the wrinkle lines at her throat, and in the flash of her eyes, and the curl of a tired mouth.

'I hope you're satisfied. I hope you understand why he couldn't come to London to see you.'

Mrs Fordham had told the Director General over the telephone that the colonel was ill and could not take a train to London. He hadn't believed her.

They stood in the panelled hallway. He thought the house and its interior were magnificent. Perhaps she read him.

'It was all my money, my family's money. The colonel wasn't interested in material reward, all he cared about was the Service. The Service was his life. And how did the Service repay his dedication? There wasn't even a party for him. More than two decades of work and the Service simply discarded him. We've had just one visit from the Service since he was thrown out, and that was some grubby little man who came here to see that there weren't any classified documents in the house.'

271

The Director General was still shaken by the sight of the shell of the man he had just seen in the large bedroom. Colonel Fordham, curled in a wheelchair near the window, unable to move and unable to speak, had kicked the fight from the Director General.

'It's a great shame, Mrs Fordham, that you didn't feel able to alert us . . .'

'I wouldn't have had your people in the house.'

They moved towards the front door. No way he was going to be offered a cup of tea. Of course they had retired the crass old fool, and years too late at that. A dinosaur, really, who believed the Service was still packing off agents to suborn the Bolshevik revolution or to run around the hillsides of Afghanistan.

'I came to ask for specific information.'

'Then you wasted your journey.'

'There was one man who was very close to your husband.'

'I'm not a part of the Service, and at this time of the afternoon I have to bath Basil.'

She dared him to stay. The Director General smiled. He fell back on his rarely used reservoir of charm. Outside his chauffeur and his bodyguard would be waiting for him, enjoying the thermos and a smoke. God, and he'd be glad to be back with them.

'The man who was close to your husband was called James Curwen. I understand he went by the nickname of "Jeez". I need your help, Mrs Fordham.'

He saw the same short slight woman, but hurt. He saw her fingers make a tight fist, loosen, grip again.

'That's what did it to him,' her voice quavered. 'It wasn't long after he'd been dismissed.'

'He read of the arrest in the papers?'

'He'd read *The Times*. He didn't finish his breakfast that morning. He walked out into the garden. It was about twenty minutes later that I went looking for him. He'd just collapsed, the dogs were with him. What you've just seen, he's been like that ever since.'

'You didn't tell us.'

'After what you'd done to him?'

'You knew Curwen?'

She shrugged. 'He lived here when he came back from Albania, before he went to South Africa. He was a sort of batman to Basil, and he did jobs in the house and he drove the car and did things outside.'

The Director General had to mask his disgust. The man had done ten years in an Albanian prison camp, and had come back to be patronized as a loyal serf. Lost his marriage and lost ten years of his life, but the kindly old colonel and his lady let him drive the car and change the fuses and make a rockery in the garden.

A desperation in her face. 'Why haven't you brought Jeez out?'

'I am afraid it may not be in our power to save him.'

'But you're trying?'

'Certainly we're trying,' the Director General said. 'Tell me about him.'

'He's a wonderful man. He came back here, after the awfulness of what he'd been through, and he just seemed to put it behind him. I'd known him before, when he was a well built, strong man, and when he came back he was a skeleton, unrecognizable. Never a complaint, not in any way bitter. His attitude seemed to be that since he'd been sent into Albania by the Service his mission must have been justified, that it was simply the rub of the green that he had been caught. He had a marvellous stoicism, I think that kept him going. Sometimes, not often, he would talk about the bad times in the camp, when men from his hut were taken out and shot, when his companions died of malnutrition, when the camp guards were particularly brutal, when it was cold and there was no heating. When he talked about it there was always his humour, very dry. He was honoured to be a part of the Service, just as Basil was. The Service was Jeez's life, just as it was Basil's. Is that what you want to hear?'

'How resolute would he be, in his present situation?'

'You'd want to know whether he'd betray you, to save his neck?'

'That's very bluntly put, Mrs Fordham.'

'It is insulting to Jeez that you even think of asking me the question. I just pray to God and thank Him that Basil cannot know what Jeez is going through now.'

'It must be a very painful time for you, Mrs Fordham.'

'His wife came here ... God, I'm going back, more than twenty years ago. We were entertaining, a weekend lunch party. The poor woman came here to try and find out something about where Jeez was, what he'd done. He said afterwards to me that it was one of the worst days of his life, having to lie to her, telling her to put her husband out of her mind. Jeez understood. When he was down here Basil was very frank with him. He had to tell him that the marriage was just a casualty of life with the Service. He told Jeez that his wife had got a divorce and remarried, that it would be wrong of him to disturb her, that he should try not to make contact with his son, however hard that was going to be. Jeez always did what Basil said. Just before he went to South Africa, Jeez went up to London and he must have gone out to where his wife and his son were living in their new home. I think he saw her bringing the boy home from school. Jeez was quite bouncy at supper that evening, as if his mind was at rest.

'The Service did all that to the man, and now you're going to let him hang. Now all you care about it is whether *he'll* talk, whether *you'll* be sacked as a consequence. You disgust me ...'

The Director General turned to the door.

'... I hope he talks. I hope he shouts his head off and destroys the lot of you, just as you destroyed Basil.'

He let himself out.

He left her to bath her husband.

The man who had been a friend of Jimmy Sandham found a telephone kiosk in the centre of Leatherhead and rang in to Century.

Villiers had been helpful, he reported. He had posed as a policeman. He had said it often enough, that Curwen wasn't in trouble. He carried identification as a policeman; he rarely used the polaroid card but it was always with him. He had been told by the Director General that he must call in as soon as he had completed his interview. He knew on the grapevine that the big man was for Downing Street that evening.

When he had dictated his preliminary report, he mentioned to the personal assistant that he had been given the name of a fellow that Curwen often worked with, and the address. He said he'd get himself down there. He said that he'd telephone back in if anything worthwhile came up.

Major Swart drove an old Fiesta out of London. It was one of four cars available to him for clandestine work, and the least prepossessing of them in terms of the bodywork, but the engine was finely tuned. It was a slow journey, appalling traffic.

Erik sat beside the major. Piet shared the back seat with the canvas bag into which had been put the tools for the evening's work.

In the bag, along with the jemmy bar and the screwdrivers, were two balaclavas and two pairs of plastic gloves.

'I won't tell you anything,' Hawkins said.

'Then you lose your licence as a blaster. Pity, that.'

'Threats won't change me.'

'Not a threat, Mr Hawkins, a promise, and I always keep promises. Anyway you've told me plenty.'

'I've told you nothing.'

He thought the place stank. He thought it was pitiful that a man should live in such conditions. Everything he saw was filthy, every surface was grimed. There was a cat mess under his chair. But he believed the old blaster. Threats wouldn't change him.

'I know he's your friend. If he wasn't your friend then you wouldn't be covering for him. I know he's in South Africa . . .'

He watched the old man closely. Hawkins looked away, picked his nose, but his eyes didn't come back. That was good enough, Curwen was in South Africa, confirmation.

'I know that you told him how to build the bomb that he carried into John Vorster Square police station. In the trade, I gather, it's called the La Mon Mark One. I don't think Curwen could have made that bomb without expert help.'

'I won't tell you nothing.'

'But he didn't go there just to blow a hole in a police station . . . What did he go there for, George?'

'Nothing.'

'If John Vorster Square which is the most important police station in the country was just for starters, then he's aiming to follow it with something that's hells big. You following me, George?'

'Bugger off.'

'I've just been cremating a friend of mine today, George. He was an awkward sod, but he was my friend. I told my friend about Jack's father, my friend told Jack . . . I'll deny I ever told you that . . . It was my friend that told Jack the truth about his father. I expect Jack told you what the truth was.'

No denial.

'Let me get back to where I was before. If it's something big, then it stands to reason that it's dangerous. You with me, George?'

Hawkins was with him. The old blaster was on the edge of his chair, hanging on the words.

'He must have been pretty lucky not to have got himself killed at John Vorster Square.'

Hawkins bit. 'Your friend that died, what happened to him?'

'Murdered . . . But that's not what I'm here for. I have to know the boy's next target. If I'm to help him I have to know.'

'How can you help him?'

'Where I work we're like the priest's confessional. We're not interested in names, we don't care where the information comes from . . . This isn't a conversation that ever happened . . . I can't tell you how we can help him. You have to believe me that it makes it easier for us to help the boy if we know what he's at.'

'You're too late in the day to come bellyaching about help. You're talking shit, it's your lot that pissed on Jack's father.'

'What's he going to do, George?'

'What would you do if it was your father?'

The gamble, the big throw. 'Take him out.'

Hawkins gazed down at the torn linoleum. Over his yellowed teeth his lips were tight closed.

'I'd try to take him out of Pretoria Central gaol, and I'd think I might know how to set about that because I'd talked to an explosives expert called George Hawkins.'

'He's on the minimum. He's no chance.'

'What sort of minimum, George?'

'Gelignite. He hasn't an ounce of margin.'

'That's tough on the boy.'

Hawkins said, 'If you betray him then it'll go with you for the rest of your life. There'll be the time, the hour before your death, when you'll be bloody sorry you betrayed him. You'll cry for his forgiveness. So help me, Christ, and you won't deserve to be heard.'

'That's well put, George.'

'I'm thought to be a hard, mean bugger. I cried when the lad went.'

'Because he's going to try to blow his way into Pretoria Central, and take his father out.'

'I'd be proud to call Jack Curwen my son.'

The light was gone, the room in shadow. The man left Hawkins sitting in his chair. He could no longer clearly see the old blaster's face. He understood how Curwen had won over Jimmy Sandham, just as he had won over a hard, mean bugger who was an expert in explosives.

There was a light on in the hall of Sam Perry's house. The rest of the house was darkened.

Erik and Piet listened a long time at the back door before they were certain the house was empty. The major had told them there was no dog, he was sure of that from when he'd called. No alarm box on the outside walls.

They taped adhesive paper over the glass panel of the kitchen door, broke it, were able to reach inside and turn the key. It was better going in the back, always gave one a head start if the householder returned to the front door and could be heard messing for the key. The major had said they should take their time, so long as they weren't disturbed. It was a great bonus that they hadn't had to wait until the small hours to break in, hadn't had to wait until the householders were in bed and asleep.

Erik and Piet were experienced burglars. They'd seen the real thing frequently enough when they were young policemen, before their transfers to security.

They knew what they were looking for.

Three streets away, Major Swart dozed in his car, head back, snoring.

The friend of the late Jimmy Sandham stopped his car at the barrier across the entrance to Downing Street. He showed his identification. He was waved forward to park.

Inside the hushed, well-lit hallway, he asked to see his Director General.

17

The Prime Minister was irritable. The Prime Minister had that day coped with hospital funding, the price per barrel of crude oil, diplomatic manoeuvres on Falklands sovereignty, unemployment statistics, and security at the GCHQ Far East listening post. He had had lunch with the Venezuelan ambassador. Finally questions in the House. When the Carew meeting was over there was scheduled a key note policy speech that would be carried on the late evening news broadcasts.

'It is purely conjecture that the son of James Carew has carried out a criminal and terrorist attack on the territory of South Africa,' the Prime Minister said. 'And I'm not going to give you a decision based on conjecture.'

'Rather more than conjecture,' the PUS remarked quietly. 'And conjecture or no, we still have to finalize a position in view of what can be regarded as changed circumstances.'

'Carew hangs on Thursday, what has changed?'

The Director General said, 'Prime Minister, we believe that Carew's son is aware of his father's true position, that his father was an employee of the Service, that is what has changed. Further, we believe that if he were arrested by the South African security police he would very probably give them that information. We also believe that if Carew were to know, before his execution, that his son had been killed or arrested, then *he* might divulge what he has so far withheld. On two fronts we confront a new danger.'

'Very well . . . what do you recommend I do?'

The PUS ducked his shoulders. The Director General was reaching for his pipe.

'Silence all around me . . . ?'

The Prime Minister smiled, mocked them.

'. . . Not normally so reticent, gentlemen. It's surely clear that we find ourselves with two choices of action, both unacceptable. I suggest we hold onto our seats, and trust that nothing happens.'

'Shifting ground is a poor foundation for trust, Prime Minister,' the PUS said.

'This afternoon, Prime Minister, we confirmed that Jack Curwen did indeed fly to South Africa shortly before the police station bombing took place,' the Director General said. 'Also that in his work for a demolition company he had acquired a knowledge of explosives. In my opinion, something *will* happen.'

'This young man, can he be stopped?'

'By calling in the ambassador and putting all our cards on the table . . .,' the Director General said.

'In the present state of our relations with the government of South Africa that would be intolerable.'

'Then as you put it, Prime Minister, we hold onto our seats and hope that we have anticipated only the blacker prospects.'

There was a light tap at the door.

The Prime Minister shifted in annoyance at the interruption.

A secretary came in, glided past the Prime Minister with a grimace of apology. The secretary spoke in the Director General's ear. He gestured his excuses and followed her from the room.

The Prime Minister reached for a worn leather case, as if to indicate that the meeting was concluded.

'If only a few small bombs are thrown at police stations, we can weather that, I believe.'

'I thought you'd like to be kept fully informed, Prime Minister.'

The PUS pushed himself up from his chair.

The Director General stood in the doorway. There was a man behind him, a creased raincoat, hair that hadn't been combed. The Director General ushered him into the room.

'Just tell the Prime Minister what you've told me, what you understand to be Jack Curwen's objective.'

The man who had been a friend to Jimmy Sandham looked around him.

It was a moment to savour.

He spoke drably, without expression, flat monotone. 'It is Mr Curwen's intention, apparently, without anyone else's help, to blast his way, using a home-made device, through the walls of the hanging section of Pretoria Central prison to his father's cell. This with a view to taking his father out.'

There was an aching silence in the room.

The Director General nudged his man away through the door, and closed it. The PUS whistled his astonishment. The Director General was stony-faced.

The Prime Minister's head swayed, right to left, left to right, slow movement, bemused.

'God help us, Director General, let's call the meeting to a halt before you spring any more surprises on us. I'm going to camp in the air-raid shelter for the next five nights and pray. Either that he makes it out safely with his father, or that they're both killed, with their lips sealed. Given the choice, which do you think the good Lord would wish me to pray for?'

Sam Perry had thought it a good notion to take his wife to the golf club social.

She'd lost nearly a stone in weight in the days since Jack had left for South Africa. She was gaunt, and moping through the house each day. She knew most of the wives at the club and he'd thought it would be best for her to be out, not sitting in the house and knitting and unpicking what she'd knitted. He'd taken to coming home for his lunch because then they had a chance to talk it through without young Will being there. They made a show for the youngster when he came rattling in from school in the late afternoon, but the child must have known from his mother's appearance that crisis touched his family. They talked in the middle of the day, but there was nothing to talk about. Her first husband was going to hang, her son was in danger and beyond her reach, and Sam Perry could only say that they had to live with it, live in hope.

On any other evening at the golf club she would have sailed into the drinking, shouting crowd, confident, happy among friends. Not on this evening. She was by his side from the moment they went through the doors and into the bar. As if she were frightened to be more than a yard from him. While he put away four gins she sipped at two tomato juices, and every ten minutes she looked at her watch.

It hadn't worked out. He wondered if it would be better when it was over, when Jeez was dead and buried, when Jack had been . . . when Jack had come home. He thought it would be a bloody long convalescence. It was a swine of a thought for Sam Perry, that she might never recover, might never regain her fun and the gaiety that he loved in her.

He knew she had made an effort to come out with him. He realized she couldn't last long that evening. He saw the pleading in her eyes, he started to make their excuses and shake hands. As soon as was decently possible. He thought of the tittle-tattle that would follow their backs out of the room. There'd be a few of them who'd get a laugh out of speculating on the problems of Sam and Hilda Perry.

It was still too early to pick up Will from Scouts.

They'd go home first . . . He heard the strong sigh of relief from Hilda when they were in the car park and clear of the raucous celebration of the bar.

A mile to their home.

Sam Perry drove slowly. He let his left hand rest on her arm, moved it only to change gear.

He turned into Churchill Close. He could hear her crying, very faintly.

'Don't hurt yourself, love,' he said. 'You couldn't have stopped Jack going.'

He looked at her. He was going to kiss her cheek. He saw her startled, staring eyes. She was peering through the windscreen and at their home at the end of the cul-de-sac. He saw what she had seen. They always drew shut their front bedroom curtains when they went out in the evening, nice curtains but not heavy curtains.

He saw the traverse of the torch beam.

Sam Perry braked. He backed away to the end of the road. He drove fast to the police station.

To the two constables the Ford Fiesta was an obvious target of interest. It was far from commonplace for an old car to be parked in the shadows between the extremities of the street lights in this sedate suburb. Via their radio link the constables had heard that two men had been arrested following a forcible entry to a property in Churchill Close. They had heard that four officers had used truncheons to subdue the intruders. They had heard that no getaway vehicle had been found in Churchill Close. They had heard that the arrested men's accents were thought to be South African. Two streets away the Fiesta and the man sleeping behind the wheel were worth a check. It was smoothly done. Door opened, keys out of the ignition before the man had tumbled awake. Major Swart was escorted to the police station.

'Twice in one day, Major Swart. Extraordinary.'

Detective Inspector Cooper thought the sullen silence of the South African amply repaid the hassle of being called out from home, of having to drive from north London into Surrey.

'There's ways for foreigners to behave in our country, Major Swart, and there are ways that are outside the tramlines. Sitting in the getaway while your muckers are managing a spot of larceny is right outside the lines.'

Three South Africans held while in pursuance of a crime was sufficient reason for a call to be made from Surrey Constabulary HQ to the Scotland Yard duty desk. The detective inspector was a member of Special Branch.

'I'm here, Major Swart, because when we searched your two

muckers we found their embassy ID cards. Now, Major Swart, I'm sure you'll agree with me that the Libyans wouldn't stop short of a spot of larceny, or the Nigerians, perhaps, or the Eastern bloc chappies, but the representatives of the South African government, that's going to raise an eyebrow or two. Is it because they don't pay you much, Major Swart? Is it a bit of burglary to supplement the overseas allowance?'

He sat on the plastic-topped table in the interview room, swinging his feet casually. Swart was on a chair, rigidly straight-backed, as though he was at attention. It amused the detective inspector to think of the turmoil in the mind of the South African. Exposure. Disgrace. Expulsion.

'I have to wonder why half the diplomatic mission from Pretoria should have travelled out of London to burgle a home in this nothing town. Very puzzling, Major Swart, because next door I have laid out on a table the items that your muckers were intending to take away with them. All pretty peculiar, but not so peculiar that I can't hold you and charge you . . .'

He saw the South African stiffen.

'Oh yes, there'll be charges. Conspiracy to rob, in your case. Your friends are in deeper trouble, of course. Theft, assaulting police officers in the execution of their duty. You might get away with eighteen months, three or four years they'll get. You'd thought of that, I expect. You knew you'd be gaoled if you were caught, surely you did? Not nice goals like yours. You'll probably all get Pentonville, that's where they send the short termers. Pentonville isn't segregated like those nice gaols of yours, Major Swart. You'll have a bunch of *kaffirs* on your landing for company.'

He thought the young constable by the door would be having a field day listening to this heap of crap. He would tell the constable that if a word of this interview got out then the boy could kiss his promotion up his arse.

'I claim diplomatic immunity.'

'Bollocks.'

'I am Major Hannes Swart. I am an accredited diplomat.'

'You're a burglar, and what's more you dress up in funny clothes and make a spectacle of yourself at funerals.'

'I am Second Secretary in the Consular Section of the Embassy of the Republic of South Africa.'

'You are a security police agent who has engaged in criminal activities.'

'I demand the right to telephone my embassy . . .'

'Refused.' The chief inspector grinned.

'. . . in order that my embassy can verify my credentials.'

'No chance.'

He turned, and he walked out. He left the constable with Major Swart. He went into the adjoining interview room and collected off the table the plastic bags inside which were the items collected by the men arrested in Churchill Close.

He carried them back for the Major to see. He laid them on the table in front of him. There was a letter in an opened envelope. There was a booklet offering South African holidays. There was a pamphlet entitled *Blasting Practice – Noble's Explosive Co Ltd*, and another *Blasting Explosives and Accessories – Nobel's Explosive Co Ltd*. There was a sales brochure issued by Explosives and Chemical Products Ltd of Alfreton in Derbyshire.

He saw the South African's eyes hovering over the display.

He played a hunch. He thought he had kept the best until the last. From behind his back he produced a see-through plastic bag in which was a framed photograph. It was the photograph of a young man. He held it under the South African's nose.

'Shit . . .'

Major Hannes Swart made the two links. He linked the photograph with the photo-fit picture sent from Johannesburg. He linked the photograph with the young man who had met Jacob Thiroko.

'Shit . . .'

Jack Curwen was the bomber in Johannesburg, and Jack Curwen was the one whom he'd seen talking to Jacob Thiroko. Explanations hammering into place.

The detective inspector watched him keenly.

'I demand the right to contact my embassy.'

'Crash job, is it, time of the essence?'

'I have the right to telephone my embassy.'

'To tell them what your muckers found?'

'It is my right to make a telephone call.'

'So it can all go on the encoder and hum back home?'

'I can establish my identity. You have no right to hold me.'

'Major Swart, this isn't parking a CD car on a double yellow outside Harrods.'

Major Swart stared at the photograph of Jack Curwen. He no longer listened to the detective inspector. His eyes flickered on, up to the table, up to the opened envelope and the spider writing that addressed the envelope to Mrs Hilda Perry. He was a trained policeman, excellent on faces. He remembered the photograph of James Carew. He looked at the face of Jack Curwen, the son.

'Shit . . . I *demand* the right to make a telephone call.'

'They all say that, every piss-arsed, common thief, they all want to telephone their embassies . . .'

'I claim diplomatic immunity.'

'I must be getting hard of hearing in my old age.'

Major Swart smiled. He thought it was his winning smile. He chuckled. He beamed up at Detective Inspector Cooper. There was a fractional wink.

'Heh, man, we're all policemen together. I'm security police, you're Special Branch. Same job, same problems. Both fighting the same enemy. We're on the same side, man. We have to help each other. If you had a problem in the North of Ireland and we could help, of course we'd help. Just a telephone call, man. What do you say?'

'I'd say you are a common burglar, and I'd say you are pissing in the wind, Major Swart.'

The detective inspector told the constable to take Major Swart to the cells.

Down a white tiled corridor. A locked door ahead. The echo of the feet and the clanging of the keys.

As if a calmness had come to the major now that he was freed from the sarcasm and goading of his interrogator.

The door ahead was unlocked. They went through. The door was locked behind him.

Closed in by the walls to the corridor, and by the bright ceiling lights, Major Swart understood.

The cell door was open, waiting for him. Folded blankets on the bed, and a bucket and a roll of lavatory paper on the floor beside it.

The door slammed behind him. He sagged onto the bed. He understood.

He understood why he was refused normal diplomatic facilities, why immunity was denied him, why a telephone was kept from him, why a senior Special Branch officer had been brought late at night from London to this shit pit town. He had grasped the importance of James Carew. He understood that James Carew was their man . . .

He ran the three steps to the door. He was beating with his fists at the steel facing, bruising his hands, bellowing his anger.

'I know who your bloody Carew is. Heh, got it, I know. He's your bloody undercover man. I know he is. I demand a telephone. I demand access to my embassy . . .'

His words rang around his head, beat at his ears.

He knew that no bastard heard him.

It was a bleak little room. There were posters of the smiling leader on the walls and boxes of pamphlets piled on the bare floorboards.

The Prime Minister's speech to the constituency workers had failed because, before it was delivered, the message had come through that the Director General was arriving for discussion on a matter of the utmost urgency.

'They're incommunicado at the moment?'

'Yes, Prime Minister. But Major Hannes Swart, an accredited diplomat, can, if he is released as diplomatic procedures require, furnish the security police authorities with information that in

287

my opinion could lead them to judge that Jack Curwen will attack the Maximum Security section of Pretoria Central prison. If those authorities were to receive such information it would, in my judgement, considerably improve their chances of arresting or killing Curwen.'

There was a gleam of mischief in the Prime Minister's eye.

'When would Curwen move?'

'Tonight, perhaps tomorrow night. I doubt he'd leave it until darkness on Wednesday, too fine.'

'Does he stand any chance?'

'Let me sidetrack . . . Recently a man called Jacob Thiroko visited London. He was a principal officer in the military wing of the African National Congress. The Special Branch officer controlling the business at Leatherhead has given us the basis of a connection between Curwen and Thiroko, albeit a fragile one. Last week Thiroko flew back to Lusaka, and immediately set off with a small team back across the South African border. He was ambushed and killed, with all the members of his group, in the northern Transvaal. I suggest Thiroko would only have ventured into his country to lead a major operation. A major operation could be interpreted as an attack on the Maximum Security gaol where four members of an ANC cadre are held and who will be hanged on Thursday with Carew. Now Thiroko's dead. Very possibly young Curwen now stands alone.'

'No chance?'

'In my opinion, no. Perhaps I exaggerate . . .'

'Tell me.'

'A few years ago three men broke out of the White Political prison. That's about a quarter of a mile from where Carew is due to hang. In the annals of escapolgy it was pretty remarkable. Every time they saw a key on a warder's chain they memorized it, and when they were in the workshops they used those memories to make a key. Their collection opened just about every door in this very secure compound. At night they used to let themselves out of their cells, with their keys, so that they could try every route that was available to them, but each time they came up against high walls that were floodlit, overlooked by watch-towers. They decided the only way out was through the front gate, and that's the way they went . . . If you'd asked me, knowing what they planned to do, what were their chances, I'd have said one in two million.'

'If he were to succeed, if he were to bring his father home, I would face the collapse of this government's foreign policy in relation to South Africa. Our position of persuasion towards reform would become meaningless.'

'Pragmatic politics demand that they fail, Prime Minister, and die silent.'

'Emotion requires that they succeed, Director General . . . It is only for his father?'

The Director General said, 'I doubt that a month ago he'd ever given South Africa ten minutes' thought.'

The Prime Minister said, 'I hope he succeeds . . . Hold them at Leatherhead, to give the boy his chance.'

'And after he's had his chance we have to face the music.'

'The man at Leatherhead, we'll shrug it off.'

The Director General left by a back exit, picking his way between the garbage bags.

It was past midnight. Ros and Jan still not back.

Jack worked methodically.

He was on the floor of the living room of the service flat.

Ros had rented it, using Jack's money, paid over the odds in deposit and said she'd be back to sign the papers the next day.

He had the tube on the floor. From a sheet of light aluminium he had cut a triangular shape that he had bent into a cone, a squat witch's hat. With pliers he had fastened steel wire at intervals along the cone and then secured the wire with heavy adhesive tape. George Hawkins had told him that the speed of the detonation would be 6,000 metres per second. The wire and the sticky tape would hold and do their job for the mini-fraction of time before the aluminium cone fused in white heat to become the boring projectile travelling ahead of the explosive force.

He placed the cone into the metal tube, the open end leading, pushing it gently forward till his arm was lost in the tube. Cautiously he took the slabs of explosive and worked them, putty-like, down the long length of the tube, squeezing them with his fingertips first into the angle between the cone and the tube's sides, and then back to the central point of the cone . . . He knew that explosive without a firing agent was harmless, but it took some faith to believe it . . . The explosive was packed round the cone. He had used 3½ pounds. Working on with care, not hurrying, because the Hawkins method was care and never hurry. He packed a further 8½ pounds of explosive, weighed meticulously, into the tube and behind the point of the cone. George had been very specific. The packing must be even, and firm.

Jack worked long and hard at the packing, sweat sheening his forehead.

George's lessons kept flickering into his head: 3¾ pounds of explosive will punch 31 inches into sandstone with an entry hole a maximum of 12 inches wide. He had a tube that was 9 inches in diameter. He had 12 pounds of explosive to use. Nine inches of diameter and 12 pounds of explosive were the only facts that mattered a damn to him.

And he had no primer, no priming charge.

George had talked to him of 6 ounces of priming charge to lie between the detonator and the Polar Ammon Gelignite for the high velocity trigger into the explosive. He didn't have a priming charge. Forget the bloody priming charge.

He had three detonators.

He taped two together. With his finger he worked a slim hole into the packed explosive in the tube. The two taped detonators into the slim hole, the beginning of the arming of the shaped charge bomb. With a sharp knife from the kitchen he cut a yard off the length of Cordtex equivalent. Very slowly, maximum care, he had eased the Cordtex equivalent into the protruding socket of one of the detonators. Making it live, powerful enough to explode him through the walls of the flat, to devastate that corner of the block. With pliers he crimped the socket of the detonator to the Cordtex equivalent. Had to be two detonators because he had no priming charge.

He made a sludge of readymix concrete. He kneaded it against the explosive and around the detonators and around the length of Cordtex equivalent. Set concrete to make the block at one end of the tube to drive the explosive force forward, undiluted, against the cone at the other end of the tube.

Later he would tie a length of safety fuse to the Cordtex, knot it and bind it.

Jack had completed the shaped charge when they came back.

When they came through the door he was assembling the last of his explosive in a 3 pound charge linked by his last detonator to Cordtex equivalent and safety fuse.

All clear in his mind. Where he would use the shaped charge, and where the smaller explosive charge, and where the Cordtex equivalent on the grilles because George had told him that Cordtex would blow away the grille bolts, slice them.

He was on his knees on the carpet when they came back, and writing on a torn scrap of paper. He had written 'rope' and 'bent metal'.

'We took a car,' Ros said.

Jan said, 'She didn't know it was so easy, to open a car up and drive it away.'

The two stared down at Jack's handiwork.

A breathlessness in Ros's voice. 'Is it going to do the job?'

'If it doesn't I'll be giving hell to an old guy in England when I get back.' Jack grinned.

'How so?'

Jack said, 'This is the first time I've ever built anything like it.'

'The first time?'

'But you're supposed to be . . .'

'It's the first time,' Jack said.

Ros turned away. She was shaking her head, broad sweeps, and the red ribbon in her hair flowing. A crack in her voice. 'And you haven't even thought how you'll get away in the car, where you'll go.'

'My father'll know.'

'I think it's pathetic.'

'I don't have the time, Ros. It's way past midnight. I've only today, I don't have the time to go running around the getaway routes. And I'm bloody tired, and I don't need lecturing. If you want to give a lecture then bugger off out through the door first . . .'

'I'll make a cup of tea,' she said.

Jan levered himself down onto the floor beside Jack. They studied the plan of Pretoria Central and Magazine Hill. Jan pointed to the place where the car would be waiting, shrugged away the distance between Pretoria Central and the car. Jack led Jan through the map points where the grenades would be thrown, where the pistol shots would be fired.

'. . . And then you'll get the hell out. You have to give that promise. You do what you're going to do and you get clear. You don't stay about to see the show. You go home and you get into your beds, and you go to the university in the morning, and Ros goes to work. It never happened, you were never involved.'

He saw the struggle working at the face of Jan van Niekerk.

Jack said, 'I have to know that you're clear. That'll be a strength to me. You have to make me that promise.'

He saw the way that the crippled boy's fingers stroked the heavy arms of the wire cutter. Light, delicate fingers. He thought the boy should never have been there.

Ros stood in the doorway. She held two mugs of tea.

'To give you strength, we promise.'

'Never hesitate, turn your backs on me.'

'I promise,' Jan said.

Ros leaned forward with the mug of tea for Jack. Her eyes were misted. He thought she was at the limit.

'When are you going to sleep, Jack?'

He smiled. 'I'll catnap when the old man's driving. Bloody old taxi driver can drive all night . . .'

The smile swiped off his face.

'Oh, Christ . . .' Furious concentrated anger spreading over him.

'I missed a window,' Jack hissed. The mug rocked in his hands. 'I have the outer wall. I have the wall onto the exercise yard. I have the window onto the catwalk. I have the grille down into the cell . . . I've all of that accounted for . . . I don't have the window between the catwalk and the grille over the cell . . .'

'You're going to kill yourself,' Ros said.

He didn't seem to have heard. He was ripping at the adhesive wrapping he had made around the 3 pound charge.

'What are you going to do?'

'Just hope that a pound and a half on each will do the two windows, and one without a detonator.'

They left him. They couldn't help him. They left him on the floor with the sweet almond smell of gelignite. They would sleep together on the one bed, dressed and in each other's arms. They would hold each other to shut out the certainty of their fear.

He lay on his bed. He could not sleep. He stared up at the frail light patterned by the grille wires.

The trap had been tested during the afternoon, the trap falling under a weighted sack.

There was a cool wind, and the cold came into Jeez's cell through the window between his cell and the catwalk, and the window between the catwalk and the night. He heard the shuffle of the feet of the guard on the catwalk above and the guttering cough as the man cleared his throat. He heard the snore of the prison officer who was locked into the corridor of C section 2. He heard the dribbling of the singing, muffled because the sound swam along the catwalks all the way from A section or B section. Keeping a poor bastard company, because there was a poor bastard who was going to hang in four hours' time. Jeez wondered if anyone slept when they were going to hang in four hours' time. Jeez had another fifty hours of living, and he couldn't sleep either.

Tuesday already started. Wednesday tomorrow. Wednesday was library day. He'd hear the trap going on Wednesday, and the sack under the trap would be of his weight.

He could end it all.

Of course he could. He had it in his power to make an end of it.

He could shout for the officer sleeping in the corridor. The officer would send for the duty major. The duty major would ring through to the night duty officer at John Vorster Square. The night duty officer at John Vorster Square would rouse the colonel. He had the promise of the colonel for his life if he coughed the details on the cadres and the safe houses and the arms caches . . . Just one shout. Fucking cruel . . . Typical of the pigs that they offered the Judas Kiss as the price for living.

It had just been a job for him, watching over the African National Congress. Just an assignment from old Colonel Basil. Wasn't supposed to get involved, not physically and not with the heart. Just supposed to be bumming on the fringe, just supposed to be a listener, and a writer of reports. He'd hang with Happy and Charlie and Percy and Tom. Fucking cruel, that it was better to hang with them than to make the Judas Kiss, and live a life sentence in a Boer White gaol.

Jeez reckoned to find friends where he was. Didn't go looking for them, found them when he needed them. There'd been a guy in Spac, good guy, teacher, they'd been friends for six years. Close enough to pick the lice from each other's heads. A good guy and a good friend, and he'd died in the snow with a bullet hole in his nape. His best friend in Spac and Jeez had been on the detail that pickaxed the grave out of the iron-frozen ground. He wouldn't have given that friend the Judas Kiss, not just for life.

He would make new friends.

He would be friends with Happy and Charlie and Percy and Tom in the corridor, going towards the door that was always closed. He'd be their friend in the preparation room, and when they went through the doorway and into the shed. He'd be their friend when it was the hood and when it was the noose. He'd not give them the bloody Judas Kiss.

No way he would shout for the bastard sleeping in the corridor of C section 2.

He did not understand why the arm of Century hadn't reached for him.

Hurt, hurt hard, lying on his bed, gazing at the dull light bulb through the mesh of the grille, to think that Century had dropped him off the team. He had the proof that they had dropped him off the team. He had the proof that they had dropped him, the proof was the bloody cell he was locked into, and the hours that were left to him.

Couldn't think about it, because thinking of the team was fucking agony for Jeez. Think of some other bloody thing . . .

Think of why Hilda hadn't written.

Think of Hilda in a nice house with a nice husband with a nice life.

Think of the boy who was his and who was Hilda's.

Think of the boy who would be 27 years old next birthday.

Think of the boy Jack.

Think of anything other than the trap hammering in practice on Wednesday afternoon, after library.

He couldn't picture, now, what the boy, his son, looked like.

First thing in the morning, first thing at his desk, the colonel called London. The London embassy told him that Major Swart was not yet in his office.

The colonel said that he would not be calling unless it was of great urgency. The London embassy told him that the major's home had already been contacted, that the major's wife had not seen him since the previous day.

The colonel said that it was an outrage that they had no contact with their man. The London embassy told the colonel that as soon as they had contact with Major Swart they would pass on the message for him to call John Vorster Square, priority.

As if a door slammed in the colonel's face. His investigation had been at a gallop. A name. An address overseas. A photo-fit likeness. Because the door had slammed, he did not know how to go forward. A piece of basic, beginner's school, detective work was all that was required from London, but Major Swart had gone walkabout and the door was slammed.

He went down the stairs to the incident room.

Expressionless, he reported that London had not yet been able to furnish the material necessary for short circuiting a lengthy investigation. He knew he had lost ground. He made a lame suggestion. He suggested that all the two and three star hotels in Johannesburg should be checked again.

'Is he standing firm, sir?'

The civil servant had brought the first briefing papers of the day. The Minister of Justice smiled.

'The State President? He's in great form. I was with him yesterday, firm as they come.'

'No question of clemency?'

'I'm surprised you ask.'

'Because of the overnight telegrams . . . Washington, the Vatican, the Speaker of the European Parliament in Strasbourg, the Security Council, the Secretary General of the Commonwealth. They all came in overnight.'

'A formality. But you have missed one.'

'Those are all the cables, sir.'

'What about the United Kingdom? No word from Her Britannic Majesty's ratbag.'

'I noted that,' the civil servant said. 'No message has come from the United Kingdom.'

The Minister of Justice clapped his hands. 'Did you see the opinion poll from the Free State? We are going to win that by-election, because I was photographed at the grave of Gerhardt Prinsloo, and because the Pritchard Five will hang.'

'But curious that the United Kingdom is silent.'

Jack stood with Jan below the wide climbing steps leading to the rearing stone hulk of the Vortrekker Monument.

Jan spoke savagely of this edifice to Afrikaner power and mythology.

As if it were something evil, a national monument to privilege and superiority. He showed Jack, with an angry pointing finger, the carved relief of trekker wagons that formed a laager around the monument, and the great hewn corner statues of the Boer leaders with their rifles, and the bronze of the trekker woman and her children. Jack thought the boy's intensity was unreal, just a drug to give him courage. For himself, he didn't listen. He stood with his back to the monument and looked across the valley to the south side slopes of Magazine Hill.

There was a wire fence at the floor of the valley, at the bottom of the hill. The ground on the slope was rough, half cleared, cut by a stone vehicle track. To the right side, as he looked, of Magazine Hill, was the sweep of the Johannesburg motorway, the Ben Schoeman Highway, that would come round behind the hill on which the Voortrekker Monument had been built. To the left side of Magazine Hill was a separate fenced area, which his plans told him was the army's firing range. Directly ahead, the crown of Magazine Hill was covered with tall and heavy pine trees, rich green, and he could see buildings in the shelter of the trees.

He made his estimates.

He tried to judge the distance from the floor of the valley to the crown of Magazine Hill. He tried to see where he could lie up if he were ahead of schedule, over which ground he could hurry if he was late.

He thought it could not be more than two hundred yards from the crown down the hidden tree-covered slope to the walls of Beverly Hills.

He turned his back on Magazine Hill and walked to the far side of the Voortrekker Monument to see down below where the car would be left. It was a hell of a distance to come back. More than a mile. His own thought . . . that in the chaos after the attack he and Jeez would be better on the scrub hills on foot than immediately into a car, but a hell of a way for all that.

In the line between Magazine Hill and the Ben Schoeman Highway was another stony outcrop. He saw the summit of it had been shaped.

'What's that?'

'Skanskopfort. Built to protect Pretoria, historic monument, colonial cannons and that crap.'

'Lived in?'

Jan shook his head. 'It's just a museum, and an army store.'

Jack walked again to the steps. He stood in the morning sunlight. He gazed again on the slope of Magazine Hill, the slope that he would climb that evening.

They went to Ros's car. Jan drove back to Pretoria.

In two heaps, Jack's possessions were laid out on the floor. In one heap was his suitcase and his coat. He had told Jan to dump them from Ros's car, once they were on the way back to Johannesburg. The other heap was what he would take with him that night. There was the metal tube, and the prepared Cordtex equivalent and safety fuse lengths, and the two charges for the windows, and the shotgun and the ammunition, and the wire cutters, and the rope and the bent metal hook that was lashed to it, all to be carried up Magazine Hill.

The bedroom door opened.

Ros had taken the ribbon from her hair. She had washed the make-up from her cheeks and her eyes and from her lips.

She was ice calm, pale, matter of fact.

'Lose yourself, Jan.'

Jan looked at her, blinking, not understanding.

'Just get rid of yourself. Lose yourself.'

'What for?'

'Because I tell you to.'

'Where to?'

'Go and check the other car, make sure it isn't being watched, walk the streets, anywhere.'

Ros came to Jan and took his arm and kissed him on the cheek and led him to the door. She opened the door and pushed him out through it.

She closed the door. She came to Jack. She reached for his hand. She might have been leading a child. She led him into the

298

bedroom. He thought she might have been crying while he had been at the Voortrekker Monument and looking over Magazine Hill. She did not look into his face. She was clumsy with her fingers as she unbuttoned his shirt, slid it away across his shoulders to let it fall from his arms. She knelt in front of him and lifted away his shoes and peeled off his socks. She reached up to unfasten his belt and to ease down the zipper. She was kneeling as she pushed her light sweater up and over her head. Jack stood in his nakedness and watched her. He knew he loved her. He loved every part of her scrubbed clean body. She stood to step out of her skirt. She drove her pants down to below her knees. Jack reached for her, he felt the loveliness of her. She stepped back from him. A slow sad smile. She took his hand, she took him to the bed.

She broke. She pushed him hard down onto the bed. She came down onto him. She was sobbing her heart to him. She tore at the skin on his back with her nails. She hurt him as she bathed him in her tears. She was stretching apart over him, reaching for him, guiding him, driving onto him.

'You cruel bastard, Jack, for coming into my life . . . for going out of it.'

18

She lay beside him, and her cheek rested on the centre of his chest.

She could feel the steady rhythm of his heart in her ear. She thought he was at peace. With her fingers, with her nails, she made shapes and patterns amongst the hairs of his chest. She formed the letters of his name, she wrote amongst the hairs of her love for him. The curtains in the room had been open when she had taken him to the bed. She could see that the skies were darkening now over Pretoria, and she could sense the thickening of the traffic on the streets below the window. She hated the coming of the evening. She felt a safety with this man as they lay against each other, damp warm and loving safety. There was a safety when his arm was around her, his hand over her breast. She knew that she could not hold him in the bed, she had seen the way that a few minutes before he had shifted his hand from her stomach to look down at the face of his watch before returning his hand to the place of pleasure and comfort. She knew that when the hour hand had trickled and the minute hand had rushed that he would leave her. She acknowledged that on this evening, on this last evening, that she played the role of second best. She accepted that she was secondary to the work of the evening that would start when he leaned across her, kissed her, pushed her back onto the pillow, and left her bed. She thought that she had helped him. Her friends had told her that the first time was awful. Ros van Niekerk, happy in her moist heat, safe with a man's hand over her breast and with his fingers over the flatness of her stomach, thought it was not at all awful. He hadn't used anything, she hadn't used anything. Not an act of gratification, not an occasion when adults who knew their minds discussed the merits of pills and coils, a time for soft urgent loving between two young people who would part when the hand of a watch had run its hour. She thought she did not care about the consequences of his not having used anything, of her not having used anything.

His hand moved.

She felt the aloneness of the skin on her stomach. She felt his fingers climbing the slow length of her body, and brushing the nipple of her breast. She opened her eyes. She saw that he looked at his watch. She hated the watch.

'How long?'

'Just a few minutes.'

'I can't keep you?'

'You knew you couldn't.'

'To have found something precious, and to lose it . . .'

'Something wonderful to remember, Ros.'

Jack kissed her, closed her eyes with his kisses. With his tongue he ran over the nostrils and the fresh lips of his girl. So calm. As if when he left her he would go for an evening walk, a stroll that was without danger.

She clung to him. Her arms were around his neck, her breasts were forced against the jutted strength of his jaw.

'Please, no hurting yourself, Ros.'

She thought that if she cried she would weaken him. She thought that to weaken him was to further endanger him. And that was absurd because there could not be more danger than where he was going. She choked on the tears, she squeezed the wetness from her eyes.

'Trying.'

'Great girl.'

'How long?'

'Less than a few minutes.'

'Will I ever see you again . . .' She faltered.

'Remember the brilliance, Ros, of being loved, and remember the brilliance that you gave me with your love.'

He looked again at his watch. She felt him start to move. And, God, she didn't want him to go. And, God, she was without the power to stop his going. She rolled away from him. She lay on her back and the bed sheet hid her knees. She laid her arm over her eyes, so that she would not see the moment of his going from her bed, from her side.

'It was only for you, Jack.'

'I know that.'

'Because I love my country.'

'That's my guilt, that I've made you fight what you love.'

'My country, Jack, that's more than a rabble of politicians.'

'Ros, my country's politicians, and the bastard desk men, they ditched my father and left him to hang. But I, too, can still love my country.'

'And I love my brother. And I hate his cause, because his cause is bombs and guns. His way is killing and loathing and fear. His way takes us to ruin, destroys the country that I love, and will destroy the brother that I love . . . How long?'

He kissed her. As if they both knew it would be for the last time. He snapped off the bed. He went to his clothes, he started to dress. She lay in the darkness, her eyes under her arm. She heard the movement of his body. She could not let her eyes see him. She felt his hands on her head, lifting her head. She felt the cold of the chain on her neck, on the skin above her breasts. She opened her eyes. She saw the gold chain, she lifted the crucifix of gold to see it better.

'Wear it and remember.'

'I won't forget you, Jack, not ever.'

She watched him go out through the door.

She heard his desultory conversation with Jan in the living room. She heard him speak aloud as he went through his check list of the items he would carry up Magazine Hill, and down Magazine Hill, to the gaol.

She was numbed. Too unhappy, now, for tears. She swung her legs off the bed.

As she dressed she heard Jack talking to Jan. They had moved on to the list of street places at which the grenades would be thrown, where the pistol shots were to be fired. Her fingers played with the crucifix. She thought she would wear it for the rest of her life, for the ever of her life. She had promised that in the morning she would be at her office desk, and Jan had promised that he would be in the lecture theatre at Wits. At home, in the top drawer of her wardrobe, there was a yellow silk scarf. She thought that when she was again in her room, that night, when she was back with her parents and everything familiar, she would leave her curtains open and she would tie the yellow scarf to the handle of the window, and she would allow the light from beside her bed to be thrown against the yellow scarf and to be seen outside her window. It was important to her that the yellow scarf should be seen, should be her beacon to save him. Her fingers were tight on the edges of the crucifix.

When she was dressed she went into the living room.

Sitting on the floor with the street map of Pretoria spread out in front of him, Jan looked up at her. He was grinning, amused. She blushed.

'Bit bourgeois, Ros, handing out home comforts to the troops before the battle.'

She ignored her brother. 'Can I do anything, Jack?'

'Have you a nail file, metal?'

'Yes.'

'Please, would you take the serial number off the shotgun.'

'Aren't you going to take it with you, to the border?'

'Just in case I get separated from it,' Jack said easily.

'You'll need it all the way to the border.'

'Wouldn't want it to fall into the wrong hands, come back to you.'

It was insane to be thinking about the border. Jack passed her up the shotgun, and he pointed to the serial number. She took it into the bedroom where she had left her handbag. She would remember him for ever, as she had seen him in her bed, because she would never see him again.

★　★　★

303

The assistant dropped Frikkie de Kok off home.

Pretty damned stupid when he thought about it, that he should have an armed escort every time he went to Pretoria Central and an armed escort back from Pretoria Central, but nothing when he took Hermione shopping nor when he took his boys to the Loftus Versfeld for rugby.

It had gone pretty well, a pretty damned good day's work.

The assistant had done him proud. Right from the start in the morning, right from the time his assistant had picked him up, he had told him to take his time, not to get himself rushed, just to go through the procedure the way he had seen Frikkie do it. It had been fine because it was only one man. The assistant had executed his first man. Not that he had *officially* executed the man, not that it went into the paperwork that he had done it, but the arrangement had been made with the governor. The governor could not really have put the spoke in, because the governor had to accept that if a man was booked for hanging on a Tuesday or a Thursday and Frikkie de Kok happened to have the influenza or he had ricked his back in the garden, then the man still had to go. Frikkie de Kok with influenza or a bad back shouldn't be a reason for a stay of execution. And the time came when an assistant had to prove himself, show that he could manage the work himself, and pretty damn well he'd done for a first time. Frikkie had been behind him, ready to lend a hand if he was needed, and he hadn't been. All right, his assistant had been a little clumsy when they brought the fellow into preparation, but who wouldn't have been, on his first time with the responsibility. A little aggressive with the pinions, a little rough moving the fellow onto the centre of the trap, a little hard when he had hooded him, a very little bit fierce when he had ringed the fellow's neck with the noose. Little things, not grounds for complaint. Little things to be pointed out over a beer. No trouble with the drop. The assistant had made his calculations to the inch and to the pound, just right the drop had been. Frikkie de Kok had shaken his assistant's hand while the rope still shivered, while a young creep on compulsory attendance was in the corner throwing up over his uniform ... Just Frikkie de Kok's view, and privately held, but it wasn't right to have youngsters in the hanging gaol, not the youngsters who had joined the prison service as an alternative to conscription into the army and service in the 'operational area'. The hanging gaol should be for professionals, not for shirkers. Just his opinion.

Afterwards he and his assistant had stayed all day in Maximum Security, because Thursday was a multiple, five on the trap. Thursday took preparation. Six was the most he could do, but that was a hell of a business even with a good assistant. Two and three and four at a time were pretty much all right, but fives and sixes were hard on everyone present. When he was busy round the trap he never looked at the spectators. Too much on his mind with the pinions and the hoods and the feet being right and the noose, but he could hear them. He could hear his audience gasping, willing him to go faster. Stood to reason that fives and sixes couldn't be as fast as hanging one man alone. Frikkie de Kok, as he always said to his assistant, would never hurry. To hurry was the fastest way to a fiasco. So, they had stayed at the gaol all day, and they had made their preparations, and because he had a combined condemns weight of 325 kilos on the trap he had gone down underneath and checked each single bolt and screw of the trap. It paid to be careful in Frikkie de Kok's job. A good day's work, and after his tea his assistant was coming back to collect him, and there would be a good evening's entertainment at the Harlequins, a floodlit Cup match. He was thinking of his shower, and of getting out of his suit, as he pushed open his front garden gate. He was thinking of the match as he came up the path, and how the second team flank forward would cope, because he was replacing the injured first choice.

He opened his front door. He could see into the living room. His two boys, singlets and shorts, red cheeks and sweat, pumping iron on his living room carpet. So they shared the weights. Beautiful to Frikkie de Kok to see his boys working on the weights. And beautiful for him to hear that his Hermione was in the kitchen making his tea. Beautiful also to be going to the Harlequins for a match.

And beautiful to know that he had a quiet day to follow before his waking before dawn on Thursday.

He thought he could smell a meat pie from the kitchen, and he thought the Harlequins would beat Defence, and he thought he would make a hell of a fine job of dropping five on Thursday morning.

The colonel listened intently.

Sometimes it was a good line from London. That evening it was a poor line. He was listening on an open line to the brigadier who headed security police operations throughout Western Europe. Major Hannes Swart enjoyed a particular autonomy in London, but nominally he reported to the brigadier.

He had forgotten the funeral, slipped it from his mind. Aunt Annie was dead, buried, gone. He had forgotten the minister's rallying words and the repetitive threat of the Afrikaners' vengeance. He had forgotten them because they were meaningless, they were rhetoric when set against the real warfare of his own battlefield.

'They would have been carrying their IDs, so it cannot be a hospital situation. If they had been in any form of accident then we would have heard from the police or from a hospital. I have checked back over the instructions that were sent to Hannes yesterday morning. I have had a man go down to this Churchill Close address. Not easy, there is a police car parked outside the house. So, I have a problem. What sort of inquiry am I to make? Delicate, eh, you understand me? This afternoon I have been to the Foreign Office and I have reported that Hannes and his two colleagues are missing. Perhaps the man I meet is lying, perhaps he is in ignorance. He tells me that he has no knowledge of the whereabouts of these three members of our staff. I cannot ask him if they are in police custody, because he will ask me why I should suppose that. I'm at a halt.'

The telephone purred in the colonel's ear. He thought the

brigadier didn't give a shit for the John Vorster Square bomb. The bastard was swanning in Paris and London and Amsterdam and Bonn, the bastard was freeloading in Europe.

He rang through to the library. He requested all communications over the previous month from Major Swart of the London embassy. He was told such records were classified. He said he knew they were classified. He was told that for access to classified communications he needed the counter-signature of the head of library on the docket. He shouted into the telephone that he knew access to classified communications required the counter-signature of the head of library. He was told the head of library was at supper, had left the building, would be back in forty minutes.

What a fucking way to run a fucking intelligence gathering operation.

He telephoned his wife. He told her he would not be home until late. He said he thought the funeral had gone well. She told him that the immersion heater had broken, the thermostat had failed, that there was no hot water in the house. He asked her what she wanted. Did she want South Africa sleeping safe, or did she want her husband as a plumber, for God's sake.

They moved all of their possessions to the corridor leading to the front door, their bags and the explosives and the firearms.

Each of them held a handkerchief underneath the kitchen tap and then set to work methodically to clean the rooms of fingerprints. Jack took the bedroom, Jan the living room, and Ros did the kitchen. Not for the sake of Jack's prints, but for the brother's and the sister's.

When they had finished they carried the bags and the explosives and the firearms down the back fire escape to the car park, to Ros's Beetle, and to the car she and Jan had stolen.

Jeez sat on his bed.

Sergeant Oosthuizen had moved his chair from the end of the C section 2 corridor, by the locked doorway, to outside Jeez's cell. He allowed Jeez's door to be three, four inches open.

It was in direct contradiction of regulations. At this time in the evening, with the lights dimmed, Jeez should have been locked into his cell.

He was like a terrier with a rabbit, with conversation. If Jeez didn't respond to him then Sergeant Oosthuizen asked a question that demanded an answer. As though good Sergeant Oosthuizen had determined that a man who was to hang in less than a day and a half was best served by making conversation.

Jeez didn't know his mind, didn't know whether he wanted to hear the retirement plans over again, didn't know whether he was better with the silence and the worm of his own thoughts. A new worm crawling. The worm was money. Money in the bank. Earning interest, accumulating. He had the account number and Century had the account number. Who would tell Hilda the number? The guy who used to know him in accounts, old Threlfall, bloody long time retired. Worry worming as a cash register, and trying to hold the thread against Oosthuizen's battering. He understood why Sergeant Oosthuizen talked about his retirement and about his kids. It was all Oosthuizen could talk about that did not drive coaches through the already broken regulations. He couldn't talk about the State President's plans for reform, because Jeez wouldn't be there to see them. He couldn't talk about the unrest, because Jeez to him was a part of that unrest. He couldn't talk about Jeez, about Jeez being the centre of whispering interest through the gaol, because it was Tuesday night and Jeez was to hang at dawn on Thursday. Good Sergeant Oosthuizen ploughed on from his exhausted retirement plans into the difficulties at his son's liquor store in Louis Trichardt.

The murmur sounds of singing.

Jeez heard them.

Not the great choir of that dawn when a single man had gone to his death, when the whole company of Blacks had sung the hymn to strengthen him as he walked the corridor to the shed of execution. A fist of voices only.

Oosthuizen heard the singing, and the slam of a door that

cut into the singing, and he was off his chair and straightening his tunic and heaving his chair away from Jeez's door and back to the proper place beside the exit door from the corridor of C section 2.

Firm, bold singing. More of an anthem than a hymn.

'I'm sorry, Carew, believe me. I have to lock you up . . .'

The singing was approaching. A few voices, along with the stamp of boots, and the shouts in Afrikaans for doors ahead to be opened.

'What's happening?'

'They're bringing the others down. The other four. They're going to double them up in two cells in here.'

'Why?'

Sergeant Oosthuizen snorted. 'You know I cannot tell you, man.'

The door closed. Oosthuizen turned the key. The corridor door opened. Oosthuizen had keys only for the cells, not for the door leading into the main corridor of C section. Of course Sergeant Oosthuizen could not tell Jeez why the Pritchard Five were to be together. Of course the prison officer couldn't chattily explain that for the final few hours it was more convenient to have all five men in one wing, one section, where the disruption to prison life would be minimized. Not an ordinary hanging because the five men were from Umkhonto we Sizwe. A hanging that raised the tension pitch in the gaol. Jeez knew another reason that of course good Sergeant Oosthuizen could not explain to him. Thursday morning, dawn on Thursday, and they wouldn't want to be bringing four men from B section and one man from C section, because they might not have their watches together, and one might walk too fast, and one might have to wait in preparation, and some might have to be scrambled down the corridors to the hanging shed. Get them all cosily together, separated from A section and B section, so that the rest of the gaol was less disturbed. Made sense to Jeez.

The door into the corridor of C section 2 was unlocked.

Jeez heard the singing.

'Rest in peace, Comrade Moloise . . .'

He heard the voices of Happy Zikala and Charlie Schoba and Percy Ngoye and Tom Mweshtu.

'Long live Comrade Mandela . . .'

Brilliant voices that were without fear.

'Long live the African National Congress . . .'

He shook his head. His chin was trembling. He felt the moisture welling in his eyes. He heard them all shout together, Happy and Charlie and Percy and Tom.

'Heh, Comrade Jeez, heh, Comrade – *Amandla* . . . Hear us Comrade Jeez, *Amandla*, Comrade Jeez . . .'

His voice was a quaver.

'Listen, you bastards. Don't you ever bloody listen to anything I bloody tell you? What did I tell you? Let's have a bit of dignity, lads, that's what I told you bastards, way back.'

He heard the shrieks of their laughter. He heard the orders of the duty major. He heard the driving shut of two cell doors. He heard the duty major demanding they should settle down for the night.

He heard the closing of the door into C section's main corridor.

They were still singing. Jeez thought his friends had found him. He called for Sergeant Oosthuizen. He saw the bulk of the man at the grille aperture on his cell door. He thought of the way they had laughed when he had called for a bit of dignity.

'Doesn't it frighten you, Sergeant Oosthuizen, that they aren't afraid?'

Jack parked the stolen car 100 yards from the turning onto the Ben Schoeman Highway.

He switched off the lights. Eyes closed, he sagged back in his seat.

It was the inevitable moment he had come for.

He felt an awful tiredness through his body. He heard Ros bring her Beetle to a stop behind him. He stepped out of his car. It was a Renault, he thought it had a decent engine and could make some speed, he had filled the tank and had checked the oil himself.

He walked to the Beetle. Jan was in the back, half buried with equipment and the bags. He settled in beside Ros. Stretching above them was the slope to the fort that Jan had said was called Skanskopfort. Ros drove away. She reversed sharply, swung and went back to the Ben Schoeman. She took them to the far side of Skanskop, to the road at the bottom of the valley between Skanskop and Magazine. She drove off the road and onto a stone chip track, and jolted them as she braked.

Jack was out fast.

Jan passed him the cumbersome shape of the metal tube that he had been cradling in his lap because the shaped charge was armed, then the bag that held the smaller charges and the lengths of Cordtex equivalent and safety fuse and the rope. He laid them on the stones, then took the shotgun that was loaded to capacity, and the opened box of cartridges that he stuffed into his anorak pocket. Last came the heavy wire cutters. Difficult in the dark, because Ros had cut the lights as soon as they had left the Ben Schoeman. He studied the luminous face of his watch. He called the time. The time was 9 o'clock and 32 minutes and 30 seconds, and he counted through to 9.32 and 45 seconds. Three watches synchronized. He had given himself one hour, less three minutes, before the decoying diversions. He slung the bag over his shoulder. He hooked the metal tube into the angle of his elbow, more than forty pounds' weight of it, he pushed the wire cutters into his pocket with the shotgun ammunition. He reached his hand into the darkness of the back of the car, he felt Jan's two fists grip his hand. Next he leaned across the front passenger seat and his fingers found Ros's chin and drew it forward so that he could kiss her mouth. Brief, an instant.

'I'll wear it always.'

'My mother gave it me. If she knew you she'd like you to have it.'

He stepped back. He picked up the shotgun. He pushed the passenger door shut with the toe of his jogging shoe. He didn't know what was in her face, couldn't see her face.

The engine exploded to life, the wheels bit into the loose stones. The car pulled away. She did not turn on her lights until she was back at the main road.

Jack laid down the metal tube and the shotgun and took a handful of earth in his cupped hands and spat on it to make the soil moist and then smeared what was mud over the pale surfaces of his face. He looked into the distance, away to the main road. He saw a single set of headlights and then the red flash of tail lights, between trees and bushes. He lifted the metal tube and the shotgun, one under each arm, and he started to walk away from the track and towards the start of the slope up Magazine Hill.

There was a sharp wind, small clouds, a half moon.

Enough light for him to move without lumbering into the thicker scrub bushes. He had thought when he had seen the slope in daylight that the ground had been cleared a dozen years or so before, then allowed to grow again.

He made himself a pattern.

He climbed for a counted 15 paces, then stopped to listen for ten seconds. When he stopped he could hear a radio playing music, ahead of him, where the prison service buildings were on top of Magazine. The stream of traffic on the Ben Schoeman was below him and away to the west, a ribbon of fast moving lights. As he climbed the sounds of the main road guttered, and he was alert to the new sounds of the hillside.

The radio playing music, the frantic wing clatter of a disturbed nesting bird, and a drumbeat on planks. It took Jack the full ten seconds of a listening pause to identify the drumbeat ... He remembered that when he had stood with Jan at the Voortrekker Monument and looked across at the slope of Magazine that he had seen a low wooden watchtower half way up the hill, away to the east of where he climbed. The tower had not been manned in daylight. He realized he had heard the sounds of booted feet stamping on a plank platform, perhaps for warmth, perhaps out of boredom. He couldn't see the tower, not high enough for it to be silhouetted against the grey blue faint light of the night sky. He could sense the general direction of the tower and he could picture what he had seen from the Voortrekker Monument. He knew that the tower was set the far side of the wire fence that he had identified when he had stood with Jan on reconnaissance. He wondered if the bastard who stamped his feet on the plank platform would have a night sight on his rifle. Sod all use having the bastard there if he didn't have a night sight, because if he didn't have one then the bastard was as blind as Jack. Had to reckon that he had a night sight on his rifle, or infra-red binoculars, or an image intensifier spy glass. The reckoning pushed Jack down on his knees, had him crawling forward. The slope was a dark and indistinct mass above him. He could only see the trees and scrub bushes that were within three, four yards of his face, less when the clouds hid the moon.

The fence seemed to rush at him, to materialize above him when he was on the point of collision.

Very gently he laid down the metal tube and the shotgun.

He wriggled the bag on its strap over into the small of his back so that it would not impede him. His fingers groped forward. So bloody insensitive, his fingers, because they were cold and bruised from when he had crawled on his hands and knees. His fingers stretched to feel the pattern of the wire mesh. A dark mesh fence against dark ground, and his fingers must do the work for him, and he must lie still and move only the barest minimum in case the bastard on the platform had a night sight or an infra-red or an image intensifier. His fingers traced the diamonds of the wire mesh.

He found the strand that he feared.

His forefinger brushed the single strand that ran along the face of the fence a foot above the ground. He touched the first tumbler wire. If the wire were disturbed an alarm would ring. He noted it, stored it, his fingers moved on and traced the mesh above the tumbler, desperately slow. He dared not look at the luminous hands of his watch, dared not see how much of his precious time he was spending in the search for a second tumbler wire.

God, if he was late . . .

Bloody stupid, Jack. Had the time he needed. Didn't know whether he had the patience he needed. Jack bloody Curwen, second-class businessman from the south of England, paid a second-class wage to drum up second-class work . . . What the hell was he at lying on Magazine Hill searching for a second tumbler wire?

He found the second tumbler wire.

The second tumbler wire was 4 feet above the ground, 4 feet above where the mesh was buried in the rough soil. With the wire cutters he made a square hole between the bottom tumbler wire and the second tumbler wire. He lifted the square mesh clear. He could feel the heave of his breath. He could hear the radio playing and the stamp of the sentry on his platform. He lifted the metal tube through the hole, and then the shotgun and then his bag. He was half way through the hole, head and shoulders and chest through, when a strand of jagged cut mesh caught at his anorak. His knees were on one side of the wire, his elbows on the other. He squirmed his trunk to reach with his fingers to free himself.

When he was through he lay on his stomach.

He was gasping.

He took his handkerchief from his pocket and looped it through the mesh immediately above the hole.

It was a risk, but everything was a risk. It was necessary to leave a marker.

Jack gathered up his metal tube and his bag and his shotgun and the wire cutters. So tired. He crawled forward. He was on his knees and using the hand that held the shotgun for leverage. He dared not let the metal tube buffet the ground. The metal tube was 12 pounds of explosive and two detonators and Cordtex equivalent, the metal tube was a primed bomb, held close against his chest. He was going forward.

He saw the light on his hands. His head started up.

The light from the gable end of a concrete building was thrown from his right, fell on him. He had crawled forward, concentration locked, nursing the shotgun and the tube, and he had not realized that he had reached the summit of the slope of Magazine Hill. He moved fast to his left, shuffling as a crab to reach shadow. He could hear the music clearly, he could hear voices and laughter. He lay on his stomach and he heard the sounds of men who had no care, no suspicion.

Shadow was his security. He stayed with the shadows as he moved away across the top plateau of the hill, towards a line of trees. He crossed paths, he ducked past buildings. He froze against a wall when a uniformed man came belching out of a doorway to urinate on the edge of a lawn.

High trees coated the skyline ahead of him, and above the trees was an umbrella of hazed white light.

The tube was an agony on the muscles of his left arm. His feet were leaden heavy, but the white light above the trees was a talisman for him, pulling him forward. He came into the trees. Going slowly, because under the conifers' canopy he could see only the white knuckles of his fingers that were tight on the stock of the shotgun.

He broke from the trees.

His path was crossed by a tarmac road. He could see darkened buildings and more trees ahead of him, and the lights above the trees were fiercer. He looked right and he looked left. He stood still and he listened. He heard dogs barking. He ran across the road and sagged against the back fence of a garden. He thought, from his map, that he had reached the line of senior officers' homes that were set on the hillside above Beverly Hills. The moon helped him. He saw a narrow track leading between two garden fences, not wide enough for a vehicle. There was another road crossing the far end of the track and he could see street lights. Ahead of him was a great cascade of light, fit to blind him.

He felt the energy surging through him. He was going forward.

A voice . . . A man talking as to a child. A voice and footsteps . . . A caressing voice as if to quieten a child. Down flat, squeezing his face, side down, into the dirt of the track. He was in darkness, short of the light thrown from the road ahead. He saw a dog handler with a German Shepherd. The dog handler was cooing soft nonsense to his animal. Jack saw that the dog handler had an automatic rifle resting on the elbow of his right arm. He heard the voice drift away. He waited thirty seconds before he slowly rose to his feet and went on down the track to where the darkness merged with the light. He laid down his tube and his bag and his shotgun. He crawled forward.

He saw the high concrete wall in front of him.

He saw the sentry tower rising above the wall, and above the sentry tower was the bank of floodlights. He could see low tilted roofs beyond the high concrete wall. He was separated from the wall by a narrow paved road and by a strip of lawn.

Jack Curwen had come a hell of a long way.

He gazed at the outer wall of Beverly Hills, the outer wall of the hanging gaol. If he had shouted then, his father would have heard him. He looked down at the luminous hands of his watch. He had six minutes before the diversion. The wall was brilliantly lit in the wash of light from the close set bulbs ahead of him. The sentry in the tower had his back to him. Jack could see the hunch of his shoulders.

He went back for his metal tube and his bag and his shotgun. He crouched down. He was shaking. He had to will himself to control his fingers. He checked the safety fuse length that was knotted to the Cordtex equivalent. He checked that the Cordtex equivalent was firm where it disappeared into the readymix block in the metal tube. He opened his bag and ran his fingers, stuttering, over the charge that contained the detonator and over the charge that did not. He felt for the lengths of loose Cordtex equivalent and of safety fuse. He found the rope that was lashed to the cold bent iron. He eased the safety catch off the shotgun, he had eight cartridges in the magazine. He emptied the remaining cartridges from the carton into his pocket. He touched the smooth weight of the wire cutters.

It was all a matter of belief . . . and arrogance.

The wall that he faced was of no use to him. The wall fronted onto B section and onto the hanging shed. He had to be against the wall that fell away down the hillside to his right, down towards the glitter lights of Pretoria.

Arrogance and now courage.

He rose to his feet.

There was a softness in his knees, there was a wetness in his belly, because he must now walk in the light along the paved road, in front of the homes of the senior officers, under the watchtower, walk for a hundred yards to the corner of the wall.

Cheek, too, because he must walk as though he belonged.

He looked at his watch. He had a minute and a half. He had the metal tube under his arm, and the bag on his back. He cocked the shotgun. He must walk. No running, no stopping.

He came off the track.

He ducked his head as the light found him, so that the smear marks of mud on his forehead and cheeks could not be seen from the watchtower. In the middle of the road he walked at a steady pace. He waited for the rasp of a weapon being cocked. He waited for the challenging shout. He walked towards the corner of the wall, along the road and towards the bend where it followed the side wall down the hill.

There was a yapping chorus.

There was a white bundle flying through the open gates from a large garden. There was a Pekingese dog circling his ankles. He saw the garden shielded an elegant bungalow. A large elderly woman in a housecoat and bedroom slippers was in pursuit of the dog.

Jack's heart hammered.

The woman saw a young man who carried a long circular length of metal and a bag and a firearm. She lived in the heart of the Pretoria Central complex, she was the wife of the major general who was Deputy Commissioner of Prisons (security). Her bosom lurched forward as she bent to catch the collar of the darting beast. She yanked it off the ground.

The woman spoke to Jack in Afrikaans, and he smiled and

317

nodded and she chastised the dog and Jack nodded again and
the dog yapped at him and earned itself a volley of reproach and
Jack took one step away and then two and then the woman was
lecturing the beast in earnest and making for her garden and
Jack was away free.

The sentry in the watchtower saw the wife of the Deputy
Commissioner talking at her front gate to a man. The sentry
knew the dog. It was rumoured that ferret dog had killed the
Siamese cat of the daughter of the Assistant Commissioner of
Prisons (personnel). He thought the man must have had business at the Deputy Commissioner's house, come there before he
had come on duty forty minutes earlier. He thought the dog
must have chased the man down the drive. He thought it was a
pity the old cow had come out so fast, a pity the man didn't have
a chance to put his boot firmly into the ferret dog's arse.

He walked on. He felt the nakedness of his back. The wall rose
beside him. The lights showed him thin, knife-edge cracks in the
wall between the faced brickwork. Thiroko had told him that
Beverly Hills was built on a rubbish tip. Heart hammering. He
wondered if that helped him, helped his 12 pounds of explosive,
the tip. Wailing siren, very faint. No. Must be singing. So bloody
frightened . . .

There was for Jeez a sort of warmth in the singing. Listening to
the singing he had put off his undressing and changing into his
coarse cotton pyjamas. He knew that once they had started they
would not finish. They would sing until the rope strangled the
breath out of their throats. And a warmth, too, from the wheezed
bronchitic breathing of old Oosthuizen. He wondered what the
other two Whites in C section 2 thought about sharing their
block with Black terrorist Commies, what they thought about
Jeez being amongst friends.

He was at the corner. He was at the furthest point from the
sentry tower, and when he was round the corner he would be at

the furthest point from the remote camera on the wall above the airlock entrance . . .

Ros drove fast down from the motorway and onto Potgieterstraat. Jan had his window down, and the grenades and the pistols in his lap.

He heard the men singing, a murmur in the night as with leaves in a gentle wind . . .

The colonel swayed back in his chair. The words, telex typed, bounced at him from the page. James Carew had written to Mrs Hilda Perry. Mrs Hilda Perry lived at Churchill Close, Leatherhead, Surrey. Jack Curwen lived at Churchill Close, Leatherhead, Surrey. He swept open the drawer of his desk. He needed the telephone directory of the Department of Prisons.

He glanced at his watch. He was on the countdown. He started to mouth away the final seconds . . .

Jan ripped the lever of the first RG-42 high explosive grenade, tossed it through the window. The Beetle was coming slowly now past the wall of Local, at the junction with Soetdoringstraat. His finger was in the loop of the lever of the next grenade as they approached the gates of SADF headquarters.

He could see the camera rotating patiently towards him. He was 50 yards from the corner behind him, 75 yards from the camera ahead.

Jack twisted, ducked towards the wall. He heard the crack thump of the first grenade . . .

God, I love you, little bastard kids.

. . . The tube down on the ground, a foot from the wall, paying out the Cordtex equivalent and the length of safety fuse, looking for the camera and the camera moving at steady, inexorable pace towards him, about to include him in the vision arc.

The second grenade explosion, the metal box thump of the grenade going. He looked again for the camera. He saw the camera swinging away from him, aiming for the main approach road that came from the direction of the grenade blasts. Struggling in his pocket for the lighter, and his fingers floundering with the car keys. The third grenade explosion . . .

Brilliant bloody kids, because you've pulled the camera off.

. . . Pistol shots in the night, soft fire crackers half a mile away. The lighter in his hand. The flame cupped. The flame held round the cut edge of the safety fuse. Jack ran back. He flung himself down onto the hard road. He pressed his face down onto the road surface. A moment of desperate stillness.

He felt the blast bludgeon over him. He felt the pain roaring in his ears. He felt the fine draught of the debris hurtling back past him.

He crawled on his knees and elbows into the grey dust cloud. He groped until he found the hole. His hands were in the hole and scraping to find the reinforcing steel cords. Coughing dust, spitting fragments. Cutters from his pocket. Finding the steel cords, fastening the cutters on them, heaving with his hands at the arms of the cutters, squeezing the arms of the cutters until there was the snap and the tension break. He was in the hole, choking, hacking. His shoulders were in the hole. If his shoulders were in then the hole was large enough. He wanted to scream, he wanted to shout that he had won. He was crawling through the hole and pulling his bag and lifting his shotgun. He wanted to shout because he thought that he had won something.

He came through. He crawled into a lit garden. Ahead of him was another wall, and the ground between him and the other wall was lit as by sunlight. He saw to his right the white flood brightness high on the stanchion poles.

He was charging forward.

It was twenty-two seconds after the exploding of the shaped charge. He fired six shots from the pump action to blow away the lights. Not darkness, there were the distant lights above the watchtower on the back wall, but shadows thrown by trees and shrubs and bushes that were the gardens around the hanging gaol.

A charge now. Only speed mattered. He saw ahead the pointed roofs of C section 1, and C section 2, and C section 3. The gaps between the roofs were the exercise yards, covered by the grilles.

He ran towards the gap that marked the exercise yard of C section 2, and his fingers were in his bag, reaching for the rope that was lashed to the length of bent iron.

19

He could hear nothing.

His ears were dulled by the explosion at the outer wall.

In silent ballet a deer that was no taller than his knee cavorted away from him. He saw between shadows the noiseless flight of a young warthog.

The piece of bent iron was in his hands, and the rope. It was his grappling hook and his climbing rope.

Jack came to the wall.

He arched the bent iron over the wall. He lost sight of its fall. He heard the first sound that infiltrated his senses. He heard the scrape of the bent iron on the metalwork of the grille above the exercise yard. New sounds now flooding his ears as he pulled on the rope, tested the strain. There was the sound of a siren, rising as if it were cranking itself awake. There was a shout. He heaved on the rope. He slid back as the bent iron slipped, fastened again, slipped again, held. Once more he tugged at the rope, using desperate strength. The rope and the hook were steady. The iron was lodged as a hook into the grille. He tucked the shotgun, barrel up, under the shoulder strap, weighed in by the bag hanging across his stomach and his thighs, and he started to climb. His feet stamped on the wall as he dragged himself upwards.

It was fifty-two seconds of time since the shaped charge had detonated against and through the outer wall. A lifetime of Jack's experience. All about speed, all about confusion, all about men staying rooted in their positions for precious seconds, all about officers who made decisions seconds after being asleep in their homes or dozing in the armchairs of their mess. Speed from

Jack, confusion from the prison staff, his certain purpose, their being taken by surprise, on these his chance depended.

He tried to walk up, throw his body back from the wall. The way the marines or the paratroopers did it. But the marines and the paratroopers weren't carrying a shotgun, and the marines and the paratroopers had proper combat packs and not a grip bag on a shoulder strap. And the marines and the paratroopers wouldn't be alone. Jack climbed the wall. His ears now were filled with the howl of the sirens.

He reached the top.

He was a darkened figure that swung first an arm and then a leg and then a shoulder and then a torso over the top of the wall, nursing his weight off the shotgun. He rolled from the top of the wall to crash onto the grille above the exercise yard. There was a moment when he was dazed, when he saw below him the dull colours of flowers in a small square of earth under the grille. If he let himself stop for more than a split second he was dead. He pushed himself away from the wall, out over the grille, the shotgun free in his hands, pressing back the safety catch.

He saw the spit of flame from the window to his right, from the window that gave air onto the catwalk above the corridor of C section 2. He was rolling, swivelling his hips to turn himself, to keep the momentum from his fall. Because he was rolling, moving, the rifle shot had missed him, and the second shot missed him. Sharp, granite chips of sound against the blanket wail of the siren. He aimed the shotgun at the window. There had been a pale face visible between the slats of the window. The pale face was scarlet, peppered, gone. A scream of pain, of fear, to merge with the siren.

Jack crouched.

Left hand in his bag. The charge with the detonator in his fingers. The moment when he had to stop. The moment when he had to put down the shotgun on the grille. He had the charge in his hand and the roll of adhesive tape. Fast movements as he pulled himself onto the sloping roof above the cell block, as he reached for the window in front of him, the window that led to the catwalk. The window was a set of vertical bars, 4 inches apart, concrete, with louvred glass slats. He slapped the charge against the central bar. His fingers were stripping adhesive tape from the roll. He was kicking with his feet to hold a grip on the metal of the sloping roof. He had the charge in place, he had the adhesive tape back in his bag, when he saw the man who lay on the catwalk and moaned and who held his hands across his face. He dropped the length of Cordtex equivalent and safety fuse back down the slope of the roof. He let his grip go, his feet slide, came to rest on the grille. The lighter was in his hand. He guarded the flame against the safety fuse. He ducked, reached for the shotgun, plucked out of his pocket more cartridges, reloaded.

The blast sang in his head. The explosion blotted out the siren sound, and the shouting, and the first rumble of booted feet on the catwalk.

Jack scrambled up the roof. A gaping hole for him to pitch himself through, left arm first with the shotgun, left elbow through, left shoulder, and his forehead caught against a shard of glass and was slashed. No stopping. He tumbled onto the catwalk and his fall was softened by the cringing body of the guard.

He stood.

He opened his lungs.

He shouted.

'Jeez.'

He heard his voice boom back at him from the confines of the catwalk, from the short corridor below him, from through the cell windows around him that were flush into the catwalk.

'Jeez. Where are you?'

It was one minute and twenty-four seconds of time since the hollow charge had detonated.

He heard a gravel voice. He heard the reply.

'I'm here.'

A babble of voices springing from the personal radios, concentrating around the controller in his glass-fronted booth beside the airlock main entrance.

'It's not in B section . . .'

'A section's fine. What's with B section and C section?'

'. . . over.'

'I repeat, nothing in B section . . .'

'Is this a fire practice, Johan?'

'Are we to stay or are we to move . . . ?'

'If you have nothing to report for Christ sake keep . . .'

'Who's giving orders . . .?'

'. . . several shots, rifle fire, I think, sounded like A section.'

'Was that a bang on the outer wall . . . ?'

'What has happened to the lights . . . ?'

'Duty Officer, do you hear me?'

'Has the military been telephoned . . . ?'

Chaos sweeping the ears of the controller.

The guard in the sentry box thought of the man he had seen with the gun and the length of circular metal, the man who had been talking with the wife of the Deputy Commissioner. He felt the crimson of panic, that he would be blamed, surging up from his gut.

There were five prison staff locked into the main C section corridor. None of them had a weapon, they were in contact with prisoners. They cowered on their haunches in the corridor.

Locked into C section 2's corridor, Sergeant Oosthuizen shouted into the wall telephone, but he could find no-one to listen . . .

Jack blew the window out that looked down onto the cell. The charge without the detonator, gone a cream cake. Back on his feet. The cell below him was a dust box, a grey cloud haze, and the ceiling light had been smashed. He peered down, trying to probe the dust and darkness to see the man. Time running, and time that was his life and Jeez's life. He fell through the window gap. He bounced on the mesh over the cell. He had Cordtex equivalent and safety fuse in his hand. Six feet of Cordtex equivalent and 12 feet of safety fuse. He laid the length of Cordtex equivalent against the angle of the mesh and the vertical wall. It was above the bed.

'Under the bed or the table,' Jack shouted.

He jumped for the smashed window. His hands ripped on cut glass and torn metal and broken concrete. He saw the uniformed man beneath him, beneath the catwalk, pleading with the telephone. Hadn't time for the bastard. He lit the safety fuse. Christ only knew what it would be like underneath.

Sirens invading the long seconds, cut off by the blast.

He saw that a length of mesh had been torn from the wall. He saw the plaster battered away from the concrete.

'Get yourself onto the mesh, Jeez. Hurry . . .'

He saw the man. He saw a small hunched figure crawl out from under the bed. The man's face was pale grey from the plaster dust. The man was dazed. Slow motion movements. Jack was back on the catwalk, reaching for the shotgun. Booted feet hammering, running on the catwalk close to him. He knew the catwalk was the causeway that covered the whole gaol. No locked doors on the catwalk, the briefing papers said. He heard the wheeze of the man's breath, he saw the white head of short hair at the hole where the window had been. He saw the face of the man, wide-eyed, staring at him. Jack grabbed the collar of the man's tunic, he pulled him over the glass edges and the torn metal and the broken concrete.

It was one minute and fifty-eight seconds of time since the charge had detonated.

Jack had hold of the man's tunic. Not stopping to look at him. He heard the voices welling through the windows onto the catwalk.

'*Amandla*, Jeez . . .'

'Fly on the wind, Jeez . . .'

'Tell them about us, Jeez, that we were singing . . .'

The man who was loose in Jack's grip stiffened. The lines cut and broke the grey dust on his face and forehead. Jack tugged at him, couldn't move him. The man broke Jack's grip.

Jack watched the man who was his father, who was Jeez.

Jeez picked up the rifle of the guard lying on the catwalk. He poked the barrel down through the grille of the catwalk.

'Oosthuizen, drop that telephone. Unlock those doors, unlock my door. You have five seconds, Oosthuizen . . .'

He fired once into the floor below him.

'Four seconds, Oosthuizen, or you're dead. You don't get to retire . . . Three . . . Don't play heroes, Oosthuizen . . . Two . . . I don't give a shit about shooting you . . . One . . .'

Jack couldn't see. He heard the rattle of the keys. He heard a door opening, another door opening.

'Clever, Oosthuizen, that's being clever . . .' He fired once more and the telephone flew from the wall socket.

The catwalk crowded as the four Blacks came up in fast succession.

Jack saw a shadow figure materialize at the corner where the catwalk over C section 2 joined with the catwalk over the main C section corridor. He fired. He pumped the shotgun, fired, pumped again, fired again. Shrill shouts of surprise. Should have been gone, on their way, and still on the catwalk.

It was two minutes and thirty-five seconds of time. Jeez and four Blacks crouched by the blown window, the route to the sloping roof. Jack motioned them gone. They helped each other, and Jack last, through the narrow window. Children on a fairground slide they tumbled down the roof. Into the night air. Out into the embrace of the unforgiving, perpetual siren. As they scrambled across the grille above the exercise yard, Jack turned and aimed a shot at the window. Keep them back, keep their heads below the window.

The controller bellowed his frustration. 'I don't care what colonel you are. I don't care about John Vorster Square. I have a break-out here, man, so clear the line.'

He slashed down the telephone. He depressed his microphone switch. He could be heard by every prison officer with a personal radio.

'This is control. The armoury is now unlocked. All unarmed personnel are to go straight to the armoury. Armed officers on B section and A section are to remain at their posts. All further orders will come from the duty major on Alpha frequency of transmission. The point of entry is believed to be the east perimeter wall. Captain van Rooyen orders all personnel to the central hallway as soon as weapons have been drawn. I repeat, further orders will come direct from the duty major.'

The controller was a senior sergeant. He looked up. The duty major was panting, red-faced and sweating. The duty major had run all the way from administration to the radio control to take charge, he weighed 18 stones.

The controller said quietly, 'C section, that's where the terrorists are.'

The duty major struggled for his voice. 'Have the police been informed?'

'More than one minute ago, sir.'

'Get the internal phone into C section 2.'

Sergeant Oosthuizen sat on his backside and his spine rested against the inside of the locked corridor door. The telephone, dead, was in his lap. In front of him, gaping, laughing at him, were the opened doors of three cells.

They went down the rope.

Jack led.

His shotgun was in his right hand. His left hand clung to the sleeve of Jeez's tunic. The Blacks ran alongside them. He led them through the gloom of the gardens. He was not aware of distance, just that the great wall was ahead. Still the siren filling the night, and then the first sporadic shots down from C section's upper windows. Searching for the bastard hole. Couldn't see it. He thought the shots were random, aimed haphazardly into the gloom light. With their impetus Jeez and the Blacks were bouncing against Jack as he slowed, as he searched for the gap. He went to his right, went 15 strides, and they were running again with him. No bloody hole, he stopped, he cursed. Fighting for breath. Again the bodies smacked against him. He turned, he went left and back over the same 15 strides. There was a jabber of voices in his ear. Couldn't the bastards see that he was trying to find the hole? They trampled through a bush. He tripped on the debris. He saw the hole, close to the grass.

God, had he ever made it through that hole? In hell's name, how had he ever made it through? So bloody small.

Two of the Blacks went first, eel-like, then Jack. Jack wriggled through the hole. He loosened his hold on Jeez for the first time since they had come down the sloping roof. His hand was back and into the hole to take Jeez and work him through.

There was a spatter of bullets. Jack saw the dirt kick close to his legs, close to where the two Blacks sheltered against the wall . . . The sentry in the high tower, and the lights above the sentry's platform. He wrenched Jeez clear. He heard the man cry in pain, he heard the ripping of the man's shirt where it had caught on a cut edge of steel cord. Jeez was through, Jeez and his rifle.

'Take the lights out,' Jeez hissed.

Jack ran forward. He must stand if he were to see the lights. He fired three times. With the shotgun it was like knocking skittles away in an alley. First time, some out. Second time, more out. Third time, most out. Most of the light gone.

They ran in a tight group towards the corner of the wall.

They were outside the walls of Beverly Hills. Ahead of them were the street lights and the road through the senior officers' quarters. When they were on the road they would be in the clear field of fire from the sentry in the tower.

They came to the corner.

'Where are we going?'

'Across the road, up that track.'

Jeez said, 'The rifle'll keep his head down. They're not soldiers, won't take it when it's coming back at them. How many shots?'

'He fired twice at me, you fired once.'

'Three left, they carry six.' Jeez was fluently taking control. 'Happy – Charlie – Percy – Tom – when I fire at the tower, run like shit.'

Jeez gestured at the track opening that Jack had pointed to.

Jeez had the rifle to his shoulder. He edged round the corner of the wall. There was the crack of a shot. The Blacks ran. They ran bent low, weaving over the tarmac, sprinting for the darkness of the track. Jeez fired a second shot. Jack ran, he thought Jeez was immediately behind him. Jack was in the middle of the road going like smoke. The sledgehammer hit him. The darkness at the track's mouth was yawning for him. He felt the crow-bar smash into him. He never heard the shot. No pain. Just the staggering blow of the sledgehammer, the crow-bar.

It was three minutes and forty-nine seconds of time.

Jack felt the hard road against his face, his chest, no breath left, and a fist snatched at his arm and held him up, dragged him across the road towards the track.

'I hit one. Definitely a hit.'

The message squawked into the headphones clamped down on the major's bald head.

'Identify your position.'

'South sentry tower.'

'How many of them?'

'Can't be sure, sir, two for certain. Armed. Shot out the tower lights before they ran for it.'

'Going in what direction?'

'Going south onto Magasyn Kopje.'

'Out . . .'

For the first time a glimmer of a smile. He had hard information.

He was reaching for the microphone that would link him to every personal radio inside Maximum Security when he heard the door click open behind him. He turned, he saw the governor standing in the centre of the room, his arms folded across his chest. The governor wore his dinner jacket, well cut, and above the folded arms was a line of miniature medals topped by vivid coloured ribbon. The governor gestured with his hand, a small movement, for the duty major to carry on with his broadcast.

He gave out the information. He issued his orders. A much rehearsed plan involving prison staff and police and military had slipped into place. He switched off the microphone.

The governor pursed his lips, there was a frown of surprise cutting deep in his forehead.

'I think I heard you correctly, that one man alone came in and took five out.'

The duty major nodded.

'Extraordinary, I would not have conceived it as possible.'

'The blocks will be in place within a few minutes.' The duty major spoke with pride.

'Perhaps in time, perhaps not . . .' The governor seemed to speak to himself, left the duty major as an eavesdropper. '. . . If they are not all back with us in time to face the penalty of the law on Thursday morning then the scandal of one man's achievement will destroy me.'

The duty major swung away and snatched for the telephone that would connect him to Defence Headquarters. He did not wish to look again at his governor, to witness the fall of a fine man.

'You have to tell me what's ahead.'

They were crowded together on the track. Jeez was bent over Jack. The sledgehammer blow was to Jack's right knee. Jeez could see the blood. Not much blood. Blood on either side of the trouser leg, as if the bullet had pierced his knee, gone straight through.

'There's just buildings ahead, then you go down the hill, and there's a fence, that's all, after that you're out under the Voortrekker Monument and the Skanskopfort . . .'

Jeez put up his hand, cut Jack off. He turned to the others.

'You heard him, get bloody going. Move your arses.'

He pushed the one who was nearest to him away. Each one

crouched, slapped Jeez's shoulder, gripped his arm. An ecstatic farewell and the last one said: 'God go with you, Jeez, and you too, friend. We'll fight together again.' And was gone. There was the patter of their feet. They were shadows and then they were nothing.

'Go with them,' Jack said.

Jeez stood and hoisted Jack up. He slung Jack's arm over his shoulder. He was on Jack's right side. They stumbled together up the track.

'I said, "Go with them." '

Jeez's fist was tight into Jack's anorak, under his armpit. Jack doubted he could have torn the fist free. They made the best speed that was possible for them. His leg was numb, useless.

The pain came later. Into the ripped hole, into the wrecked ligaments, into the broken cartilage, into the splintered bone. The pain was in water surges, damned and then rushing in intensity. Flash floods of pain in Jack's whole leg as they went forward, up the hillside and through the trees. Skirting the buildings and holding to the black holes where the lights did not reach. Silence around them. No cordon. No dogs. Only the sirens pulsing behind them. Together, Jeez supporting Jack, they started down the hill, down the south slope of Magazine. They couldn't crawl because Jack's wound would not have permitted him to crawl. Jeez walked, Jack, leaning on his shoulder, hopped beside him. In the pure darkness they went down Magazine.

Jeez said, 'Where are the wheels?'

'Far side of Skanskopfort.'

He heard the whistle of surprise.

'What I was trying for . . .'

'Save your strength.'

Jack found the hole that he had cut in the fence. He found his handkerchief. They slithered through. Jack, in his life, had never known such agony as when Jeez worked him through the wire and over the lower tumbler strand. He thought they should have been going faster, he knew he was incapable of greater speed. They crossed the road at the bottom of the valley between

Magazine and Skanskop, and they climbed again. They climbed over the stone hard earth and the broken rock, and through the matted thorn scrub.

Against the clean night sky were the ordered plateau lines of the old fort's ramparts.

They looked down.

Jack gazed down the south face of the Skanskop slope to the road and the place where he had parked the Renault. The triumph was bolted in his gut, the words were blocked in his throat. He could see the Renault. The Renault was illuminated by the lights of a jeep. There were many lights, many jeeps and transport lorries for moving troops. The lights of the vehicles shone on to the hillside where it fell to the road. He heard the rising drone of engines to his right, and to his left, and away behind him. His eyes squeezed shut.

The voice grated in his ear.

'You bastards took your time, and now you've blown it.'

'It was the best . . .'

Jeez snapped. 'Bloody awful best, and after I've been sitting there thirteen fucking months. Bastards.'

'Who are the bastards?'

'Your crowd.'

'What's my crowd?'

Teeth bared, 'The team.'

'What team?'

'Where's the back-up?'

'There's just me, me alone.' Still leaning on Jeez's shoulder.

'Where's Colonel Basil?'

'Never heard of him.'

'Lennie, Adrian, Henry.'

'Don't know them.'

'Who sent you?'

'I sent myself.'

Jeez looked up at him, searched his face. Didn't understand, couldn't split the mist.

'So who are you?'

'I'm Jack.'

'And who the hell's Jack, when he's at home?'

'He's your son.'

Jack hung on his father's neck. Jeez buried his face in his son's shoulder. And around them, far beneath them, was the tightening circle of lights.

They had come off the motorway, they were close to their parents' home.

After Jan had thrown the grenades at Local, and the SAAF recruiting office, and the creeper-covered fence of SADF HQ, and after he had fired a whole magazine of pistol shots at the sentry box at the bottom of Potgieterstraat, Ros had taken a circular route to Johannesburg. Not a word was spoken. Ros's knuckles were white on the wheel all the way. Their nerves were stretched like wire. They expected every moment the flail of the siren in pursuit, the roadblock in their path. The number plates were mud-smeared. She did not think that the sentries would have noted her number plate, they'd have been lying in the dirt and shielding their heads from the shrapnel and the pistol bullets. She had driven 50 kilometres out of her way, across to the east before doubling back through Bapsfontein and Kempton Park and Edenvale. She hadn't been followed, there had been no roadblocks. They had heard one explosion. Jan had said it was the main charge going against the wall, and then they had finished with their diversion, and he had wound up the passenger window. They had heard nothing more.

Now the radio was on in the car.

The midnight news bulletin. A bland English accent.

'. . . English service of the SABC. Good evening. In the last ten minutes police headquarters in Pretoria has announced that the area to the south of the capital between Verwoerdburg and Valhalla has been declared an emergency military zone. All persons travelling through that area until further notice are subject to SADF and police control. Residents in the area are advised to stay in their homes throughout the hours of darkness . . .'

'They made it,' Jan squealed. 'They're running.'

'. . . Late this evening it was reported that explosions and firing were heard in the area of the SADF headquarters on Potgieterstraat in the capital, but as yet there is no official police confirmation of these reports.

'In London a demonstration by an estimated two thousand people outside the South African embassy was broken up by police after violence . . .'

Jan switched off the radio.

'It didn't say he made it,' Ros said bleakly. 'It just said he was being hunted.'

'Wrong, not a military zone unless he's taken his father out.'

She drove on. She held the wheel lightly with one hand. The fingers of her other hand played listlessly with the shape of the crucifix at her neck. She wanted only to be home. She wanted to tie the yellow scarf in the window of her bedroom.

'Did you love him, Ros?'

She turned the car into the driveway of her parents' home. She parked beside her father's BMW.

'You're best to go straight to bed, Jan, or you'll be sleeping right through your classes in the morning.'

All Pretoria had heard the gunfire and the explosions. Frikkie de Kok had heard them.

Pretoria is a valley city. The gunfire and the explosions on the southern hills were cradled above the community by the northern slopes. Distant gunfire and muffled explosions, and the city was an armed camp and the sounds were insufficient to disturb the celebration between himself and his assistant. Right that they should take some beers in the Harlequins bar after the assistant had performed well at dawn. A celebration for the two of them in the corner by the window going on long after the field floodlights had been switched off, away from the talk at the bar.

When it came to be time to go home, the bar closed, the hangman did not know whether the gunfire and explosions were part of an army night exercise or the result of a terrorist attack.

335

At his front gate he waved his assistant goodnight. He came up the path. The porch light showed him that Hermione had been weeding in the evening after he had gone to the match. A fine woman, the rock of a fine family. He let himself inside, moved quietly into the darkened hall.

He could hear Hermione snoring softly. Down the corridor he could see the edge of light under his boys' bedroom door. He thought they would be interested to know the score of the match, and how the Springbok who played for Defence had performed. Fine boys, with a fine future. Boys such as his would survive whatever. He pushed gently at the door. The flicker of a frown played at his forehead. Erasmus was curled in his bed, asleep and facing the wall and avoiding the light that was between the beds. Dawie's bed was empty, the coverlet not pulled back. He was annoyed. Dawie had been working so hard, and there was talk of a university scholarship, and all the school exams were important, and the boy should have been in his bed. He would tell Dawie of his displeasure, perhaps he was too soft on the boy . . . He went into the living room.

He saw the white sheets of paper on his desk. He went to them. He picked them up, and recognized the papers that had come that morning from the school, the entry forms for university application. The envelope was beside the papers. The boy was normally so tidy. His leg brushed against an obstruction. He glanced down and made out the black leather, wide-built attaché case with which he went to work. The lock catch of the black leather case was unfastened. He cursed himself for his own carelessness in leaving the bag unlocked. He was as careless as his Dawie – heh, that was rich – father and son as careless as each other. The smile extinguished. So fast developing, the picture in his mind. His Dawie skimming through the university entrance form, and his Dawie seeing the bag that had never been opened in his presence, and his Dawie succumbing to curiosity, and his Dawie feeling for the lock and finding it unfastened, and his Dawie opening the case that carried the tools of the hangman's trade.

Chilled, Frikkie de Kok stood for a moment motionless. He lifted back the flap of the black case. The ropes were coiled neatly in see-through Cellophane bags. To count them he did not have to lift them out. New ropes, drawn from the prison store that day, signed for that afternoon. He loved his boy, and he did not know how his boy would react on finding that his father was the executioner in Pretoria Central.

There were four ropes. When he had brought his case home there had been five ropes. The ropes he would use at first light on Thursday. Only, because he loved his Dawie, Frikkie de Kok had never summoned the courage to tell his boy what work he did for the state . . .

He thought that he knew where to look.

Frikkie de Kok went to the window. He stared out on to his back garden. The ceiling lights of the living room threw shadows across the lawn. The lights groped as far as the old pear tree from which the autumn frosts had stripped the leaves.

Cold, shivering now, the hangman saw the slowly revolving shape.

The colonel stood beside the stolen Renault car. Above him the bleak outline of the hillside. With him was an army brigadier. Between the palms of his hand the colonel held a warming beaker of coffee. Technically the military had been called in to aid the civil power, in practice they had taken control, and the colonel was outranked and deferential, and damned tired because he'd not slept, and he had left his office at a quarter past two in the morning for the drive to Pretoria. He had no place in the cordon line. He could not have stayed away, could not have borne it in John Vorster Square with only the telephone and the telex machine to feed him the news.

The brigadier munched at a sandwich.

'. . . I tell you this, we were pretty poor getting the act into place. The operations room had us under sustained attack at Defence Headquarters, so we lost critical minutes. I'll kick someone's arse for that. It's why we've only got two of them up there for definite, but those two are bottled, and anyway there's a blood trail so they're not going anywhere.'

'Which ones, which two?'

'A sentry on Magasyn had an image intensifier on them when they came off the hill. Can't be sure, not through that thing, but he reckons they are both White. There was only one man came into Maximum Security and he was White . . .'

'So the other is Carew.' The colonel heaved his relief. 'What'll you do?'

'It's what they're going to do. If one of them's hurt he'll need the medics. When they're cold enough and hungry enough and hurt enough, they have to come down. They've nowhere to go.'

'I'd like them alive.'

The brigadier smiled sardonically. 'So you can put them back inside, hang them?'

'It's no help to me to have them dead.'

'They have a rifle and they have an automatic shotgun, and I'm not having my men shot up by desperate men who are going to end on the rope anyway. If they shoot first, they're dead. If they don't shoot, they'll live. It's pretty simple.'

'Would you allow me to broadcast that to them?'

The brigadier snapped his fingers, brought his adjutant hurrying. He asked for a loudhailer.

'You can tell them that if they don't shoot first they will not be harmed.' The brigadier's voice dropped, 'Then they'll be able to meet the hangman on another morning.'

The colonel drank from his beaker and stared again up at the silent hillside. Around him were quiet voices, the occasional clatter of weapons being checked. There was the low throb of running engines. The crackle of brief radio messages. If there were only two on the hillside then he knew those two were James Carew and his son.

The loudhailer was handed to him.

The dawn was coming.

The blast of the message had slipped away, dispersed amongst the surrounding hills.

A mauve streak in the east.

They had talked through the night. They had met as strangers, and during the dark hours, in faintest starlight, they had lurched through understanding towards friendship. Jeez sat with his arms gathered round his knees as if to find warmth for himself against the cold on the Skanskop. Near to freezing on the hillside and he wore only his prison tunic and cotton trousers and his thin prison shoes. Jack lay prone beside him, sometimes twisted by the agony in his leg, sometimes able to rest in relief between the spasms of pain.

They were together, it was as if they had never been apart.

They talked of Hilda Perry and her life with Sam and the house in Churchill Close, and Jeez seemed pleased at what he heard. They talked of Jack's job and Jeez chuckled at the stories of the blaster George Hawkins. They talked of the Foreign Office and of the man called Jimmy Sandham, and Jeez spat into the dew damp earth. They talked of a girl called Ros van Niekerk and of her brother with a club foot, and Jeez heard his son through. When the pain came to Jack then Jeez held his hand. When the pain spurted then Jeez's fingers clenched over his son's fist.

They could see the lights of the vehicles around the base of the Skanskop, a mesmerizing cage of lights. When they were not talking they could hear the idling engines of the trucks and jeeps.

'You won't be afraid?'

Jack shook his head. Enough light seeping onto the hilltop for Jeez to see his son's face. Through the night he had talked to his son and he had not known his son's face. Jack gazed at the face of his father. A thin pinched face, stubble on the chin, short back and sides where there was hair to cut. Jack thought he saw a love in his father's face.

'Not having been a talking man, Jack, not any of my life, it's hard for me, to say what I want to say to you . . . To say thank you, that's not enough. Just crap to say thank you. I'll tell it better if I say what you've given me . . .'

Jack watched his father's head, clearer against the sky.

'It won't be by them, that's rich to me. It'll be in our time, not at the time they'd open my cell up, the time they've decided. Because it'll be us, by ourselves, who decide the time, that's bloody fantastic to me. Free hands and free arms and free legs. No pinions on my ankles, no hood over my face, that's wonderful for me. Yesterday I couldn't have imagined how wonderful. You understand me, Jack?'

'I understand you, Jeez.'

'You're the son that I made with your mother, you're the son that I bloody failed, and you came here to take me out when none of the other bastards were coming. You've given me the thing I wanted most.'

Almost a shyness on Jeez's face. 'Where I've been you don't get to see the morning coming, and you don't feel the wind on your face. I wanted most to see the morning coming, the sun rise, and feel the wind. And I don't have to be counting. Got that?'

'Got it.'

'In that place you may be counting in months; weeks, days, I was down to counting hours. I'd got to counting meals. Day before yesterday I was counting how many socks I'd be needing. Day before yesterday they gave me a new uniform, but it wasn't new, oldest they'd got, look at it. You mess your clothes when you're hanged, Jack, so they give you an old uniform before they drop you off. You got me out of the counting. You got me to see a morning coming. You got me to feel the fresh wind on my face.'

He was between the pain. He was lying back. He was aware of the light building in the sky.

Jack said, 'Everyone I spoke to, they all said it was impossible.'

A dry smile from Jeez. 'Probably was.'

'The car was wrong.'

'Just as wrong as when I said we had to stop and take the boys. We had to bring them, Jack.'

'You don't get a choice. You had to take the boys, just as I had to come for you.'

'They *might just* make it. Us going so slow might have drawn the flak off them. You know what, if they do make it, you *might just* get to have a street named after you in some real African shit-heap up in 'saka or Dar.'

'I don't blame you for anything, Jeez.'

'You're not afraid?'

'It's like I'm happy.'

'You screwed them proper.'

'Cheated them.'

'It's the best morning of my life, the cleanest air. Thank you.'

'For nothing, Jeez.'

'So let's get this fucking show on the road.'

'They don't take us.'

'No way they take us.'

'It'll be what they wanted in London.'

'They'll be breaking open crates in Century, swilling champagne.'

Jack said, 'There must be some people who know, who'll want to tell the truth.'

Jeez said, 'They'll promote them. Promotion and the honours list, they're good silencers.'

'I wanted to walk you down Whitehall. I wanted to take you into the Foreign Office. I wanted to see those bastards' faces.'

'The bastards don't get to lose that often, not there, not here.'

Jeez stood. For a long time he looked away to the clipped, half rising sun. He breathed in. He dragged the morning air into his lungs. He wondered how long it would be before the dandelion weed showed again in the garden of the exercise yard of C section 2. He clapped his hands. Jeez took off his tunic shirt and started to rip strips from it. He made five strips. He came behind Jack and put his hands under Jack's armpits and lifted him up. With the strips from his tunic, Jeez bound Jack's right leg. He knotted the strips tight.

Jeez checked the shotgun. He checked the rifle.

'You heard their message, what they want of us.'

'They don't take us, Jeez.'

'We're close as family, boy.'

They stumbled forward to the edge of the hill. The pain swam again through Jack. Behind them were the walls of the old Skanskopfort, and the light of morning, and a gathering wind. It would be a short pain, the pain would not last. They were stiff with cold. It took them a few strides to find the rhythm. He wondered whether he could live with the pain from his stiffening, ruptured leg. He looked into Jeez's face, saw the chin jutting bloody-minded defiance. He saw his father's face, the face he had grown to know in a dawn haze.

They came to the edge.

Jack clung to Jeez's shoulder, supporting himself, trying not to shake, trying to hold back the agony tremors. Jeez had the rifle to his shoulder, aimed. Jack saw a jeep far below, a bristle of aerials. He saw the pygmy figures evacuating the jeep. He could hear the faint alarm calls. One shot, one bullet left. He understood the controlled pleasure at Jeez's mouth. Hitting back, after thirteen months. Aiming on the jeep, finger squeezing over the trigger, the report of the shot, the kick in Jeez's shoulder.

Jeez whipped the rifle down, gave it to Jack as a support, as a stick. Jeez took the shotgun. They came down the slope. They were juddering forward, faster. Jack's arm tight across Jeez's shoulders. They were one, father and son.

Down the slope, and the pain gone from Jack's knee. Just the echo cracks of the shotgun and Jeez's laughter. Laughter pealing at the sun and the clean cold of the wind, and the blast of the shotgun. Jeez firing from the hip at the vehicles that seemed to soar to meet them, and all the time his laughter. No pain for Jack, only the laughter and the shotgun blasting. He didn't hear the shouted order of the brigadier. He didn't see the barrel of a Vickers machine gun waver and then lock on their path. He didn't know that the colonel of security police howled his frustration in the ear of the brigadier and was ignored.

He only knew his own happiness and his father's freedom and the hammer whip of the shotgun.

They were wrong, all those who said it was impossible.

They were wrong because Jack had come for his father, and had taken him out.

THE CORPORAL'S WIFE

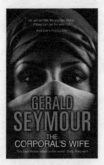

'Seymour is, quite simply, one of the finest thriller writers in England,
every bit the equal of Frederick Forsyth and Robert Harris.'
Daily Mail

A young woman determined to live her own life in an
oppressive society.

A rag-tag team of men sent to bring her out of it against all the odds.

THE CORPORAL'S WIFE is a hugely suspenseful thriller
about escaping one of the world's most explosive hostpots – Iran.
It is an epic, nail-biting story of courage and betrayal, a brilliant
glimpse into a closed society and the way the secret services
operate on both sides of the line between politics and morality.

'This is another masterly performance from an author whose
recent work turns individual spying missions into ambitious ensemble
dramas mixing action scenes and love stories with espionage.'
The Sunday Times

HODDER

THE OUTSIDERS

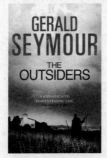

'Once again demonstrating his ability to probe the moral murki-
ness of the spy trade and create an absorbingly diverse ensemble,
Seymour crafts a sophisticated, reader-teasing tale.'
The Sunday Times

MI5 officer Winnie Monks has never forgotten the death of a young
agent on her team at the hands of a former Russian Army Major-
turned-gangster. Ten years later, she hears the Major is travelling to a
Spanish villa and she asks permission to send in a surveillance unit.

There is an empty property next door, perfect to spy from –
and as a base for Winnie's darker, less official plans.

But this villa isn't deserted: the owners have invited a young
British couple to 'house sit' while they are away.

Jonno and Posie think they are embarking on a carefree holiday in the sun.
But, when the Secret Service arrives in paradise, *everything* changes.

'Those [Seymour] sends off into dangerous territory are, in fact,
his readers. With each book, we enter a dangerous universe, and
are totally involved with utterly plausible characters, faced with
moral choices that are rarely straightforward.'
Independent

HODDER

A DENIABLE DEATH

AN EPIC NOVEL OF HIGH COURAGE AND LOW CUNNING, OF LIFE AND DEATH IN THE MORAL MAZE OF THE POST-9/11 WORLD.

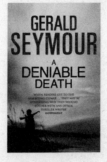

'Gerald Seymour is the grand-master of the contemporary thriller and A DENIABLE DEATH is his greatest work yet. Gripping, revealing and meticulously researched, this is a page-turning masterpiece that will literally leave you breathless.' Major Chris Hunter, bestselling author of *Extreme Risk*

YOU WATCH. YOU WAIT. THE HOURS SLIDE SLOWLY PAST.

A WHOLE DAY. THEN TWO.

YOU LIE UNDER A MERCILESS SUN IN A MOSQUITO-INFESTED MARSH.

YOU CAN'T MOVE, LEAVE, OR RELAX.

YOUR MUSCLES ACHE FROM CLENCHING TIGHT FOR SO LONG.

IF YOU ARE DISCOVERED, YOU WILL BE TORTURED THEN KILLED.

AND HER MAJESTY'S GOVERNMENT WILL DENY ALL KNOWLEDGE OF YOU.

'Great storytelling . . . you just have to read this novel . . . absolutely gripping' *Eurocrime*

HODDER

THE DEALER AND THE DEAD

THE ARMS DEALER BETRAYED THEM.
THE SURVIVORS WANT REVENGE.

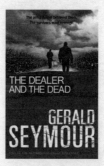

'*The Dealer and the Dead* is Seymour firing on all cylinders
and his rivals need, once again, to look to their laurels'
Independent

In a moonlit field near the Serbian border, Croatian villagers waited for an arms shipment that would never come. They
will never forget that night, or the slaughter that followed.

Eighteen years later, a body is discovered in a field, and with it the identity of
the arms dealer who betrayed them. Now the villagers can plot their revenge.

For Harvey Gillott, it was all a long time ago. But now the
hand of the past is reaching out across Europe, to Harvey's
house in leafy England. And it's holding a gun . . .

'The final scenes are brilliantly orchestrated . . . Without doubt, *The Dealer
and the Dead* is one of the finest thrillers to be published so far this year'
Yorkshire Evening Post

HODDER

THE COLLABORATOR

CORRUPTION. BETRAYAL. REVENGE.

'A dense, intensely satisfying thriller from one of the modern
masters of the craft, Seymour's latest novel will remind the world
just how phenomenally accomplished a thriller writer he is.'
Daily Mail

Eddie Deacon has a new girlfriend. She's beautiful, clever and Italian.

And then she disappears.

What Eddie doesn't know is that Immacolata Borelli is the daughter of a
merciless Naples gangster. She can no longer live with her conscience and
has decided to collaborate with the police to bring down her own family.

But the Borellis will not lose their empire without a fight. They will
use or destroy anything and anyone to prevent her from talking.

Including Eddie.

'Tight writing and meticulous research . . . Seymour paints the
streets of Naples and their dark denizens with an artist's brush
that lingers equally on the grime, the glitter and the blood'
The Times

HODDER